Sophia Tobin worked for a Bond Street antique dealer for six years, specialising in silver and jewellery. Inspired by research she made into a real life eighteenth-century silversmith, Tobin began to write *The Silversmith's Wife* which was shortlisted for the Lucy Cavendish College Fiction Prize, judged by Sophie Hannah. She is currently Library Secretary for the Worshipful Company of Goldsmith's and lives in London with her husband. This is her first novel.

'A dense, intricate historical thriller centering around the murder of a silversmith – in the tradition of Iain Pears' *An Instance of the Fingerpost* and Hilary Mantel's *Wolf Hall*'
Sophie Hannah

'Self-assured, page-turning debut which leaves you guessing until the last – a GREAT read'
Daily Mail

SOPHIA TOBIN

The Silversmith's Wife

SIMON &
SCHUSTER

London · New York · Sydney · Toronto · New Delhi

A CBS COMPANY

First published in Great Britain by Simon & Schuster UK Ltd, 2014
A CBS COMPANY

This paperback edition published 2014

1 3 5 7 9 10 8 6 4 2

Simon & Schuster UK Ltd
1st Floor
222 Gray's Inn Road
London WC1X 8HB

www.simonandschuster.co.uk

Simon & Schuster Australia, Sydney
Simon & Schuster India, New Delhi

A CIP catalogue record for this book is available
from the British Library

PB ISBN: 978-1-47112-810-3
EBOOK ISBN: 978-1-47112-811-0

Typeset by M Rules
Printed and bound by CPI Group (UK) Ltd, Croydon, CR0 4YY

To my parents

PROLOGUE

November, 1792

'Who's there?'

Edward Digby heard the hoarseness of his shout as though watching himself from a distance. He felt his breath catch in his throat. For a moment there was no reply, and his right hand went instinctively to the hilt of his knife, feeling the reassuring texture of the cloth-bound handle beneath his fingers. Even in the open space of this elegant square, every dark corner was threatening. He was alone on the watch and it was past midnight: late, too late for anyone respectable to be hiding in the shadows.

'Show yourself,' he shouted.

'It's Bright Hemmings,' came a familiar, plaintive voice. 'I came to find you. Someone's stolen my pig again.'

Digby almost laughed out loud with relief, but instead began to cough. With every inhalation of cold air he felt a nagging pain grate in his lungs. He had caught a cold, and he knew he wouldn't shift it until the sun broke through winter again and the daffodils were blooming in St James's Park. If I live that long, he thought grimly. Predictably, the coughing fit brought little relief. Even as he caught his breath, he could feel the corruption, flickering and insistent, in the back of his throat. 'Evening to you Bright,' he croaked eventually, his voice splintering and dying. 'Another one lost, eh?'

Bright had emerged from the shadows: a slight figure, his black eyes shining in the lantern beam, with an exaggerated expression of outrage on his face. He was a local joke. Every time he acquired a new pig it was gone within a week, leaving only the reproach of its smell and a few handfuls of soiled straw fluttering in its empty stall. At the sight of Digby he launched himself into a litany of complaints about pig-stealing and the treachery of neighbours.

'Foes are all around, Edward Digby, you mark my words. They've taken her: my Sunbeam. There's not a person this side of Piccadilly I'd trust to leave my livestock be.'

He was about to continue when Digby cut him off. 'That's enough,' he croaked. 'I don't have Watkin with me tonight. I'll make enquiries in the morning.'

'No you won't!' cried Bright, his voice growing shriller. 'You'll leave me complaining to the air, just as you did before.'

'I swear it,' said Digby. As he walked away he swore under his breath. His heart was still hammering in his chest. 'Stupid bastard,' he muttered.

He walked swiftly down Hays Mews. The smell of

horseshit and hay didn't disturb him, thanks to his blunted senses. Behind the grand terraces of Berkeley Square the mews buildings crouched in darkness and near-silence apart from the occasional shifting of one of the equine inhabitants, a faint nicker or the sound of a shod hoof on poorly covered stone. Their human attendants were still, probably lying in death-sleeps of fatigue. Digby wished he could join them. He hurried on, thinking of his bed. On Hill Street the pale moonlight picked out details here and there, like highlights on a watercolour.

Normally Digby was glad of a full moon – at least he could see his way across the ground and identify potential hazards without hunching over his lantern beam. But tonight, patrolling alone without Watkin, the sight of it made him shiver. He felt there was something malevolent about it. The wind rustled through the trees to the north of the square. He put his collar up and hurried on, stopping once to succumb to another coughing fit. This was the only stretch he had to do alone tonight: he would meet with other members of the watch on Hay Hill. Damn Watkin and his pointless reading society; now, he would be poised over some volume of poetry, his lips moving. Digby knew the learning he got would be of no use to him on London's streets.

Candles were still burning in the tall town houses on Berkeley Square; Digby saw their soft glow beyond fan-lights and windows as he passed alongside the facades of the houses. Some were tall rectangles of dark brick; others had frontages of chalk-white stucco. No one house was the same, as though the rich families contained within were asserting their individuality. The square had been built only fifty years before, raised out of the mud by prospectors with building leases and high hopes. Digby's grandfather had told him stories of it as a child; he knew where the buildings had come from, and he knew what had been here before: Brick Close, a patch of land that had once been a farm, with a sewer at its south end. This knowledge, he fancied, gave him a kind of superiority to the grand ladies and gentlemen that lived there. He tried to remind himself of it. The houses were just bricks and mortar, even those set behind high walls like separate estates, and the people within, living souls, just as fragile as him. Yet the houses seemed as inviolable as churches, and as serene, as though they had always been there.

As he walked, Digby felt his jaw tighten, the old familiar resentment. It was the same every night. He never considered how often he repeated himself; each night he picked at the scab of his hatred. Past his fortieth year, he hated with the intensity of a young man, just as he still yearned. The women who had come and gone in his life had all urged him to pray – strange, that, how he drew them to him, all these holy women – but he always ignored attempts to force serenity upon him. The only prayer he ever said was a line from the evening service: *lighten our darkness, we beseech thee, O Lord; and by thy great mercy defend us from all perils and dangers of this night.*

He felt it fitted him, for now he was a private watchman, paid by the wealthiest inhabitants of the square to keep watch over the hours of darkness. He was nothing to them, but he kept his sharp eyes trained on their lives. On a summer's night he might pause, and try to see in their windows from a distance, as though by glimpsing a silk-covered wall, a candlestick or even – if he was lucky – a face, his curses might have more meat to feed on.

But this night he had an overwhelming urge to huddle into his coat, to fold his arms and suffocate the infection out of himself, so he was denied the pleasure of watching the houses. He was in pain, and felt as if his bones were sewn together with threads of ice, crystals forming in their marrow. He wasn't stopping for anyone.

Stepping off the path he dodged a young man driving a phaeton too fast: it passed him with the clatter of hooves and wheels, heading for the mews. Digby stayed against the railings, glancing warily behind him at the dark heart of the square. They had planted young trees there, as though trying to create a country estate in the midst of the city of filth and ashes.

At a quiet stretch on the square, where a house stood vacant, a faint cry made him stop and look about. A woman? He paused and listened. In the distance he could still hear the sound of Bright Hemmings wailing about his bloody pig, and wondered that his reedy voice could carry so far. He supposed it was for his benefit. Who else would listen to him at this time of night apart from thieves and vagabonds? He thought about going back and telling the man to be quiet if he valued his life.

As he walked on a shiver ran through him, from the top of his head to the depths of his guts. He looked around. Something was wrong.

Then he spotted it. There was a dark mound on the other

side of the railings bordering Berkeley Square: an irregularity in the chill depths of the grass, the edge of something protruding from shadow. He marvelled that he should know his beat so well; that the moonlight sliding off one curved surface should draw his eye.

'Who's there?' he said.

There was no reply.

He grasped the ring of keys in his pocket, wincing at the cold of them, and went to open the nearest gate into the square. It moved at his touch; it had been left unlocked. As it creaked open, his hand found the knife hilt again.

The irregular shape was a man asleep, face down in the grass, beside one of the young plane trees. Digby relaxed a little. A drunk.

'Come on, you,' he said. He tried to inject some levity into his tone. The man did not move. Digby was faintly aware that in the distance Bright Hemmings had fallen silent. He and this man were alone in the heavy darkness of the London night. 'Wake up,' he said, giving the inert mass a sharp, practiced kick. It did not stir.

He changed the details in the telling, of course, but that was how Edward Digby found Pierre Renard dead.

CHAPTER ONE

28th April, 1792

*This book has been ordered special for me from Mr Laveen.
The best marbled paper, the finest calfskin, although we had a
dispute about the quality of the gilding; but it is well enough.
One day, all of the things in my house will be as beautiful as
this book.*

*I wish to keep a record of my thoughts; not just for myself (for
there are few persons I can confide in), but because the generations that follow me will wish to know of Pierre Renard. Founder
of a dynasty of silversmiths. Gentleman. This is not mere intention, but resolution; I have my eyes set high. This precious record
will serve as a reminder of the rough road I have travelled, when
I one day come to write of my life. For now, I will keep it tucked
away: as safe as silver.*

*

She did not know what prompted her to turn her eyes away from the full moon on that winter's evening in 1781. She had waited, unmoving, for so long, her face cold against the windowpane.

That was when she saw him. Even before she could make out his face, she recognized the way he moved, each step with a confident spring to it. Hope died in her, as quietly as a candle snuffed out by a draught. She had allowed herself to hope he would not come.

All day she had listened for the sound of her brother Eli's footsteps on the stairs; she kept forgetting that he had been taken to stay with her aunt. Without him the house seemed to have lost its soul, and the silence was heavy and charged, like the air when a storm is approaching. She longed to hear his laughter and his quick, lively footsteps. But Mary had been made to understand that Eli's absence was absolutely necessary: the survival of her marriage prospects depended upon it. A clean, healthy bloodline, Pierre had said: strong, wholesome sons. Pierre Renard esteemed Mary, but the small brother who sat watching him, staring as though he could see into the very soul of a person: he was a problem.

'Look at the silversmith's moon, Marie,' Mr Renard said that evening, her name becoming French under the influence of his voice. When they had first met, she had thought it was mere affectation, for though of French parentage, he had been born in England. But now she realized his accent strengthened by habit rather than will, when he was trying to make love to her, or persuade a stranger of his artistic heritage. She said nothing.

'What do you see?' he said.

'The night sky,' she said. He gave a little sigh: the wrong answer. She tried again. 'The full moon?' she said, and was relieved to feel his hands squeeze her arms, a gesture of approbation.

'When you see the moon,' he said, 'I see silver. A blank disc of silver, waiting on my bench to be worked. It is the moment I love the most.' His voice lowered to a whisper, as though he was telling her some profound secret. 'The moment of potential.'

After he had gone, she stood at the window, and thought: it is not too late, not yet. I must do something, now. I must end this.

Mary came to with a start. The memory stayed with her, fading only as she looked around her, and she realized she had been dreaming of a time long ago, and of events that were fixed and irreversible. Eleven years had passed from that November night to this one – but still, the words moved through her mind, as slowly as a piece of cotton pulled through the eye of a needle.

It is not too late. I must do something. I must end this.

Dazed and half-asleep, she rubbed her eyes and breathed steadily, waiting for her heartbeat to slow. She was alone; in her little parlour, the fire was burning low, casting shadows on the wall behind her. She shifted in the hard chair: mahogany, with a shield-shaped back, chosen by her husband. She wondered if he wished her always to be uncomfortable. As she put her hand back to rub her neck she felt that her skin was damp with sweat.

'Pierre?' she called, and heard her voice falter. She was relieved when there was no response. But of course: after dinner he had left with the words 'I may be late', by which she knew that he would be gone for most of the evening, and possibly all night. She had said nothing and tried to keep her expression neutral, an approach that sometimes calmed Pierre, and sometimes maddened him. For a man who had made his way from obscurity to a goldsmith's shop on Bond Street, he had a surprisingly thin skin.

Mary glanced nervously at the clock: it was nearly one, and her hands went to her keys before she remembered that she had secured the doors straight after dinner. Some instinct had urged her to make the tour of the house then, locking the inhabitants into their rooms – customary in many houses, but strictly adhered to at Pierre Renard's establishment on New Bond Street. Had she fallen asleep without doing it, she would have been culpable indeed.

In the long evenings when he left her alone, she would step on to the street for a moment before locking the door, casting one brief look up and down, lest her husband was approaching. She could not recall doing it this evening, but her slippers were damp, so she must have done. She closed her eyes, and massaged her temples: two glasses of red wine at dinner had dulled her nerves, but now she could not remember the evening, only her intention to be safe, and her fear of her husband's displeasure. It was the monotony of trying to please Pierre; each nerve strained in one direction, so that every other part of life was peripheral. Her husband's approval was a thin line to walk, and she often stepped off it by accident. At the thought of it a cold, hard little bead of anger rolled in her stomach; every day she felt it sitting there, insoluble, like one of the pills her husband bade her take to help her breed, Dr Taylor's scrawled writing on the label.

A noise. She tensed.

Someone was knocking on the front door.

There was a short pause, and when the sound came again, it was harder. Soon it was joined by another noise – was someone calling? She sat, immobile with fear. The silver and gold plate were never far from her mind, and the house was vulnerable without its master. Her maid would be fast asleep; Grisa, the shop manager, was in his lodgings a street away; and though the apprentice slept in the shop downstairs he was merely a boy.

'Marie.'

She heard the shout; heard her name, indistinct, but pronounced as only he would. If he was shouting in the street he was in drink and in a vengeful mood. She ran downstairs and took to unlocking the door, her hands clumsy and fumbling in the near darkness. Luckily she had left the bar off, not feeling strong enough to lift it. When she finally opened the door the face that appeared out of the night was not that of her husband, but his friend, Dr Taylor, the physician.

'Oh,' she said, giving a little sigh of relief.

He leaned against the doorframe, as though trying to diminish his height – six foot in his stockinged feet, as he was proud of saying. 'Mrs Renard,' he said. And his words, too, came out with a sigh, as though after all his knocking he was sorry she had come to the door.

'Dr Taylor,' she said, with a small curtsey. 'It is very late, sir.' She wondered whether he was in liquor; there was something not quite right about the expression on his face. He was always a plainer dresser than Pierre, but normally so fastidious that it was strange to see him in dishevelled clothes, and the wig he normally wore – a little old-fashioned, but elegant – left off. It made him look curiously vulnerable.

They regarded each other in the moonlight. His eyes were shining, watery; he looked as though he was on the brink of tears.

'Do you wish to come in?' she suggested helpfully, then cautioned: 'My husband is not at home.'

'No,' he said. 'But it is for him that I am here.'

Talking in riddles, she thought in her befuddled brain. *Perhaps it is some game they have been playing again* – she knew how Pierre and Taylor delighted each other with wordplay, though she often thought they sounded like overgrown children. She let him in, and directed him up to the parlour. If he was going to speak cryptically to her, they may as well be warm; and as for respectability – there was no one respectable out to know that she was receiving him without Pierre in the house. She followed him up the stairs wearily.

She thought later how strange it was that he should make such a mess of it. Dear Dr Taylor, who was normally so authoritative; so used, as a doctor, to presiding over birth and death. Yet there he was, walking up and down her parlour, the floorboards protesting beneath his heavy feet, his hesitant speech fading to a mumble as he groped for words.

He said her husband's name several times, as though by saying it, it would give him the momentum to speak on, but each time his voice trailed off, and he muttered the name of Digby, and spoke of Berkeley Square, and of footpads.

'Please tell me what has happened,' she said, eventually. Taylor ceased his pacing. He stood over her. It was odd to see his face, which usually bore an expression of jovial kindness, twisted with sorrow, the shadows and the fire-light laying contrasts on it, making him seem gargoyle-like.

'He is dead,' he said. 'Someone has taken him from us. I am sorry. So very sorry.' Then, hesitantly: 'Marie.' It was the use of her Christian name that most clearly showed his distress; until this night, he had never said it. A fat tear rolled down his cheek.

Mary stared at the floorboards, and the Turkey rug that Pierre had made such a fuss over. 'Make sure it is brushed, Ellen, and brushed properly,' he had said to the maid before he left. There was a spot of dirt on it. She had to resist falling on to her knees and picking it up, pincering it between the nails of her thumb and forefinger, before Pierre came back and saw it.

'Has the constable been called?' she said.

'The watchman will make his report to him, but – when he was found – there was no one nearby.'

'How did he die?' she said. She knew it was an unlady-like question, but she also knew that in his current state, Taylor would tell her; tomorrow, it would be too late, but for now, all delicacy and convention had flown.

'They cut his throat,' he said. His voice was barely a whisper.

Tick, tock, went Pierre's lantern clock, and as Mary's eyes darted around the room, all she could see were things chosen by her husband, for he had crafted his home carefully. She gazed on the dull brass colour of the lantern clock; it was over a hundred years old, he had told her when he bought it. She would have preferred something else in this room: something made of wood, 'something feminine', he had scoffed. Everything in the house had been done to his liking. Except for the papers in this room: cream, with little scarlet fruits. They had agreed on the choice, startling each other with acquiescence.

She heard the doctor pull a chair towards her, and felt him take her hands. They were unexpectedly rough. He was an accoucheur, and she had always assumed his hands would be soft, silken, for attending to a woman's most delicate parts; but no, these were large paws, chapped, as though if you stroked them the wrong way the skin would rise up like scales.

I never had a child, she thought. And I never will, now. In this, as in so many ways, I failed my husband and my family. She closed her eyes and thought: my poor, dead father, and his promises.

The night he had proposed to her, Pierre had made her come to him on the front steps of her father's house. He was standing just beyond the front step, looking up at the night sky. He seemed elaborately posed; had her father given him a few minutes to prepare himself? Beneath his cutaway coat she glimpsed the lilac satin waistcoat and the large watch he was so proud of, the gold case chased with putti and clouds, and bordered by thin slices of coloured hardstone. He treasured that watch; he never let anyone touch it but him, keeping them at a distance with one hand as he showed it to them. His shoe buckles were new additions, set with glittering white pastes, and were larger than any she had seen before. He stood as though he was acutely aware of them, and wanted to show them to their best advantage. Every movement said: you are lucky, madam. I have chosen you. Every movement had spoken of self-confidence, and his certainty that he would rise in the world. Now, someone had cut him down.

She did not know how long she sat with Dr Taylor, only that her reverie was broken by the house itself, warning her of the people within. She heard footsteps on the wooden floors upstairs; the suggestion of her servant's and lodgers' voices. 'I'd better unlock the doors. They'll have heard you come in,' she said. But instead of going up she went straight downstairs, to the door that divided the hall from the shop. Again, she had to fumble with the keys to get the door open.

On the other side her husband's apprentice was standing. He alone of the house's inhabitants had stayed quiet, but he was dressed and awake. She had guessed he would be most afraid, and she could see he was trembling. She put a hand out to him in reassurance. He was still recognizable as the fifteen-year-old sent to them from the Welsh borders some five months before who had taken to following Pierre around with the grateful look of a rescued cur. The dim candlelight glanced off his blonde head, his blue eyes in their bruised hollows wide with misgiving. He did not take her hand.

'Come on, Benjamin,' she said. 'There are bad tidings. Your master is dead.' Her voice wavered only slightly on the word: dead. The boy looked at her dumbly. She gave him the keys. 'Go upstairs. Unlock the others. I haven't the strength.'

It was unprecedented for her to hand over the keys, but Benjamin took them without a word and bolted past her. As she went back into the parlour, Mary heard the thumps and creaks as he ascended the upper stairs in his lumbering, heavy-footed way. She sat down again.

'You may go, Dr Taylor,' she said. 'It is late. You must be needed at home.'

The doctor stood up, but did not show any sign of going to the door. 'He was a good man,' he said. 'He was my best friend, in all the world.' At the sight of her face, he seemed to remember himself. 'My sincere condolences. Are you sure you wish me to leave? Can I not be of assistance in some way?' He stayed where he stood, looking her over as though she was one of his patients. She felt the piercing intensity of something just out of vision begin to strum at her nerves.

'I am sure,' she said. 'Please go. If you would come again in the morning?'

He bowed, and withdrew. 'Ho, there!' he called in the passage. Mary heard Benjamin descend the stairs and let him out; then the locking began again, concluded by the apprentice grunting slightly as he heaved the bar across the door, the bar she had left unhooked.

She heard the voices of her servants and lodgers in the passageway. But Mary stayed still. She realized she had not asked Dr Taylor where her husband was now. He must be somewhere; they would not have left him out there, lying on the cold ground. She felt the weight of her incapability descend upon her. Her sister Mallory would have asked, and made sure things were dealt with properly.

Her housemaid came in, dressed in her outside cloak over her nightgown. She crouched down beside Mary, and took her hands.

'You are icy cold, ma'am,' she said. 'I thought you were walking again, when I heard the footsteps; but I was locked in, and could not come to you. I was afraid you would go out into the night, and have no one to bring you back.'

Mary looked down, feeling the familiar shame. She had sleepwalked for years, and only once had her husband shaken her awake. At the memory of it she could feel the primal horror it had awakened in her: a seam of terror running from her throat to her breastbone. Her scream, like an animal, he said, had woken every inhabitant of the house. He had cursed her for it, and never woken her again, always rousing Ellen from her bed to talk Mary soothingly back to her room or to a chair in the parlour.

'I am cold,' said Mary. 'My feet are damp, from standing on the doorstep. I wish my sister was here.'

'But it's too late to go out,' said Ellen, and Mary saw the fear in her eyes. 'Who did it, Mrs Renard?'

Mary shook her head. 'I do not know,' she said, and covered her face with her hands.

The girl slipped out and returned with a glass of red wine. Her hand trembled as she put it down on the table next to Mary. She banked the fire, then brought a shawl in, and wrapped it around her still mistress, gently pulling Mary's reddish-brown hair free from it and smoothing it over her shoulders as one would to a child.

The other inhabitants of the house did not go back to bed. Roused by the news of a sudden death they stood around, conferring, in low voices. Who could have done it? He was, they all agreed, a difficult man – but this?

Mary watched the flames rise and fall. She was hardly aware when Benjamin came into the room, and put the keys by her with a clunk, scratching the flawless surface of Pierre's tea table.

She realized she was hunched tight, her arms folded around her body as though she sought to hold herself still. As her hand slid down she felt a dull pain, just above her wrist, and pulled back her sleeve. On the underside of her arm there were three bruises: three small perfect circles in a line. As she saw them, she heard her brother calling her, a voice from eleven years ago.

Mare-lee. Mare-lee.

A door slammed shut.

'It's a full moon,' she heard the maid say in the passage. 'It makes my flesh creep.'

Mary began to laugh; and once she started, she found she could not stop.

CHAPTER TWO

1st May, 1792

I must begin by saying that my blood is French. It is a century since my mother's family came to this country, silk weavers driven here by cruel religious intolerance, and though I may pass for an Englishman, the name of France is engraved on my heart: for it is the source of taste, of true art and of craftsmanship fit for kings. My father was descended from a goldsmith's family, creators of some of the finest silver and gold plate this country has ever seen; but he died before I was born and my mother, denied by his family, gave me her name. She died when I was barely walking, and I knew only of a cousin living in some distant part of the country, only lately reconciled to me.

From such sad beginnings, I have come, and my present circumstances, to some, would be enviable indeed. I own a fine shop on Bond Street, where I live with my wife, Mary, and our servants and lodgers. People of quality flock to my shop, for I know how to match each man with the piece of silver or gold plate that will appeal to him: for this man, beauty matters; for this man, utility. I am a master at it.

Yesterday, a newly married couple came calling to the shop when I was not there. It sounds as though they are prepared to spend a good portion on plate, but Grisa – my shop manager, an emotional fellow – was apparently all of a fluster with them, and instead of serving them well, took the gentleman's card, and said I would call upon them. Their names are Mr and Mrs Chichester, and I go to Berkeley Square to see them, this morning.

In the morning light, Joanna Dunning laid out the pots on the satinwood veneer of her mistress's dressing table, the silver cold beneath her hands. Here the powder pot; here the pin tray. Each piece had its place. After laying them out in their prescribed positions, she looked at them. Then she straightened them again: sometimes moving each box an inch or two, sometimes merely touching it, careful not to scratch the polished mirrored surface of the dressing table with the ornamented surfaces.

It passed the time, she supposed. Which was the business of life.

In such moments she would reflect on the journey she had taken, from the milliner's shop where she had begun her working life to the coveted role of lady's maid. Time in service had taught her that it was best not to look too closely at things. She saw evidence of life's baseness everywhere; for all its grand furnishings, the air in the room was thick with the closeted fug of the bedroom, and for all her care the silver bore the traces of a hundred touches by her fingertips.

She glanced over her shoulder at her mistress. Harriet Chichester lay propped up on a mound of pillows, her golden curls spread around her, sipping her chocolate lethargically. Joanna had hoped a young bride would be easy to work for – she had been engaged by Harriet's mother only days before her wedding – but the new Mrs Chichester had rapidly disproved this notion by displaying a fierce temper. Just this morning she had lashed out at Joanna on waking. Luckily, Joanna had stepped back, so the pretty little claw met nothing but air; in servitude, as in life, anticipation was all.

You have known nothing of suffering, Joanna thought, and thus nothing of life. To her, the girl's face seemed unfinished; unlined skin set with moist, china-blue eyes across which thoughts moved as clearly as clouds across the sky. It was a countenance unmarked by experience. Joanna supposed it was this very blankness that had meant Harriet was referred to as a beauty. For the last seven months, she had searched that face with her gaze as she tended to it; but try as she might, she could not see anything beautiful there, and could see no trace of a soul behind the eyes. Mrs Chichester seemed to be merely the sum of her wants and desires, and a voracious seeker of novelty.

I must have been muddle-headed to pursue this situation, she thought; I must have taken a thimble too much of gin with Mallory. She moved the pin tray again and tilted her head to gauge whether she liked its new position.

'Joanna?' came the small, fretful voice from the bed.

'Yes, madam?'

'I want to wear the white muslin today.'

'It's rather cold for that, madam.'

'I don't care.'

'Very good, madam.'

The white, always the white. And in the midst of winter. Out she'd go, stepping out of the carriage and on to the filthy London streets, wandering around just long enough to cover the hem in mud. How in Christ's name was she supposed to get it clean? How would the weak winter sun bleach that out?

I am not the only one, she thought, who finds you hard to bear. For it was evident that Harriet's husband, Nicholas Chichester, was growing more despairing by the day. He was only a year older than Harriet's twenty years, and it was the opinion of the servants' hall that he had married his wife for her father's coal pits, and the money they brought him, under command from his own father. Joanna felt sorry for him; he seemed too young, and clever, to have been saddled with such a torment as Harriet. But there was something discomforting about him, too: he had the air of a person who preferred his books to people; and he had some odd notions. Like the silver-gilt toilet service she stood over now.

Joanna had been there the day Mr Chichester had explained all to Harriet. His mother had had such a set, handed down from her mother, and they had been forced to be rid of it at some time (he had hinted at a mystery – but Joanna suspected it had been sold, for she had heard the family's fortunes rose and fell like mercury). Never one to eschew a new purchase, Harriet had agreed to the commission with enthusiasm. Mr Renard of Bond Street had been called in to design and execute it.

So far, all had been sweet between the newlyweds; or as sweet as could be, thought Joanna, for two strangers pushed together.

But over the silver, their innate incompatibility had emerged. Harriet had insisted on choosing her own designs, on veering away from the restrained, classical direction her husband had favoured. No, smooth lines and elegant, plain surfaces were tedious to her; there were to be flowers, and perhaps a cherub or two? Mr Renard had been called to the house repeatedly. Designs had been drawn up, rejected, and drawn up again. He had trudged up and down the grand staircase, a self-approving, amused smile playing over his mouth, for he found her pettishness engaging, it seemed. Barely a week after agreement had been reached, Harriet had complained that it was not ready.

Finally it had arrived. A set of sixteen pieces: boxes, trays, snuffers. Each box's silver lid finely chased with flowers. The silver covered with a wash of gold, by her insistence, each surface glowing, so it seemed to light up the room, especially in the evening when the candles were burning. The mirror, set in an elaborate frame, was so large and heavy it had taken two men to carry it up the winding marble staircase. How they had grunted and sweated, rolling their eyes at the voluble directions of Mr Renard. And everywhere, Harriet's initials. As Renard told Mr and Mrs Chichester, it was a toilet service fit for a duchess.

Some bloody duchess, thought Joanna. Harriet had barely had it a month and already she was careless of it; dropping things, banging the boxes against each other. In the last day or so it had seemed as though she intentionally wanted to damage it. Joanna wanted to tell her to be careful of it; that she wouldn't get another. This would be hers for her lifetime now, just like the husband that she treated as an amusing toy.

You could tell Mr Chichester hadn't wanted to have the initials engraved upon it. She had watched him when it was unveiled, he and Harriet standing awkwardly side by side like two children pushed together against their inclinations, his eyes veering away from the HCs everywhere. Joanna understood. He wanted the service to be passed down through his family, an heirloom unsullied by Harriet's name. He had suggested that the initials be left off. But when he had said it, holding the designs in his pale, long-fingered hands, Harriet had made a fuss, her eyes brimming with tears. Mr Renard had looked askance at him: come on, indulge the lady, his expression had said, his fingers running over his elaborately embroidered waistcoat; gold thread, as gold as the dressing set. And Mr Chichester, so nearly a man, but still with something of the student about him, had allowed himself to be bowed down, and submitted. In a moment Harriet's tears had been transformed to smiles, and Renard was laughing, looking at her face as though she enchanted him.

Joanna pushed away the memory; it annoyed her, and what good did that do? In the past she had been able to dismiss her envy of those she served. But there was something about Harriet, and about the relationship between the Chichesters, which was creeping in under her defences. Some nerve had been found and pressed; and she did not know how to dissolve the irritation that welled up in her every day.

'Joanna?' Harriet had taken her place at the dressing table.

Joanna started to tease out her hair. She did it carefully, as precisely as she arranged the pots and boxes on the tabletop, and as she did so she could not stop her thoughts from returning to her master.

Mr Chichester had, at first, made nightly visits to his wife's bedroom. As a paid confidante to a green young woman, Joanna was spared no detail. It was only in the last month or so that his visits had tailed off, and now ceased. Less laundry, she thought, which was good; then she realized that Harriet had not bled for some weeks, and the thought of a child halted her hands for a moment.

She wished she didn't know half the things she did. She wished she was still the innocent girl she had once been, before service forced her to know too much of others' lives. Coming to this house on Berkeley Square had been a step too far on a long road. These days the experience weighed her down, hardening not just her heart but her face too: setting valleys and ravines into skin that had once been fresh and soft. Had he lived, she thought, Stephen would hardly recognize her now.

Her hands moved; a little involuntary tug on Harriet's hair. But, unusually, her mistress did not cry out.

'What are you thinking of?' said Harriet.

'Only how I should do your hair,' said Joanna.

'You looked so thoughtful,' said Harriet. Joanna opened the silver box that contained black pins.

'I will tell you what I was thinking of,' said Harriet. 'I was thinking of how my servants lie to me.'

Joanna looked up at their joint reflection in the huge mirror. Harriet's blue eyes watched her, her lips compressed. Joanna saw her own face, and it looked strange to her: the dark hair drawn tightly back, her brown eyes, her features oddly passive and immobile. She thanked God for the lack of expression on her face: a cultivated inscrutability, worth the years of practice.

'For example,' said Harriet, 'I know that my husband was not alone last night. That he was in the library with someone. And yet, you told me he had gone to his club.'

Joanna's mouth was dry. She continued to dress her mistress's hair, turning her eyes to the task in hand. Let her talk, she thought, let her run the stream of her thoughts dry, and I will see what I am dealing with. It had not been a malicious falsehood; it had been a way of freeing herself from Harriet's company. The master had dismissed his staff yesterday evening, for it suited him to have privacy. It was rare that the servants were all together, but they had played cards in the basement room known as the servants' hall. Unusually, Joanna had enjoyed herself, even breaking through her brusque shyness to risk a remark or two. Now and then the butler had run upstairs and checked the silent staircase hall and the dim seam of light under the library door.

'I heard something,' said Harriet. 'I suspected you had

lied to me. I went to my window; and I saw a figure on the steps, all wrapped up in a cloak, so I went down. There was no one there. I could barely spend a moment on the steps. It was so cold.'

Joanna imagined Harriet tiptoeing down the stairs; opening the front door, and stepping tentatively out on to the front steps, arms bare, her breath misting in the winter night. 'Forgive me, but you should not go outside, madam,' she said. 'It is not right. What if someone had seen you? It would ruin your reputation.'

They would know you are not a lady, she thought. That you are counterfeit, with the blood of a pit-owner flowing in your veins. She did not say it; for all her bitterness, she did not have the bent for deliberate malice.

'no one saw me,' said Harriet. The pettish tone had returned to her voice; her normal tone of a child, thwarted in her will.

Joanna felt on safer ground. 'It is for your health I worry the most,' she said. 'The cold is dangerous; what if you had caught a chill? I sought only to soothe you, madam. I believed Mr Chichester had gone to his club.'

'Help me dress,' said Harriet.

Joanna laced her, and the knowledge that Harriet had not had her flux made her do it looser; there was no need for tight lacing with the current fashions, and she thought her mistress would not notice.

'You lace as quickly as you sew,' said Harriet, a little smile darting across her face. Joanna said nothing, but as she began to fasten up Harriet put her hand out, and took one of her wrists. 'Tighter,' she said. 'I do not wish to be one of those fat old wives, neglected by her husband. I wish always to be a girl.'

Joanna stared at her.

'Go on,' said Harriet.

Joanna took a breath, and pulled. It was good the mistress couldn't see it, she thought, her one chink of weakness. Because when she did it, she had to close her eyes.

CHAPTER THREE

2nd May, 1792

The Chichesters will do well for me, I think; they wish for a fine toilet service to be made. Such a quaint idea, but one that takes a good deal of bullion, and a good deal of fashioning, so I am satisfied. The husband asked me how I had come to be a silversmith, and I spoke lightly of it, but as I walked away I thought further on it, and of how no man knows the truth that lies in my heart.

After my mother's death I was taken in by a family she had known. They were prosperous, charitable people and the father, Mr Pelletier, took to me and thought me worthy of his time. In his company, I saw my first jeweller's shop. How my heart leapt at the sight of such wealth: the precious stones glittering, and the silver plate casting light over the room. I decided, earnest beyond my years, that this was where my vocation lay, and begged him to help me find an apprenticeship. Before long, I was apprenticed to a goldsmith in Cheapside; Mr Pelletier paid my premium partly in furs and partly in money. I believe his children envied the affection he had for me, for when he left this world they did not send word to me. I felt that, and resent it still. It is strange, with life, for my resentments seem to pile on top of each other, so that they all together build into an anger that haunts me. Why should things that happened so long ago cause me to crumple up a sheet of good paper, or make me wish to snap the pen in my hand as I stare at my ledger?

As she emerged on to New Bond Street, Mary bowed her head. She had often thought there was something cruel about the morning light, and now splinters of it seemed to be embedding themselves into the sensitive membranes of her eyes. She felt the delicate, papery skin around her eyes crease in discomfort. With a pang of guilt she thought it was lucky Pierre was not here to see her, and tell her that she was not the fresh young girl he had married, her outward disintegration the sign of her inward inferiority.

She had been left alone in the parlour all night, and even as the sun began to shine her people did not want to come and stir her. She hadn't noticed the glow of sunlight around the shutters until Ellen came and took the keys again. 'Are we to open up the shop, Mrs Renard?' she said. She had taken on the role of spokesperson, the men of the house shying away from the mistress's unpredictable state. Mary opened her mouth, but couldn't formulate a reply. She felt empty of all emotion; anaesthetized by a general numbness.

She heard Ellen pad back to the passage and report to the others that the mistress was insensible. There was a short debate, and Mary decided not to go out there and interrupt it; she had the vague sense that they were enjoying it. Whatever they had to say, she was not interested in it. She was saved from further decision-making when Grisa, the shop manager, arrived noisily on the scene. She heard his voice, heavily accented as always in imitation of her husband, expressing his shock and alarm as Ellen told him the news. He was a theatrical man who always wished to be attired appropriately, so she wondered whether she might hear him beg leave to return to his lodgings to don full mourning. Instead he began to shape a response that the others could follow: ordering black cloth to drape the counters, chiding Benjamin for his uselessness, and weeping flamboyantly. All of these things he did loudly enough for her to hear from the parlour.

As he gave directions for the others to rearrange the shop, Mary left quickly and quietly, unnoticed in the midst of diversion, like the most enterprising of prisoners. She ran down the stairs and out into the light, without even putting on her hat or cloak, still wearing the clothes of the night before. As she passed the window she saw Grisa waving his arms as he berated the apprentice. For all of his fastidiousness, she noticed that his wig was slightly askew.

She had acclimatized to the light before she reached the end of Bond Street. She turned left along Piccadilly and walked without looking up until she came to Castle Street, where her sister lived. It had been months since she had last come to this door. There she knocked, persistently, until Mallory yanked the door open, cursing under her breath.

The sight of Mary seemed to drain all of Mallory's aggression away. She put her hand to her sister's forehead. 'Are you sick?' she said.

Mary shook her head. 'It's Pierre,' she said. 'Someone killed him. They wouldn't bring you to me last night.'

Her sister stared at her. Her brown eyes, so dark they seemed almost black even in the morning light, showed nothing. 'You look like hell,' she said, and taking Mary's wrist, she pulled her into the house. Weakness wasn't for the London streets, not at any time of day. 'It's a wonder you arrived here unmolested, looking like that.'

Mary followed Mallory in and sank into a kitchen chair as her sister bellowed at her children and coerced them into going upstairs. The house, though tall enough to be impressive from without, was only two rooms deep, and much of its life revolved around the kitchen, its gloom only assuaged by the flickering of the fire. Mallory's second husband had been dead a year and she often complained that her children's noise swelled up and filled the space he had left behind. 'Will you never give me any peace?' she shouted after the retreating backs as they raced each other upstairs. Mary thought kindly of poor, complaining Francis Dunning; her brother-in-law had known her since childhood. Had he been here, he would have embraced her.

Mallory did not; she moved around quickly, here and there, tidying things, as though at any moment she might start butting at the confines of the house. There had been no love lost between Mallory and Pierre. Even now Mary could sense that it was not grief agitating her sister, but rather the tension of words left unsaid. Mallory was so direct that she could sooner ignore the thrust of a knife than her own thoughts, always pushing to be spoken.

Finally she sat down by the fire, opposite Mary.

'How?' she asked.

'His throat was cut last night in Berkeley Square,' said Mary.

Mallory left a barely decent silence. 'He ruffled too many feathers,' she said. 'He was bound to push someone too far, one day.'

'You think someone killed him purposely?' said Mary.

'Drawing a knife across someone's throat is hardly accidental,' said Mallory. 'Though for the number of enemies he had, it will not be worth you engaging the Runners to investigate. Unless there is someone they are thinking of for the crime?'

Mary shook her head. 'I thought footpads,' she said. 'I don't know what I thought.' It crossed her mind that she had not even considered a motive, in the same way that she did not question why the rain fell or the sun rose.

'Look at the state of you.' Mallory got up, took out her comb from her pocket, and began to untangle her sister's hair, carefully but firmly, ignoring Mary's intake of breath when she tackled a knot.

'Dr Taylor will call a coroner's meeting. I should go,' said Mary.

'No reason for you to be there, even if they let you.'

'I feel I should. Perhaps it would be real for me, if I saw him.'

'With your nature?' said Mallory. As a child Mary had been plagued by nightmares; small traumas brushed off in moments by Mallory had lasted weeks for her. 'It's real enough as it is. No husband, no income.' She finished the combing to her satisfaction, and sat back down.

They looked at each other. 'Can you be our plain old English Mary again, no more madame this, and madame that, now he is dead?' said Mallory.

'You're glad of it, aren't you?' said Mary.

Yes. The word appeared in her mind as if Mallory had spoken it aloud.

'Don't snap my head off,' said Mallory sharply. Mary wondered how, on such a morning, she could still be rebuked. 'It's a terrible thing and I'm not saying it's not. I just thought you could be an Englishwoman again. It's probably his French mouth that got him into trouble. Someone fancied him a Jacobin, all the stuff he was fond of spouting. He'd say anything if he could vex someone.'

Mary regarded her sister carefully; the way she had gathered her teeth together under tight lips, she was just about suppressing a tut. She was right, she supposed, in her remembrance of Pierre talking in that way: after the Revolution, he'd really laid it on.

'Who's at the shop?' Always businesslike, Mallory was. 'I hope you haven't gone and left all the doors and windows open, in the care of that fool Grisa.'

'Ellen and Benjamin are there,' said Mary. 'People will come. Everyone will have heard.'

'Of course they will. What do you expect? They're probably rummaging around in the plate chest as we speak.'

'No they're not. Grisa is a faithful guard. I trust him as I would a brother.' She felt unbearably tired. She had come to Mallory for comfort, but now she could almost hear the chime of silver on silver, the greasy fingerprints left on valuables looked over. 'Oh for goodness' sake,' she snapped, irritation breaking through. 'no one will touch my plate.' Mallory tutted out loud this time, as though to indicate that, on a normal morning, she would have said more. She trusted no one; not even a theoretical brother. Mary took her arm.

'Will you not ask me how I feel?' she said.

Mallory was stilled at last. She stood, and it seemed to Mary that her words had dissolved her sister's rage. 'No,' she said, eventually. 'No, I will not.'

'I feel nothing,' said Mary.

Mallory put her hands on Mary's shoulders. 'Hush,' she said. 'It is over.'

When she walked back to Bond Street, the crowds, the noise, the cold sunlight all made Mary feel giddy. She tried to hold her shoulders back, to walk as Mallory would, but the effort only lasted for a moment, before the fear came, overtaking everything. I said my silver, she thought. I said it was mine. She glanced over her shoulder. And for a moment it was as if Pierre walked beside her.

'Everything,' he said. 'Everything you have, you owe to me.'

There was almost nothing Edward Digby liked more than a good coroner's meeting, and Pierre Renard's was no exception. He arrived early at the tavern near St George's,

Hanover Square, and dallied around outside greeting some of the tradesmen he knew. It was a cool evening, but it had been a day of pale sunshine and a vein-blue sky, and the light had cheered him. When he'd amused himself for half an hour he went inside the tavern, the customary place for coroner's meetings in the parish, and watched the men as they arrived. The constable did not come; he had told Digby he had a particularly profitable case to pursue that evening, and besides, Digby himself was the key witness.

He'd felt better today, and not just because it was a bright day. When he'd got home after discovering Renard he had slept in the arms of a woman – a tart, but still a woman. He could not remember how long it had been since he had been held like that, but her embrace had imparted to him a liquid warmth that had clung to his skin, blood and bones. He felt happy. He thought if he had that warmth every night, he would soon be cured of his ills.

In the chill of the evening the cold was finding him again and he was obliged to rub his hands together for warmth, cursing the innkeeper for his meagre fire. Though he stayed to the side, trying to disappear into the shadows and merely observe, his red hair and jiggling limbs made this almost impossible. Dr Taylor, the coroner, was first to arrive. He had been appointed as coroner only a year before, and Digby wondered how the well-connected Taylor found balancing the needs of the dead with those of the expectant mothers of Mayfair. The man certainly looked tired.

After Taylor, the members of the jury followed. Most of them didn't care to speak to Digby, of course; they had their own concerns, and merely glanced at him before looking for someone more useful to converse with. Before long the air in the room seemed thick with self-importance. The tone of their voices rankled with him, and he could feel his good mood slipping away.

Henry Maynard, the foreman of the jury, was one of the last in, and the first to acknowledge the watchman. He had the relaxed demeanour of a man past fifty who had nothing to prove to his fellow men. Digby liked him: Maynard was a real gentleman; unobtrusive, not flashily rigged up, and always free with his coins.

'My good man,' Maynard said, by way of a salute. Digby managed a smile, although it didn't quite reach his pale eyes.

'What's your business here today?' said Maynard.

'It was me who found him,' said Digby, nodding to his right, where they were bringing the body in. He said it in the same voice he always used: emotionless. But he felt cheerful about his find. He was the talk of the watch. Long would Watkin regret staying in and reading poetry.

'You did?' said Maynard. 'I thought perhaps you were an old acquaintance of his. You were a silversmith once, were you not?'

A deep one, that Maynard, thought Digby. He remembered everything, even the things you didn't want him to.

'Yes,' he said. 'That is, apprenticed to one. But life don't always take you the line you want to go, does it?' In a brave attempt to change the subject, he again directed his gaze towards the bearers of the coffin. 'I didn't know him to speak to. Knew *of* him, of course.'

'Yes, yes.' Maynard nodded thoughtfully as though what Digby had to say was of special interest. 'A strange character, Monsieur Renard. Shouldn't speak ill of the dead, of course, but I have a feeling half of the people here have come to be sure they've seen the last of him.' He smiled, and went to greet Dr Taylor, who, as coroner, was to preside over the meeting and report back to the magistrate, who was probably at home and on his second bottle of port by now.

Digby noticed that Dr Taylor's face was as green as unripe fruit. It wasn't difficult to see how uncomfortable he was; and certainly not for someone like Digby, who liked watching people. Despite Taylor's attempt to present a stoic expression, Digby's sharp eyes noted the sickly distress on his face as the coffin scraped on to the table, wood on wood. He saw him take his handkerchief out to wipe his forehead and then hold it, clenched tight in his fist.

Digby decided he wasn't going to waste pity on Taylor, not after their disagreement the night before. The man was too puffed up for his own good. Digby had been proud of himself: it wasn't as if Renard and Taylor were his own people, for they did not live on Berkeley Square. Yet he had remembered that they were connected, for he had often seen them coming home arm-in-arm in the hours of darkness, clearly having spent the night roistering – usually Renard was shouting about cards or women. Remembering their fellowship, Digby had called another member of the watch and told him to fetch Taylor, and the doctor had thanked him for it. Yet when other members of the watch had arrived to help move the body, and Digby had suggested carrying the body to the dead man's house on New Bond Street, Taylor had spoken sharply to him as though the suggestion was disgusting.

For Digby, it was simple, almost a matter of housekeeping; Renard was to be taken where he belonged. He couldn't understand Taylor's anger. He had also found it hard to shake off, and had been obliged to take home Cissie, who normally plied her trade on Piccadilly's side streets, so that he might have a little company. She had been most disconcerted when he had asked her only to lie alongside him, and put her arms around him.

Even now Digby found it hard to shrug off the look of angry disgust Taylor had cast him. In an attempt to divert himself he dwelt on Cissie's embrace, and reflected on the fact that he could have told the good doctor a thing or two about women. Like: it was a bad idea, an exceptionally bad idea, to take the corpse to the Taylor house, and leave its blood darkening Mrs Taylor's kitchen table. It was no excuse that he was seeking to spare Mrs Renard's delicate nature. Just thinking of it made him chuckle under his breath. Mrs Taylor was the kind of woman who wrapped her hair in bindings then slept still, untouched, like an effigy on a tomb in one of the old churches. The idea of her stumbling across a corpse in her kitchen was the funniest thing he'd thought of all week.

In its coffin the silversmith's body looked as lifeless and sallow as wax, a model in a show. But Digby saw the coroner was avoiding looking at it. It had never happened before, but Taylor seemed to be acting like a squeamish old bird. Still, what could you expect from a man who turned a profit from dealing with ladies' privates?

Eventually the doctor called the other men to attention. An expectant silence fell on the company, which became tinged with embarrassment when he fought to control his voice, clearing his throat several times. Eventually, he began. 'We are, gentlemen,' he said, 'called to enquire into the death of Pierre Renard, Esquire, of Bond Street, a fine Christian gentleman, who was regrettably killed in Berkeley Square.'

A murmur passed through the company. Digby folded his arms and looked on with interest. Pierre Renard was no Esquire, he knew, despite his pretensions. Henry Maynard stepped forwards, hat in hand, but with a sour expression on his face. He gave his condolences to Dr Taylor 'on the sad loss of his friend, *Mister* Renard. We should be exact, for the record.'

Taylor nodded in acknowledgement of the correction. A suggestion of a smile flitted across his face. 'He was rising in the world,' he said to the other man, as though they were alone in the room. Maynard looked unimpressed, and Digby admired the sardonic way he raised his eyebrows in response. 'As I say, exactness,' he murmured.

Regaining his composure, Taylor brusquely called Digby as a witness. Digby came forwards slowly, with measured steps. When he reached the table, he looked evenly around at the faces observing him. 'Gentlemen,' he said. The acoustics of the room made his voice resonate in a particularly agreeable way.

'Will you tell us what you have to say?' said Taylor. His voice had a harsh ring to it. Still angry, thought Digby, and for no reason. There, there, Doctor; calm your temper, now.

Digby recounted his discovery of Renard, although he left out the kick he'd dealt the body. He concluded by saying that Renard's watch chain had been hanging, loose and empty, when he turned the body over, and that his pockets had been emptied. 'I think it must have been theft, Dr Taylor,' he said, and murmurs broke from the circle of jurors. 'Theft,' he said again, for good measure. 'And a bloody job the killer made of it, for the gore had soaked the ground for several feet around.'

'Enough,' said Taylor harshly. There was an uncomfortable hiatus as the coroner stared at the floor. Digby felt the heat gathering in his cheeks. Eventually one of the younger men in the group stepped forwards and took control. 'Thank you, Mr Digby,' he said. 'You have discharged your duty.'

Digby looked him up and down suspiciously. It was beneath his dignity to be dismissed by someone just out of the nursery, but he wasn't prepared to do battle over it. He nodded, and backed into the shadows, to continue watching.

'Mr Digby may well be right,' said the young man, with careful ambiguity. 'And the watch will be advertised for, of course; but has anyone enquired as to why Mr Renard was in the vicinity of Berkeley Square at such a late hour? And what his business was there? Could he have been meeting somebody?'

Taylor glared at him and gave a little shake of his head.

'No?' continued the man. 'Perhaps enquiries should be made. Perhaps Mrs Renard—'

'This is no place for a lady,' said Taylor. Digby saw a little tremor of irritation move across the other man's face at being cut off.

'I agree with you there, Taylor,' said Maynard, a smile briefly flickering across his face as he spoke up. 'And if one were to look for a motive, you would be forced to cast your eye over the hopeless entanglements of Mr Renard's life. I do not doubt there were many. He was ever where he had no business to be; and last night was obviously no exception. I understand the constable has no notion of who could have done this other than a thief; and if Mrs Renard were to be put to the expense of an investigation, those she hired would hardly know where to begin.'

'Berkeley Square is but a stone's throw from where Pierre lived,' cried Taylor, his voice reaching an uncomfortably high pitch, as though it was being drawn painfully through his tight throat. 'We have no way of knowing why he was there but no reason to taint his reputation by suspecting that he was involved in some kind of scandal or bad business – if that is what you are implying, sir; and I see from the look on your face that it is.'

'I am implying nothing,' said Maynard.

'Now, gentlemen,' said another of the men. 'It is a cold evening, and the case seems clear enough to me. Mr Renard was murdered by some unknown person.'

There were nods and muttered agreements. Digby saw Maynard look at Taylor, but the coroner did not want to meet the foreman's gaze, and only nodded. 'Then, sirs,' Taylor said, 'let us set our hands and seals to that.'

In his pocket, Digby's hand closed around the watch. It was a risk to carry it with him, but he couldn't bear to be parted from it, and his landlady might find it if he left it in his rooms. It was the finest thing he had ever seen but, as he was discovering, it had a feel of its own too. His fingertips brushed over it: the chasing of clouds and cherubs, the smoothness of hardstone.

CHAPTER FOUR

10th May, 1792

After my liking period with my master, I was bound over as his apprentice; there were three others in the same workshop, and I was the most junior of them. These three were all sons of gentlemen, and they lived very well, almost as if nothing counted on their completing the work. They were more in Covent Garden than at home, leaving me in the kitchen to eat the stale bread and rancid butter which it pleased my mistress to feed me. I worked hard to ingratiate myself with my master and his wife, and learned ways of pleasing them. Before long, I shared in the food from their table. The way the other apprentices lived still sat badly with me, and though Mr Pelletier gave me a coin or two as an allowance, there was no way I could partake of the same pleasures as my fellows. Yet I was the hardest-working of all of them.

I learned of the injustice of life early, you see. Now I will never take a gentleman's son as an apprentice; and to me, a so-called born gentleman is worthless, except for the money he pays me. It is the self-made man that I respect, and raise my glass to.

Twenty-six hours on the mail coach, thought Alban Steele, was enough to kill a man. He felt as flattened and reduced to essentials as one of the letters he had travelled alongside. Longing to rest, to stretch, he looked out at the bustling crowds of Charing Cross, and wondered how he would fight his way through them to reach his cousin's house.

He had crossed the unimaginable gulf from his quiet world to this place, which had lived only in his memory for years. As the coach had slowed on the congested roads he'd looked out at the black night and seen the lights of the city glittering. It was true. He was in London. And if the view from the coach was anything to go by, she was just as he had left her.

He climbed down carefully, clinging to his pack, ready for the onslaught. Seven in the evening at Charing Cross. In the winter's darkness he felt the energy of London: the charged night. He was warier than he had ever been, for the newspapers talked of insurrection and riot, of fires lit all over, and coaches riding away from a burning city. Had he come here in time for revolution?

Through the noise he picked out a voice calling his name. He looked around. The sound came again, a thread tying him to this place, preventing him from pushing through the chaos: consistent, a pause for breath, then again. Finally, he found the source, a boy whose mouth opened repetitively like a cuckoo's. The child had pale flaxen hair, green eyes, and milk-white skin. Alban immediately saw the similarity to his cousin: the boy had to be Jesse's. He waved, then fought his way through the crowd.

'I'm your second cousin,' he said, as he reached him.

'I'm Grafton,' said the boy, and held his hand out. 'Pa says I'm to call you uncle.'

Alban smiled, and shook his hand. The boy had been a baby when he visited last. Grafton: Duke of, he thought. He wished his cousin would stop naming his children after patrons. It wasn't as if they would know or care. Had the Duke of Grafton been asked to recommend his silversmith, he would have said: Pierre Renard, at the sign of the Golden Acorn on Bond Street, for Renard liked to keep his sign as well as his number. His Grace the Duke had no knowledge of the man who had actually fashioned his favourite silver bread baskets. Alban had reasoned thus with his cousin years ago. 'It doesn't matter,' Jesse said. 'The plate on their tabletop was made by me, not that bloody Frenchman.' He refused to admit that the silver had Renard's maker's mark stamped all over it, obliterating Jesse's own.

Alban followed Grafton as he weaved his way through the crowds. He knew it was some way to Jesse's house, but he was glad of the walk, and glad too that Grafton was taciturn.

The action of walking helped him shake off the melancholy that had settled on him during the journey. Everyone had agreed it would be best for him to come here, to help Jesse. After all, that was what kin was for. The family silversmith's firm in Chester was doing well enough: his cousins there hardly needed him. But Jesse did. He was sickening, and there was talk of a large commission from Renard, which he wanted a part in. So Alban had come, with hardly any need of encouragement, back to the city he'd once cherished hopes of establishing himself in, but which he never had, kept to his place by habit and, he supposed, weakness of will. He had begun the journey electrified with hope and the knowledge that he was doing good.

He had travelled under the light of the full moon. They had just left the city and reached the open road when the driver had to pull up for an obstruction to be cleared from the horses' path. As the coach swayed to a halt the three other passengers, all ladies travelling together, started murmuring to each other. Their eyes were wide with alarm and one even gave a little shriek. Alban hardly blamed her; the roads from Chester were notorious for footpads. 'Be calm,' he said. 'Remember, we are armed; there is no need to stir yourselves.' But his words had little effect and he turned aside with irritation. As they waited in the moonlight, Alban looked out at the fields he had walked as a child and watched the long grass ripple in the wind.

I am leaving here for ever, he thought. The conviction that he would never return surprised him; for though no dates had been discussed, he'd initially thought his stay with Jesse would be temporary. What surprised him still further was that he felt no sorrow at his leave-taking. He tried to bring himself in touch with it. He tried to bid the familiar landscape goodbye as the mail coach started forwards again: to forge into his memory the view of the fields and the sky, blue-black in the moonlight.

His family had always told him he was too sensitive, too fastidious, too careful: and yet as the landscape of his childhood, so loaded with memories, had receded from him, he felt nothing. The nothingness was familiar to him. It approached him sometimes; he felt it in the middle distance, nearing him.

There is a gap, he thought, where my heart should be.

The house on Foster Lane was the same as he remembered, but Jesse was not. Something had left him, although he was Jesse well enough, and not visibly ill. He came to the door at Grafton's knock, and gripped Alban's hand strongly.

'I see no invalid,' said Alban, trying to make light of his purpose. 'Am I really needed here, or have I come all this way for nothing?'

Jesse gave him a weak smile. 'Some days are better than others,' he said. 'Yesterday I came in late from a visit to a customer and could hardly lift my limbs at all. I'm lucky I have my best apprentice here.' He slapped Grafton on the shoulder, and the boy smiled.

Jesse's children provided a welcome distraction. They swarmed towards him as he entered the parlour, all seemingly identical at first glance, differing only in height. Every child had the same milky blonde hair, green eyes, freckled skin and mouths overfilled with crooked teeth. They were all lean and long-limbed, like their father. They parted easily for him. 'It's good to see you, Alban,' Jesse said. 'Children, let him through to the seat by the fire – how long has it been?'

'Eleven years,' said Alban; he had the date he'd left London written down somewhere, probably on the back of a design sheet. He wished he could name it now: he enjoyed precision.

Jesse sucked the air in through his teeth. 'Have we lived that long?' he said. 'You don't look a day older than when you left. Does he, Agnes?' He turned to his wife, who had stepped quietly in behind them, carrying a small child neatly on her hip.

'Always so handsome,' said Agnes, kissing Alban on the cheek. 'And your hair is still black, while mine . . .' Laughing nervously, she tucked a grey curl under her cap.

'You are still as lovely as ever you were,' said Alban, and he didn't lie. Agnes looked to be the same uncomplicated, cheerful girl he remembered his cousin plighting his troth to. There were lines around her eyes and her figure was thicker. But she didn't have the sadness that ricocheted off the spaces in Jesse's eyes. She wore her exhaustion proudly, as though it was an honour that she was happy to bear.

'How many children now?' Alban said, looking around. 'I can't even count them.'

Jesse laughed, though his eyes flickered. 'They move too fast. Seven.' He lowered his voice. 'A man must work hard to support them all.'

Alban fixed his gaze. 'I'm your hammer man now,' he said. 'I work quicker these days, so whatever Renard throws at you, I'm your man.'

'I appreciate you being here,' said Jesse. 'I'll make sure you don't regret it. Tomorrow we will go to the Hall to have some silver touched, and you will see some of your old friends. I've spread the word to every worker of the metal in London. Soon we'll be striking the leopard's head on that fine silver of yours.' He watched Alban produce a coin from behind his youngest daughter's ear. 'How old are you now, cousin?' he said.

'Who knows?' said Alban, and their laughter sent the little girl scurrying off to her mother. Alban took the seat offered to him.

'We can register a maker's mark for you, if you wish,' said Jesse.

Alban shook his head. 'I work for you,' he said. 'Anything I make can bear your initials.'

'Always in the shadows, cousin?' said Jesse.

'Always,' said Alban.

They had just finished eating when there was a knock at the street door. Jesse went to answer it, walking slowly, holding his arms a little wide of his body, as though he sought to fill whatever space he was in. The familiarity of his gait moved Alban; unlooked for, he seemed suddenly in the past. He heard Jesse open the front door and greet someone, his voice low and cheerful. Goldsmiths' Hall was but a few steps away, and other silversmiths often knocked on the door in passing, sure of the welcome they would find at Jesse's house.

Agnes leaned forwards, and put her hand over Alban's. 'He is gladder than he can say that you are here,' she said. 'He does not wish to be the weak link in the chain.' Alban nodded; he understood. To create silver of true beauty needed a network of craftsmen, for there were so many skills involved: raising, casting, chasing, engraving. Although well established, Jesse would not wish to fall behind, to lose his reputation as a craftsman of worth. Thinking on it, Alban saw Agnes's eyes widen as Jesse came into the room.

'My dear?' she said. The children had been telling stories to each other, but their murmuring voices fell silent.

In the dimness, Jesse's face had a ghostly pallor. His eyes seemed blank smudges of darkness. 'That was Ovick from the Hall,' he said. 'Pierre Renard's dead. Someone did for him last night, in the middle of Berkeley Square.'

Agnes murmured a prayer under her breath.

'How?' said Alban. The word broke from him before he could suppress it. Mindful of the little ones, Jesse turned his back to them and drew his finger across his throat.

'It's time for bed, my dears,' said Agnes. As she ushered the children out, Jesse pulled across a chair, and sat down heavily, his shoulders sagging forwards. Only when the last of them had gone did he look up at Alban. 'I cannot believe it,' he said. 'I was up that way last night. I went to deliver a commission to another shop.'

'But you did not call on Renard?' said Alban.

Jesse shook his head. 'No, no, but,' he blinked, and shook his head again, 'it does not matter. Forgive me; it is the shock of it all. And things have been so unsettled recently. We are relying on him for most of our work.'

'There's still a business there,' said Alban. 'There will still be work.'

Jesse smiled, a little colour returning to his cheeks. 'I'd forgotten, cousin,' he said, 'how placid you are. I bring you news of a murder and you look just as if I'd remarked on the weather. If only I had your sense of serenity.'

Alban smiled uncertainly. He took the notion of his stillness as a compliment, but he also felt it to be wrong. He was far from calm. He had a thousand questions moving across his mind.

'We will call upon them when it is decent to do so,' said Jesse. 'Though I may need to go to the West End sooner. Mallory has some repairs which need carrying out.' He rubbed his eyes. 'It is strange,' he said, 'how everything can change in an instant.'

Agnes had slipped back into the room. 'It's late now,' she said. 'There will be enough time tomorrow to speak of all this.' Alban saw from the expression on her face that she was concerned for Jesse.

He did not respond to her touch on his shoulder. 'Go up to the children,' he said, after a moment. 'Let us converse a little. It will bring me to life again, I promise.'

Alban smiled a goodnight to Agnes as she turned away, and sipped his beer. It was a good few minutes before either of the men spoke. Above them small footsteps traversed the floor again and again, as though a game was being played. Eventually Alban formed one of the questions that had been moving around his mind.

'Was Renard a good man?' he asked. 'I met him once, but I could not form an opinion.' He kept his tone quiet, and emotionless.

His cousin gave him a lopsided grin that emphasized the

sad expression in his eyes. 'Not really a good man,' he said. 'He was a flatterer, a salesman. He didn't care too much whether he spoke truth or lies. I called him an oily bastard often enough, behind his back, of course. But his death is – inconvenient, at least. At the worst – well, I will not speak of that. He had spoken of some large commission, and without him – I'm worried that we may have a loss of income, when we need it most.' His eyes met Alban's questioning gaze. 'Agnes is expecting again,' he said.

Alban sat back in his chair. He could not imagine another child in this dwelling: another whole presence clamouring for food and care. 'How does she feel?' he said.

Jesse gave a mirthless laugh. 'She's pleased about it,' he said.

Alban knew he did not need to ask how Jesse felt. The answer lay in the silence between them. He also knew that it was the wrong time to ask about Pierre Renard, to stir up thoughts of the past when there were more immediate concerns.

'Alban,' said Jesse. 'I worry for them. I am so very tired.' He looked up at Alban's face. 'Do not tell me I will get better.'

'Go to bed,' said Alban. 'Sleep. We have work to do tomorrow.'

'Yes,' said Jesse. 'And we'll have a gallon of porter, for your handprint remains on my wall, so we must honour the tradition and drink your health.'

Alban stared at him. 'Still there,' he said, remembering his last day in London all those years ago, his cousin chalking his hand, and him laying his hand on the wall, as was the custom when a craftsman left the workshop, the hand-print left there to await his return. He had forgotten it, and at Jesse's words the past seemed to breathe over him again, filling his head with a hundred memories and feelings that made him afraid to speak in case his voice betrayed his emotions.

When Jesse had gone Alban dragged out his truckle bed from its place by the wall, took his boots off and lay down by the embers of the fire. He felt weariness weigh his limbs down. There was too much to consider and he pushed away the concerns crowding his mind. Instead he focused on the journey he had just made; on how far from him London had seemed ever since he had returned to Chester all those years ago.

Here at last, he thought, breathing out.

My silver will be marked with the leopard's head, for London.

A doubt moved fast across his mind, like a single magpie seen from the corner of the eye, flying too fast to be greeted, a harbinger of sorrow gone in a flash: I've come too late, perhaps. London is for a young man to seek his fortune, and I am not that.

He sat up, and drank back the remainder of the beer. Its tang pleased him, and sitting in the warm, he could comfortably reason with himself. What would be the point in coming so far, to bring himself low like this? He had made the resolution that, in London, he would be a new man. He would go to Bond Street with his cousin, present his condolences and his compliments. Even with Renard dead, the business would go on. He would do whatever was necessary – bow and scrape, if need be. Though he doubted his ability to do that; the idea was more palatable than the reality.

He had not asked, though. He had not asked who would be there at the shop; he had not even asked whether she lived. The question came to the front of his mind, for at the first mention of Renard's name it had flared into life, from ashes he had long thought cold.

What of her? he thought. What of Mary?

He pulled the coarse blanket up around him. Forget it, he told himself. The business is what I am here for. The rest can wait, for it has already waited long enough. He felt the tension leave him, his back unfurling. He was practised at pushing away his worries and tonight his exhaustion assisted him. As he lay still his eyelids drooped as though weighted down with lead.

He slept deeply, and dreamed many dreams. When he woke the next morning, all he could remember was the sound of a child's laughter.

CHAPTER FIVE

A most disagreeable encounter today. No, I am wrong to say that, though I do not wish to cross it through and spoil the page. It was source of both pleasure, and pain. Whilst on Bond Street, seeing Mrs Jacobs into her carriage, I glimpsed a lady I once knew, who – it pains me even to write it – I once thought would be my bride. Her name then was Miss Laycock, though I hazard to say I knew her as Sarah.

She was the daughter of a wealthy mercer, but she had charms beyond her father's money. Miss Laycock had such grace and softness, that within a week of knowing her, I formed the strong intention of making her my wife, though there were scores of suitors buzzing around her at the time.

All did not proceed as I wished, though she looked kindly upon me. Her father was a rough man; he pretended that his uncouth manners were a virtue, calling himself a 'plain speaker'. He and I could not agree on the terms of the marriage, or anything else, if truth be told. Not long afterwards, she married a mercer approved by her father, his name being Blackwell, and I met the woman who is now my wife. Mary's father, a maker of gold and silver boxes, was desperate to be rid of her. He persuaded me, and I, still raw with regret for my lost love, made the marriage more quickly than I should have done.

You can imagine with what regret I saw the former Miss Laycock, now Mrs Blackwell, come down from her carriage followed by a little train of children, two boys and two girls. She looked most devoted to them, and they were a pretty picture: dressed in the finest clothes, all of the children most handsome and well formed. Although she looked a little older than I remembered, there was still that softness of expression that I had once cherished and hoped to make my own. When she saw me, she moved quickly on through the crowds. I did not wish to follow her and trouble her; and I needed a moment to regain my composure; so I was able to inspect the equipage. I have not seen such a fine pair of horses for many a day, both dappled grey, and perfectly matched. All of these things added to my keen regret.

As she watched her mistress sleep, Joanna longed for a rummer of something to take the chill off: garnet-coloured liquid, potent and purifying, rolling down her throat into the depths of her empty stomach. It would be something to satisfy the hunger: a sop to throw to the black demon roaming its way around her belly.

It had been a bad day. As she had carried in the breakfast tray she had found Harriet, pale and still, sitting straight up in bed, her eyes wide open, her stare fixed. Joanna had almost cried out with fear, and set the tray down heavily. But once Harriet was roused by the clatter of porcelain and silver, she had begun to weep.

'What is wrong, madam?' said Joanna.

'I am forgotten so soon,' said Harriet. 'I did think he would return, and yet he has not.'

Joanna said nothing; she was concerned with rearranging the tray. She wondered how Harriet had such a wrong-headed notion of what a wife was; had she really thought she would be the subject of constant devotion?

Later Joanna had taken the tray downstairs. 'When I first came here, there was talk of us going to Reismore for Christmas,' she said to Mrs Holland, the housekeeper. 'A change of scenery would be welcome to me.'

'That decaying lump of masonry?' said the butler, who had served as a footman on that estate. 'Unlikely. The master's valet says madam's family is refusing to pay out half of her dowry – and that is what would have furnished your room, along with most of the others in the house. It's lucky that Mr Chichester has his aunt to lend him this place.'

'Some luck for me. How am I supposed to run a house of this size with just eleven servants?' said Mrs Holland.

Harriet had remained melancholy all day, refusing to go out. She wrote a letter, and read listlessly, casting various books aside. In the afternoon, Joanna had sent a note to the master, telling him of Harriet's state. She had thought he might come, to calm Harriet's agitation. But he had not.

He had gone out at eight o'clock. At the window of

Harriet's room, Joanna had watched as Mr Chichester had left the house, descending the front steps without looking back. She glimpsed his pale face, moon-like at the window of the carriage, and sought some meaning in his look. But the uneven pane of glass in the carriage door had shifted the light of the flaming torch that blazed, suspended from the front wall of the house, and she was unable to make out his expression, or report back a moderated version of it to her mistress.

It had taken her hours to get Harriet to sleep. Like a fractious child, the girl kept rising up from her bed, fighting unconsciousness. Now that she slept, Joanna regretted the promise she had made to sit with her until the master came home.

She had listened all evening to the sounds beyond the house; horses' hooves as riders rode hard around the square; the carriages; the distant voices of the London night: imagining revellers and street sellers, drunks and vagabonds. She thought that the watch must have already done several circuits of the square, and the noise had been damped down now these two hours. From the distant chime of the clock in the hallway she knew that it was long past midnight. The carriage had returned to its mews; the link-boy would guide the master home through the London streets, carrying his blazing torch before him. The only light in the room was the flickering illumination provided by a small fire dying in the grate.

Joanna got up and, bending over the fire, lit a half-burnt candle in a chamberstick taken from the dressing set. In her hand, the silver felt like ice, its ornate surface reminding her of Monsieur Renard, for it had come from his shop. A sardonic smile twitched her lips at the thought of him. He was full of sugared words, so much so that the master had taken to sending him straight to Harriet rather than suffering his compliments. Whenever Joanna thought of Renard's narrow, handsome face, she remembered that strange curl his lips had, as though whatever he saw was a dumb show for his own amusement, and other people merely his puppets. It was for this reason that Joanna didn't care much for him, even though he had slipped her a trinket here or there, to ensure her favour. She didn't bother to tell him that she never promoted any trades-man's cause. When he had invited her to his house on Bond Street to partake of a dish of chocolate, she had gone, but only out of curiosity, for she had wished to see his wife, a woman she knew a little of.

She put down the candle and watched the flame, remem-bering an argument of long ago: her first employer, an old woman who had reprimanded her for burning too many candles. It seemed that her life since then had been a con-struction of small lies, excuses and alibis to make it bearable. She thought of her lover, dead long ago. Stephen, you promised you would always work in the world for me, even though you are with God. It was too much to think of, all at once; in the darkness, the grief blindsided her. It was because she had felt weak today, foggy-headed; tomorrow, she would be her old self, sharp and clear-sighted.

Her eyes were closing in the gloom and her head was nodding forwards when she heard footsteps on the pave-ment outside and the familiar voice of her master. She had promised she would wake Harriet on his return. But now she longed to sleep, and knew his arrival would only bring trouble. Sick with tiredness, she could have wept with exasperation.

She only dallied a moment, then was spared the decision. Harriet sat up with a little cry. Joanna rose and watched her nervously. 'Madam?' she said, keeping her tone low and neutral.

'What time on the clock?' said Harriet. Her voice had not lost the throaty rasp she had had from crying.

'It's about one, madam,' said Joanna.

'Did I hear my husband?' said Harriet.

Joanna nodded.

The gesture seemed to startle Harriet into action. She swung herself out of bed. Joanna hurried to put the little silk slippers on her feet, and felt Harriet's hand on her shoulder, its coldness soaking through the material of her dress. Silently, Harriet padded over to the door and pulled it open. She gave a little gasp of exertion as she did it. At the sign of weakness Joanna felt suddenly afraid for the girl.

She followed Harriet out on to the landing. In the darkness, the entrance hall seemed as vast as an abyss. Far below there was a cloud of light, where Oliver the footman stood, holding a branch of candles. In the gloom, Mr Chichester was taking off his gloves.

'Love never comes in through the front door,' Harriet whispered with a little smile, as though to herself. Certain that Harriet was about to succumb to some kind of hysterical crying fit, Joanna took a step towards her, but before she reached her Harriet had leaned over the balustrade and said in a stage whisper, 'Nicholas!'

There was no response, and she whispered again, more urgently. 'Nicholas!'

Dutifully, Oliver did not look up, only held his arm out for his master's cloak. After what seemed like minutes, Nicholas Chichester turned his face up to his wife. He took off his hat. 'Madam?' he said.

Harriet stood, frozen. Joanna sensed that she had finally woken up; that her training had reminded her that her behaviour was indelicate: calling downstairs like an ill-trained servant.

Trailed by Oliver carrying the candelabrum, Mr Chichester began to climb the spiral staircase, one hand gripping the rail, his head bowed. His approach was slow, and Joanna watched the glint of Oliver's eyes as he held the candles before them.

Harriet put her hands to her head, and gave a panicky little start as she touched the unruly mass of curls. Then she tried to flatten her creased gown. Joanna moved back against the wall into the shadows, knowing she could not help her. The master loved order and neatness; Joanna would have laid a wager that, before her marriage, Harriet's mother had made sure her daughter never had a hair out of place. She had even ordered a portrait of her, a portrait she had given to the master: the painted image of an ideal dynastic beauty.

As he reached the top of the stairs, Chichester looked his wife up and down dispassionately. 'You are *déshabillé*,' he said.

Harriet paused, as though unsure of what to do; then she came forwards, and placed her hands, palms down, on his chest, so they rose and fell with his breathing. 'Will you not come to me tonight?' she said, a girlish little curl to her voice, higher in pitch than usual.

Joanna saw his lips part in surprise, and heard his breath catch in the back of his throat. He shook his head. 'No,' he said. 'No, I will not.'

Joanna's eyes met Oliver's, and though each of them had the steady, unreadable gaze of the good servant, they sensed the shock in each other.

With an attempt at coquetry, Harriet put her hand to her husband's face, then tilted her palm up and touched the skin of her wrist and upper arm against his jaw and neck: the softest skin, where a man would wish to kiss her.

Nicholas took her wrist, and gently lowered it. 'Harriet,' he said. 'What makes you play the drab tonight?'

Joanna saw the distress dawn on Harriet's face, and the girl took a faltering step backwards.

Her husband sidestepped her and walked past her. 'Goodnight,' he called over his shoulder, Oliver following him as silently as a shadow.

Joanna waited until she heard him at the distant end of the corridor, opening the door to his chamber, where his valet would be waiting with a banked fire and a decanter and glass. When she heard the door close she stepped over to Harriet, and encircled her waist with her arm to support her back to the bedroom. 'Come now,' she said softly.

Harriet allowed herself to be steered back into the room, then sat on the bed as Joanna shut the door and lit several more candles. When Joanna returned to her, she was counting under her breath, as though carrying out some complicated equation that she could not solve. The tears were already in her eyes when she put her head against Joanna's shoulder. 'I have done enough already to keep myself safe,' she said, her voice a pitiful sound, almost a squeal. 'I have, haven't I?'

Her voice reminded Joanna of the mewling of kittens in a sack in her father's fist, on the way to a watery grave. She stared at her mistress blankly. 'I am sure you have,' she said, not knowing what question she was answering, offering comfort from habit.

'Please God, I have done enough,' said Harriet. She began to cry, and laid her hands over her stomach.

Joanna held her tight, and shushed her. Some distant part of her brain noted little light footsteps passing the door: the link-boy, his light long since extinguished, running through the halls like a midnight mouse. She heard a door open at the end of the corridor. I am harder than I was, she thought, as she stroked Harriet's hair. I should pity you, for though you are a spoiled child, you seem truly wretched. But I have nothing left in my heart for you. Nothing at all.

CHAPTER SIX

16th May, 1792

The image of Sarah and her children stayed with me throughout the day. Her face appeared before my eyes when I tried to concentrate on writing my business correspondence in my chamber this evening. I could not help but feel what a poor creature my wife is by comparison, and my imagination conjured up the life I might have lived had my marriage to Sarah taken place. I have achieved much, yet I have a cold bed, and no children of my own. In truth, I find it unjust that I, who have succeeded in all my endeavours, should be tripped up by a mistaken choice in marriage.

In my prayers, I asked that blessings be rained upon Sarah. I was sitting, thinking of her, when my wife came up to see me. I spoke to her with tolerable kindness. She tries often to be in my confidence, to wheedle things out of me. It takes all of my patience to be gentle with her.

*

Mary thought she must have been small when her father first took her to the Assay Office, the place in Goldsmiths' Hall where silver and gold were tested before being hall-marked. For when the memory came to her, she had the sense of being held high in his arms, her face against his, as she stared over the shoulder of the man at the touchstone. The man took the slim piece of metal (the touch needle, her father said) and drew it across the black stone deliberately slowly, taking pleasure in her delight. He did the same with the ring her father had given him, then, so delicate with his large hands, laid a drop of acid on each line.

'Look at the colour,' her father said. 'One line, that drawn by the needle, is gold; the King's gold; and the other is a baser kind of metal.'

Mary had leaned forwards, almost overbalancing, wanting to touch the black stone with its magic. Had she touched it, she thought, even now, she might have known better; known the difference between base and noble, true and false.

'One day,' said her father, 'you will have a brother, and he will work silver and gold.'

Many years later, he had been sure, even before Eli was born, that his last child would be a son.

'Mary?'

Mallory's voice, low and loud, broke through Mary's thoughts, bringing her back to the parlour. In the morning light, every object was harshly delineated, unsoftened by the shadows and candlelight of evening. Mary was dressed in the black bombazine dress she had worn to mourn her parents, and the garment had wrapped her in memories which constantly claimed her attention.

'What in the name of Christ are those men doing down there, gathered as if it is a hanging day?' Mallory said. 'And why are you not there? Are you not mistress of this house?'

Mary recognized the look on her sister's face: as though she had been lumbered with a recalcitrant child who was sorely in need of a good hiding. Instead of answering her, Mary huddled deeper into her shawl. The taste of her breakfast roll still lingered in her mouth, sour and grainy, as though someone had put chalk in the flour. It was not out of the question, she supposed.

There was the sound of a chest being dragged across the floor downstairs, the sound of wood and metal scraping on stone. 'They are being too loud,' said Mary faintly. 'They will tear the house apart. Why must men destroy everything?'

'Will you answer me?' said Mallory.

'They are looking for Pierre's will,' said Mary. 'He told Dr Taylor he had made him executor. They asked me, but I know nothing of it. And now they cannot find it either.'

Mallory shook her head, as though to indicate she was valiantly keeping her temper in the midst of the most absurd situation she had ever heard of. She had been executrix of both her husbands' wills. When Francis Dunning had said he preferred to wait until he was ill to make one, she had clapped him around the side of the head so hard he said he had seen stars for a week.

'Are you sure he made one?' said Mallory. 'He was just

the kind of man to think he would live forever, and said all kinds of fiction with three bottles of claret inside him. Oh,' she gave a cry, 'how he went on about it: I am a three-bottle man, at least, as if that qualified him for some high position.'

'It was not long ago that he wrote it,' said Mary. 'Do you remember when he took to his bed with that cold? He was convinced he would die.'

'I do not, unfortunately,' said Mallory.

'I tended to him all night, and the next day he wrote it. Scratching away, behind a locked door. He was always stowing things in dark corners. He trusted no one, though you would not think it to see him smile.'

'Did you not ask him where he kept it?' Mallory was relentless: her strong voice, so toneless, so sure.

'No, I did not,' said Mary, struggling to keep her self-control. 'You knew him. You know it would have been pointless to ask him. He would never have told me.'

She knew what would have happened had she asked Pierre where he kept the will. He would have insinuated that she wished for his death. Pierre seemed to search automatically for the vice in everything she said. His face was not expressive, but in his last days, his eyes had clouded with dislike every time she spoke. She wondered if he had felt that way for years, and simply become less adept at hiding it. His eyes would seem to darken, and there would be a frozen aspect to his face, pale patches around his nose, as though her words had shocked him enough to stop his blood from flowing for a moment. At such times she would touch his hand, and say 'my dear' to him, as though the words carried some kind of opiate effect, the marker of a partnership that neither had completely abandoned.

'You are over-tired,' said Mallory. 'I have sent for Avery, and she will not thank me for it; there will be so much for her to do when she arrives, if you let things run on as they are.'

Mary had a vague memory of their cousin as a slim, blonde girl with a ready smile and a caustic wit. 'I have not seen her for years,' she said.

'Thanks to Pierre,' said Mallory. 'But she will come readily enough now. She is needed; you cannot live here without a companion. You are causing enough talk as it is. I found your girl Ellen out on the street, gossiping. I heard her tell Alice Barber that her mistress is not right in the head. And though I gave her a good talking to, I can see why she thinks it. You are active enough in your sleep, it seems, locking and unlocking doors, moving the furniture; but now, when action is called for, you are sitting here, staring at nothing, letting a group of so-called gentlemen take your shop apart.'

There was a crash, and the sound of a man's voice damning everything to hell.

Mary swallowed Ellen's betrayal. 'I promised her extra tea and sugar for her trouble,' she said. 'I cannot offer an explanation for what I do in my sleep. That she speaks of it on the street . . .' She wrapped her shawl tighter around her. 'Perhaps Pierre was right. He always said that, left unchecked, people would become unruly and out of hand.'

Mallory said nothing for a moment, and Mary guessed that she had been shocked into silence because she agreed with Pierre.

'Did I see one of your lodgers dragging his trunk along Bond Street?' she said, after a moment.

'Mr Pickering?' said Mary. 'Yes, you did. He says he will not stay. He feels the chill of death in this house, and claims he heard Pierre's footsteps the other night.'

'Fool,' said Mallory.

'Do you think so?' said Mary. 'I am in agreement with him.'

Mallory ignored her. 'Have you opened the boxes for them?' she said. Mary nodded. Pierre had kept his documents in a number of secure chests, soundly locked and stowed in the cellar with the plate chests.

'I thought so. Give me your keys,' said Mallory. 'I will watch over them while they look.' As Mary handed her the keys Mallory could not help one further burst of advice. 'When will you learn?' she said. 'Your servants live to rob you. Bright Hemmings is probably in the back yard with a hand cart.' She turned, with an exhalation that sounded like a sigh, and ran through the door down the stairs quickly and lightly.

Mary settled back in her chair. The house felt like a galleon in full sail, groaning and creaking, voices rising and falling in every room. In Pierre's lifetime, the inhabitants of the house had done their best to be quiet, by the master's command. Though he didn't seem to mind the noise of the workshop and the sound of the hammer on metal, within his home Pierre had been sensitive to every voice and footstep. He had even sent a maid packing because she was too heavy-footed. The household had been muffled, everyone closing doors quietly, keeping their voices lowered, as though in mourning.

Now, when everyone was dressed in black, they seemed to be making enough noise to wake the dead.

After a few minutes Mary decided to follow Mallory. The shop door was closed, and as she came down the stairs she saw that beyond the velvet-draped window Bond Street was quiet. The inhabitants of her house were concentrating their attention on the workshop, and the passage that ran between the front door and the cellar. Grisa saw her first, and fell silent. Then they all turned, one by one, and looked at her as though she was a ghost.

Taylor was holding a document in his hand, holding it with his fingertips as though he did not want to sully it. Mary saw the large dollop of sealing wax on it. There was more wax there than necessary: Pierre must have poured it on with his trembling, feverish hands, and caught it with the side of his hand as he sealed it, so a smear lay across the parchment, the colour of dried blood. She came through the group, Grisa and Mallory moving aside, then Taylor's assistant.

'You have found it,' she said.

'Quite so, my dear,' Taylor replied.

'Holy Jesus!' cried Grisa. Everyone followed his gaze, turning to see a man's face pressed to the window, white, the nose squashed so it was deformed by the glass. It would have been ridiculous at any other moment, something a child would have laughed at. But as Taylor went to the door Mary saw all colour had drained from his face.

'Maynard,' said Taylor, opening the door with a jerk so that the bell jangled wildly. 'Good God, man! You scared the ladies half to death.'

'Speak for yourself, sir,' said Mallory.

'You are causing concern on the street,' said Maynard smoothly. 'Did you think you would attract no attention, rummaging through the house of the departed – God rest his soul? Has more evidence been uncovered? Do you wish the constable to be summoned? I have just passed Mr Pickering, who was giving a most colourful account of this house as a haunted one.' He caught sight of Mary's face, and flushed. 'Forgive me, Mrs Renard. I did not see you there.'

'It is the will, sir, that is all,' said Taylor. 'An important matter for those close to Mr Renard, but not to you.'

'In that case, I hope that Mrs Renard will forgive the intrusion,' said Maynard, tipping his hat and withdrawing. Grisa was still breathing in a laboured way, one hand splayed across his chest.

'Come now, Mr Grisa,' said Mary, patting his arm.

'Do not interrupt him,' said Mallory loudly. 'He is seeking to outdo you in the matter of extreme nervousness.'

'My dear Mrs Renard,' said Dr Taylor. 'This is no place for you. Will you allow me to escort you upstairs?'

Mary placed her hand on his arm, and they went upstairs slowly, Mallory two steps behind them. Mary could not help but feel grateful for the doctor's calm, steady manner; his arm felt as solid as she felt insubstantial. When they reached the parlour and she took a seat, he stood over her, a kindly smile filling his face, his eyes searching hers with concern.

'Your grief is most natural and a credit to you as a wife,' he said, 'but you must be careful of your health, Mrs

Renard.' He had stopped calling her Marie; his sense of decorum, unseated by grief, had returned.

'The doctor and I are in agreement on this,' said Mallory, sitting down opposite her. 'I've ordered your girl to make caudle. You need it. You are fading, Mary; there is no flesh on your bones.' To belie her harsh tone, she put her hand to her sister's cheek, and let it rest there for a moment, as though half in appraisal, half in caress.

'I do not think I can drink caudle,' said Mary. At the idea of its cloying, milky, spicy sweetness, she felt her stomach roll in rebellion.

'You have to eat,' said Mallory.

'Mrs Dunning is right,' said Dr Taylor. 'And I see she will make a good nurse. I can, at least, take the burden from you of reading the will, and arranging the funeral.'

Mary saw Mallory's features tighten, but she said nothing. The doctor took his leave, and the two women heard him go out through the shop door. Mary resumed her former position, settled in the chair, swaddled in her shawl.

'Will you let them take over everything?' said Mallory. She took Mary's hands; her sister was unresponsive. 'What are you thinking of?'

'The manner of his death,' said Mary. She saw irritation flash across her sister's face again: how vital Mallory was, how full of life and feeling. She observed this dispassionately, as the doctor, she thought, would observe a patient.

'Then you are wasting your time,' said Mallory. Her voice was harsh and loud. 'For he is gone, and you should be glad of it. Open your eyes. There is a business here;

there are many things to be dealt with. This house and shop needs a mistress: you must be strong.'

'You speak as though it is simple,' said Mary. 'As though my life is my own. But Pierre has not gone, do you see? I feel him in this house, as though he might walk into the room at any moment.'

As she looked at her sister, Mary could have sworn she saw a slight shiver move through her. 'Did you go and see the body?' Mallory said. 'I told you not to.'

'I did not go,' said Mary. 'This is not about that. When I wake in the morning, all I see is the life he created, and that includes me. It is as I knew, the night he came to speak to our father, to say that he would marry me. I had watched the craft of silversmithing my whole life, from dark corners of workshops. I knew that from my softness, he would make a clay maquette, a waxen form, then cast me out of sterner stuff. And he did: I am, now, his creation. Every dress, every word, almost every movement, I measured and weighed before he himself could measure and weigh it. Day by day every piece of me was stolen away. You look at me as though I should be my old self, but the old Mary is gone and I do not know the way back to her. Our parents and Eli are gone too. It is only you who remembers me as I was; and it is too late for me to make amends for what Pierre did. Do you understand?'

'No,' said Mallory. Mary saw distress stir in her dark eyes, and knew her sister was fighting it with all the obstinacy of her nature.

Mary pulled up the black sleeve of her dress, turning her wrist to show the underside of her arm. 'On the night

Pierre died, when Dr Taylor came to tell me, I was asleep by the fire. And somehow, I had gained these.'

Mallory stared at the bruises in silence.

'Did Pierre do that to you?' she said.

'No. I told you,' said Mary. 'It happened in my sleep.'

'Not this, again.' Mallory shook her head. She crouched down beside her sister, and took hold of her hands with a gentleness that surprised Mary. But her gaze was firm, and her tone had a warning note to it. 'My little sister. Cover your arms. Do not show the world your bruises. At night, blow out your candle, keep your eyes closed. Tell yourself: the dead do not walk. They cannot love, and they cannot hate. You must be strong.' She sounded tired. 'You will drive yourself mad, and me too. Speaking of spirits and spectres, rather than the practical matters you should be thinking of.'

'Surely you can see that he will not leave me in peace,' said Mary.

'I do not believe that,' said Mallory, holding her hands tight. 'It is the real world that you must deal with. Do you know what our mother would have said?'

Mary nodded, and said the words as though by rote. 'Bear what you must bear with patience and resignation; give thanks to God for your blessings.' Their mother had said it often: when trade was poor, when their servant stole from them, when little Eli refused to sleep, shaking his head and smiling as though it was sunrise at two o'clock in the morning, his blue eyes wide with curiosity.

Mallory smiled. 'I never much cared for patience and resignation; nor for giving thanks, come to that. But bear up, Mary. For God's sake, bear up. Do not listen for foot-steps where there are none.' As though shaking off her sadness, she gave a short laugh, and turned her face away. 'What a commotion it was down there. And how it made me laugh, the way that man scared them all out of their wits. Such fine gentlemen, they are. Who was the man at the window?'

'One of the coroner's jury,' said Mary. Her head was beginning to ache.

'He seemed mighty inquisitive about everything. What did they decide on Pierre's death?' said Mallory.

'They have agreed it was theft; killing by person or persons unknown. Dr Taylor told me the streets are thick with villains. Whoever killed Pierre took his watch. Do you remember it? Such a fancy thing. How he loved it.' It occurred to her that she hadn't wanted it, that she had surrendered it with no anguish at all.

'It didn't seem so cut-and-dried from the look on that man's face when he came knocking at your window,' said Mallory. 'Nor is it settled in the gossip up and down Bond Street, if what I heard today is anything to go by.' She caught sight of Mary's face. 'We will not think of it any more,' she said. 'Whatever happened, it was Pierre's own fault. Wandering round the streets at night. Going places he had no business to be. His fault, Mary, just as this whole situation is.' She looked at her sister, long and hard.

But Mary was elsewhere, thinking of the distant past. Why did it come back to her so clearly now? Being held tight by her father as she gazed at the Assay Office dishes of bonemeal, and the man's voice telling her: 'We wrap it in lead, Mary, and then, through heat, we separate the noble metals from the base; because as the heat grows strong, everything base is burnt away.' But you are wrong, she thought, and she wished she could go back and tell the man so. I have been tried, and all that is left of me is the ash of my impurities.

CHAPTER SEVEN

18th May, 1792

Whilst lying awake in bed this morning, I conceived of an excellent plan. I will write to Sarah and offer an apprenticeship to her younger son, gratis. I am sure she would be most grateful for such a prestigious place. I will reassure her that there is no obligation in the case; and assure her that she will always have a friend in me.

I went to see my good friend, Jones, this afternoon, to purchase some tablets for my wife's headaches. Jones is my age and, like me, was a poor apprentice. He served the apothecary whose business, and wife, he now has, for his former master died some six years ago. He has done me many a service, for at the time we bemoaned our state often and it forged an unbreakable bond between us. It raised my spirits to see him.

*

When Alban woke, he thought: this is the day, and the jolt was immediate. He and Jesse had put off the visit to Bond Street by two days, not wanting to appear gawpers at a scene where blood had been spilled. As the sleep cleared from his eyes, he saw Jesse, sitting at the table, not watching him, but staring at his hands. Alban sat up, and Jesse put a finger to his lips to signal that Agnes and the children were still sleeping. Alban joined him at the table, moderating his voice so it was a near-whisper, watching Jesse fiddling with his own fingers. He seemed to quiver with nervous energy this morning. 'We can wait,' Alban said, wondering if it was wise for his cousin to venture out. 'It's a long walk for you.'

'Only if it's a bad day,' said Jesse, with a slight lopsided twitch of his mouth upwards. 'And it's not, today: I know it. I feel I could walk to Chester and back, take over your business, cousin, rather than have to deal with all this, hawking for trade at a house in mourning.'

They both dressed as though they were going to church, and set out just as the children were waking, their small voices pealing through the morning air as Jesse shut the door behind them. The sky was dark blue, suggesting evening rather than morning, and they walked briskly in the cold air. They travelled without speaking, peaceably, as they were wont to do as young men, threading their way through the narrow streets of the City, the cries of the street sellers beginning, the black shapes of kites hovering above.

As the sun rose fully their spirits rose with it, both of them walking with their shoulders back, turning their faces up to the light. Jesse looked at Alban and smiled.

'Your face is like a sundial, cousin,' he said. 'By the fire of an evening you seem ageless as silver, but catch you in the morning light and I can see the days and hours there, in the way the shadows fall.'

Alban shoved him. 'Damn the light,' he said, and at the sound of Jesse's laugh he wished they could walk forever, and never reach Bond Street.

Imagining this moment had been uncomplicated; after all, what was it but the putting of one foot in front of the other? But Alban had not reckoned on the feelings that grew ever more intense as they neared their destination, the inner world that distracted him from the cold and the searing blue sky. His physical reactions gave the lie to his normal stillness. I will not stop, he thought, his stubbornness saving him: I will go forwards, I have decided it. But as they turned off Piccadilly he paused, for half a second, and hoped that Jesse did not notice it.

The street they found was at once foreign to Alban, and familiar. His memories of it had grown fainter over the years and he had dwelt on it for two nights; flashes of the past, seen through his own eyes when he had been an altogether different man.

When he had first known Bond Street, Pierre Renard had not owned a shop there. Now Alban tried to think of him dispassionately, as a stranger whom he could at least shade with the neutral respect one gave to the dead. But always, when he thought of Renard he thought of the day he had met Mary, and it was impossible to be neutral. He could not trust his own judgement in the case.

Today they reached Bond Street at an early hour, so there

were no throngs of fashionable shoppers as there would be later in the day, and he was tempted to stand still and look around, to place the template of his memory over the subtly changed landscape.

Alban was thankful for his cousin's presence. Had Jesse not been there, he suspected he would not have turned down the street at all, would have instead kept walking down Piccadilly. He would have been the Alban of old, taking himself away, dissolving into the tides of London, lost in the comfort of being anonymous. He would not have gone far; perhaps only to St James's Piccadilly where, he thought, if he would not pray because he believed in nothing, he could at least find silence.

Jesse said nothing and they continued walking, until he put his arm out and halted Alban. 'There,' he said, and pointed to a handsome double dwelling on the other side of the street. The building had bowed windows chequered with fine glass and their surface rippled and caught the light. Alban noticed that the windows were empty, and the shelves draped with black velvet.

Alban found his cousin watching him with nervous intensity. 'It's Renard's, yes?' he said, and Jesse nodded. 'So why are we standing here?' Alban said.

'You think I don't have a memory?' said Jesse. 'You're a close one, alright. But I know why you went back to Chester all those years ago. She lives, you know. But she is much altered.'

Suddenly Alban had an image of Mary as a plump matron, surrounded by Renard's unattractive children. 'Should I laugh or cry?' he asked.

'Make a jest of it if you wish,' said Jesse.

They crossed the street, dodging a carriage, and Jesse tapped on the window of the shop, catching the eye of a dark-haired man in the shadows, who came straight to the door. Alban could feel the tension vibrate through him; he felt sick in his stomach. But, once inside, the shop was empty, the only noise someone whistling in the small workshop beyond. Alban felt suddenly empty and deflated. Trust you, he thought, anticipating everything when really there is nothing. He looked around the fine, handsome room, its walls covered with glazed presses. A long counter displaying trays of mourning rings, jewellery and seals was dotted with pale marks; fingerprints, he realized, and when he saw Jesse looking at them too, he warranted Pierre Renard would have had them cleaned away.

Jesse introduced the man as John Grisa, Renard's shop manager. He was a slim man with quick, dark eyes, a mobile, expressive face, and dextrous hands in constant motion. He nodded to Alban, and even Alban could see the spark of interest in his eye.

'My poor Monsieur Renard,' Grisa said, and with a flourish produced a square of silk that he used to dab his dry eyes. 'We found his will earlier today.'

'May we present our condolences to Mrs Renard?' said Jesse. He glanced at Alban, who was staring stolidly at the floor in front of him.

Grisa clicked his tongue. '*Non, non*, there is no need for that. She receives no one but family at the moment.' He rolled his eyes upwards. 'And she would not know who you are. She is – what? – *insensible*.'

Jesse swallowed hard. Alban read the irritation in his seemingly calm expression; his cousin had known Mary and her family since childhood. To be dismissed so was irritating, but he was obviously used to it. 'Will you tell her, though?' he said.

Grisa nodded, and clicked his fingers, which seemed to be a sign to move the conversation on.

'Do you have any work for us?' Jesse said baldly.

Grisa's imperious expression cracked open with grim amusement. 'Of course, of course. I have no idea why the English find violent death so enthralling, but we have more orders than ever. Yesterday, I have to send the boy to turn people from the door, at this season, can you imagine? Monsieur Renard would have been in ecstasy. And yes, we have work for you: if you hadn't come I would have sent to you today. There was no need to come here with sympathy.'

Alban's heightened senses faded Grisa's voice out as he heard someone descending the stairs: the light footsteps of a woman, the sweep of heavy skirts. The door linking the house to the shop was shut, but he fixed his gaze on the crack beneath the door, as though he might sight movement there. Sure enough, he did: the movement of dark over light; feet halting, then heading off again. He heard the front door open and shut, and saw her walk past the window. She was moving quickly so he had only the briefest impression: of reddish-brown hair, lightly powdered, haloed by the winter light, a tiny figure, not dressed for the cold, and pale skin. He could not see her face: she did not glance back at the shop. But there was something indefinable about the way she moved, about the curve of her cheek. It was her; it was definitely Mary: ten years older, thinner, and fading; the life almost gone. What remained was only a signifier of what she had once been, like the painting of a saint on a church triptych.

He had turned to watch her pass the window, and felt Jesse's warning touch on his arm. When he turned back, it seemed Grisa had not noticed his interest; his eyes too had followed his mistress. His lips were pursed in amusement. 'And she flies again,' he said. 'No hat, no cloak. See how she races towards death? It is no surprise that she is desolate; how do you replace such a husband? Come into the workshop, and I will give you my orders. We must be quick; my day will be full once the agents arrive.'

Grisa seemed to speak forever, his voice running on and on until Alban's attention faded away. Half an hour later, Alban and Jesse emerged into the light, their heads full of instructions.

Alban looked down the street in the direction he had seen Mary walk. 'She looked like a ghost,' he said.

'I told you,' said Jesse, tucking some papers into his coat pocket. 'She's a weak, bloodless thing now. He sucked the life out of her. Never let anyone near her.' He touched Alban's arm. 'Stop staring after her. Let's have a pint of something. Celebrate our commissions, and my new child.'

The close, dark-panelled room of the Red Lion in Crown Passage was nearly empty, but the smell of sawdust, burnt meat and ale sent Alban back eleven years. As he accepted a cup of porter from Jesse, he saw a man watching from a bench in the corner. The man had red hair, and though he was sitting in a hunched position, had a kind of contained hauteur that drew the eye. He looked at Alban with unashamed directness.

'Jesse,' the man said. 'Who's this you've brought with you?'

Jesse twisted round and smiled. 'My cousin from Chester, come to seek his fortune in the city,' he said. 'Alban, this is Edward Digby.'

'We've met before,' said Digby, his hand curled tight around his pint pot, though he had not drunk from it since they'd entered the taproom.

'You'll forgive me when I say I don't remember,' said Alban.

Digby took a large gulp of his drink. 'I never forget a face,' he said, and a smile dawned over his features, followed by a low gasp of laughter that graduated into a cough. He did not get up, or offer his hand, but Alban had the sense it was more through his weariness that he did not observe the niceties of introduction. It was his policy to refuse to see malice unless it declared itself.

Digby ground his jaw. 'This city is a cruel mistress, sir,' he said. 'She will chew you up and spit you out. Best go back to Chester, where the air is pure and business is straightforward.'

Alban smiled and took a mouthful of porter. 'It's clear you don't know Chester,' he said, and Jesse laughed. 'Besides, I'm no stranger to London. She is my old sweetheart, and perhaps she'll welcome me back.'

'Don't say I didn't warn you,' said Digby. 'Where've you been, this time of day?'

'Bond Street,' said Jesse.

A snigger escaped from Digby's throat, then he began to cough again. 'Easy there,' said Jesse.

Digby came up for air, gasping. 'Bond Street,' he said. 'Full of gentlemen. I was followed down it by our gracious Mr Maynard today, wishing to speak to me urgently. No,' he shook his head, 'you can't move for gentlemen round here.'

He tutted under his breath, took a final swig of his drink, and got up to leave without another word.

As the door banged behind him, Jesse looked at Alban and smiled. 'Don't listen to him,' he said. 'The man has black humours sometimes, and when he's in them he puts a sour cast on everything.'

'I didn't listen,' said Alban, taking another mouthful of porter. He watched as Jesse gulped down one pot and ordered another. After some time, he tapped his cousin's arm. 'But should we not go, Jesse? We have much to keep us occupied.' His cousin assented with a grunt.

The streets were busier now; the air filled with the sound of voices and the clatter of hooves and carriage wheels. On Piccadilly, Jesse turned right. He was walking quickly, and as Alban accelerated to keep up, he saw his cousin's breath misting before him in the cold air; he was breathing quickly. The early sunshine had given way to a darkening sky. 'Jesse,' he called. 'Where are you going?' It certainly wasn't the quickest way home, he muttered under his breath. If they carried on in this direction before long they would hit street walkers and villains and be carried along on a tide to God knows where.

'Jesse,' he said again.

His cousin stopped so suddenly that an old woman selling eggs walked into the back of them, and cursed them. As Alban mollified her, handing her a coin for the crushed eggs, he saw disquiet writ plain across his cousin's features.

'Agnes asked me to call on Mallory,' he said. 'I promised her.' He had the look of a man whose courage had failed him.

'A good idea,' said Alban. 'You said the other night you meant to visit her; that she had some repairs for you.' He could not help but feel hope rise in him; it was the thought of hearing more of Mary. Her elder sister could always be relied upon for frankness: that, Alban remembered from the way Jesse had talked about her. When he had come to London long ago, as a child, the families had been close. Jesse had been apprenticed to Mary and Mallory's father before being turned over to another silversmith, and he had once been thought of as a match for Mallory. It was all long ago, but Jesse had maintained a brotherly affection for both girls. Though he hardly saw them, it was always there, underlying everything, to be called on at times of trouble.

'The turning is there,' said Jesse, tapping his foot. After a moment, he reached a decision. 'We will not go,' he said. 'Not today. She gave me a poor welcome the last time I called on her, and I do not have the temper for another one. Besides, there is too much to be done at home.'

'It will not take a moment to call,' said Alban. 'Was Agnes worried about Mallory? Why did you not mention it before?'

'Agnes should worry about herself,' said Jesse, looking about him. 'She is too kind a soul. When folks make poor choices – like welcoming Renard into a family – they should live with them. We have work to do, and I have had enough of widows for today.'

CHAPTER EIGHT

19th May, 1792

Having served my apprenticeship, I found some clients of my own who were happy to invest in me, and this is how I gained my own firm and finally landed on Bond Street. It was just before I came here that the sad story of my marriage began.

It is impossible to think of my wife with an unpolluted view, for so it is when you are deceived. Yet when I married her, she had bright skin, and seemed healthy, and altogether had an appearance of malleability, which I thought would serve me well. But that placidity was little more than a veneer; and all the impressions I had hoped to make upon her seemed to fade beyond the moment I suggested them. She did not respond to my delicate shaping, only remained her own obstinate self.

Now, she is cunning enough to be docile to my face, to pretend that she obeys me. She thinks she keeps me content with her

pretence of supplication. But I know she has a rebellious heart.
She thinks herself cleverer than I. Now and then, proof of it slips
from her tongue, but when I reprimand her she only says that I
twist her words, and cries.

With her constant weeping, and her feigned melancholy, she
would make me out to be monstrous. Yet I would be a good hus-
band if she were a good wife; I want only the chance to prove my
goodness. Had I married Sarah, I might have augmented the
delights of my profession with the joys of a warm bed and a large
family. As it is, I am left only with her, and she is but the shell
of what I was promised.

Joanna was going to the kitchen to drink a dish of tea when
she found Harriet in the staircase hall, walking towards the
library. She had hoped for a few moments of respite after
breakfast, but when she saw the determined look on her
mistress's face, she knew it was not to be.

Harriet's eyes lit up when she saw her. 'Come, you are
to stay with me,' she said, holding her hand out. Joanna
noticed the glance of the footman nearest the door, before
he gave a slight bow of the head.

Joanna sensed Harriet's agitation; the girl's hand was
hot and clammy in hers, and she pulled Joanna through
the door with some force. Even crossing the threshold felt
like an intrusion; for all its marble fireplaces and lush dec-
oration, the library was a masculine room, decorated in a
dark claret, red and gold and with mahogany furniture
that absorbed the light from the three tall windows that ran
along one wall. Mr Chichester sat at his desk in a deep
library chair, one arm lying along the swept-up arm of the

chair, holding a letter in his hand, looking up as though to form a tableau of surprise. There was an empty glass on the desk beside him, and a fire crackled in the grate. When he finally put down the letter, rose and bowed, it was with clear reluctance. Joanna curtseyed, then stood with her eyes on the exotic details of the carpet, only allowing herself the occasional glance up.

Joanna could not gain any lasting impression of Mr Chichester; despite much thought on the matter, she could not pin him down. She wondered whether it was his youth that made his looks and manner so malleable, for every impression she gained of him was as fleeting as a shadow. If you took each part of him individually he was unremarkable; the miniaturist who had painted his portrait for Harriet had made free with his looks to transform him. The face painted on the small oval of ivory that hung on Harriet's wall in its silver-gilt frame was smooth and wide, its features depicted with an almost feminine delicacy. In reality the young man's cheeks were faintly pitted, and his wide brow tapered on a long journey to a small chin. Around his mouth and beneath his nose the hair was trying to break through, so that he looked like a boy trying to grow a beard, each individual bristle painful to contemplate. Yet he dressed elegantly; his French valet had seen to that. Joanna found the certainty of his gaze compelling. She, who had wandered directionless for so long, never quite knowing the difference between good and bad, right and wrong, longed to bask in such certainty.

He settled himself back down in his chair and graced Joanna with a fleeting smile. 'Miss Dunning. Do you wish to speak privately, Mrs Chichester?' he said. Joanna curtseyed for the second time, and took a small step back in the hope that she would be allowed to withdraw.

'Stay here,' said Harriet.

The master pushed his chair away from the table. He was all angles, like a long puppet folded into a box. Long, crooked nose, visible cheekbones, wrists, knees, all shone out as points on a diagram, the white of bone showing under the skin. As Harriet sat down opposite him, Joanna thought how incongruous they looked together. Harriet was all blonde softness, especially now, with her slightly swollen figure. Her face was rounded, pink, and dominated by her glistening blue eyes; her husband was all cold, dry brownness, like the winter landscape outside the window.

As Harriet gazed at her husband, a smile tinged with triumph settled over her face, as though she had drunk glasses and glasses of wine, or held the perfect hand at cards. The high carriage of her head conveyed the message that she was winning some silent war, and was prepared to be charitable with him.

'What do you have to say, madam?' said Chichester. 'Have you come to warn me of your extravagance? Have you been emptying Bond Street of goods?' There was a hard sarcasm in his tone which shocked Joanna.

'I think, perhaps, you will be more careful of my feelings,' Harriet said, 'when I tell you that I believe, that is, the signs seem to show, that I am with child. You will forgive me for waiting some weeks before I told you, but I wished to be sure.'

Nicholas Chichester let his hands rest on his breeches

like a pair of spindly white spiders. His stare fixed on his wife's face. His eyes were glazed and Joanna could not tell his thoughts. To her mind he looked like an ice sculpture, his self-containment frozen, yet dissolving imperceptibly moment by moment. She heard a slight creak beyond the door and wondered if the footman was looking through the keyhole. She glared in that direction and narrowed her eyes.

'Well,' Nicholas said eventually. He rose, took his wife's hand, and kissed it. 'You have done your duty. My dear girl.' The last sentence sounded more like an insult than a term of affection.

'Perhaps we can now send for Mr Renard,' said Harriet. 'Our commission, sir; a new silver service. We discussed it with him.'

'I put him off some days ago,' said Chichester.

'Oh,' said Harriet. Her voice was faint, childlike.

'Is there anything else?' he said, looking at the letter again. There was a long silence.

'You sent away my coachman,' she said. 'He was trained in my father's stable.'

'And he was very much your servant, Harriet,' said Nicholas. 'But the horses are my concern. He hobbled my best grey.'

'I am sure it was not his fault,' said Harriet. 'The roads are a disgrace in some parts of town. May I request his return? He was a good servant. Trustworthy. And it is so hard to find trustworthy servants, especially in London. I have heard you say it, sir.'

'Touching as your concern for the government of this

household is,' said Chichester, sounding bored, 'you need not worry yourself. His replacement has already started and I am perfectly satisfied. A lady should not concern herself over her husband's coachman. And Harriet – you must write to your father. He can no longer deny us your portion.' He glanced quickly at Joanna, and she thought she saw something like shame in his face.

Harriet gave a forced laugh. It sounded ugly in the grandly furnished room, reverberating off crystal and marble. 'Is that all you have to say?' she said.

'I will engage Dr Taylor as your accoucheur,' said Nicholas. 'I understand he attended my cousin's wife, and is a respectable man. He studied at Oxford, I believe. I trust you do not object?'

'It hardly matters,' she said. 'I must go and rest. Joanna?'

Joanna tried not to look at Chichester as she followed Harriet, but she could not help glancing back once. He caught her gaze, and held it, before she looked away.

'Joanna,' he said, as she turned. 'I require your presence here for a moment – once you have seen Mrs Chichester to her bed.'

She nodded.

As she supported Harriet up the stairs she glanced up, and blinked in the white winter light streaming in from the cupola in the staircase hall. It was so beautiful that she paused, and felt Harriet tug on her. If only I could breathe it in, she thought, like vapour; it would make me new again.

In Harriet's room, Joanna helped her to the bed. As she passed her secretaire, Harriet let her hand trail over the polished veneer of purple tulipwood and mahogany. The key sat in its lock, the lank ribbon hanging from it. Once, the ribbon had been pale blue, but Harriet had taken to wearing it around her neck, and now it was grey from its proximity to her skin. She must have put the key back in the lock that morning.

'You may open it if you wish,' she said, catching Joanna's eye as though daring her to do so. 'For in there lies what was once the promise of happiness.'

'I won't open it, madam,' said Joanna. God knew what was in there, but she didn't want to. And for all Harriet's dramatics, she thought, it probably contained nothing but the detritus of a privileged childhood: a feather here, a piece of ribbon there, a jewel.

She excused herself from the room with a low curtsey, and ran back down the stairs. Mr Chichester was waiting in the staircase hall. He did not respond to her smile with one of his own.

'Renard, the silversmith, has been murdered,' he said. 'Do not tell her; she should be spared the shock of it, for now.'

Joanna could say nothing; her face was frozen in its customary blankness, but her lips parted with shock, and she felt heat gathering in her face. Mr Chichester's gaze softened. 'It is a terrible thing,' he said. 'Our streets are not safe.'

Joanna shook her head, and managed a poor curtsey as he walked away. She was glad he had instructed her not to tell Harriet; she had been particularly fragile of late, and Joanna had the feeling that the loss of the silversmith would send her into a fit of the vapours.

'Did I hear aright?' said one of the footmen, approaching her as she stood immobile, one hand on the balustrade. 'Is the French silversmith dead?'

'Yes,' she said, and turned away. She ran up to the first landing, then through the hidden door so she could go up the back stairs. She needed movement, and solitude, to calm her feelings. She made her way up to the servants' floor, where she had a room to herself.

When Harriet was at her most trying, she asked Joanna to sleep near her, but Joanna preferred her garret room. She had requested it specifically when Harriet's mother had interviewed her, and on her first day Mrs Holland had handed over the key, raising her eyebrows as she did it.

Once inside the room she closed the door behind her, turned the key, and sat on the bed. She still felt hot, and slightly sick, as though she was beginning a fever. She put her head in her hands.

Damn Renard, she thought. Damn his sly looks and his cold eyes and his flattering tongue. Even in death, he had found a way to disarrange everything. It was not just that she would have to deal with Harriet; there was something else, infinitely more precious to her, another loss that she could not afford.

She dragged the wooden locking box out from under the bed.

From the candle compartment she took what she was looking for: a small packet of paper. She opened it, and gazed at the tiny curl of dark brown hair there. She had retained just a strand or two, for she wanted some always before her eyes so that she would not forget the colour. She had given the larger lock of hair up for setting; it had been in Mr Renard's possession, and now she feared it was lost. She folded up the packet and kissed it, stifling the sob which had taken hold of her throat. She had no time to grieve, not now. She must go back to Harriet, and behave as though everything was normal.

She went to her window and looked out over Berkeley Square, trying to think herself out of sorrow, and the view did offer some relief. She had waited for snow for a long time, and now it was getting colder, she had the hope of it. Disciplining her focus, she imagined Berkeley Square blanketed in white, the young trees bowing with snow, the black prints of animals and early risers criss-crossing it. There will be beauty, she thought, for the snow made everything new, transforming dirt into purity and muffling the harsh noises of the city. The places she had long grown tired of seeing would seem lit up by some internal light, redeemed by the silent fall of snowflakes.

Without thinking, her arms formed a cradle against her chest, and she looked down upon the face of an imaginary baby, her right thumb stroking the cheek. 'Maybe there will be a Frost Fair, my love,' she said, out loud, then caught herself. But she only felt foolish for a moment. What did it matter if she spoke out loud, in an empty room?

As Digby emerged from the pawnbroker's shop he told himself it was impossible that anyone could have followed him. The place was so hidden in the maze of alleyways off the Strand that he would be hard-pressed to find it again. So disturbed was he that he even passed a tavern without pausing, keeping his eyes on the ground and pushing forwards to the main thoroughfare. He wanted a drink, and badly, but he also wanted to find his way out of this place, the light falling like mist into the dark and polluted air. If he felt guilty, he didn't want to admit it.

The pawnbroker had a tiny room, with a barred window, and a few meagre trays of seals and rings set out there. It seemed strange to Digby that the man even bothered with those trays, for surely to find him you would have to know where he dwelt. You wouldn't simply pass by such a place. The man, his eyeglass permanently held in his eye socket with a spasm-like squint, had looked over the seals and the small gold pendant with its lock of hair set under crystal. Then he had dropped the eyeglass from his eye and caught it in one smooth movement. When he first named a price Digby didn't hear him; he was too busy looking at the man's face, disliking the cynical expression there, the one raised eyebrow.

He hit the Strand. His hand was clenched around the watch; he was stewing it with his own sweat. He let go, feeling its weight in the depths of his pocket, thinking perhaps the heat and moisture would hurt the precious thing in some way. He had meant to lay it on the table, for the man would have given him such a price for it. He had half-relished the idea of seeing the man's expression at that. Such a masterwork would never have ordinarily found its way into this back alleyway full of greasy brooches and rings. But when the moment had come, he had not done it.

There was the doubt, after all – if the pawnbroker had seen the handbills circulated by Taylor telling of the watch's theft, Digby could not count on the man's dishonesty to save him. Before he had left his room, he had separated off Renard's seals and pendants in his other pocket, making them easy to hand over separately, so now he wondered whether he had ever meant to do it at all.

Digby muttered and sang to himself as he strode along, leaning forwards, uncomfortable and eager to be on home turf. He felt as though there was a knot in his brain that he could not untie. Pawning the watch would have given him a substantial sum of money, perhaps even enough to win the favour of a woman, for even had he stowed most of the money away, there would have been enough to buy her a new bonnet and as many ribbons as she wanted. It was all the pretty ones wanted: a few coins flashed before their eyes.

The streets were busy; the sedan chairs were halting, almost piling up on each other; there was the clatter of hooves as the horse pulling a hackney carriage shied at a street seller. Two men were arguing over a debt in the middle of the street. As he hurried on, weaving his way through the other pedestrians, Digby felt the disquiet and conflict of the city grate on him; he had enough to deal with, starting with the rattling contents of his own brain. Renard's death had seemed to him some kind of happy accident; he had only seen the watch, snatched up the beauty, seen an opportunity and taken it. But as the days passed he had began to wonder: what had he been thinking of to take the valuables of a murdered man, and one he had known? He was divided between distress at his actions and fear for his own safety. He had even begun to fancy that the murderer had stood nearby when he found the body, watching from the shadows, and it had disturbed his sleep last night, his own cry of panic waking him.

At the top of it, there was Mr Maynard to worry about. Fine Mr Maynard, stopping him on Bond Street the other morning to ask questions about Pierre Renard. When he'd started talking, Digby had clamped his hand around the watch, feverish with fear, mumbled his excuses and gone straight to the Red Lion. If they found it on him, he'd be stretched by the neck in no time, and the thought of it made him want to weep with terror.

His pace quickened further. Finally, he reached the west churchyard of St James's that fronted on to Jermyn Street. In the shadows, he coughed heartily. He thought of the coroner's meeting for Pierre Renard. He remembered how he had stood, feeling secure and comfortable, with something like optimism framing his thoughts. He had never given himself to it completely, but its loss was still bitter.

He leaned against the wall, hoping it would support him for a moment. He knew what it all came down to, really; he had kept the watch because it was his secret. Having it with him gave him strength: its beauty was something he alone could enjoy. When he was able to hold it in his hand, and examine its details by the light of a candle, it was worth enduring the fear of discovery. It seemed to him to be fated, telling him of the life he was destined to live. Once he had thought he would make such objects, that he would finish his apprenticeship and be a maker of beauty. Owning it was a compensation, for it seemed to have its own kind of life, and it tempered his bitterness. To let another human being set eyes on it would taint its sanctity. He realized now that he could not let it go.

He was standing in the churchyard when he saw Dr Taylor come out of the church, followed by his wife. They'd been at prayer, he presumed, pulling his hat down to shade his face. You like praying, don't you, Doctor? he thought. Such mealy-mouthed little prayers before you go to touch up all the fine ladies. You like taking possession of your godliness before you take possession of those women, summing them up, dismissing them, as you dismiss us all. And yet you have a wife who is happy to walk beside you. He couldn't stop his thoughts running along dark channels, his heart beating faster, poisonous black bitterness in his heart's blood. I lived a good life until now, he thought. Do I deserve this, the only comfort I have a piece of metal stolen from a corpse?

He wondered if he would be able to sleep before he went out on the watch again. He dreaded returning to his poky lodgings, to lie alone in the greyness of the winter afternoon. He breathed slowly, trying not to cough. Unseen, he listened to the good doctor whining to his wife.

'It is a mess,' Taylor said. 'I would not have credited it: a man of his stature and exactness.'

'But of course,' said Amelia Taylor. 'He thought he would live for ever.'

'How do I explain it to her?' he said.

'Tell her the truth,' she said. 'That her husband wished her to marry a dead man; and that, since he is gone, her fate is to be decided by you.'

CHAPTER NINE

1st June, 1792

A letter from Sarah came in response to my own. On seeing the letter and recognizing her hand, I could hardly contain myself, and felt like a child being kept from a treat. I waited until I was alone to open it. Her phrasing was formal; even with my willing eyes I could see in her words barely a trace of the affection she once bore 4for me. She says her second son is not yet reconciled to choosing a trade, and is some five years too young. She does, however, ask that I consider a nephew of hers who lives in Shrewsbury, and wants for a profession. I will send for him; I have space for an apprentice to learn the running of the shop. I wrote back to her, and then on to Shrewsbury, to the address she enclosed. I thought one day my own son would learn my trade from me; and that still may be so, God willing. But it is my duty to ensure that my knowledge is passed to others lest I fall silent; and it does me good to help Sarah.

*

It was early morning when Mary took her seat on the south side of St James's Piccadilly. She went there to see Eli's stones. After his death, she had been frightened of losing the memory of her brother, but in one corner of this church it had always been clear and vivid. It was as though he toddled before her: six years old, but small for his age and often unsteady on his feet, so that he seemed younger. A decade old, this vision had grown more intense as time passed, as an oft-repeated prayer settles into the memory. As he walked, he trailed one small hand along the surface of the church wall, feeling each irregularity with his fingertips, his fingers as nimble as his legs were unsteady. He paused when he found his favourite stone: a patch where some plaster had come away, exposing a facet that was black and rough, as though the surface had been chipped away by some ancient tool, a flint split open, its texture changing from sharp to smooth. His small fingers had always dwelt on the roughest surface, as though he found some particular pleasure in it. The feeling of texture beneath his hands made more sense to him than words, for he rarely spoke. This had been his touchstone. It had been covered over long ago, but she knew the spot, and ran her fingertips over the inscription there.

I AM THE RESURRECTION, AND THE LIFE.

Eli turned, and smiled at her. His face was pale, as smooth as a sea-washed pebble, with a tiny, flat nose, and large, almond-shaped blue eyes. He often seemed to be in his own world; but he knew who loved him, and in those blue eyes that watched, his family saw a soul as wide and deep as the sea.

Many people had looked at Eli as though he was a curse to her family. They had learned soon enough to hold their tongues; for Mallory and Mary had spoken in the harshest terms to anyone who dared to speak against their brother. Still, the words 'idiot' and 'imbecile' had hovered just out of her hearing for years until Pierre had voiced them, only months after her marriage.

On that last terrible day, the last time she had ever ventured to the City, she had said: he is ours, and we love him. I love him.

Loved, he said. He has gone; and he will not return while I live.

She closed her eyes. I will not remember the parting, she thought. I will think of Eli happy.

In this aisle of the church, she had sat with her family the Sunday her banns were read for the third and final time. All seated together, jammed in the pew in their best clothes, grim-faced: Mary, her parents, Pierre, Mallory and her husband. And Eli, toddling away from them, taking advantage of the attention being elsewhere, as they held their breath.

I publish the banns of marriage ...

If anyone knows of any lawful impediment ...

In the midst of the solemnity and tension, there came the sound of Eli's giggling. Toddling down the aisle, he had found the arms of a man who had picked him up and thrown him in the air. His laughter rang out, and continued until he was breathless. Some of the congregation laughed with him, others shook their heads with disapproval and took sharp intakes of breath. Mary didn't notice Pierre's annoyance. She turned, and smiled at Eli's delight, and her eyes met those of the man who held him. The memory of that moment still made her catch her breath, half in recognition of its joy, half in mourning for its brevity.

The man was a visitor to the church, a cousin of her childhood friend, Jesse Chamac, her father had said. She had curtseyed to him, listened intently as her father had passed a few words with him. He had a soft, agreeable voice, and when he smiled it was as though a shaft of sunlight had fallen on his face. 'We met long ago,' he said to her. 'When we were children. That is, I was a boy of fourteen, and you were not even as tall as this young man.' And he had rested his hand on Eli's head. Eli, still for a brief moment, had looked up at him.

Mary had nodded, for though she had not known him immediately, there was something familiar about him. After a few minutes' worth of polite conversation, her father had guided Mary away, to tell her of Pierre's displeasure. She hadn't known it then, but that would be the last time her family would be together, united, with some sense of hope. She had never said goodbye to the man, but remembered glancing back, and seeing him speaking to Pierre.

Now, she remembered. They had met first on the day her father had taken her to the Assay Office. Letter by letter, his name emerged in her mind, as though it had always been there. Alban Steele.

'Ah, Miss Dunning,' said Mrs Holland, as she surprised Joanna coming down the back stairs from the garret. 'We'd all been wondering where you'd got to, disappearing to your room again.'

'What's going on?' said Joanna, ignoring the remark. The housekeeper was holding a pile of folded linen in her arms, but had stopped beside a landing window, as though something had arrested her attention during her climb up the stairs.

'They're all out there with the new coachman,' said Mrs Holland, glancing at her. 'A fine fellow he is, too. He'll be charging for the girls to look at him soon.'

Joanna came down the two steps between them and looked over the woman's shoulder.

The coachman was below them. His back was turned and he was brushing off the master's horse, dressed in a linen frock coat that he had put on over his other clothes to protect them. Mrs Holland was right: he was a fine, strong man, just as Joanna's Stephen, also a coachman, had been. He had broad shoulders and she could see from the way he moved that his limbs were powerful. She doubted that he had her lover's gentleness, and his almost occult sense of horsemanship. But if she stared for long enough, and allowed her eyes to blur a little, he might almost be Stephen. For Stephen had worn such a shirt, and he too had dark brown hair beneath his wig, that curled at the nape of his neck; such a curl as the one she had given to Mr Renard to be set in a pendant.

She felt the tears rising in her eyes again and blinked them back, cursing herself for having left her room at the wrong moment, before she had fully gained her composure. In the day since she had been told of Renard's death, she had found little time to be alone. She was sure Mrs Holland knew that something was wrong, and she did not wish to expose herself to more questions. The groom made to turn, and Joanna moved sharply away from the window.

'Remind you of someone, does he?' said Mrs Holland, gazing steadily at Joanna's reddened eyes. The light from the window made the downward turn of her mouth seem harsher and deeper than Joanna recalled.

'No,' said Joanna. She managed to summon up a haughty glare. 'I'd best go to Mrs Chichester, if you'll excuse me.'

The housekeeper said nothing; she stayed where she was, and Joanna felt her gaze following her as she descended the stairs.

'I am sorry to disturb you, madame,' said Grisa, leaning on the doorframe and examining his fingernails. 'Bright Hemmings wishes to speak to you. I told him to leave, but he would not go.'

Mary was by the fire, leaning forwards, her hat on the chair beside her. When she looked at the clock she realized she had returned from the church two hours since, and had not moved. 'I will come down,' she said. 'Do not let him up here.'

As she walked down the stairs she tried to summon some kindness for her visitor. Poor Bright, who lived in the perpetual shadow of his own absurdity. Feeling so out of place herself, she had sympathy for him. His story had been repeated so often that it was the stuff of local legend. A shop sign had fallen on his mother when he was a child, and the shock of her sudden death had altered Bright's mind, it was believed, making him impervious to good sense. It was the first thing one thought of when you looked at him: a falling shop sign, on a street of swinging shop signs. Or pigs. He had long borne a partiality for Mary, not because she had shown him any particular favour, but simply because she was not harsh, unlike most of the others who spoke to him.

Bright was waiting in the shop, looking at one of the shelves of silver with attentive interest, as though he might be tempted to buy a piece. He even placed one hand on the glass in front of a salt cellar, causing Grisa to clear his throat severely. Grisa stood near him, clearly agitated at the idea that one of his customers might see the visitor. When Bright addressed a remark to him he gave a one-word answer into which he injected as much contempt as possible, his eyes darting to the door and back again.

By the look of him, Bright was dressed in borrowed clothes: tight breeches, a yellow and blue striped waistcoat, and with a grubby cravat tied in a large bow beneath his mud-stained greatcoat.

As he turned to Mary, with a self-important toss of his head, she found her compassion for him evaporating. It was all very well being patient from a distance, but he had the gift of converting sympathy to irritation. For, surely, she thought, as he executed an exaggerated bow, he would always have had that ridiculous cowlick of a wig, no matter what had happened to his mother? Always that face with its currents of cunning, his expression infused with the belief that he was cleverer and more dignified than everyone else? Faced with him, one was inclined to think he might have made up the story about the shop sign.

'Madam,' said Bright. 'My honourable compliments and condolences.' He bowed again.

'What is it, Mr Hemmings? Pray hurry,' said Mary, thinking that he had never dared enter the shop when Pierre lived.

'If I may trespass on your time for a brief five minutes. May I be honoured with a private interview?' said Bright, as though continuing on a course he had set for himself, to which Mary had become an irritating obstacle.

'No, not now,' she said, and saw Grisa shaking his head, his eyes directed out of the window at the street.

'At a future time, madam, you may be grateful for the addresses I have come to pay to you,' Bright said. He gave her a ghastly smile. 'For I come to offer you protection from a dark world. But I see you are being shy due to the delicacy of the situation, and the public nature of our meeting.'

Mary looked around her. At Grisa, his hands clasped behind his back, his eyes fixed on Bond Street and the people passing the windows. On the shelves of silver, each piece reflecting cold light. On the counter, where rings and brooches glittered. At Bright, his face full of misplaced confidence, as though he anticipated a quick sale. I am here to be bought and sold, she thought. No matter how I dress it up, that is all there is.

'Go,' she said. Her mouth was dry. 'There are no pigs for you here.'

She looked at Grisa, who sniggered at the mention of livestock. He walked towards Bright, hands up, herding him backwards towards the door, not caring when Bright stumbled and almost fell, cursing them as he went out on to the street.

Mary went back up to her parlour, but directly heard a commotion on the street outside. When she looked out of the window she could see Bright standing there, but there were others too; even Ellen was out on the street, her arms folded across her chest in the cold. Mary saw her glance up at the parlour window.

'What is going on?' she said to Grisa a minute later, breathless from running down the stairs.

'You are not to go out there,' he said.

She pushed past him and went out of the door of the shop. The crowd were looking in the direction of Dr Taylor's house.

'What are they doing?' she heard a woman say.

'It's that table,' said another. 'They couldn't get the blood off.'

'She's having it burnt,' said another. 'You can hardly blame her. There's something bad about this business; why would a bloodstain not shift?'

Ellen had noticed her mistress, but as she approached, her eyes full of alarm, Mary put her hand up warningly. She knew now what they meant: Pierre had lain on Mrs Taylor's kitchen table, where they had carried him on the night of his death. Many times she had imagined the gore pooled, so dark it was almost black, as it seeped into the wood; of the poor kitchen maid who would have to try and scrub it away; of Pierre, left there as though he was a piece of meat on a slab.

Two men came out, lugging the table into the full glare of the day. Bright Hemmings pointed and laughed at them. Mrs Taylor was nowhere to be seen. As the table emerged, Mary thought she could see the evidence of death upon it, and she put her hand to her mouth, a small cry escaping. Bright turned, and she saw his smile fade at the sight of her.

She couldn't move; she put her hands over her eyes, but she had already seen it, and now could not erase it from her memory. The sickening, dark stain, the physical reality of Pierre's murder, and she could only think that the blood-stain would smell of him. Her legs buckled as sweat-beaded nausea rose in her. She felt hands on her shoulders: two strong, capable hands, and she could not look up to see who it was that guided her. Head down, she allowed herself to be supported, back into the safety of the shop. She heard the bell above her head with relief, smelt the beeswax: no meat, no blood. Just the shop; never had she thought of it with such relief. Her head was pounding; unthinking, she rested her forehead on the glass of the counter.

'That wasn't for her to see.' It was a man's voice. His alcohol-tinged breath sank through the air.

'I could not stop her,' said Grisa.

As the shop door opened again, Mary looked up. She saw the back of her helper, saw him turn, just once, and caught only the keen sympathy in his blue eyes before he was gone.

CHAPTER TEN

2nd June, 1792

We had many customers today. I kept good cheer; it is my business, and has been the habit of my life. I am skilled at hiding my true thoughts. Yet despite my smile one thought enflamed my mind, and shaped my prayers this evening, my frustrations brought to fruition by Sarah's letter.

Dear Lord, give me a son. That is all I ask for. I am prepared to accept that I may never have a wife who is worthy of me, but if I had a child, that pain would be dulled. A son of my own, to carry my name. Late this afternoon, I called my wife to my chamber, but – oh, it pains me to think of the efforts I made, for she lay as though dead beneath me. Her lack of passion for me is why she cannot conceive. My good friend Dr Taylor has told me before, his tongue loosened by an evening's drinking: the woman's ardour is needed.

*

In the basement workshop on Foster Lane, Alban started early and finished late, straining his eyes in the dim light. He was working on a small cup, fashioning it from a blank of silver. He loved the beginnings of making something; he had hammered it round once, heated it cherry red, and soused it in the pickle. Now it was pale, cratered and chalky, like the surface of the moon. He looked at it, turned it carefully on the bench, and began to work it again: hit, rest, hit, rest, each strike firm and landing with a sweet chink, a note played just right.

He knew most other silversmiths didn't love the metal as he did. He couldn't remember how he had grown to love it; its presence in his life was a given. But he knew that once it had been his enemy. As a boy of thirteen, apprenticed to his uncle, he had found it nothing but noise and hard work, a war between his puny arms and the obstinate metal. But in the calm, unblinking stare of Alban's eyes there had been a will, a desire not to be beaten. He had grown strong so quickly that the skin had stretched on his shoulders and arms, leaving pale welts that had never quite gone away. He had learned his skill; he had conquered the metal; and now he loved it.

In London he had worked harder, and faster, than he could remember. Watching the silver yield and shape to his will had calmed him after seeing Mary. His skill was something to be relied on. Even in near darkness, he didn't want to leave it to go upstairs and eat. To look at Jesse, hunched in his chair, drumming his fingers on the kitchen table. He preferred to stay in the dark workshop, its walls pasted with tattered handbills of songs and verses. The light was so dim he could only read them half a foot away. And somewhere, on that wall, the shape his chalked hand had left the day he had returned to Chester, so long ago.

He heard the door to the workshop open and shut and looked up, prepared to see his cousin and discuss how their commissions were coming along. There was some elaborate casting to be done, and in a day or so some of the plainer pieces that they had made easily would need to be taken the few steps to Goldsmiths' Hall, for marking and to pay the duty. But it was Agnes, coming towards him with a strange half-smile. In this setting she looked out of place, and as though she felt the strangeness, she was moving awkwardly.

Alban pushed his hair out of his eyes, felt the sweat slick the back of his arm. 'How d'you do?' he said, smiling at her.

'I've come to fetch you,' she said. 'You must eat. I have a slice of fine Gloucester cheese for you, if you can be parted from your mistress.' She tilted her head and looked at him playfully. He looked at the piece of metal in front of him and laughed.

'You've left the children to burn the house down just to fetch me,' he said. 'I'd never have thought it.'

'My good husband is watching them,' she said. 'I've told them to say their prayers.' She came closer to him, bashfully, into the light, and looked at the silver he was working on. 'It's good to see you work,' she said. 'When we were first married, I would watch Jesse at the bench sometimes, though he told me to leave him alone unless I wanted to burnish something. He said he could never work properly when my eyes were on him.' She gave a low laugh, one finger tracing a pattern on the bench. 'We are so grateful to you, Alban,' she said. 'We are lucky to have you as kin. Jesse was worrying himself into the grave.'

Alban shook his head. 'There is no need to thank me. I should have come here sooner, as I promised all those years ago. But I am here now, and there is plenty of work from Renard's shop. Jesse can put his mind to rest.' He worried as he said it that there was, perhaps, some uncertainty in his tone. There was still a faint smile playing over Agnes's face.

'He used to say he wanted to be a gilder to make more money,' she said. 'I said if I'd wished to marry a dead man I'd have trimmed my bonnet and paraded around the churchyards looking for one. I said I wanted him to have the full span of his life, and have it with me.'

Alban nodded and smiled. It was rare to see a gilder live beyond thirty; subsumed in mercury fumes all day, they were paid well but died young. Yet it sounded like something Jesse would have offered to do: a rash promise, made with no expectation of fulfilment.

Agnes's smile faded. Away from the fireside and her normal wifely exertions, she looked unlike herself. With the smile gone, her full face fell slack. Her cheeks were not rosy, but a pale colour that reminded him of the dough she was forever kneading.

She looked up and caught his eye. 'When I told him

about the new babe, he could barely raise his head and speak to me,' she said. 'He is melancholy. Does his soul make him sick?'

Alban put the hammer down and leaned on the bench. The sudden intimacy of the question made him uncomfortable. 'I doubt it is that,' he said. 'Illness comes. There is no reason.'

Agnes nodded, and crossed her arms over her chest, staring at the floor intently as though she was seeking answers there.

'Agnes Chamac,' Alban said. 'You are a worrier, and I never knew it.'

She answered his smile with one of her own, though the worry stayed in her eyes, behind it; how long had her fear been there, he wondered? Poor, jolly Agnes, who everyone believed was well and strong all the time; who never faltered.

He put his arms around her, held her briefly, tightly. 'Do not think on it,' he said. 'Jesse lives for you.'

As he released her, she looked at him as though she wished to believe him, and he looked back at her, trying to stay steady and strong, but feeling as empty inside as he had on the night journey from Chester. He could only see the rutted road, the grass waving in the wind, the full moon, and the faces of his fellow passengers, frightened that someone might come and take all that they had.

They both jumped at the sound of the workshop door slamming. 'Won't you come up into the light?' said Jesse. He was standing at the top of the stairs. 'Don't you get sick of the darkness?'

'I never think of it,' said Alban. 'But as you both ask so well, I will come with you.'

The children were sitting tamely enough by the fire when the men took their place at the table. As Alban bit into a slice of bread a deep sense of well-being spread through him: the soft warmth of Agnes's bread, the salty butter prickling his taste buds. As he chewed it Agnes ladled pickled cucumbers on to his plate alongside a large slice of cheese.

'Enough there,' said Jesse. 'We don't want him so fat and lazy that he can't work.'

Agnes sat down at the end of the table, her gaze moving backwards and forwards between the two men. In the background, Anne, Agnes' and Jesse's eldest daughter, was reading a psalm to her brothers and sisters.

'I should take my break more often,' said Alban. 'Though it only makes me realize how much I would like to sleep in front of the fire.' He bit into a pickled cucumber, and as he crunched on it noticed that Jesse had not yet eaten anything.

Jesse placed his palms on the table in a slow and measured movement. 'Go to the children, would you?' he said quietly to Agnes. Alban watched warily as Agnes moved away without looking at him. 'Is something the matter?' he said to Jesse.

'I was speaking to some acquaintances at the Hall today when I took those pieces to be assayed,' said Jesse. 'They had news of Bond Street.'

Alban scanned his cousin's face. Robbery was the greatest hazard for those who dealt in precious metals, and his first thought was for Mary, undefended in her late husband's establishment. 'What's happened?' he said. 'Have they found out who killed Renard?'

'No,' said Jesse, glancing away. 'It relates more to what happens next. One of my acquaintances raised a point that might be of interest to you. I had not thought of it, but I warrant you have. Mary Renard will have to marry again.'

Silence.

Alban bit into a pickle with a savage crunch, and sat chewing defiantly under his cousin's grave stare.

'Her husband's barely cold,' he said, once he had swallowed it. 'Have you all chosen a candidate?' He couldn't help the tarnish of bitterness on his words; his eyes flickered down to his plate then up to Jesse's face again, searching for information.

'No,' said Jesse. 'Dr Taylor is meant to be dealing with the will, but one of the trustees – a crony of his – has a looser tongue than him, and spilled it all to a friend of mine who keeps him in seals and trinkets. Renard left his affairs in some disorder. It seems he had some idea that Mary should marry a cousin of his, but the cousin is dead. Thanks be to God: one Renard husband is enough for a lifetime, I would think.'

'Why does she have to marry again?' said Alban. He felt anger flare up in him as Jesse rolled his eyes. 'If it is all left to her she may manage it in some other way, surely?' He thought of Mallory. He remembered her as a child: her hard, glittering eyes, even then, the flame of animal vitality in her. She was his hope for a moment: he was sure she knew more about business than both her dead husbands had, put together.

'A woman cannot run such a business without help,' said Jesse. 'I know, some do, a woman such as Mrs Bateman. But she had a lifetime's more experience than Mary, as well as a more indulgent husband who allowed her to share in his affairs. Mary knows nothing of the business, I imagine; Renard never let her near it, no, nor anyone else either. She has no friends to step in, apart from Grisa, who is ...' He waved his hand in the air, a disparaging gesture. 'It seems Taylor is in a rush to marry Mary off. He thinks she is in need of protection.'

'What business is it of Taylor's?' said Alban.

'He is the executor, and main trustee,' said Jesse. 'In charge of her too, as well as the money. It's no surprise. Taylor and Renard lived in each other's pockets.'

'We do not know the true situation. It is pointless to speak of it,' said Alban.

'It is good to anticipate,' said Jesse. Finally, he took a bite of the bread and butter, and crammed a pickle into his mouth. 'You should ask her,' he said, his mouth full.

Alban sat back in his chair. He was half of a mind to leave the table, go back down into the cellar, and begin work again. He need never say anything; he need never even acknowledge that he had heard Jesse's words. But something about the way his cousin was watching him made him think that he would not leave it. Not this time. Things had changed in the last eleven years; Alban would not be left, unchallenged, to do as he wished. There was something driving Jesse; an imperative to secure Alban's happiness, to break through his obstinate silence. Alban wished heartily he had stayed in Chester, where those he knew would have left him to pursue a quiet life.

Jesse swallowed his food. 'What do you say to it?' he said. Alban could say nothing: he shook his head.

'There was a liking between you,' said Jesse, ploughing on. 'That day in the church. I saw it, plain as day. And if I could see it . . .' He shrugged.

'You saw nothing,' said Alban. 'You saw nothing but me look at a pretty girl. That is all.'

'And all your questions afterwards?' said Jesse. 'Your sudden desire to leave London when I said the match was settled? You couldn't get to the mail coach quick enough.'

Alban pushed his chair back. 'Thank you for the victuals, Agnes,' he said, and left the room, descending the cellar steps, closing the door quietly behind him.

The workbench was as he had left it; the piece of silver there, waiting. But as he touched it, he knew he could do nothing with it, his concentration spoiled. He swore under his breath. As the fury surged through him he wanted to pick it up and hurl it across the room with a force that would crumple it against the wall. All he could do was stand there, leaning forwards against the bench, waiting for it to pass. He heard Jesse come down the steps, and when he looked up his cousin was waiting.

'There is nothing, nothing to recommend me to her,' said Alban.

'Your accounts are all in order, I understand,' said Jesse.

His tone was blunt, unemotional; it had a kind of formality that Alban was grateful for, however fleetingly. 'You have funds,' added Jesse. 'I know you do.'

'Yes. But.' Alban couldn't describe the weight that sat on his chest.

'Is there some other woman?' said Jesse. 'Some prior attachment?'

'No!' he said, in outrage. He walked up and down alongside the bench, his hand running across the smooth wood.

'I vowed I'd be a man such as Renard,' he said, after a moment. 'Better than him, even. I knew that was what I should be, and that I had the capability. But I didn't hunger for it, I didn't reach, or push, or attain. Mine is a history of lost chances. She is just another, you see.'

'No, I don't,' said Jesse. 'Understand me. There will be men crawling all over that shop in Bond Street tomorrow like maggots on meat. You have another chance. She could not ask for a better husband, a better man. Let her decide it.' He blocked Alban's path as his cousin tried to pass him. 'Let her decide it,' he said again. But Alban had already pushed past and was running up the stairs.

The daylight hurt Alban's eyes. He walked quickly away, not wanting to be caught by Jesse. At the first dram seller he saw, he took a drink. It tasted foul and hot. He walked on, haltingly, winding his way through the streets. He remembered the day in church when he had heard Mary's banns read. He recalled her brother's face, and the sunlight on the stone floor of the church as he spoke with Mary and her father before they moved away from him. Then, Renard had come to him, standing tall and straight in his finery. The man had a handsome face, and an easy smile. 'You are Jesse Chamac's cousin, are you not?'

'I am, sir,' Alban had said. They had stood there for a moment, Renard speaking of the trade, his voice ranging pleasantly over subjects as though Alban was his equal, but his dress and his watch indicated otherwise. He seemed perfectly relaxed, and his smile never wavered; Alban thought how engaging he was, and imagined him charming his customers.

Several aisles away Eli gave a little cry as he was lifted up by Mallory, struggling with her, but with a smile on his face. Renard's face changed, and though Alban could not remember the colour of his eyes, the content of his stare had remained with him: cold, and full of spite, as though the child he watched was an inconvenience, a blemish on the pleasant picture of a morning at church.

'That child,' he had said, in the same lyrical tone, with a hint of a French accent. 'I cannot look at him without wishing to raise my hand.'

Alban left the church; and for days he had been haunted by the memory of Mary's smile when her father had introduced her as Renard's bride.

Eleven years later, Alban walked quickly down the London streets. He had not put on a coat and the winter air crawled over his skin. Jesse's words had angered him, raising emotions from the past that he had no wish to confront. He had meant only to escape the workshop, but as he walked his route bent towards the west. He reasoned that his feelings had been just the tremors caused by memory, echoes of something that no longer truly existed. If he could look her in the eyes again, and use logic to decipher his thoughts, perhaps he could lay it all to rest.

He followed the route he and Jesse had taken four days before, stopping every time he came to a taproom or a beerseller, throwing down spirits after ale. He tried to unpick the past, but underlying his thoughts was the question that had always haunted him: why had she married Pierre Renard?

The drink desensitized him. It was two and a half hours before he reached Bond Street. He told himself he was walking straight, yet he felt that numbed hesitance: a precursor, a whisper not yet loud enough for him to heed, that he would think of this later with shame. For now, the drink had taken the edges off life, so he proceeded with confidence.

On Bond Street everything seemed brighter than before, the colours more intense, the edges sharper. The sky's blue was a mixture of ice and lapis, without a cloud. The grey of stone against it, the burnt-wood brown of bricks cut from the London mud and stained by the city's smoke. Had he never noticed these things before? he wondered, he who prided himself on recognizing beauty, on seeing detail where others saw only the mundane essentials of life. Where there were carved details, be it a bunch of grapes or only a volute, double-lined, cut in stone, he stopped and looked at it, as a child looks at a ladybird crawling on a wild flower: with fascination and excitement. The window displays and people did not interest him as much as the buildings did; the busy road, the noise, he could ignore. His progress down Bond Street was slow.

The ladies and gentlemen had come to buy things: silver, jewels, sweetmeats, furs. Their carriages and sedan chairs filled the road, and their feet the pavements. More than once, in his unsteady state, Alban's shoulder caught another, earning him a sharp reprimand, but he continued on, expecting at any moment to be pushed into the path of a horse by an officious manservant, but somehow knowing he would deal effectively with trouble when it came. The liquor he had drunk gave him the certainty that he was able to defeat the hundreds of foes, natural and unnatural, that had barred and would bar his way in the world; it gave him the conviction he could survive. This new view made everything possible, suddenly; even the possibility of love. With it came an intense desire to see Mary's face and gauge if there was any trace left of the girl he had once known.

He found a space opposite the Renard shop. Or, more accurately, he carved a space out with his sudden stillness, refusing to be carried on the relentless crowds of shoppers down Bond Street. People flowed around him. How he stared, intensely, at that shop front, looking for meaning (like a fool, he thought) in something dumb, unseeing and unfeeling: as if glass, bricks and mortar could speak to him. The tumult and excitement in him, the flame lit by Jesse and the drink, began to gutter and die. For though he knew he could live whatever came, he could not find the words to speak to Mary, even to ask for her, without drawing ridicule on himself.

He was not like Renard. He had no words. He never wished to explain, or excuse himself. He had lived with acceptance, at a distance from the things that could have given him joy or pain. He had nothing to account for: the sheet was clean. He did not wish to apologize for himself, and yet he felt unworthy.

He kept telling himself that he could lay it to rest. For it seemed so strange that this ache in him, this sense of loss, had been based on such brevity of acquaintance. He had never said the word love in his mind when thinking of this cherished stranger, and did not want to account for why she should be so precious to him, dearer than his own flesh, when they had spent so many years apart. If it was love he felt – and he could think it, after so much drink – then it was a love long buried and based on unknowing.

He stood watching for some time; minutes passed, then an hour, and still he did not move on. When the shop door opened, and Mary came out, he felt shocked, though he had waited for that reason, with that hope. She was dressed in black, her hair up, her dark eyes paled by the sunlight. There was a wildness about her look that reminded him of Grisa's word. *Insensible*. She was alone, divorced from propriety. Then she looked up from adjusting her cloak, and saw him.

They were separated by Bond Street; carriages, horses, people moved between them in a blur of colour and noise. She was the fixed point he kept his eyes on, and she did not draw her eyes away.

He saw her lips move; he could not tell what she was saying. One word. Sir? You?

He did not know how long they stood there. It was she who crossed the road, eventually; he could never after think of that without shame. When she reached him, they kept a good foot apart, for all the others moving around them.

'Mr Steele?' she said. She looked down when he nodded, took a breath. 'You probably don't remember me,' she said. 'My name is Mary Renard.'

'I know who you are,' he said. In his mind he begged whatever watched him, whether it was God, the sky or just his own thoughts, to keep his voice steady, to stop himself from slurring the inane things he was going to say. But already reality was breaking in: he was unkempt, dressed in his work clothes, smelling of a tavern. He bowed briefly. 'I would not have chosen to meet you like this,' he said.

'You did not wish to meet me?' said Mary, and he saw the hurt in her eyes.

'No!' he said. 'Not as I am now, dressed only for the workshop, and the smell of drink on me. I am not normally so. Let us move a short way; I would speak with you.'

She acceded by following him. They walked in parallel, still apart, as though each separate and unseen by the other, buffeted by the shoppers, and unaware of them. Near the junction of Old and New Bond Street, at Grafton Street, they were able to turn off the main thoroughfare, and stood awkwardly as the flow of people continued without them, both looking on at the ongoing rush that moved ever forwards like a river. 'And this is low season,' he said, looking around them. Then, he knew he must finally turn towards her. 'How are you?' he said, quickly. 'I must give you my condolences.'

Mary stared at him. 'I am well, thank you,' she said. She forced a smile, while her eyes remained unreadable. 'And what of you? Where have you been, all these years?'

'In Chester,' he said. 'It does not seem so long. When one does the same thing every day, the years fly.' The evenings in a small, dark room in a lodging house: drawing by candlelight, putting the elements of his silver designs on paper. The days: never realizing the designs, only doing the bread-and-butter work. One woman in those years, her white back turned to him, her dark plaited hair so long the end rested on the bed. He had not cherished the sight of her as he had the stacks of drawings, littering the table and the floor, drawings he would one day categorize, one day fulfil, one after the other. He had sworn it; he had sworn many things. One evening he had even sworn he would return to London and seek out Mary, when, drawing a design, he had found beneath his hand a cypher: her initial, and his, intertwined, drawn without calculation or thought. The memory of it was a small stab in him; it made him catch his breath, for he had been a younger man then, and he wondered if he might have saved her from the sadness that now enveloped her.

'I will be in London for some time,' he said. 'May I call on you?'

She was about to respond when a shout went up. 'Thief!' There was a scramble, of people turning, of men checking their watches and women their jewellery. Mary had taken a step backwards towards Bond Street. Later,

Alban thought he must have been emboldened by the drink still filling his blood, but he was not sure if the instinct would have overridden politeness anyway. He took her wrists, gently but firmly, and drew her out of the path of the crowds, towards him. His hands were still upon her, when she caught sight of something over his shoulder.

'Here is Dr Taylor,' she said. 'He has come to protect me again. I keep going out alone, and it is thought to be unseemly.'

Alban turned and saw the lumbering figure dressed all in black. He squeezed his eyes half-shut to focus, and noted the grim expression on the doctor's face. He bowed briefly to Mary. 'My compliments,' he said. Then he did the same to the doctor, barely hearing Mary's introduction of him as Mr Steele, a fine silversmith, from Chester. It was evident that the doctor wished him gone; so he went, glancing at Mary's face, her suddenly downcast eyes.

As he reached the junction of Grafton Street and Old Bond Street, a man in a burgundy coat tipped his hat to him. 'I see you know Mrs Renard,' he said.

'I cannot see what business it is of yours, sir,' said Alban. He would not have shown such sharpness, normally; he hardly knew where he was.

The man smiled, looking around as though he sought to take in every detail of the scene. 'A stranger,' he said. 'How curious.'

He briskly joined the flow of people before Alban could say another word. Frowning with annoyance, Alban looked back over his shoulder: Mary was speaking, and the doctor was still watching him.

As he began to walk, he dwelt on the moment when he had taken her wrists, and moved her aside. It was in that moment that he had known there was something beyond logic in all of this. Whatever he felt for Mary Renard, it was not dead.

CHAPTER ELEVEN

5th June, 1792

Lately I have kept to myself when not working, and shied away from pursuits that might divert me, for I have needed the quiet to think on the past. But tonight I sent word to Dr Taylor that I would care for his company, and sure enough he came.

Taylor is a good man and I prize his high connections. I first met him when I took the lease here on Bond Street; he lives nearby, and has earned a high reputation doctoring women, but is a man of great skill and learning, and now serves as a coroner. He took to me at once when we met, and has been a useful friend. He has no children, and being some fifteen years older than I, I believe he values me almost as a son, for there is something of that tenderness in his treatment of me.

I am wont to speak to him at least with the impression of openness, and sometimes I am frank even beyond what I intend.

I confided in him of my desire for a family. He, huge man that he is, had tears in his eyes. He has not spoken to me of his own marriage, which has lasted twenty years, but remained childless. Yet there was such emotion in his face when I spoke that I felt sure he knew my anguish.

'None deserves that better than you,' he said to me. 'If it is God's will, you will be given a son, but you must be patient.' His words, though meant well, did not soothe me. My agitation is great.

Digby had left the watch house late. It had been a busy night. He'd broken up three brawls, and then some house-breakers had been caught and delivered. He did not feel tired; he and Watkin had been dissecting the night's events with good humour and vigour. So he decided to go to the Red Lion and have a pot or two of beer.

The beer was good, but it made his head spin. He thought perhaps he'd got a good barrel for a change, before the landlord could water it down. Whatever was wrong with it, it had had a stupefying effect, as though stronger than usual, and his energy melted away. He stumbled along in a cloud of fatigue, bumping into a man or two as he walked, raising his hands in apology. 'Half-dead with tiredness,' he muttered, when he hit one man's shoulder particularly hard, and was sworn at. He speeded up on Piccadilly; not long now until his bed, and he was so ready for it he knew the vermin would not disturb him.

A flash of a burgundy-coloured coat insinuated itself into his peripheral vision as he walked slowly along, and it was half a minute or so before he realized Maynard was beside him, swinging his stick as he walked and smiling with his usual determined good humour.

'Sir,' Digby said, wondering how long he could delay the action of taking his hat off without being accused of insolence. Every movement was an effort, and especially any movement that went against his will.

'What a fine morning it is, Digby,' said Maynard, in a good-natured tone. He was slightly breathless, the colour high in his cheeks. There was an aura of enquiry about him, Digby thought, and he found the very awareness of it exhausting and disquieting. Still, though his liking for Maynard was diminishing, tempered as it was by suspicion, he did not actively dislike him. Which put Maynard above most of the people that crossed his path in the average day.

'As you say, sir.' Digby stayed on the right side of politeness.

'And what a fine coincidence to see you here.' A large woman descended regally from her carriage into their path, her enormous hat pinned precariously to her towering hair, one gloved hand holding it in place. Digby and Maynard swerved as one, Maynard tipping his hat.

'Begging your pardon, sir,' said Digby, in a tone which did anything but. 'I could've sworn you live on Half Moon Street, yet I cannot move but you are near me.'

'It is hardly my place to consider where you shall be when I walk out in the mornings,' said Maynard, a little more loudly, but still cheerfully. 'And shouldn't you have been abed several hours since?'

Digby opened his mouth, then closed it again. His bed

was not a welcoming place, but he did not want to risk the truth, and he could not trust himself to utter a falsehood without making it a little smart. He had a sense that Maynard would not enjoy more smartness from his lips.

'Besides,' said Maynard. 'You must have thought I would come and find you again. You never did answer my question the other day.'

His hand closed around Digby's arm, bringing him to a halt. Digby looked at the hand. Yet, for the suddenness of the gesture, Maynard's touch was firm but unthreatening, as though they were friends, and he was simply supporting him.

'Isn't Ma Blacklock's near here?' said Maynard. 'We could have some coffee. You look like you need it. And this kind of discussion is better had off the streets. Good morning, sir!' He tipped his hat at another acquaintance. 'Everyone's up early, ain't they?' he muttered, after the man had passed by.

Digby wondered whether he could possibly steer Maynard back to the Red Lion, but then realized it was too long a walk. 'I don't know how a gentleman of your sort knows of Ma Blacklock's, sir,' he said.

Maynard gave a hearty laugh by way of reply, and cheerfully led the way off Piccadilly.

Ma Blacklock's was situated in a small courtyard, and was styled as a coffee house, but all kinds of dubious services issued from its centre. Digby watched Maynard's face, and noticed that the man looked undisturbed, cheerfully handing a coin to the girl that came to serve them.

What had once been a parlour was lined with benches and two trestle tables, panelled with dark wood, and lit by guttering reed lights. It had a stale smell, as though shut up too long, and the lights gave the air a constant smoky tinge of animal fat. After Maynard spoke briefly to the girl they were directed to a small box of a room in a section of what must have been once the back parlour, where Digby sat down and longed to put his head on the table. A coffee pot and cups were banged down next to them. 'I didn't know there were private rooms here,' he said, his voice slurring with tiredness.

'This is it,' said Maynard, sitting down. 'Apart from upstairs, of course. It's been years since I came here last. A gentleman seasons his experiences with places such as this. What kind of man would I be if I spoke only with the womanish Taylors of this world? You and I know what life is, Digby. I hear you carry a dagger with you rather than your watchman's rattle.' He took a sip of the coffee, and winced.

Digby yawned. 'My voice carries pretty far, sir,' he said. 'I've no need of the rattle, and the knife serves me better.'

Maynard smiled. 'You've got sharp eyes, Digby,' he said. 'I'll give you that – yes, a hundred times over. I always knew it; I always saw it in you. The most acute perception. Surprising.'

Digby was unimpressed. Was this the man's idea of flattery? 'Just because I'm no gentleman it doesn't mean I am dull-witted, sir. Not all of us are.'

'Then we agree,' said Maynard. 'As I said to you the

other day, I require your assistance. I am certain, as certain as I am that this coffee is mostly not coffee, that there will be many rumours about Pierre Renard's death. Some have said he wanted the Terror brought to England.'

'Hardly a reason to kill a man,' said Digby reasonably.

'Unless you're hot-headed,' said Maynard. 'But like you, it seems, I think Renard's trouble was closer to home. Recently, he had become more arrogant, and careless of making enemies, even amongst his customers. Much more to this than meets the eye, my good man, much more.' There was an edge to his cheerful tone. 'What have you heard?' he said.

The watchman raked through his recent memories for a recent titbit. 'Bright Hemmings,' he said, this throat croaky, 'is telling everyone who'll listen that Mary Renard is sweet on him, and that she'll be his. Exham, that engraver of Renard's, was ready to combust when he heard him say it. Chased him halfway down the street.'

'And what do you think of that?' said Maynard. 'Drink the coffee, Digby.'

'I think Bright Hemmings is an idiot who thinks more of pigs than he does of women,' said Digby. 'The idea that he had someone do Renard in is nonsense.'

Maynard nodded. 'There we agree, again.'

Digby took a mouthful of the coffee. It tasted foul and gritty and he had to fight every instinct to stop himself from spitting it out. He swallowed it with a gulp. 'I don't know why you think you need me to work all this out, sir,' he said.

'Because it is not simple,' said Maynard. 'For Renard

was the kind of man who had a thousand threads weaved together, and it will take thought to untangle it all. I want to know if there is so much as a hint of who might have wished to kill him.'

'And why do you think I can get near it?' said Digby. Looking up from his coffee cup, he met Maynard's eyes for the first time: steady, unblinking grey eyes. 'Oh, I see,' he said. 'Because no one will notice me. I am not a gentleman. I am nothing.'

Maynard left a brief pause. 'I did not say that, Digby,' he said.

Offence had already risen up in Digby; he was feeling more snappish by the moment. 'What I don't understand is this: why do you care so much anyway? What was he to you, I wonder?' He tried a small leer.

'Oh, nothing,' said Maynard. 'You may think me a hard man, but I am not – and it is the plight of his wife that touches me. I have heard she is delicate, and as Taylor seems concerned only with keeping her out of the daylight, she is not likely to make a move herself to ensure her own safety, or discover if there was some dark dealing by Renard which may come back to haunt her. I worry for her. He was a wretch, that man.'

'Handsome, though,' said Digby, thinking he would rub it in. 'Ladies liked him.'

'That too,' said Maynard, with a grim smile. 'But I don't talk out of jealousy, Digby. Renard had a dark heart, and in seeking to make himself out as a gentleman ... he took people in, people like Taylor, who should have had more sense. He thought he was clever, that he could line people up like pieces in a game of chess.' He shook his head. 'Shortly before his death, I heard talk that he'd promised to get votes for one of his patrons, in exchange for a big commission. God knows how he thought he was going to get them, I don't know. Blackmail, perhaps. I was going to expose him, make the world see him for what he was.'

'And now you can't,' said Digby. 'Speak no ill of the dead.'

'Quite,' said Maynard. 'But the puzzle remains. What kind of bad business was Renard involved in? Surely correcting an injustice appeals to you? And protecting an innocent lady, who may still be in danger? You have a strong sense of justice, I can tell.'

Digby swung himself off the bench with some difficulty. 'I need to sleep. I wish you a good morning, sir, and I'll think on it,' he said.

'I'll call on you again sometime,' said Maynard. 'You're in the Red Lion mostly, are you not?'

'I am,' said Digby, wondering how Maynard knew, but not caring to enquire any further.

He went directly home. But when he got into bed, sleep would not come. Maynard's words had disturbed him. Eventually, he dozed, and when he woke he panicked, going to his coat and feeling in the pocket for the watch. He decided he would buy a cheap chain for it, so he could secure it in some way even if he could not wear it openly. He raked his fingers through his hair. A headache was beginning behind his eyes. He decided to take a breath of air.

*

A stagecoach had disembarked at the White Bear on Piccadilly, and to Digby's jaded mind as he walked through the people every face seemed to shine with hope and expectation. There was a radiance about them all, he thought; young people, come from the country. Were they all so young? He wrapped his coat around him, coughing, and that created a clear enough path.

'You again,' said the landlord of the Red Lion.

'And a good day to you, too,' said Digby. 'Give me a friendly word for a change, would you? I have had precious few this last week or so.'

'Well, you might be of some use,' said the landlord. 'You know him, don't you?'

Digby looked over his shoulder to see Jesse Chamac, sitting on his own. He was gulping quickly from a pint pot, and when he put it down he drummed his hands on the table. He nodded. 'He's been here for hours and he's putting some of the regulars into bad humour,' said the landlord. 'Speak with him for his own sake. Old Paynter doesn't like strange 'uns and I don't want blood spilled at this time of the day.'

Digby took his own pint and went to sit down with Jesse. 'Visited Bond Street?' he said, as Jesse looked up. Jesse shook his head. His eyes glowed with a kind of feverish excitement, and with every breath he exhaled the scent of an afternoon's drinking. He drummed his fingers on the table.

'Leave that, now,' Digby said. 'What's ailing you?'

'Woman,' said Jesse.

Digby said nothing, took a sip.

'It's not *that*!' cried Jesse. 'I see the way you are looking at me. She's like a sister to me.'

'I'm sure,' said Digby.

'She will not sh-peak to me,' Jesse said, tilting his head, observing the grain of wood on the table closely, as though it was deeply interesting to him. 'I keep coming to her, I keep trying. I am neglecting my work, I am neglecting my family. Today I came to her, and I said, I cannot keep inventing pretexts, madam, to visit you, but if I must protect you I must know why.'

'Did she tell you?' said Digby, swilling his beer around and rolling his eyes in the direction of the landlord.

'No, shur, no, she did not. She cursed me, and said she wished I was long gone. And I said to her, but I saw you. I was visiting some of my fellows and I saw you on the street that night, that night, you know when, you passed me and you did not see me but I saw you, I would know you anywhere, and she said, what night, and I said the night your sister's husband met his maker.' He gave an exaggerated, triumphant nod, then clumsily mimed a sawing action to his throat. 'She could be strung up for it. I keep it quiet, I say nothing, I ask only for a word of explanation to rest my conscience, and she curses me.'

'Who are you talking about?' said Digby. At Jesse's silence, he swallowed hard and put his pot down. In his mind he damned Maynard before he asked the question. 'Is this about Pierre Renard?' he said. He lowered his voice. 'Jesse, you know me. Is it him?'

Jesse's face changed. He closed his mouth; he shook his head.

There was a burst of raucous laughter from the far corner of the room. In the gloom, Jesse looked about him, chewing his lip. He leaned in to Digby.

'They've been watching me, those men,' he said. Digby drew away from the stink of his breath and followed the direction of Jesse's gaze to see a group of disgruntled regulars. 'They want to steal from me. They know I'm a silversmith. They're planning to follow me, I can see it in their eyes. I'll give them it back tenfold, I'll make them regret it. I have my family to think of.' He punched one hand into a fist and smacked it into the palm of his other hand. Then, with barely a moment's pause, his eyes welled with tears. 'My dear Agnes,' he said.

Digby sighed. He must be going half-mad to listen to the ramblings of a drunk. It was the watch; it was his duties on the street; it was Maynard. He needed to calm down. He looked at Jesse. 'Go home, man,' he said. 'Before you drink London out of hops. Regain your wits. Keep your mouth shut. I don't want to hear any more and neither does anyone else here. Go and seek your wife at her fireside and stop worrying over troublesome wenches.' He banged his pint pot on the table, and he was relieved when Jesse stood, and staggered his way out on to the street, mumbling to himself.

Digby opened his mouth to call for more porter, but for the first time in a long while, he'd lost the taste for it.

'Mary,' said the voice, a woman's voice. 'Mary.'

Mary sat up in bed. Her cousin was standing over her, dressed in her cloak, with her bonnet on, a small locking box on the floor beside her.

'Oh my God,' cried Mary. 'I did not lock the house up. Where are my keys?'

'Here. And I am glad you did not,' said Avery. 'It made it easier for your girl Ellen to let me in.'

'I was sitting by the fire in the parlour,' said Mary. 'Who carried me to the bed?' A single candle was burning on the table next to her.

'I am afraid I cannot answer that,' said Avery. 'I have just arrived. I am sorry if I startled you. Your girl had just let me in when we heard you cry out.'

'I did not know you were coming today,' said Mary.

'I received Mallory's letter and I barely stayed another moment,' said Avery, with a wry smile. 'It was a perfect excuse to leave the dullness of my brother's shop. There was not time to send ahead. Besides, it was not hard to find my way here from the White Bear. What a crush Piccadilly is this time of day.' She smiled, and held her arms out.

Mary embraced her, but felt disorientated as she stood. 'I must call for some refreshment for you.'

'Your girl is seeing to that,' said Avery, untying her bonnet. 'And I will sleep in with you tonight, seeing how I found you. What were you dreaming of?'

'Pierre,' said Mary.

In her dream, Pierre's blood had been as thick as molten candle wax, the white skin of his throat so delicate that the knife had slit through it as though it was silk. The gaping wound was pumping, his strong heart propelling his blood into the void, his face resting in a slick of scarlet that spread wider by the moment, an expression of panicked

142

astonishment on his face. He had stared at her, his eyes growing duller as the minutes passed, until they looked like those of the fish Ellen had cut up in the kitchen that day. And she had watched him, doing nothing, feeling nothing. 'Did I call his name?' she asked Avery.

'No,' said Avery. 'You called out "forgive me".'

CHAPTER TWELVE

12th June, 1792

The summer will be here soon; my patrons will leave their town houses and journey to clean air and country pursuits. I have no country estate to flee to yet; I will stay here in the stinking city, with too much time to think as we restock the shop.

I am glad, at least, that Grisa improves in his manner with customers. I can hardly flatter the ladies and gentlemen better myself. He is a devoted and loyal employee, who has never stolen from me. Early in his employ, I made him drink with me one evening: a lot of fine wine that quickly overcame him. He confessed to having been born very poor, in Southwark, and said that he had not always behaved as well as he ought – how dramatically he flashed his eyes at me. It amused me greatly, for he had led me to believe that he was of a respectable family of French origin. Now, he is bound to me by my knowledge of him; I have never spoken of it since. He told me he had saved himself by becoming a dancing master at a small school in Stockwell. That, I can believe.

The melancholy toll of a single bell sliced through the bustle of the London streets. It was late afternoon, and already the light was fading, the shadows thick and vaporous. Here and there, candles were lit in the windows of the shops, stars of light to attract customers to their firmaments. But not at Pierre Renard's shop on Bond Street.

'Listen,' said Mary to Mallory, turning her piece of rosemary in her gloved hands. 'I can hear the bell. Surely that is not the bell of St James's? It is too far?'

Mallory did not answer; she only flinched in irritation. Beside her, Avery looked much more acceptable: neatly but plainly dressed in black, her neutral expression shaded with kindness, she gently handed the weeping Grisa a new handkerchief. Grisa shook it out with a flourish, momentarily pausing from his grief to do so. 'He is moved to tears much too easily,' said Mallory.

They were seated in the parlour, and Pierre's open coffin lay before them. Mary tried not to look at him. His wound was hidden by a large, perfectly tied neckcloth that was whiter than his face. The dark shadows of the box defined him, and his cheeks were strangely hollow. The line of his mouth at last showed his cruelty. In rest it lay in a faint sneer, though she wondered if she was the only one who saw it.

Dr Taylor was instructing Ellen to go and get some glasses of red wine. He had followed faithfully the instructions of Pierre's will regarding the funeral, though it had taken a day or two more to arrange it than anyone would have wished. Mary was grateful to him; he had ordered the black gloves, the rosemary and the mourning rings. She knew it was her duty to remember such details; yet she only dully observed and accepted them. She watched him instruct Ellen, speaking with a gentle authority, and noticed the girl's unquestioning respect for him.

Mallory leaned towards her. 'What did the inscription cost?' she said, in a harsh undertone.

'It is all settled in the will,' said Mary. 'Pierre specified it. It is not a large funeral; there is no procession from the livery hall. His only firm wish was that he should be buried in St James's, with a stone inside the church.'

'He'd have been put in St George's, Hanover Square, if he could,' Mallory whispered. 'Lucky for us they don't do burials there. He can't even die without making an exhibition out of it.' She glanced at the coffin, her eyes gleaming with venom.

'Do stop glaring, Mall,' murmured Avery.

'He did not think he would die now,' said Mary softly. 'It was part of his great plan; to be a gentleman.'

Had he lived longer, Mary was sure there would have been a much more lavish funeral procession, perhaps from Goldsmiths' Hall; and a memorial designed by him, probably in marble, a refined design in the latest taste, with urns and swags of bellflowers. But because he had died much too soon there was nothing but the sketchiest of details to fulfil, and a grave in the prestigious church. Of course there would be some inscription, he had paid for it, but it would be plain. I could almost weep for him, she thought; but she could not. It reminded her that there was once a time when she thought she had used up all of her tears, crying for Eli, then for her parents.

She did not tell Mallory that Pierre had not bought a double grave, so that his wife might join him; when she had asked Dr Taylor this, he had only looked at the floor, and shaken his head, unable to meet her eyes.

Taylor had asked her no questions about the funeral, and she couldn't blame him: she had accepted the role of helpless victim. She knew her appearance couldn't be helping matters: the grey shadows beneath her eyes, the suddenly visible bones in her décolletage. With careful kindness, Taylor had offered her a draught to calm her, but she did not want to be drugged, and said she did not need it. Controlled for so long, she felt that dissolving her defences would lead to God knows what. Whatever lived beneath her pretence of serenity frightened her; she preferred to occupy the space between her imagination and reality, a silent watcher.

The door opened, and Dr Taylor greeted Mr Exham, Pierre's engraver. He looked disturbed, and after greeting the ladies, he returned to Dr Taylor and began conversing with him in a low voice, but with some urgency. Mary saw Mallory look in their direction, but after a few minutes she sighed and leaned towards her sister. 'I cannot hear them,' she said, 'with Grisa snivelling so loudly.'

Everyone was glad to see Ellen re-enter, carrying glasses of red wine on a silver salver. She spoiled the effect by unloading them with indecent swiftness, averting her eyes from the coffin, then running from the room, letting the door go so that it closed with an incongruous crash.

Beneath the spire of St James's Church Mary could not help but remember that she had come to this spot once as a bride, and that this day, like her wedding day, had a kind of unreality about it. On this winter's evening she had a little more composure than she had had as a bride, when her fear had seeped out of her as irritation. But now she lacked her father, and it was this loss, and the others that had accompanied it, which pierced her numbness, and set the dull ache of grief going in her body.

In St James's the service passed quickly, the priest's words a ceaseless murmur. In the north churchyard stones had been prised up to gain access to the vault beneath the church. When one of the undertakers slipped on the steps and the coffin descended with a crash, there was a collective gasp from the onlookers, for though none of Pierre's patrons had come, many of his outworkers had ('They all wish to be seen,' said Mallory, 'so they are not overlooked as the business goes forwards.'). Mary noticed that Exham was standing towards the back, glancing to his right and left, and even occasionally behind him, as though he was looking for someone. It struck her as strange that he should take his handkerchief out and wipe his brow, as though he was sweating in the cool of the evening.

When the ceremony was over, Mary noticed Alban Steele, his cousin Jesse, and Jesse's wife Agnes. It was Agnes who came forwards first. Her face, Mary thought, seemed to reflect the dull winter light, or perhaps it was just the warmth shining from her eyes. She took Mary's hands, then kissed her cheeks. 'Every blessing on you,' she said.

'You are kind,' Mary said. 'I have not seen you in years.'

'When did you last come to the City?' said Agnes. 'My husband tells me you rarely venture from Bond Street.'

It was when I said goodbye to Eli, Mary thought, and the sharpness of the memory silenced her, the pain of it showing on her face so fiercely that Agnes and Avery looked at each other in dismay.

'You must come and have a glass of wine, Mrs Chamac,' said Avery, seeking to break the silence, as Mary struggled with her emotions.

'That is most kind of you,' said Agnes. 'I must speak to my husband.'

Alban came forwards and bowed, his hat in his hand. Mary felt that his eyes were searching her face for something, and, aware of her pallor, she glanced away from his scrutiny and saw Exham, standing with his back to her, looking up and down the thoroughfare in the near-darkness.

'My condolences, Mrs Renard,' said Alban.

'I hope Mrs Chamac will forgive me for my silence,' said Mary, looking at him finally. 'She mentioned my last visit to the City. It was years ago, and I had almost forgot it: the last time I saw my brother. These past few days, I have thought of him more than ever.'

Alban's eyes were full of sorrow. 'He was a blessed soul,' he said. 'His memory should give you strength.'

'I am sorry,' she said. 'But you do not understand at all.' Her widow's veil fluttered in the wind; she pushed it back with one gloved hand.

'I understand some things,' he said, in a low voice. 'You must take care of yourself. You look as though you have not eaten for days.'

'I have strength enough yet,' she said.

'When I met you here, long ago,' he said quietly, 'there was such joy in you, such spirit, as there was in your brother. I believe you worthy of happiness in this life. I would wish to see the day you recover it.' He bowed to her as his cousins approached, then he, Jesse and Agnes moved away swiftly, pausing to speak briefly to the priest.

'It's a cold evening,' said Mallory. 'We'd best hurry on.'

Mary stood still, and Avery came and put an arm around her.

'If you are thinking of Pierre, do not dwell,' said Mallory. 'He thought of no one but himself, on a good day. He thought himself such a great man, but where are all his worthy clients?' She looked around at the emptying church-yard. 'It's your life you need to worry about, troublesome bastard that he was.' She glared at the warden who stared at them, pale with shock. 'And what are you looking at, Reuben Savery? Your Christian duty extend to prying on conversations, does it?'

'Hush yourself,' said Mary. She watched Taylor speak-ing to his wife, with the occasional glance in her direction. Several times she had caught him looking at her, as though he was on the brink of saying something momentous he couldn't find the words for.

'I believe Dr Taylor is worried about the will,' she said. 'It will be bad for me, I know it. I did not do my duty; there is no child.'

'And you should be grateful for it,' said Mallory. 'A child of Pierre's would have sent you half-mad with the pretence of loving it. Though I grant you, it would have guaranteed you a roof over your head.'

'Had I done so,' said Mary, 'our parents might still be living, perhaps even Eli. Pierre promised me things would be different between us if we had our own children.'

'Promises were worth nothing from his lips,' said Mallory.

'I would have loved the child,' said Mary. 'No matter what you say.'

Mallory shook her head. 'Love comes too easily to you; and hate too easily to me,' she said. Then she frowned. 'What's Edward Digby doing here?'

'Who?' said Mary.

She only saw him for an instant, a man with red hair, as he turned and walked away, quickly, and she remembered that the man who had taken her away as they carried the kitchen table on to the street had red hair too.

But at that moment she heard a shout, and saw Exham break into a run. He was pursuing another man, that much was clear; but she saw only a back, retreating into the winter darkness.

'What was the matter with Mr Exham?' said Mary to Dr Taylor, as she entered the house. It was already filling with visitors, and from the parlour upstairs she could hear the hum of voices.

'Oh, nothing of any matter, Mrs Renard,' said Taylor. His wife, Amelia, stood beside him.

'We must speak with you, my dear Mrs Renard,' she said. 'Privately.'

They moved from room to room, but every corner of the house seemed to be filled. Mary heard the lodger in her top room banging on the floor, protesting at the noise. Eventually, in exasperation, she took the Taylors to the kitchen. Ellen was upstairs attending to the visitors.

'Come now, James,' said Amelia. 'Mrs Renard would care for the truth, I am sure. Give it to her quick and clean, like an honourable blow.'

Mary looked at the woman in the half-light of the room. So often Amelia Taylor had seemed cold and unfeeling, but now she looked straight at her with a quick and humane comprehension Mary had never noticed before.

'I am sorry to speak to you in these circumstances,' said Taylor. 'But we are to read the will, and I thought you should be warned of the contents. Mr Renard has specified me and some gentlemen of my acquaintance as his trustees. He did not wish to make it a burden for you, I am sure.'

'Yes,' said Mary.

'There is less money than we thought,' said Taylor, looking uncomfortable. 'But you are to have a small portion to maintain you, and your husband has honoured your marriage settlement; the furniture, porcelain and books are all yours. You are allowed to remain in this dwelling for the term of your life. But, it was his wish for the firm to continue. He stated that his cousin should inherit the business, his only living relative, and that he be joined in matrimony to you, if you both wished, but,' he rushed on, catching her eye, 'when I wrote to the cousin, I was told that he had died some months ago.'

'Oh,' said Mary. The relief unhooked the muscles in her shoulders; she had been holding herself as though she was about to be struck.

'Pierre had also written a codicil, very recently, stating that his apprentice Benjamin be included in the firm, and that he be made a partner in it, once he has reached his majority. It states that if there be no children – as there are no children – the business will pass to Benjamin on your death. I and the other trustees are to act as guardians, in a sense, of your fortune and marriage.'

'What he means to say,' said Amelia, 'is that their approval is needed, if you remarry.' Her gaze had a hard sympathy to it. 'Your inheritance may be revoked if you do not marry as they wish; you would have no roof over your head.'

'Madam.' Taylor's tone was grief-stricken, not harsh. 'There is no need to say this. I am sure Mrs Renard would not act in any way that would cause such a thing to occur.'

'Benjamin?' said Mary. 'To inherit the business?' She felt dull-headed, as though there was some lesson she was struggling to learn.

'Benjamin is little more than a child,' said Taylor. 'We will keep him in check. Pierre loved you dearly, and he has asked me to ensure that you are safe, to protect you as he, now, cannot.'

Amelia put an arm around Mary, and Mary inhaled her unfamiliar scent, of sweat and damp sable. The gentleness of the gesture reminded her of Alban's hands on her arms a few days before. The kindness of it had shivered through her. After years during which the only physical contact she experienced was in the clammy brutality of her marriage bed, the remembrance of a kind touch had been lost; she had missed it without knowing it.

'Why should he have done such a thing?' said Amelia, in a whisper.

But Mary knew and she could imagine the look on her husband's face as he had written the words, one of bitter satisfaction.

One evening, carefully, slowly, as though luxuriating in it, he had told her the story of the woman Sarah; how he had loved her, and she should have been his wife, but her father had prevented the match. How he had taken on the boy Benjamin, her nephew, as some kind of cure for the past, to be linked to her still (though he did not say that last part; only presented himself as a man of charity and kindness, a veritable saint).

'Am I like her?' she had said. Even now, she did not know why she had asked that question.

'Yes,' he said. 'Selfish, and wilful.'

What a joy it must have been, she thought, for him to write the words in his will. Now, neither she nor Sarah could ever escape his memory. But before she could say anything, there was the sound of raised voices from upstairs.

'What on earth ...' said Taylor. He bowed hastily then walked quickly up the steps. Mary and Amelia followed him.

The shop door had been slammed shut the moment before; the cloth-wrapped bell was still banging dully against the wood. In the shop, Exham was standing. He was holding Bright Hemmings by the collar. Bright's eyes were bulging with alarm. He was pale, his black hair loose about his shoulders.

'See here,' snarled Exham. Mary had known the engraver since her childhood, and never had she seen him like this, wild-eyed and trembling. He glared at Dr Taylor. 'I told you,' he said. 'The coffin should not have been shut!'

'Mr Exham?' said Mary, and her voice seemed to awaken him to reason.

'Begging your pardon,' he said, with a brief bow in Mary's direction as he held the struggling Bright. 'This villain has been walking up and down the streets telling anyone who will listen that he will marry you, Mrs Renard. We all know how he has been behaving. I told Dr Taylor I planned to find the rogue, and that he should be brought here to touch good Mr Renard; so that if the blood seeped from him, we would have our answer. But he would not delay; and now it is too late for that. It is my hope that in seeing you, good madam, the truth will be brought forwards.'

Mary had heard of it before. When she was a child old woman Moore had been murdered by her husband, and she had bled out when he had touched the corpse, as proof of his guilt.

Exham dragged Bright closer to Mary. 'Will you look this good lady in the eyes, you wretch?' he said. Bright whined, and shook his head, twisting away.

'Then we have our answer, do we not?' said Exham.

'Wait,' said Mary. 'How can you believe Bright capable of such a thing? Did you tell the watch, or the constable, of this?'

'I did tell the constable,' said Exham. 'And he laughed at me. I see he has fooled you all. But I recognize the cunning in his idiocy.'

As he said the last word, she saw the shame enter his eyes, the flash of colour in his cheeks. *Eli.*

'If you will excuse me,' he said. 'I meant no insult to . . .' His voice trailed off.

Mary dismissed his words with a short shake of the head. She turned towards the man he held, leaning over, his hair around his face. 'You have known me a long time, Bright?' she said.

He stared at the floor. 'Yes,' he said.

'Take your courage, then. For if you are innocent nothing bad will befall you. Look at me.'

Slowly, Bright raised his eyes to her face. 'It is true I said I wished you were my wife,' he said. 'But I did not harm him, milady. I swear it.' His bottom lip was trembling, and as he concluded his speech, he began to weep.

Mary turned to Exham. 'You will need better evidence than his foolish tongue to convict him, sir,' she said. 'I will leave you to converse with Dr Taylor. But I advise you to let him go.'

She felt overwhelmingly tired, but as she turned to go upstairs, she heard Exham shift. 'Mrs Renard?' he said.

She looked back.

'I meant nothing against your brother, madam,' he said. 'He was a good, sweet boy. I do remember his face.'

'As do I,' said Mary.

They left her to climb the stairs, thinking she would go to the parlour and see to her guests; but she did not. She was glad she had gone against the old custom, and kept her chamber locked. She went to it, unlocked the door, and closed and locked it again, so that she could be alone.

Sitting there, waiting for the minutes to pass until her house was empty again, she was haunted by an image that had returned again and again in her mind despite all her attempts to forget it: a letter, burning in her fireplace, with a poker thrust through its heart. With this before her eyes, she bent her head, covered her face, and let herself weep, fully and openly, at last.

CHAPTER THIRTEEN

13th June, 1792

This morning I dealt with agents from the Duke of Grafton, and various Earls and Lords despite the time of year. Then, I went, hastily, to the Chichesters. Mrs Chichester was in bed with a cold, but her husband bade me go up to her. He spoke to me most insolently, as though I am merely a tradesman. But his wife has great delicacy of character. She is, also, a beauty. I spent some time with her, enjoying her wonder and delight at the pieces of silver plate I showed her. I was pleased to hear that she will not be leaving town for the summer.

As I left, I passed a portrait, and recognized the semblance of the fair lady I had been granted an audience with. It captivated me: this image of perfection, somehow different from the woman I had just been conversing with, and yet adding to my impression of her.

Her maid is a sour thing. 'I cannot wait all day, sir,' she said, as I stood looking at the portrait. I will slip her a trinket or two; she will warm to me soon enough.

Walking away from the Chichester residence, I found myself smiling, and with real feeling. It was almost as though ten years had fallen away, and I was a young man again, unmarried, unhindered, bright with ambition and with faith in God's grace.

Harriet had spent too long neglecting her duties, sending the footman to return calls for her with a handful of cards, knocking on doors outside the usual hours. At last, she was forced to go out herself, and she left Joanna at home.

Joanna locked herself in her room to sift through her belongings. She liked looking through the things she owned; she felt they rooted her in the present, and made her more real. Employers had been generous over the years with their gifts: a piece of ribbon here, a piece of spider lace there. Once, four gowns at once, from dear Mrs Higgins, as she lay dying. Today she wore one of these gowns, of grey silk, above a stiff black petticoat. She liked the grey: it suited the steely resolve she sought to cultivate, the self-control. It was a colour to help the soul, she thought, to bleach it of its colour: staid, calm, all passion gone. Some ladies' maids sought to emulate their mistresses, flouncing around with feathers in their hair and the latest cut of dress, but Joanna prided herself on her invisibility. She was saving her coins for something. She didn't know what, only that it would come, one day, and she would be ready, as she had not been ready for Stephen.

There was a little silver thimble that Pierre Renard had given her as a bribe to keep her in his favour. She had smiled and taken it when he had given it to her; but it was an insult, really, she thought. Not for her the heavy, crafted silver he sold the quality; but some flimsy thing that he had probably bought by the handful from a toy maker. But for the loss of the lock of Stephen's hair – which she must find the strength to investigate – the loss of the man meant nothing at all.

The coins she looked at last, and she inspected each of them, rubbing them gently, biting one or two, as though they held some sacred mystery. One day, she knew, they would buy her something she had never had before: freedom.

Then she closed the box, locked it, pushed it under her bed, and wrapped a cloak she had extracted from the box around her. It was woollen, patched in two or three places. It was another habit she enjoyed; huddling into it, her mind returning to a familiar scene of the past. Within its warmth she could remember the comfort of a summer's afternoon, grass working its way into the cloak as she and Stephen lay down upon it in a small hidden glade of the park. In the distance, she heard the sound of the bells that hung around the necks of the cows that grazed there. As he leaned close to her she smelt the leather of horse tack, and his hands were grey with dust. She had worried about her dress being crushed, her hair, so artfully arranged back then. But each movement was seamless and flowing, and there seemed no one moment when she leapt into the unknown. It shocked her, the easiness with which she had lent her body to something she had warned herself against, for almost only a moment after the pleasure came the cold emptiness of vulnerability.

As she struggled to cover herself, and to straighten her clothes, Stephen had watched her, chewing a piece of grass, a little paler than before. 'I did not know I was your first,' he said. 'I saw the blood. I won't leave you.' He looked changed, pensive, as though shocked by what they had done, when he had acted with such confidence.

She had not believed him, but he had told the truth. He had not left her, though she would find out later that he was not the man she thought he was. Friend, protector, traitor: these three strands twined into one when she thought of him. Some days he was always in her mind, as constant a companion as if he walked beside her; some days she couldn't bear to think of him at all.

She had used the same cloak to cover him when he had been unwell, visiting him in his room above the stable during his last winter. He was racked by the headaches that destroyed his vision. He lay, white-faced, with her hand resting on his forehead. 'It's doing for me, Jo,' he had said. He had already been chased by death for some time then. He had managed to dodge it, blocking out pain with some kind of natural ability to ignore. It was impossible to imagine him dead, he with his ready smile and quick tongue.

No person had witnessed her love for Stephen and their mutual suffering. Only this cloak, this object; not long after he had gone she even fancied it carried the scent of him. But that was years, so many years ago, she thought. She could not give the thought any credence now, not without admitting herself half-cracked.

In the real world, Harriet's periodicals and two new novels had to be collected, and Joanna went gladly, still clutching her cloak around her. It was a short walk to the bookseller, and she walked quickly so she could pay a visit to her sister-in-law. Now that her brother was dead, his widow and children were all she had for family.

She found Mallory in her dingy parlour, cursing over papers from the pawnbrokers' business her husband had left her a share in. When Joanna entered the kitchen Mallory cast her pen aside, leaving a large black blot on the sheet she had been adding accounts on.

'We'll have tea,' she said.

Joanna put down the bound stack of books on the kitchen table with a thump. 'Where are the children?' she said.

'Upstairs,' said Mallory. 'Lisbeth is quite the teacher now.' Lisbeth was the eldest, and Joanna's favourite: the only one who would not protest when Aunty Jo hugged and kissed her, but rather smile with an angelic sweetness, as though she understood perfectly her aunt's need for affection though she did not need it herself.

'It's been a while since I've seen you,' said Mallory as Joanna sat down. 'How are they treating you in Berkeley Square?'

Joanna had promised herself she would be non-committal, but she could not help giving a sour little smile, as though her thoughts asserted themselves on her face without her wishing them to. 'Well enough,' she said. 'Madam barely shows, but she is parading around the place patting her stomach.' Her voice caught on the words, suddenly changing the balance of the conversation.

'Can't be easy for you,' said Mallory, unlocking the tea

caddy and scratching around one of the lead-lined com-
partments with a spoon in the hope of gathering enough
tea for the pot.

Joanna shrugged. 'No matter. As I grow older I have less
patience with the young, that's all. Do you find that?'

'I never had the patience to start with,' said Mallory.

'Her life would be much easier if she spoke in a more
kindly way to her husband,' said Joanna. 'If she contrived
to keep his interest. He is a fine man.'

'Think he's worth effort, do you?' said Mallory bluntly.
Joanna glared at her. With characteristic sharpness,
Mallory had put her finger on something buried, not even
considered or ready to be brought into the light.

'I didn't say that, witch,' she said, not without malice.

Mallory laughed. 'I think whatever that young madam
did you would not be satisfied with her. You and I were
not made to be servants, Jo,' she said. Then she put her
hand tightly over Joanna's. 'But I know what it must cost
you to see that girl with child. I'll say what I've always
said: it would never have worked. You did what was best.'

Joanna let her hand rest under Mallory's. 'As if I don't
know that,' she said quietly. 'And you mistake my tiredness for caring. How is your sister?'

As she left Mallory's house and turned on to Piccadilly,
Joanna looked over her shoulder at St James's, casting the
sharp shadow of its spire over the busy thoroughfare. Since
the death of Pierre Renard, she had been aware that she had
lost her dislike for Mary Renard. It was then she realized
that it was a burden shed: one that she had carried and

nursed, heavy on her, an ill-feeling, one more bitterness. It had unfurled itself, like a knot pulled free at one stroke.

As she walked, she revisited the memory, wondering if she would find it again. For it had seemed to her that Mary Renard had the perfect life, the protected life that Joanna had not. Once, she had seen Mary in the street, and made to speak to her, but the woman had looked over her head, as though she saw nothing. Are we not the same? Joanna thought. Our lives are only made different by the throw of a dice. But no, she thought, I fool myself. I would never have disliked her, except for that one day.

It was the day that Stephen had died. Joanna had held him all night, listening to his breathing slow, then stop. She didn't move even after he had died, didn't care for the cramp in her limbs. She held him until the sky began to lighten, and he was quite cold. Then she got up and left his body tucked up in bed. She went out on to the streets of London, dishevelled and disorientated. It was still early morning. She thought she would give herself one hour before it was real. For now she would pretend he was still there, waiting for her. no one would know; if she saw an acquaintance and they asked after him she could pretend that he still lived.

She couldn't remember how long she walked for; she knew only that she was in disarray and that people were staring at her, thinking her drunk, probably a street walker. She was younger then, just out of the beginnings of love, and in her distress more than one man saw a delicate vulnerability he was prepared to pay for: something pure, probably fresh from the country, easy pickings.

One man even pulled her towards him, and she struck him so hard, with such an intention to wound, that later she would wonder why she had dried blood under her fingernails.

She knew she must have walked for hours when she found herself in the churchyard of St James's Piccadilly, because the clock was chiming eight. She took shelter in the green portion of the churchyard, the trees harbouring her, a small, dark, half-yard of peace. Even now she didn't know why she had gone there; perhaps to say a prayer for Stephen, who was still waiting in his room for the world to mourn him.

It was just after eight when a carriage pulled up on Jermyn Street at the gate of the church. Joanna watched in fascination as the door opened, and a bride descended, landing heavily on the path. As she watched, dully, she realized that she recognized her: Mallory's sister. She did not know her well; only remembered seeing her here and there, a quiet girl who had little interest in company and was always running after her younger brother. The little boy was nowhere to be seen. The girl was dressed expensively in a dress trimmed with silver lace. Her shoes had fine square buckles, with white stones that glittered in the light. She looked like a walking piece of silver, a creation that had been fashioned with intent and worked on for hours: polished, clear, reflecting light. But when Joanna looked at her face, her expression was sour. The only natural thing about her attire was the flower in her powdered hair: a white rose. As she climbed down, it fell to the ground, and the girl tutted, her face contorted with irritation.

'Papa, look,' she said, as her father descended and took her hand.

As they walked towards the church door, Joanna came out from her hiding place on to the path behind them, and stood there, watching them as they walked into the church, their pace almost funereally slow. After they had turned down the aisle, Joanna slipped into the back of the church, and heard the marriage ceremony of Pierre Renard and Mary Just.

Joanna had dreamed of being Stephen's bride. In her mind she had come to such a church many times. She had imagined walking slowly down the aisle, the light pouring in on them from the huge windows. Stephen waited for her at the altar, turning to smile at her.

In the freshness of her grief, Joanna saw Mary Renard as a bride, and the contrast between them had sown the seeds of bitterness in her heart. She thought her vain, complacent, and unaware of the gift she had been given. She could not forgive someone so careless of their happiness.

She heard the vows said, then left the church. In her pocket was the slim bundle of folded banknotes that Stephen had given her the night before, dry as tinder under her fingertips. He had once been married, he had said; he still was. Now that he knew death was close, he had to clear his conscience by telling her the truth. He was choosing to give Joanna, his true wife, everything he had. But she knew it would not be enough, for she was pregnant.

Carrying Harriet's books, the church behind her, Joanna walked on. Life had evened out their fates. At one time, her resentment towards Mary Renard had been such that she would not even stay with Harriet when Mr Renard called; she would pass him on the stairs rather than sit in the room to hear him babble about himself. On the night she had commissioned the pendant with Stephen's hair in, Renard had invited her to have a dish of chocolate in the Bond Street shop, and she had gone, wondering if she would see Mary again, and if Mary would, at last, speak to her. But Mrs Renard had been indisposed on that night, and Mr Renard had dealt with her, smiling his strange smile as he took the lock of hair with his fumbling fingers.

As she walked back, so swiftly she was almost running, the air stung her eyes, and she felt the pain of another's sorrow, a swelling tightness in the base of her neck. I envied you, she thought: and I am sorry. Thinking of the young bride she had seen stepping on to the churchyard path all those years before, she sped through the crowds, and back to Berkeley Square, clutching the bound stack of books to her breast.

CHAPTER FOURTEEN

14th June, 1792

I am dull, and scratch over the past in the evenings; but I must do this, for from my misspent days, my new life must be born and my purpose reinvigorated.

My wife had a brother, an idiot child who she nevertheless doted on. In the early days of our marriage the thought of him was a sore spot in my mind. Even on the Sunday before our marriage, I sat in St James's on Piccadilly, and wondered what fate God had in store for me. I closed my eyes, and prayed for serenity: to feel as I did when I looked at the night sky. But instead all I could hear in my head was the laughter of that idiot child. That wretched boy. I suppose the anger stayed with me.

'What news, my good man?' Maynard said. He was standing casually, his hand tucked in his pocket, as though he was surprised to meet Digby, but the watchman wasn't fooled. He had seen the way Maynard had pushed the tavern door open with his shoulder and looked in, his face all curiosity, bright eyes taking in all the inhabitants. His bluff, over-cordial tone was a warning, unnatural and piercing, alerting the tavern guests. A couple of men sitting nearby stared at the visitor.

Digby's long-standing regard for Maynard had been waning over the last day or so. It waned even more now, when he noted Maynard's flushed cheeks, and specks of the good dinner he had eaten on his face and cravat. The presence of food spattering was, in itself, an affront to Digby, who didn't waste a crumb. 'Sir,' he said, and took a swig of his porter. Maynard sat down next to him; a large man on a small stool.

'I hear our mutual friend Renard was buried yesterday,' said Maynard. It seemed to Digby he was already retrenching his good cheer, and his customary coolness was returning. 'All very hide-in-the-hole, wasn't it? Taylor could hardly get the words out when I met him just now.'

'At another coroner's meeting, were you?' said Digby, his interest piqued.

Maynard nodded. 'A suicide,' he said. 'Collings, the jeweller. I believe he supplied to Renard occasionally. Seems the season for it. So. Go to St James's to see the Frenchman put away, did you, Digby?'

Digby paused, his lips twitching in a silent curse. 'Don't know why you need me to keep a watch out, when you clearly have spies everywhere,' he muttered.

He looked at his pint rather than Maynard's face. 'So I went to the church,' he said. 'A prayer can do no harm, can it?'

Maynard gave a boisterous laugh. 'No, indeed,' he said. 'And Renard would need it.'

'Thought you might be there yourself,' said Digby.

'I?' Maynard raised one eyebrow sardonically. 'I have better things to do with my time than feign mourning for a tradesman – and a dishonest one, at that.'

'Coffin slipped,' said Digby. 'It made me wonder. Disquiet, you know. The dead not resting, not avenged.'

'How did Mrs Renard look?' said Maynard. For all his apparent lightness a moment before, his eyes glittered with interest.

'Sickly,' said Digby.

Like a wineskin slit open, he thought, her soul all emptied out.

'Does she really grieve, I wonder?' said Maynard.

'God give her good fortune,' Digby said, the words finding their way out of him almost against his will. He had surprised himself, and raised his cup to the surprise more than anything else.

'As I said, you have the sharpness to see it all,' said Maynard, a brief, indulgent smile fading to seriousness. 'I am a little tired of chasing around after you. If you come across anything, Digby, that pertains to this case, what say you tell me?'

'And why should I do that, sir?' said Digby. 'I'm tired enough watching the streets. Or am I to be rewarded for my trouble?' He liked the way Maynard needed something from him, how he shifted in his seat. 'Sounds to me like a lot of work,' he said.

Maynard stayed silent for a moment. His face was expressionless when he leaned forwards towards Digby. 'I hear you've been drinking the health of Tom Paine,' he said, in a low tone. Digby did not think Maynard could even speak like that, in a voice as soft as a woman's.

'I have not,' said Digby. 'And you know it.'

'With all the disorder people don't like that, Digby. Our watchmen are paid to keep the peace on the street, not cause unrest.'

'I'm no Leveller,' said Digby. His mouth was dry. The porter in his cup looked dark. He would have taken a sip but thought it would taste as bitter as poison at this moment. If he choked on it, it would show weakness. 'I don't care for politicking,' he said. 'And every man that knows me, knows that.' His voice was gruff, and defiant. He was glad to hear it, for it was proof that he was able to hide his fear.

'Politicking,' said Maynard, 'is the least of your troubles. Been to a pawnbroker's recently?' Digby stared at him, felt the rapid falling away of fear, real fear, that could not be countered by show. 'Where did you find things to pawn?' said Maynard. 'Could it possibly be that you pick up treasure during the hours of your work? Do I need to ask what you have been pawning?'

He sat still. Digby could see no trace of triumph on the man's face.

'I see my meaning has hit home,' Maynard said. 'Keep your eye on things for me, Digby, and I'll look no further.

You want to keep your place, don't you?' He seemed almost sorrowful as he drank back the contents of his glass.

Digby gave a slight shrug, and said nothing when Maynard got up and left. He knows nothing, he thought: thank God I kept the watch with me. I am hemmed in on every side, I am royally fucked, just like Renard's poor widow.

It was dark, the full, uncompromising darkness of a winter's evening that seemed to fill every corner of the house. Mary had sent Benjamin to visit his relatives, telling him to come back with his tears dried, and to begin his work again as the person who would one day own the shop. He had gone, but she sensed that he was unwilling to obey her, and she saw that already his youthful features were hardening with the knowledge of his power.

Mary told Avery she wished to make the tour of the house alone before locking up. It took courage to enter the dark workshop, even though she carried a candle. During her marriage the night had always been her enemy, the time of day she feared the most.

She went straight to the place that Pierre called his own: a small space of bench, its large pouch of leather below, that he would occasionally show visitors, sweeping out his arm. He would always say the same thing: 'This is my bench. I may be a goldsmith, a seller of fine things, a master of many men; but I am also still a working silver-smith, even after all these years.' And he would pause and nod, as though communing with some part of himself where his vocation still lay, a seam of precious metal running through his heart.

Mary knew his performance was part sentiment, part business sense. To her the two did not belong together, but he had melded them seamlessly. The truth was, he hardly ever worked the metal in his last years, and the vague memory she had of him at the bench in the months after their marriage was a picture of discomfort. She remembered him swinging the hammer, his face sheened with sweat and his expression hard. He had always maintained a sentimental liking for the camaraderie of the workshop, and his sense of himself as a master of craft was something he had clung to. Yet swiftly Pierre had become a man that dealt with people: a salesman, a builder of networks. He kept his apprentice and a couple of men, but more and more the silver had been delivered to him, finished, from outworkers.

Of course, many patrons were under the impression that Pierre alone produced every piece of glowing plate that graced his shop's walls. And before candlesticks and salvers were sent to their owners, his maker's mark was struck over that of the workman who had made them. It was common practice, but Mary still disliked it. Her husband had seemed a world away from the men that made the objects. His arms had grown thin, and he was happiest when his hands were stained with ink rather than grazed and hardened by the tools on the workman's bench.

Beneath the full moon long ago he had promised to make her a marriage cup of silver, but he never had. She remembered staring at that moon, feeling his hands on her arms as he held her there. In that moment, she had thought he was right: it was the silversmith's moon, for it was as cold and hard and unyielding as unannealed silver.

She still associated him with the empty bench, and as she stood there, the candle trembling in her hands, he seemed only a breath away, the scent of him hovering in the air. There was something touching about the space: the tools of his craft all neatly put away, an ancient mark here and there where a piece of silver had been worked. It would be easy, she thought, to love the space he had left behind; something unreal to fill the emptiness. The memory of his face was slipping from her mind, leaving a disembodied impression beyond specifics. The unhappy memories of the hideous closeness of marriage faded too: the smell of his skin, and the taste of him.

Over the last few days Mary had thought over the past, turning it and looking at it from every angle as a jeweller inspects an unset stone; and she had become convinced that Eli had been brought back to London too soon after her marriage. It had been her own fault; her confidence had grown too quickly when Pierre had promised her that all would be well.

'I never wish to be parted from you,' he had said, with the air of one bestowing an honour. She had been grateful for it, and taken her chance.

'Will you let Eli return?' she said. 'It pains my parents to be parted from each other, and Eli's health suffers. If he returns, he need not travel about freely as he was wont to do. But he only flourishes amongst the people he loves.'

Pierre was in lyrical mood. 'When you look at me in that way, with your eyes alight, how could I do anything else?' he said.

Mary had written the next day, and her mother and Eli had returned ten days later.

It had been in her father's parlour that she had seen Eli again. His face had lit up at the sight of her, rising to his feet, his arms reaching up to her as he tried to say her name. Mary had been lost in her joy, but when she turned to see her husband's face she had been frightened by his tight expression, the flex of his jaw as he stared into the middle distance.

'Come now,' she said, settling Eli on to the floor by the fireside. 'Hush, my love.' In his excitement Eli continued to babble as she stroked his face. When Pierre moved suddenly, the child at last turned his eyes to him: steady, unblinking blue eyes that did not look directly into Pierre's own face, but seemed only to gather him as a shape, some dark mass that Eli did not wish to see. The little boy looked away.

Pierre was holding a coin. 'Here, little fool, if you wish to jest with me,' he said. The smile on his face was strained. 'I will give you this, if you will be quiet.'

Eli looked at him. Then, without even blinking, he snatched the bright coin and threw it into the fire.

'I should have told you,' said Mary, rising to stand between them, her fingers twined with Eli's. 'He is very quick. He does not mean to anger you; he only sees something bright and moves for it.'

Pierre said nothing. His face was white with anger.

When her parents entered the room, he stared silently into the fire. He had made his anger known later.

'I have done everything for your sake, for the best, and God's glory,' he had said to her, one day. By then, all her family but Mallory were gone. She thought she saw, compunction in his eyes. In the vow they had made to each other, before God, she had sought sanctity. It had been the foundation of her marriage, the reason for putting away the bad memories, and for telling herself that love could be built on such broken foundations. Now knowing the contents of the will, she knew with certainty that the vow that had lain between them had never been sacred in his eyes; and she felt his betrayal more bitterly, realizing that she had borne with him out of duty, in the belief of love.

I did not know, she thought, that it is possible to love and hate at the same time. But you cannot truly feel both at once; one feeling must lie dormant, sleeping, while the other burns itself out.

When did you last come to the City? Agnes's soft voice in the churchyard, so full of kindness. In response, a memory came, a memory that, like Mary's heart, had long been suspended, in frozen winter.

One day long ago, she thought. She had gone to the City, to her parents' house. The front door had opened with one push.

In the hallway, her mother stood, holding shut the parlour door. Even in the grey January light, as dull as evening, Mary could see the tears on her face. Beyond the door, she could hear the sound of her brother's feet as he circled the floor again and again, and the peaks and troughs of his voice as he chattered to himself, small inconsequential noises expressing curiosity and agitation.

'Mother?' said Mary.

'He cannot see me weep,' said her mother in a whisper, one hand holding the door as she wiped away her tears with the other. 'He is breathless already. It will distress him.'

'Why are you crying?' said Mary.

'You should not be here,' said her mother, turning her gaze to the floor. 'The carriage is coming directly.'

It was then Mary knew.

'Pierre,' she said. Her mother said nothing.

'Why?' said Mary.

'There is no other way,' said her mother. 'Pierre will not have him here. We have promised him. I will not tell you what he said, I will not speak ill to you of your husband. We will go to my sister. Please, Mary, do not speak. It is absolute. You know your brother's health is not strong. He will not make this journey again.'

From within, Eli's footsteps ran faster. His breathing was faster too, rasping a little, a sound they had long been sensitive to.

'Let me in,' said Mary. Her mother released the door.

At her entrance, Eli turned, his mouth forming a little O of wonderment at the sight of his sister. He smiled broadly and ran to her, then, when she crouched down beside him, planted a kiss on her lips.

'There, my little man,' said Mary, holding him in a tight embrace. 'What are you chasing?'

Eleven years later, she remembered the scent of his hair as she held him tight; the warmth and life of him in her arms.

There was the sound of a carriage beyond the parlour window, her father's voice as he spoke to someone.

'They will take us to Charing Cross,' her mother said. 'And we will go from there.' And her mother, who Mary was used to seeing so stoical, broke into sobs.

A little noise issued from Eli, and Mary held him back to look at his face. At the sight of his mother crying, his expression had faded from happiness to fear. He began to cry, then to shriek. When her father entered the room with Mallory, he had to hold Eli as her mother forced his fingers free, each small hand clamped tightly around his sister's arms. When one hand had been moved, he held tighter with the other, so that the next morning, there were bruises where his fingertips had dug into her skin.

In the workshop, there was a noise behind her. Mary turned sharply, her sight blurred by tears. But the only noises were in her mind; the voices of those long gone. She remembered the tightness of Mallory's arms as she held Mary back from running after the carriage. Mallory, she thought, always protecting me.

In this moment there was just the darkness, barely ameliorated by the light from her single candle.

She put it down. She leaned against the bench, battling the grief and fury that rose in her. Her one urge was to destroy the room, to throw things, to set light to it and watch it burn. She breathed slowly, hoping that it would recede. Images from the last eleven years came to her mind, once colourless, now too intense. She longed to empty the contents of her mind to begin again tomorrow. But there was no going back.

You have tainted everything, she thought, remembering the moment Pierre had pushed the wedding ring on to her finger. Like a drop of ink in water, it is impossible to rid my life of the colour of you.

CHAPTER FIFTEEN

15th June, 1792

My wife had barely settled here in Bond Street before she asked for the idiot child to be returned to the family. I smiled at her, but the anger I felt made my mind turn black. I had given her everything, and I was her husband, and yet still she harked after this small, broken child. It all ended badly, as I knew it would, and I persuaded her father that the boy should be removed from London, and for good. Yet still, Mary would not forget. The last night she asked me, I denied her. That night, I held her down. I feel some shame at that. Her wrists felt so thin and fragile beneath my hands I thought I could crush them to powder if I willed it. It pains me to think of it: trial as she has been, I am sorry for having hurt her. But I will not torture myself over it. In her eyes I saw a will that needed to be broken, lest she become a scold, like her sister. It was my right.

I had hoped she might temper my disquiet through goodly obedience, but I was sorely mistaken. I had the means to always procure transport for her, but she would insist on walking everywhere. She also insisted on maintaining at least some relations with a sister whose reputation is questionable. These days, she tries to soothe me, but I see her lies everywhere.

Harriet, dressed in a pale pink quilted nightgown with a hood to protect her against draughts, sat at her secretaire like an obedient child. She was slowly writing a letter to her mother, her novels piled neatly on a chair nearby as an inducement to be good. The scratching sound of her quill on the parchment set Joanna's teeth on edge. She was further irritated by the fact that when Harriet finished a sentence, she would mouth it silently to herself.

Their chief conversation that morning had been about what colour ribbon would go with Harriet's newly ordered gown. It was Joanna's policy to produce a definite opinion early on in such a conversation. Certainty was usually enough to bring Harriet's gabblings to an early and satisfactory conclusion. It created the impression that Joanna was, indeed, an authority on the subject of ribbon, and that Mrs Chichester had, within her employ, a ribbon connoisseur. But she had not been sharp enough today, not nearly firm enough in her pronouncements, even though she knew from long experience that vagueness was death. The conversation had meandered on for so long, she thought if she had not managed to direct Harriet's energies towards writing the long overdue letter to her mama, she might well have smashed one of the silver boxes against the wall.

Now, there would be no Monsieur Renard to fix it. No Monsieur Renard to bow, one leg stretched out before him, as though he was at the court of Versailles rather than a London town house. Joanna had not mentioned his death to Harriet. She had known of a house where a servant had been turned away for bringing news of a death.

Joanna excused herself to go and give instructions to the new cook. Mr Chichester's fashionable French chef had departed the week before, and Harriet had not taken to the new man, who mangled his vowels tortuously in a vicious approximation of a French accent. As a result Harriet had decided to start giving her instructions through Joanna, initially writing them in laboured characters, then giving them verbally, so it gave Joanna a few minutes' respite at the kitchen table every morning, questioning whether quite so many sauces were needed on that evening's dinner.

Downstairs, Joanna sat and instructed the inattentive cook. She was just resting for a moment when Oliver ran down into the kitchen. In the distance she could hear the faint tinkling of the silver table bell used by Mr Chichester to call for attention. 'You'd better get up here, Miss Dunning,' said Oliver. 'She's screaming the place down.' The fearful expression on his face had Joanna on her feet in a moment.

She ran past the footman and up the stairs, into the staircase hall, where an eerie wailing sound could be heard, barely recognizable as Harriet's voice. Two of the other menservants were already there, looking pale. Mr Chichester had emerged from the library, the table bell in his hand. 'What is the matter with her?' he said. He looked terrified. 'For God's sake, will you go to her?'

As she ran up the marble staircase, silence fell. She must be miscarrying, Joanna thought: I must prepare myself. There will be blood. She will have cramps. There must be brandy and hot water. Someone must call for Dr Taylor, due to make his first visit that afternoon. She opened the door.

Never had the bedroom, with its pale blue silk-covered walls and draped sash windows looking out over the square, looked so huge as when she opened the door, and never had Harriet looked so small to her. She was crumpled in a heap on the floor, next to the bed, moaning. She looked up at the sound of the door and saw Joanna; then she took a breath and started to scream, like a child who has seen her parent, and knows she can unleash hell at last. Joanna ran to her. She thought of the men downstairs, the footmen, and Mr Chichester, peering up, their hands over their ears.

'What is it?' she said, over the noise. There was no blood, no signs of the miscarriage she had expected. She got hold of Harriet by the shoulders. The girl sobbed convulsively.

'Are you bleeding?' she said, and Harriet shook her head.

On the bed, she saw a letter, and pulled it down with one hand while she held Harriet with the other.

It is with regret, madam, that we write to inform you of the untimely death of Pierre Renard.

'You need to be quiet,' Joanna said. 'Be quiet.' A movement caught her eye and she saw that Jane, one of the maids, had come in through the open door and was approaching them. Even with only a glance Joanna saw something in the girl's expression that disturbed her. 'I didn't tell you to come in,' she said. 'Get out. Get out now!' She raised her voice high enough to cut over Harriet's sobs. The girl turned and walked out, briskly, her head held high.

Harriet was rocking herself, pulling Joanna with her. 'I shouldn't have said no. She'll have killed him,' she said between gasps. 'He said she hated him. He said—'

'I don't care what he said,' said Joanna. She felt the pressure bearing down on her head. Her mind, her imagination, only had room enough for her own secrets. 'I do not want to know,' she said. 'You must quieten yourself, for the sake of the baby.'

The mention of the baby seemed to break into Harriet's thoughts, and she began to breathe in a laboured rhythm, though there was a look of surprise on her face at the fact that she had been reprimanded. Joanna stroked her hair, wondering whether the maid was still standing just out of sight, against the wall next to the door. 'Hush,' she said. The word, meant to soothe, came out as a hiss, as a warning.

Joanna had expected Dr Taylor to be a small, sprightly man with a feminine face; her strong imagination had made him so real that the lumbering man who met her at the bottom of the stairs, with his large curved shoulders and his cheerful, blunt features, seemed an impostor. He moved slowly but with a grace that was surprising in a man so large, as though he thought carefully about every manoeuvre. He had greeted Joanna with bright-eyed kindness, but at the sight of Harriet his expression lost some of its warmth. When he rested one of his large hands on the silken arm of the pale blue daybed, Harriet shrank away. He smiled, his gaze distant, as though his eyes were fixed on some faraway horizon rather than his patient. 'Mrs Chichester,' he said. 'You must not worry yourself. I will be as gentle as possible. Lady Whiteacre said she had never known gentler.'

Harriet smiled. 'I am a little afraid,' she said.

'There is no need to be afraid. You will have the best care. Your husband told me you were in great distress,' said Taylor, rising and beginning to lay his hands carefully on her stomach. 'Is there some discomfort?'

'No,' said Harriet, her voice small and wavering.

'If I may, Dr Taylor,' said Joanna, trying to make her tone clipped and cheerful. 'It is an excess of sensibility. Mrs Chichester has been reading novels. She is very susceptible to them. They provoke strong emotions in her.'

The doctor paused, as though he was trying to process what she was saying. Then he smiled, and spoke with a mock severity. 'I would put them in the fire, if I were you,' he said. Joanna forced out a laugh.

'They are from Mr Holt's,' she said. 'I will return them.'

'Without delay,' said Taylor, holding Harriet's wrist. 'If you could wait in the next room, Miss Dunning?'

As Joanna waited in the dressing room, her hand went to the small indent between her collarbones, the place where she had planned for the pendant to lie. Having initially despaired, she had begun to hope that it might be waiting for her in Renard's shop. She had a ribbon ready for it: a small and simple glazed locket, containing what he had described as 'artfully arranged' hair, though the weeping willow shape he had suggested didn't seem to fit with Stephen's memory at all. Her fingertips pinched the spot where her neck met her décolletage, and the skin felt slacker than she remembered it. A storm was approaching: the rain slapped angry streaks on the windowpane, and she heard the distant threatening heave of thunder. She was glad of the noise; if Harriet cried out, she didn't want to hear her.

When the doctor left he told Harriet that he believed it was true: she was to have a child. He recommended rest, plain food and quiet occupations to calm her spirits. Joanna sat with Harriet and they ate oat biscuits, warm from Mrs Holland's oven, and drank milk together, fresh from the cows in St James's Park. Later Joanna tucked Harriet into bed and she promptly fell asleep, exhausted by her exertions. Warily, Joanna sat beside her for some time, watching her sleep.

It was long past the dinner hour when Joanna went downstairs. When she opened Harriet's door the staircase hall was dark, chill and empty, and from the upper floor she could just make out the black and white tiles below, and the glistening streaks of water on them where someone had come in out of the rain. There were no footmen in attendance; she warranted they were off drinking and dancing somewhere, playing cards with the valet and losing their money. And crooked Mrs Holland would be melting candle ends into the fat pan, before she sold it on tomorrow.

She was tired, and her flux had started, the pain tweaking at her, beginning its monthly test of her endurance. She looked forward to lying down in her room. But as she walked towards the hidden door to enter the back-stairs section of the house, the library door opened, revealing a vertical rectangle of dim flickering ochre, and a figure silhouetted there.

'It's you,' said Nicholas Chichester. The way he spoke was not as precise as usual, she thought, though she could be mistaken for his voice was echoing in the hall, and she was tired. She curtseyed unsteadily on the stair she had halted on. 'Will you come down?' he said, and turned away to walk back into the room.

As she entered the library, she saw he was more than usually dishevelled, dressed in a dark nightgown over his breeches, shirt and cream waistcoat, his neckcloth undone. His dark hair had shed its powder and it stood upright, as though he had passed his hands through it many times. He was wandering aimlessly up and down in front of the far fireplace, as though lost in thought. The fire blazed happily, and its light jumped and flared, casting shadows on the wall. 'Sir?' she said, wanting to alert him to her presence.

He stopped pacing, and looked at her. 'You look done in,' he said, concern in his voice. 'Sit down.' His voice slurred slightly; the decanter on his desk was nearly empty. There were piles of books there too. As she sat down on one of the fauteuils covered in fine French tapestry, she noticed *The Gentleman's Magazine*, carelessly thrown aside.

'You must be exhausted,' he said. 'Would you like a glass of wine?'

She said nothing, startled by the question, but his eyes followed hers to the decanter, and he smiled.

He poured the liquid out unsteadily, slopping some on to the surface of the desk. The fancy silver wine label chimed against the side of the glass as he put it down. Joanna thought of Renard when she saw it. She took the glass and drank the wine back in two gulps: ruby red, iron rich.

'Dr Taylor said my wife is well and healthy,' said Nicholas, standing before the fireplace. 'That her scream-ing and yowling like a dying fox was due to a temporary derangement. That ladies sometimes have strange fancies when they are increasing. What is your experience in the matter, if you will excuse the indelicacy of the question?'

Joanna was still savouring the taste of the wine. 'Every lady is different,' she said.

Nicholas was nodding, as though he had expected her reply. 'Yes,' he said. 'Yet it was unusual, was it not? All Taylor would advise me to do was let her eat what she has a fancy for, though not in excess. I believe she mentioned sweetmeats from Gunter's.'

He laughed, and as the firelight flared she noticed a slight tic, that shivered his skin in the side of his face. She fought off a wince as the squeeze of cramp claimed her. She longed for another glass of wine, but knew she couldn't ask.

'I don't think of you as a servant,' said Nicholas suddenly, and, surprised, she brought her eyes to his face. 'Harriet's mother said you are a woman of gentle breeding, who has been brought low in the world. But I hope you will always feel more than a servant in this house.'

Ah, she thought. My false character. Perhaps I went a little too far. She had wanted to leave her past employer so much that she had written herself a lavish character and faked the signature. She said nothing.

'Why do you always wear black?' he said. 'Grey, or black? Are you in permanent mourning?'

She said nothing, trying to think of some answer that would satisfy him. Seemingly aware that his sally had failed, Chichester sat down opposite her.

'I feel I can talk to you,' he said. 'You seem calm – always the same.' He was drunker than she had first thought. His neck, close to, was mottled with red. Four bottles at least, she thought. He leaned back in his chair.

'I first saw my wife,' he said, 'in the ballroom of some house, not far from here. I told the doctor, she seemed so perfect, if it were forty years ago I would have transacted a Fleet marriage that night.'

Perfect and rich, thought Joanna. Best not to treat the doctor like a fool, if you wish for his candour. The doctor knows all about the marriages of his betters. She imagined the round-shouldered Taylor reading the marriages section in *The Times*, noting the day on his pocketbook, counting the months and making another mark, waiting to bestow his patronage on another birth. In his own way, he was like her, she imagined: always keeping his eye on things; after all, it was good to be prepared. It was necessary for survival.

'I speak to you with more candour than I should,' Chichester said. 'But only you can comprehend, living so close to her. She was trained for the marriage mart. And she is not what she seems. You know that.' He groaned. 'I have feared for you. It has vexed me to see the burden you have been under. And as for me.' He seized his glass, and tossed back the contents. More for me too, if you please, she thought, but managed to look attentive.

'I feel as though I am cursed,' he said. 'She seems to me to be unstable in her temperament. I am told things will change with time, but I am a logical man, and with the material I see before me,' he waved his hand, and she feared he would send the glasses crashing to the floor, 'I doubt it.'

They sat in silence, their glasses empty, the flames in the fireplace rising and falling.

'But what are you to do about it?' he said. 'Forgive me. You need your rest.'

'If I may be excused, sir,' said Joanna. 'I am rather tired.'

He stood and bowed. The motion was slight, yet it had the weight of a revelation for her, the gesture cutting dead her cynicism in a way that words never could; for in that moment it seemed he looked at her as though she was a lady, and not a lady's maid.

CHAPTER SIXTEEN

16th June, 1792

This morning I delivered my designs to Mrs Chichester, so for an hour or two I was all delight. I came home, and wretchedness wrapped itself around me. Dinner. Then, to a rat pit, where Mr Rowan's bitch did well. It does me good to see a little blood let. It releases some of the anger from me.

Afterwards I played some cards. Dr Taylor was always near me, a benevolent presence, but I got into a vicious contest with young Maynard. He is a fiery, headstrong creature, with something missing in his eyes. I was so in my cups, I told him so. He laughed at me: 'They say the same about you, Frenchman,' he said. I played him then – on, and on – it was like taking money from a child. Then I thought that half the money he was playing with was lent by me – and I could not help but laugh and laugh, and that got him into a temper. When he set a snuffbox on the

table, I played him for that too, and took it. Even in the half-light,
I would have recognized it anywhere, for it was of a type that I
had looked over many times. The chased gold mounting was the
work of Mary's father.

'If that child makes any more noise,' said Digby, 'I'll kick
him down the stairs.'

His neighbour looked up at him, silently, from the lower
stairs. In the morning light her pale hair, only partly covered by a cap, looked like a halo to his blurry eyes. He had
meant to shout more, but the image made him pause, and
slowed his tongue. 'If you please, keep him quiet,' he said.
He rubbed his eyes. Sleep was departing from him: chased
away by the child's footsteps, it fled down the stairs like a
mocking ghost.

She turned away without a word, or a smile. He went
back to his room, feeling foolish for having softened
towards her, and slammed the door.

Holy women, holy women: in the past they had all come
to him, seeking for something, and now it seemed he saw
them everywhere. He had come close to marrying one
once – what had her name been? He was not so cynical
that he did not feel ashamed at forgetting her name. He
could still conjure up her face, the look she had often given
him: as though he was the source of her joy, the object of
her worship, a kind of alchemist who could transform the
dirt and ashes of their lives into gold. It had not lasted;
over the years of their long engagement that joy had faded,
and she had found it more in response to the priest's words
than in Digby's company. One day, there had been no more

words to say, and they had both realized that whatever glue had held them together had melted away.

He did not remember the ending of it. Only that she had said, with a half-smile on her face so that he didn't know whether it was an insult or a sign of affection: you have no soul, Edward. And if he could bring her back now, back to his door, and walk her up the shadowy stairway to this room, with its dirt in the corners even though he tried to keep it clean, he would say to her: Alice, or Jane, or Emma, whoever you are, you are wrong.

There was a gaping tear in him. Not in his body, but in some other part of him. He felt it. And thus he knew that, though he had never considered it before, he had an immortal soul. Before he had seen himself only as a physical entity, a collection of features and habits, ruled by the world: he could point to this or that and say, that is why. His mother had told him that he'd been born from a tumble with a nobleman. Much as he scorned her words out loud there was part of him that believed it. His features were fine: his aquiline nose and pale blue eyes seemed proof of it. He had kept the secret of his birth in his heart, occasionally uncovering it and looking at it. It had bred a sense of entitlement that had unseated him from the one real opportunity that had been given to him.

As a boy, he had been apprenticed to a silversmith, and had gone to a rich man's house to deliver a message. He was a child of fourteen, standing dwarfed in the entrance hall as a priest is dwarfed by St Paul's dome. He had heard of how the rich lived, of course, but he had not seen until that moment: one had to see it. Paintings. Silk. Marble.

Silver. In their presence, these things had moved through him, given his hitherto disparate resentments focus and force. His bitterness made him difficult; so he had lost his place.

Over the years he had cultivated that bitterness, stoking it by dwelling on the lives of those he watched. There were times when he walked around Berkeley Square and the streets nearby even by daylight, hardly knowing why, only feeling the compulsion to know and see everything. But now he knew he was more than just the sum of his resentment and bitterness.

He tried to pick out what had triggered it. When he had turned Renard's body over with his foot, he had still been the same old Digby, rooted in the world. Perhaps it had been that moment at St James's, when he saw Mary Renard glance at the sky, her eyes full of some emotion he somehow recognized; perhaps it was the feeling of Renard's watch in his hand as he had walked home from the Red Lion after Maynard had threatened him. No, there was no one moment; it had all happened in degrees.

You and I are trapped, he thought, Mary's face before his eyes. We are mourning what was, and what could have been. And he knew, in himself, in a place beyond bitterness, that there was a kind of holiness about her, something within her that had remained untouched by the world. She was not a woman he wanted to possess; he wanted to protect her.

He remembered the smell of meat and wine on Maynard's breath, the driven look in his eyes, and wondered what really motivated him.

He wrapped the blanket tight around him, trying to gain some warmth from the rough material. If I watch her, he thought, if I try and put the puzzle together, perhaps I can save myself, and her too. Perhaps we can both be free.

'I will have to Londonize myself,' said Avery, smiling broadly as she sipped the dish of tea Mary had just handed her. 'The moment I set my foot on London ground I realized I need a dozen new caps just to get me through the day. I have already been to the draper's and used your name, my love. I am in jest. Of course I am in jest! I have come to be your respectable companion. I will wear only this dull rusty black dress and fade into the corners of rooms.'

She was trying to lighten the atmosphere, and she did it well. She won a smile from Mary: a sweet, effort-full smile. Both of them were pale, with shadows beneath their eyes.

The last few nights had been difficult. When Mary went to sleep, Avery would sit with her, watching her, stroking her hair and putting the candle out. Mary seemed to sleep peacefully enough for the first hour or so but then would wake screaming, beating at the locked door of the chamber with her fists. 'You are fearsome strong,' said Avery, the first time. 'This great old door rattles in its frame.'

'You should leave me,' said Mary. 'I will wake myself, and go back to sleep. I do not wish to be a burden to anyone: I wish to fend for myself.'

She did not say so, but now she imagined she saw Eli everywhere. Standing on the window seat of the parlour, watching the street below, his head golden in the sunlight.

Swinging on the banister at the top of the stairs. Seeing him was a comfort, but with only one drawback. In her visions, he always had his back to her; she never glimpsed his face. As he watched Bond Street she could sense his absorption, see the little movements of him as he looked at things, but he never turned and smiled at her.

Below, the shop bell rang. Mary flinched. Avery watched her.

'Do you not wish to venture out a little more?' she said gently. 'Mallory tells me you confine yourself to the house overmuch.'

'She is probably right,' said Mary. 'Pierre preferred me to stay indoors, unless he could take me somewhere. And I was always a dormouse. I am a little like Eli, I think. He liked things to stay the same, would walk around the house touching this and that, as though by rote. It comforted him.'

'I remember when he came to stay,' said Avery. 'Your mother said you and he were companions in everything.'

'We were,' said Mary. Tears came to her eyes. The grief welled up in her; one light scratch of the surface would release it. 'When he died, and then my mother and father, I felt as though the very roots of my life had been pulled up. I have been in darkness, since then, I think. Except for those first few days after I heard of his death: when I woke in the mornings, before I remembered, I would hear Eli's footsteps. They were as clear as the church bell. I would think he was there, just for a moment; and when I remembered, it seemed worse somehow.'

'It is perfectly natural,' said Avery, taking her hands, 'to grieve in such a way.'

'To talk about him is a joy,' said Mary. 'But I cannot forget ...' Her voice trailed off. 'I chose Pierre. Eli would not have died so soon, if I had not made that choice. And having done so, I found that I could not honour it; every hour, it ate at me. My father told me, and so did Pierre, that it was my one duty to be a good wife. But I could not.' The tears were drying on her cheeks; she looked at Avery, an unflinching gaze that reminded her cousin of Mallory. 'I did not have it in me.'

'Mary,' said Avery. 'You have not done anything.'

'But I think I have,' said Mary.

She saw then that she had her cousin's attention; for Avery paused, and in her blue eyes Mary saw, for the first time, a trace of uncertainty.

'In my early days as a wife,' said Mary, 'I kept my old character, I believe. When my parents were forced to take Eli away, I spoke to Pierre, I made my anger clear. But he had his methods for quietening me; I will not speak of them. Before long, I cared only to protect myself – not to anger him more than was necessary. I looked only to soften his temper, and his sense that I had been unfair to him. One day, a letter came from my mother. Pierre was not at home when the maid brought it, so I took it and opened it, before he could see it. The moment I saw her hand, I could not help myself.

'She wrote that Eli was unwell. That she would never have written, but that he was near death, and that his searching gaze bore such power that even her prayers could not overcome it. That she wished only that he and I could see each other again. Foolish wretch that I was, I took it to Pierre. I thought her words would move him.'

She sat still. It had been in the parlour; Pierre's face twisted with disgust. She had waited until the evening, hoping that he would have made many sales that day, putting him in a good mood. But when she handed him the letter, she saw his expression change.

'Am I always to be haunted by that idiot child?' he said. 'By God, you will never learn. You will never know your duty to me.'

'He is my brother,' she said.

His movement was swift, silent, slicing through the air. She felt the breath of it before she felt his hand around her wrist, twisting her arm behind her, pushing her towards the fire. 'You will not yield in any other way but through pain,' he said. For a moment she thought he intended to burn her to death, and it surprised her that she did not feel afraid. Tiny drops of sweat broke out on her face as she gazed into the flames, her eyes stinging. She was silent; in that moment, she thought – or was it only now she thought this? – she longed for death. Below, the shop bell rang. Grisa was still serving customers, customers gazing in admiration at the smooth, cold silver, lined up on the shelves.

'You are mine,' Pierre said. His voice was thin, high, wheedling; the voice of a teenage boy. 'You will always be mine, in life and in death.' His hand tightened on her wrist. 'You will honour at least one of the promises you made me,' he said. 'To obey me.'

Mary had to remind herself that she was not there, in that distant time. She held the arms of her chair, the smooth wood, and looked at her cousin's face.

'And I did,' she said. 'I made no effort to escape. He burnt the letter. He put a poker through it; I watched until every last fragment of it had turned into ashes. He held me there, as I wept. And now, what a coward I seem, looking on at this distance. At the time, I felt tied to him; bonds that no one on earth could untie. But now, I think, why did I not leave? Find some way to reach my brother, my family? Do you understand? I could have changed everything.'

'It is easy to say that now,' said Avery. 'But you do not consider the obstacles that lay in your way. Your parents would not have thanked you; you would have disgraced them.'

'Better that, than to become what I am now. Weak, weighed down with bitterness and sorrow. I have no Christian heart. Bound up in my own guilt, in my hatred. There were days, weeks, when I lived more in my own mind than in this world. And my imaginings, so dark. Waking, screaming with all the fury I should have shown him in life. Knowing nothing about the preceding hours. What have I done? What am I capable of?'

'Do not say it,' said Avery. 'Do not.'

Mary leaned forwards. 'I see Pierre's death,' she said. 'Too vividly.'

'Hush,' said Avery, and she looked serious, glancing over her shoulder before she continued. 'You may say it to me. But do not say it aloud, any more.'

'But it is the truth,' said Mary.

'There is no need for the truth now, when it can harm,' said Avery. 'You have done nothing, Mary. You are incapable of harming anyone.' She leaned close again, so that she could whisper. 'I wish you could have done it,' she said. 'For Eli. For him alone. But you did not. That is all I know, and that is all I need to know.' She sat back, drummed her hands on her knees with nervous intensity. 'We will not speak of it again. You need some fresh air; we will go to the park today. I have decided it.'

When they returned from their walk, the door connecting the shop to the house was open. Beyond it, Grisa was carefully arranging rings, and Benjamin was leaning against the doorway of the back room, staring at Mary, a cloth in his hands. He no longer shied away from looking at her directly, although his glance had a strange quality to it, as though she was insubstantial and he looked through her. He was standing taller too, not bowing forwards, and not responding with a jump to Grisa's every command.

'I saw Mr Renard last night, madam,' he said.

Grisa stopped his work and glared at Benjamin.

'What do you mean?' said Mary.

'I was putting things away in the back room,' said Benjamin. 'And he walked past the door. Just walked past, without a glance in my direction. When I came out, he was gone.' He took a step towards her. 'It was him, madam, it was most certainly him. He wanted to check on things. That's what I think.'

He continued to wipe his hands, slowly and deliberately. When Mary looked at Grisa he shook his head.

'Shake your head if you choose, Mr G,' said Benjamin. 'It will all come to me in the end.'

Mary stood, and watched him. His expressions, his tone

of voice, his very movements seemed to be a grotesque imitation of her late husband's. Revulsion rose in her.

'Benjamin,' she said, and her voice was clear and hard. The apprentice did not trouble himself to speak; he only raised his eyebrows. She held his gaze. 'Mark me,' she said, 'will or no will, you raise your voice to me again and I will beat you out of doors.'

Her heart was beating hard, the rage thrilling through her. He stared at her, and said nothing. Avery put her hand on Mary's arm.

'Mary, come now. The Taylors will be here at any moment.'

But Mary would not turn away while Benjamin still stared at her. He could not keep his eyes on hers; after only a moment, his gaze flickered to the floor.

It was half past seven on the clock. Dr Taylor spoke interminably about recent events on the continent. As he droned on Amelia shivered feverishly, and a small, cloudy drop of perspiration trickled its way down her face. 'Damn it, James,' she snapped eventually, and Mary realized with surprise that the shiver had been one of annoyance.

Dr Taylor seemed unmoved that his wife had taken on the habit of swearing so enjoyed by aristocratic ladies; perhaps, thought Mary, it was a point of pride for him. She thought of swearing at Pierre, with his labyrinthine sense of grievance.

'Patience, my dear,' said Taylor. He turned to Mary. 'I have been discussing matters with Grisa,' he said. 'He thinks it best, for reasons of security, if he moves into the house. He has couched his request most reasonably. If it would be bearable for you, perhaps . . .'

It surprised Mary, the overwhelming surge of gratitude she felt. 'I think it a good idea,' she said. 'It will be much more secure; I lost the last of my lodgers a day after the funeral. He may have two rooms on the second floor; we will take the parlour and the two rooms upstairs. It is quite convenient.'

'You are most gracious,' said Taylor. 'I would not have put you to such inconvenience. If the living arrangements are to be made so, I will arrange for a builder to come in. Your floor should have its own access; perhaps another wall, with a stronger door, for decency's sake, that you can lock at night as well as the inner door.'

'Oh, James,' said Amelia. 'Why would she wish to be walled in?'

He said nothing; but something about the quiet, regretful way he stared forwards showed Mary he would not be moved on the subject. She glanced at Avery's face and saw disquiet there.

Anger stirred in her again, the sea-change, as though there was water within her, rushing and switching direction. She thought of the roiling Thames. As a child she had looked at its waves from the riverbank, her mother and father behind her, Mallory holding Eli's hand and pointing at scavengers digging the liquid mud on the foreshore. Eli, laughing, pausing only to scoop some up and try and taste it, Mary rushing to stop him, laughing too at the disconcerted look in his eyes as she covered his small, purposeful hands with her own.

Taylor leaned back, and fanned himself. The chair back groaned under his weight. 'Are you quite well, my dear Mrs Renard?' he said. She saw the shine of acute distress in his eyes. 'It is for your own sake; it is my duty to protect you.'

Pierre would have mocked his vulnerability, she thought. His kindness was like a break, a crack in his defences, where nameless anxieties had crawled in. She smiled gently, and tried to reassure him.

A man came the next day trailed by another with a pile of yellow London bricks. They mixed mortar, and gave Mary another wall, leaving lines of pale, muddy seams scattered in the passage like dead caterpillars. And she thought: who do you wish to protect me from, Doctor?

CHAPTER SEVENTEEN

18th June, 1792

A good evening with Taylor; we talked of my business, and how it thrives. Mary sewed in the corner. If only Taylor knew what it cost me to smile at her, and speak to her gently. When I speak of expanding the premises he must always mention how this and that will surely suit Mary. I maintain a sanguine appearance, but my heart rages against his consideration of her. I have cosseted her for too long. If it were not for her, what riches would I have in this world.

After she had gone to bed, we sank another bottle, and talked agreeable nonsense. He could not stop praising the silver kettle I supplied him with a month or two ago; but then I did not tell him I bought it in five years ago, and the man has little knowledge of taste.

*

The dust covers were coming off the furniture in the great rooms, by the master's command. Harriet, mistress of the house, did not seem to care. 'I would like to go to church today,' she said to Joanna. 'Alone.'

She asked to wear a piece of lace given to her by her mother. As Joanna unfolded it from its paper, bringing the perfume of lavender with it, she felt a spark of sensuality strike, a small joy in the sombre grey morning. She pinned the lace carefully over Harriet's hair, leaving the golden curls unpowdered, for in her pregnancy the girl couldn't stand the smell of half the cosmetics laid on her table in Renard's silver boxes. Then she placed Harriet's hat on her head, the mistress sitting with an air of patience and penitence, like a novice about to take her vows. As Joanna put the boxes back in their separate places on the dressing table, Harriet leaned forwards and kissed her hand. The unexpected tenderness of it made Joanna catch her breath.

'Thank you,' said Harriet. 'You have been so good to me. Will you help me down the stairs?'

Joanna gave Harriet her arm. She walked her down the stairs and across the staircase hall, where Will and Oliver stood looking queasy in their livery after an evening drinking rhubarb wine. She watched as Harriet was handed into the carriage. As it moved off, Harriet raised her small gloved hand to Joanna, and waved. Joanna raised her hand in response, instinctively. But the carriage was already lurching away. She turned back into the hall to see Will the footman waving his hand mockingly.

'Watch yourself,' she said.

'Listen to you,' he said, folding his arms. 'Why should I?'

'Because I'm above you in this house and all other things,' she said.

'You think you're so much better than me, don't you?' he said.

'There's no thinking needed,' she said, and bodily pushed past him, cannoning her elbow into his chest. Feeling her own strength gave her a flush of pleasure; for a moment she imagined leaping on him, bringing him down and beating him with her clenched fists until he was silent. But he was saved by one of the maids, who came tip-tapping down the stone staircase at great speed.

'Master wants to see you, Miss Dunning,' she said. 'He's in the Grand Salon. He told me to leave the sweeping for later.'

'Master wants to see you!' said Will in a mocking, whiny tone of voice. Joanna cast him a glare as she ascended the staircase.

She stopped at the threshold of the room. The double doors were open. Nicholas Chichester was standing at one of the sash windows.

She had only ever seen the room swathed in white dust covers. Uncovered, it was majestic. The walls were covered with emerald green damask, its colour bold even in the winter light. Details shone with the gold of ormolu and the glitter of glass. The emerald colour, with gold trimming, had been used to cover the chairs and settees. So vibrant was the room that Joanna felt it touched her senses, in the way music sometimes made her heartbeat fall, or scent recovered memories.

Mr Chichester glanced at her, and smiled at the expression of astonishment on her face. 'Come in,' he said.

She realized she was gaping, and closed her mouth. As she stepped on to the sprung floor, she wanted to walk on tiptoe, in reverence to the space. More than anything she wanted to touch the fabric of the walls and furnishings, but she knew any touch would sully it. Two enormous fireplaces of Siena marble had recently been cleaned, each with a pair of caryatids bearing the mantel on their shoulders, watching her with glassy eyes from either end of the room. Above the mantels were large looking glasses, each reflective expanse bordered by a frame carved with fruit and ever-scrolling motifs she could not quite disentangle with her eyes, even if she squinted. Either side of each glass, there were silver-gilt sconces to reflect the candles that would be lit there.

She looked up at the ceiling, and took a breath. Above her was a painting of a classical scene, in a frame of carved plaster, of such richness and complexity that she could not take it all in. 'Jupiter,' said Mr Chichester. Beneath the god's feet was a golden sunburst, from which hung a rain of crystal drops: an enormous chandelier, its diamond-cut drops ready to reflect the light of a hundred candles.

'You will see it lit,' he said. He stopped half a yard from her, his hands clasped behind his back. 'Breathtaking, isn't it? Not quite Devonshire House or Lansdowne House, but still a miniature work of art. All my aunt's work. She lived here alone, you know, for many years after her husband died.'

And she was a miser in the servants' bedrooms, thought

Joanna, who had fought to have even a small table in her room. One woman: all these candles, all this damask, all this gold and glass. One woman to breathe this air. The pleasure she had taken in the room curdled. 'How is your aunt, sir?' she said.

'Tolerably well, but not well enough to return to London,' he said. 'She dictated a letter commanding me to open up the grand rooms and use them. She says she has seen nothing of me in the London papers, and is disappointed. As her favourite nephew, I must obey her commandments. A small gathering and a long letter would satisfy her. I only just ordered for the dust covers to be taken off the furniture.' He put his hand on the gilt carved arm of one of the chairs. 'Extraordinary.' His head bowed, he looked up at Joanna. 'I see you appreciate beauty,' he said. 'I admit I am rather fearful of ladies and their teacups around these silks.'

'What kind of gathering, sir?' said Joanna, mentally running through Harriet's gowns and their suitability for such an occasion.

'I think a hundred for tea and bread and butter one evening won't do any harm,' he said. 'Will my wife manage that, do you think? Are two hours of pleasantries within her power?'

Joanna curtseyed.

'I did not mean to burden you, the other evening,' he said.

'Please, sir, do not think of it,' she said.

'I have confidence in you, that is all,' he said. He smiled, and his face looked boyish, despite the formality of his fine clothes. 'I would like to think of us as allies. I will be away for a few days. Some urgent business. Mrs Holland tells me my wife has been eating oysters by the barrel, and I can only surmise that she is perhaps not looking after herself and the baby as she should.'

Nasty old bitch, that Holland, thought Joanna. She said nothing.

'While I am away, watch my wife,' he said. 'Perhaps make a note of what she eats, and what she asks for; her general health. Please see that she eats nourishing food, suitable for her condition. It would do me good to know there is someone caring for her in that way.' He put his hand on hers briefly; the heat of his touch warmed her cold skin. 'I trust you, Joanna,' he said. 'You will have whatever you wish for: extra fires, ink, paper, more candles. Things that befit your status in this house.'

'Thank you, sir,' said Joanna.

When Harriet returned, she was in a sulk. 'I saw Miss Williams at church,' she said as she walked past Joanna, who followed her up the stairs. 'I had thought I would be alone, at that time of day. That I might confess,' she stopped, smiled, and leaned into Joanna's ear, 'like a Papist.'

Joanna smiled, and immediately felt the expression did not suit her; it was an indication of guilt. 'How was she?' she said, tempering it.

'She looked very fine,' said Harriet. 'She wore a green silk gown with silver lace, and a green ribbon a mile long threaded through her hair beneath an enormous hat.

Her curls were tumbling everywhere. She put me quite in the shade.'

'But, madam, you always look so beautiful,' said Joanna, mechanically. The familiarity of it soothed her. Flattery had been one of her first lessons, learned when she was still sewing ribbons on to bonnets in a milliner's shop. Now she flattered like an automaton, and so convincingly that even she didn't consider herself a liar. It was a duty she had to perform well, that was all. 'If you wish, we can experiment with the curls, but I think the more structured look you have now suits you very prettily indeed.'

Harriet had picked up a letter that had been placed on her table. She took her gloves off and threw them on the bed, then broke it open and began to read. She put a hand to her mouth.

'My own mother,' she said, looking up. Her voice vibrated, but no tears came. 'She writes to me as though I am a stranger; and she knows I live through my letters.'

Joanna remembered Harriet, hunched over her secretaire, writing laboriously: words, and more words, her lips moving.

'A few lines on duty, and that is all she has to say to me,' she said. 'And the letter is closed by my father, on money matters. At least my husband will be pleased.'

She got up and walked backwards and forwards by the bed, then threw herself down in the chair. Joanna went to her, took off her hat, and unpinned the lace. She made her hands gentle, knowing how to soothe without words. Harriet's voice had stopped on a little break, but no, she would not cry: it was simply her voice, so overly expressive, as though she had a perpetual sore throat. 'She sees me as a family portrait now,' she said. 'That is all. What comes after I have done my duty? Nothing, it seems.'

'Your mother will write again soon,' Joanna said, softness and briskness mixed together to make her sound definite. 'I hope, in the interim, to be of some comfort to you, though I am but a poor substitute.' You are a wifely scion now, she thought. I have waited a long time for you to turn from child to adult, and now you have realized the truth in mere moments. She wondered what exactly Harriet had written to her mother; she was sure it had not been too much, for Harriet was in awe of the woman. She certainly would not have breathed even a hint of her connection with Monsieur Renard.

Harriet went to her dressing table and laid her hand on one of the silver boxes. 'I have done what they asked of me,' she said. 'I wear the diamonds my father bought from some poor purse-empty family. He thinks to make us an old family, but you cannot do that so quickly, can you? My father's house in Northumberland covers acres, but not the house my mother was raised in. My grandmother was a fearsome woman, but practical, with forty keys swinging from her chatelaine. Counting the provisions, counting and mending the linens, supervising the cooking. Even her recipes were kept under lock and key. She ran the house in every sense; she was of use.' She stopped. 'What did your mother do?'

'She was my mother,' said Joanna. 'I don't remember.' She didn't dare to utter the truth: father a bookbinder, mother a drudge, apprenticed to a milliner at fourteen.

One never knew when some stray remark would be taken up against you, especially when you had submitted a false character. Joanna had scrubbed enough floors to last a lifetime; she was determined to keep this place.

Harriet looked at her for a long time. 'I knew, Joanna, the moment I saw you, and Mama knew too. There was a goodness about you, a steadiness. She left you here for my comfort.'

Joanna said nothing. She folded the lace into its paper.

'That woman, Mama said, will guide you, will keep you as you need to be for Mr Chichester. I never told you that till now because it made me sad to think I should need chaperoning. I was a little afraid of you when you arrived.'

Something like dread turned in Joanna.

'But then, how could Mama be expected to stay near me?' said Harriet. 'It would be impossible. I am the first of her children to go out into the world, I must lead the others by showing an example of perfection. There are eight of us, you know.' She paused. 'Eight living, that is.'

Joanna felt the knowledge break over her that while she congratulated herself on being the perfect servant, she had failed in something. She had been entrusted with something and she had not realized it. She had been given a child in Harriet, a child that would have to be a lady, handed over by her tired mother.

'What must it have been like to live my grandmother's life?' said Harriet again. There was no sharpness in her tone, only insistence.

'I would not know,' said Joanna.

'I wish I did. I thought myself sensible until I came to

London,' said Harriet. 'But my head was so easily turned. The clothes, the entertainments. So many whispers, so much gossip. And then, him.' She looked at her hands. 'I did not see the man. Only the name, only what a prize he would be, and for my family too. I was pointed at him; I looked at no other. We were engaged within a few days. I made it so easy for him. I try to remember if he ever smiled at me – I think he must have done, once. He must have done, surely? But if he did, I cannot remember it. One brief season of merriment. And now, my world is this house. A prison of the most exquisite kind.'

'Have you been reading those novels again?' said Joanna, wondering which of the servants she had sent to get books.

'I see it all,' said Harriet. 'I know it is beautiful. My mother gasped when she first saw it, and I did too. I thought it would make me the wife my husband wishes me to be. That it would flow through me, make me of itself, in the way that other things do. But it does not touch me: I rebound off it; I am temporary.'

'I will fetch you a drink,' said Joanna. 'Sit here, be quiet.'

Do not fight life and the path it takes you, she thought. Do not waste your energy, beating against the beautiful enclosure of your jewelled box; and she felt something like pity stir in her heart.

CHAPTER EIGHTEEN

19th June, 1792

*To the Chichesters again, with more designs, adapted for the lady.
I admit they are taking up much of my time for new customers.
I know it will be a long time before I am paid for this service, but
the wife is an enchanting creature. It does my heart good to see
her. She has the bluest eyes I have ever seen, so bright and innocent; there is nothing haggard about her, she is unsullied, and
seems to walk always in sunshine.*

*I cannot look at my wife without a pain in my guts, as
though I have drunk bad wine; whereas Taylor remarks on her
delicacy, her feeling, as though it is some admirable quality, I
see only how her imagined cares (what cares does she have,
when a woman is as lucky as she?) have left their mark on her
face.*

*

Daylight had long left the winter sky when Mary Renard's household was woken by a small fist hammering on her front door. Mary was sitting in the chair by the fire's embers. She heard Grisa open the front door, and begin a tirade of some sort. When she arrived at the top of the stairs she wondered whether she was dreaming, seeing Grisa remonstrating with a small figure, all the time wearing the most extraordinary red embroidered headgear.

'What a fine nightcap you have, Mr Grisa,' she said, as she came down the stairs, before she noticed that he was reprimanding her nephew, Matthew. Luckily, Matthew was his mother's son, and did not heed Grisa's annoyance, or look impressed by him. He only waited dispassionately for his aunt to descend the stairs. 'You shoulda locked him in,' he said when she reached him, nodding in the direction of Grisa.

'What is it, my love?' she said.

'Ma's going through her chests, throwing things out,' he said. 'She wanted you to have this. Said it was urgent. Says it will make you feel better, Aunt Mary.' And he handed her a letter.

There was just enough light to see him run off along the pocked surface of the stone paving flags. A fine drizzle was falling and as she stood in the doorway Mary heard a watchman's rattle sound in the distance.

'Inside if you please, before we are all murdered in our beds,' snapped Grisa. He pulled the door shut and heaved the bar up. A faint smell of smoked mackerel still hung in the air, a reminder of their dinner.

'How like Mallory,' said Avery from the top of the stairs.

'Sending the poor child out at night. Could she not have waited until morning?' She padded off to bed.

'Poor child?' said Grisa after her. 'I pity any soul who gets in his way between here and Piccadilly.'

Mary went to her parlour, Grisa stamping up to his rooms and slamming the door hard. She sat on the edge of the chair, leaning close to the embers in the fireplace, the only source of light in the room.

She had seen at once that the address was written in the firm, elegant hand of her mother, the characters sloping forwards. The sight of the familiar, long-stilled hand gave her a jolt, reminding her of the letter burnt by Pierre so long ago. She unfolded the page and read it slowly. It was written after their mother had left London with Eli. It seemed so strange to see a new representation of her mother's voice. She wrote of preserving vegetables, of a new maid her sister had engaged, and Eli. She smiled as she saw his name. Then, as she read on, her smile faded.

Tell me how Mary does. I dream of her sometimes. Eli does not say her name any more, nor yours, nor your father's. He still laughs and plays, but sometimes he sits very still and stares ahead of him, and I know he is wondering where you have all gone. His health is never good, and I fear this loss worsens it.

I repent of that marriage. We were wrong to have encouraged Pierre Renard, and to have silenced all Mary's doubts, for he had no kindness for her, and that is the one thing that is always needed in marriage.

Beneath the last line was fresh ink; Mallory had underlined it. So you all knew, Mary thought, remembering their blank faces when she had wavered in her resolve to marry Pierre. How her parents and Mallory had looked at her: uncomprehending, puzzled, a wall of faces. Their lack of expression had silenced her, so there was only the noise of Eli playing in the background, and the clatter of the char-woman's pail as he upturned it.

'He will provide for you,' said her father on the night before her wedding. 'I am convinced of it, my dear.' He had kissed her on the forehead, and turned to watch her as she began to climb the stairs by the light of one candle. 'You said you liked him, when you met him that first time.'

She knew that Mallory had sent the letter to comfort her. But the image of Eli sitting on the floor, cross-legged, his blue eyes looking into the middle distance, hit her deeper than she could have anticipated. The letter was clasped tight in her hand now; carefully, she spread it out on her lap, and smoothed it. Then she pushed up the sleeve of her black bombazine dress. The bruises were fading; they were now pale yellow. She hardly knew why, but she could not bear for them to fade completely. She could only think, 'not yet', and press her index finger into each of the faint circles. She needed to keep Eli with her a little longer; to make his memory stronger in her mind than that of a destroyed letter, dissolving in flames. He was with her, watching the carriages and the people going up and down Bond Street; he was urging her to live.

*

Before he began his evening's work, Digby went to Half Moon Street with the intention of speaking to Maynard. The man's interest in Renard was vexing him, and he had resolved to know more. He was angry that he had allowed himself to be intimidated. He walked with a purposeful briskness, not wrapping himself against the damp evening air but keeping his head up and shoulders back, as though his proud gait would invest his old clothes with some kind of dignity. They were well enough, he supposed; he paid a woman in his lodgings to keep them well-mended, and was proud of his shirts. But they were not the kind of clothes he longed to wear; plain broadcloth, rather than the rich damasks, satins and figured velvets that gentlemen such as Maynard enjoyed, and the thought of meeting with his insistent patron made him feel even poorer.

As he neared Maynard's house, his bravado began to drain away. He pulled his collar high so that his face was half-hidden. A couple of fine carriages passed him, and there were several sedan chairs carrying people to their clubs and to engagements. He passed one containing an old woman, her face white with powder and fur around her neck. She glanced at him with a mixture of disdain and fear, and he wondered whether she was anxious about the white pearls hanging from her elongated lobes. He almost fancied making a lunge towards her just to see her jump, but she might recognize him, and he had no wish to lose his place.

Maynard's house was fine enough; a tall town house of London brick with an imposing door studded with iron. The torches were lit, and a carriage waited outside it, the horse twitching its tail this way and that. Digby bit his lip and surrendered, turning away. He was unable to imagine himself mounting the steps and knocking on the door, but he had no wish to go around to the back of the house, and face the curious stares of the servants, for he was a free man, he thought, not a servant. He began to cough, and as he fought it, trying to catch his breath, the front door opened, and Maynard came out.

Digby took a step back, not wanting to be seen. Maynard was dressed for dining out; Digby saw a flash of white and black beneath his greatcoat. The woman that walked beside him Digby took to be Mrs Maynard. Her hair was piled ridiculously high and covered with an enormous confection composed mainly of feathers. But through her grand appearance Digby noticed her eyes: a piercing blue, full of sadness, her fine skin lined, so that she looked older than her husband. She smiled at Maynard as he handed her into the carriage, a smile that spoke of trust and perfect confidence, and it stuck in Digby's heart.

Before the carriage even rolled off, Digby walked on, passing through the scent of roses that the woman had left to linger in her wake. He was glad they had not seen him; his heart was beating hard with agitation, and he wanted always to be calm when dealing with Maynard. It was drizzling, and the dampness soaked into his clothes, so that before long his agitation calmed to dull misery.

When he reached the watch house he found his partner in a rebellious mood. 'I'm sick of covering for you,' said Watkin.

Digby had heard it all before. 'Quit all your mouthing,'

he said. 'We can go out now; it's barely chimed the quarter hour.'

'Not so quick,' said the beadle, shifting his clay pipe in his capacious mouth. 'I've already got two lots of you patrolling the square. I'm sending you round to Castle Street; there were housebreakers at number twelve on the square last night, and the maid says she saw a silver coffee pot like the one that got taken in the pawnbroker's window. Go and visit the woman who owns it.'

'Where's the constable, then?' said Digby. 'We should be led by him, and we've no warrant. Besides, it's off our patch.'

'I decide that, Digby,' said the man with a tone of self-importance. 'The constable has other things to attend to, and if it pertains to the square, it's our business. It's owned by a widow Dunning. Go round and see if you can get anything out of her.'

Digby blocked out Watkin's moaning as they trudged around to Castle Street. It had taken a moment before he had realized that they were heading to Mallory Dunning's house, but now he had, the tension crackled through him. While Watkin squared his shoulders, Digby shoved him out of the way and knocked on the door.

It was opened just a crack, and Digby raised his lantern to make out the woman's face as he said his name and business. She opened the door without a word.

'Make sure you scrape your boots well,' said Digby to Watkin. 'We don't want to be dragging dirt through Mrs Dunning's house.' He received a nod and a flash of approbation from her fine dark eyes, and she led them into the kitchen, shading the candle flame with her hands. It was a dark room, with bare floorboards, and a young girl was rolling pastry at the table, watched by a smaller girl.

'You're too early,' said Mallory, following Digby's gaze. 'Apple tart, but not ready yet. Matthew,' she addressed a young, stocky boy, who was watching the men with his mother's eyes. 'Go and fetch a pot of beer for Mr Digby and . . . ?' She let her eyes rest on Watkin's face.

'W-Watkin,' Watkin stammered, and Digby longed to give him another shove, for it was evident that his partner wasn't used to dealing with the fairer sex.

'What's your business with me, gentlemen?' said Mallory. 'But where are my manners? You should sit down in the parlour. There's no fire there, though.'

'That is well,' said Digby. 'We are hardy. We'll leave your girls to do their cooking.'

The parlour was a small room, and there were signs that it had once been neat enough. But with a stranger's eye Digby noticed how sparsely furnished it was, and though it was clean, any elegance had long since ebbed away. The paper, once à la mode, had greyed with the London smoke, and was peeling from the wall. There were a few ornaments here and there, and a rug on the floor, run to threads from the children's shoes. When Watkin sat down, the spindly chair he had chosen creaked under his weight.

'How can I help you?' said Mallory.

'We're calling about your business, Mrs Dunning,' said Watkin.

Digby sat back in his chair. If anyone was going to be the bearer of bad tidings, he was happy for it to be Watkin.

'The fact is, housebreakers visited Berkeley Square last night,' said Watkin. 'And we've been told a silver coffee pot from the robbery ended up in your shop. I think you know how grave it would be, if that were the case.'

Mallory took a breath. Digby didn't know if it was just his imagination, but she seemed slightly paler; though in the low light, he could not be sure.

'I doubt it, Mr Watkin,' she said, without a tremor in her strong alto voice. 'My shop is run by a manager, and it has done me more harm than good, I'll grant you. But I keep a tight rein on it, sir, and I can tell you that no new stock has been brought today. I send my boy there to check every day, and Mr Ibbotson, the manager, must always report to me if he has bought anything; and I have no such report. You are free, good sirs, to go to the shop, and search there, in the morning. He is there at eight every day.'

The parlour door opened, and Matthew entered with two pint pots.

'Thank you, young man,' said Digby, as he took his. 'You're old enough to be a 'prentice, now, aren't you?' The boy nodded, the dimples beginning in his cheeks. 'What do you want to be?' said Digby.

'A silversmith like grandpapa,' said Matthew, without hesitation, and Digby frowned.

'My father was a silver box-maker,' said Mallory. 'And his father before him. Though no one remembers that now; my good brother-in-law eclipsed him, with his fancy Bond Street shop.'

'Mr Renard?' said Digby. 'Get on with him, did you?'

'Mattie, go into the kitchen now,' said Mallory. After the

door closed behind him, she turned back to the watchmen. 'I didn't think well of him,' she said. 'And I don't mind telling you. He made my sister's life a misery. And, at the last, he brought a stranger into his house, and now he has left him everything.'

She was an astonishing woman, thought Digby, as he stared into her eyes. Animated, as she was now, she seemed lit up from within.

'Your husband, Mrs Dunning,' said Watkin, showing signs that his memory was groaning into life, like a slow-moving automaton. 'Was he not had up for receiving? Taking in melted-down silver plate in ingots?'

'He was acquitted,' said Mallory sharply. 'My late husband was a good man, and too trusting of others. He never did a dishonest thing in his life, and the same goes for me.'

'We believe you, ma'am,' said Digby, downing his pint. 'Come on, Watkin. We have troubled this good lady long enough.'

As he bundled Watkin down the hall towards the door, Digby turned back to Mallory. 'Who do you think killed your brother-in-law, Mrs Dunning?' he said.

Mallory did not seem moved by his words. She stood as though considering the question, a long tear of tallow running down the candle, the glitter of the flame in her black eyes. 'Someone who hated him,' she said. 'But God knows, there were enough of them.'

CHAPTER NINETEEN

20th June, 1792

Young Maynard came to me: sickly, hollow-eyed, without his chest puffed out. He told me that he wanted only the snuffbox back, and that his father would settle up all he owed me. That it was a family piece. When one has been treated as I have, you learn to savour moments such as these. Did the young dog think he would shake me off so easily? I told him no; that the box had been made by my wife's father, and that I liked it. That it was mine, and I would keep it.

Of course, he lost his temper; swore, put his hand to his sword – an empty gesture, for he cares too much for his young face and too little for his honour to fight me.

After he had gone, I hid the box well, for I would not put it beyond his father to come to the shop when I am out, and tell Grisa to turn the place over for his sake.

*

'All this flummery about your widowhood,' said Avery sharply, as she cut a slice of fruit cake for Mary. 'I forever hear Dr Taylor referring to it, as if you are a fine lady with independent means, when it is clear your income does not support such pretensions. There is decency to think of, of course, but they cannot expect you to be shut away in mourning for two years. Where I come from, if a tradesman dies, it is the duty of his wife to find a good replacement. Do not look so shocked! You are Mallory's sister, after all.'

Mary yawned. 'I think you speak to me of marriage because you are tempted yourself,' she said. 'I saw you downstairs in the shop, speaking with a very fine-looking gentleman.'

'He was newly engaged,' said Avery, with an attempt at primness. 'And wanted advice on what silver plate his wife would wish for on the dining table.' She smiled as Mary took a bite of cake. 'Besides, I did not have long in the shop before Grisa saw me and chased me out. I alarmed him terribly, I believe.'

She leaned forwards, took another piece of cake and put it on Mary's plate. 'Eat it,' she said. 'I would have some colour in your cheeks.'

'Am I improving well enough for you?' said Mary.

'No,' said Avery.

'Then you must make a plan of action,' said Mary, with a smile. 'Will you excuse me for a moment? I think I hear Mr Exham below.'

She had purposely left both doors open, to hear what was happening in the shop, and now she tiptoed out on to the landing. At the foot of the stairs, George Exham was talking to Benjamin. Mary had not seen him since the day of the funeral. Today, he was the man she remembered from times of old: neat and calm. He was wearing what looked like his Sunday clothes: a smart, moss-green coat, and a hat with a brilliant buckle that caught what light there was in the dark stairwell. She stood back, not wanting him to see her.

'I thought Taylor would be open to offers. But if things are as you say,' he said slowly.

'They are.' Benjamin's voice was harsh. 'There's no need to mention marriage to her, dried-up witch as she is: I'll save you the trouble. Why do you want her, anyway? I understood your affections were engaged elsewhere, as Mr Grisa would say.'

'They were,' said Exham. 'That is, they are. But these are difficult times. The situation in France ... the prices ...' He let his voice trail off.

'Wanted some ready money, did you?' said Benjamin. 'Well, you'll get none of it here.'

Mary's heart was beating hard at their words, yet in her shock she had enough awareness to wonder why Exham, who was Benjamin's superior in age and craft, did not reprimand him. But then she realized: of course, they know that he will inherit one day. He is to be cultivated. He is to be flattered. He could lock me in the cellar, she thought, and no one would help me, unless it was worth their while.

'It seems I've wasted an afternoon,' Exham said, putting his gloves on. 'You'd best tell people. More will come.'

'Let them,' said Benjamin. He had assumed a rough

edge to his boyish voice. It was artificial, and grating. 'The answer will be the same. One day I will be master here, and she'll get what's coming to her.'

The coins Digby had given to the girl had been worth it, though as the immediate release of pleasure passed, he felt shame creep into him. Was she clean? he thought. It would be just his luck to be given the pox. She'd said she was just off the coach, fresh and clean from a hamlet near Oxford, 'a few houses only, sir'. But now he remembered the precise way she'd said 'fresh and clean' and he began to doubt her. To his lust-clouded brain she could have said 'French and dirty' and he still would have done it.

Damn his lust, he thought, damn his sinfulness. She was haring off into the night now, a distant figure, carrying the coins with her, moving quick as a louse through dry hair. He wanted to call out to her retreating back. Come back here, just for a moment. Put your arms around me. I only wanted some comfort.

He picked up his lantern and began walking back to the watch stand on Hay Hill, where he knew he would find Watkin complaining. When he heard a cry it took him a moment to focus. He made out a struggling pair of figures, and began to run towards them.

'Who's there?' he shouted. He was lurching a little; for he'd drunk so much porter at the Red Lion the landlord said he'd have to start a new slate for him. Then the cough came, drawing him up; and a small figure ran into the night, leaving a man, brushing himself off.

'You alright there, sir?' said Digby, catching his breath and coming towards him. And a fine gentleman he was too, with silver lace at his throat and wearing a waistcoat – which Digby just glimpsed – that looked as though it had taken seventeen hands to make it, all silver tissue and spangles.

'Do not trouble yourself,' said the young man. He was breathing noisily. His face was white, and pinched, and for a moment he put his hand up, as though he sought to shield his expression. 'I'm in your debt,' he mumbled, opening his purse with trembling hands.

Digby knew the face well; he took the coins that were offered. 'It's a bad time of night to be wandering around here, sir,' he said. 'There are villains all about.'

'It was the link-boy,' said the man. 'I didn't know him. I paid him to see me home. The wretch.'

'I didn't see his light,' said Digby.

'He extinguished it when he tried to rob me,' said the man. 'I swear he could see in the dark, like the devil himself. It serves me right, I suppose. But all is well. I will wish you goodnight.'

'Goodnight, and be careful,' said Digby, his words slurring slightly. 'This city's a whole mess of darkness, you know, Mr Chichester.'

He turned back in the direction of the watch stand and walked away, glancing at the coins he had been given. Yes, the man had been generous: far too generous. He was sure the boy had been paid to do more than light him home. You could hardly blame the poor child for the scuffle. He shook his head as he pocketed the coins, and when he glanced behind him, wondering where the child had gone, he could see only darkness.

CHAPTER TWENTY

20th June, 1792

My new apprentice arrived today. His name is Benjamin. He is a very slight, timid kind of boy, but I think I will beat him into tolerable shape with strong words and the example of discipline. He will sleep in the shop, for I cannot favour him too much lest it draws attention from Grisa, who is a jealous employee, but he will be fed well with the remains from our table. I much prefer having a boy here such as him, with no youthful arrogance, for I am sure he will take well to instruction. I will be firm enough to teach him; but fair enough for him to give a good report to his aunt Sarah. It pleases me to have served Sarah in some way. There is something of her in him, I fancy.

The household had gone to church, but Joanna had cried off with a sick headache. She was not sick in body; but a glimpse of the front page of *The Times* from the day before had sent her mind spiralling and turning in on itself. It was why, she thought drily, a lady should never read the newspapers.

Foundling Hospital
Admission of Children

Persons desirous of obtaining Admissions of Children (such as are the proper objects of this Charity) into this Hospital, may apply between the hours of Ten and Three.

She had read it in the kitchen, the master's abandoned newspaper brought downstairs for the servants to pore over, for he had sped away in his carriage that morning. Normally she controlled her imaginings, using them as a consolation even if they made reality a little more sour, but that small square in the newspaper had unlocked a jumble of sensations and images. It was then she thought that she had been exercising her mind too much with memories of Stephen, for the intensity of her thoughts threatened to overwhelm her. She locked herself in her room, and sat on the bed, her breath catching in her dry throat.

In her hand it was as though she could feel the small disc of metal, cold and hard, held so tight it left marks on her palm.

No, she thought, no. You are imagining things. You imagine too much. You are here, sitting in a small room in a house on Berkeley Square. The past is gone; it lives only in your mind. But there was no escaping it, whether she closed her eyes or kept them open.

The walk to the Foundling Hospital all those years ago had been the longest of her life, every step slowed by her exhaustion and her knowledge that these were the last moments she would spend with her child. Her daughter had slept against her chest, tied there with a piece of cloth, and Joanna kept her fingertips against the baby's warm cheek as she walked. There had been no need for a token, no need at all. Everything is written down, the clerk had said. We have your name, from the petition. But she had pleaded for the small metal disc to be taken in anyway and, with a sigh, the man had eventually held out his hand. It was a token from the Frost Fair of 1776; an ineffectual souvenir of a distant girlhood. She had nothing of Stephen; nothing that signified their love, but the lock of hair. She would keep that, she had decided, for her sanity, else she began to think that she had imagined him. There was the money he had given her, but it was nearly all spent; and you could not leave money with a baby.

The worst thing was that she had believed she could be strong. As if her discipline and training as a servant could have prepared her for it. She maintained that illusion until she untied the child and put her in the arms of the clerk, and then everything fell away. Pray keep her safe, she said. She fought to get the words out, for she was sobbing. I will call for her again. I only need time. One last glimpse of the baby's face, an image burnt into her memory, and her life had diverged from that of her child. Part of her had died that day.

Her breathing began to slow. She had ridden out the memory, and was becoming calmer. She thought of Mr Chichester's face. His generous gaze, the way he spoke to her. She thought of Harriet's little mutterings as she patted her stomach. As she settled, she felt again that cold hollow emptiness in the pit of her stomach, and thought: I have no responsibility for you, Mrs Chichester. Whatever slight affection she had begun to feel for her charge, she aborted by force of will.

She could hear the distant sound of church bells as she went to Harriet's room. She adjusted the boxes on the dressing table as though her purpose there was normal. She had persuaded Harriet to keep the key to the secretaire in one of the boxes in the dressing set, hidden by pins. She opened it, took out the key on its lank ribbon, and opened the box, remembering Harriet's words: *in there lies what was once the promise of happiness.*

The interior of the secretaire was decorated delicately, the marquetry of different coloured woods forming images of flowers. The drawers were tiny, and the whole looked like something made for a doll to use, rather than a woman. Hastily pushed away were a few letters from Mama, for Joanna recognized the handwriting. The secret mechanism was simple enough; she supposed it had been made to suit Harriet's simplicity, and it took her only a moment to work it out.

Joanna pulled out the letters; there were so many jammed into the compartment that they tumbled out, collapsing on to the leather-covered writing surface, bringing a faintly musky smell with them. They were jumbled, in no discernible order. Her heart beating hard with alarm, Joanna only glanced at them, her gaze sweeping over each page, absorbing some words and leaving others.

232

My dearest girl,

This, as a reminder of the memory that touches heaven for me.

I cannot stop my thoughts from racing. If I were free.

I want but one word from your dear sweet lips; my name.

I will not suffer her forever.

All of the letters were in handwriting that had its swirls and flourishes, yet the characters were strangely laboured and childlike. All of them were signed with the same initials.

P.R.

For a moment, Joanna froze. She had learned what she had come here for, yet she felt a cold sinking, then the realization that if she could put the letters back and unlearn it, she would. She had long suspected Pierre Renard, but the new reality of it, his initials before her eyes, was too sudden. She read more slowly, but that made it worse, for she began to pick up the full content of the letters, and some of it was explicit, sparking sickening images in her mind.

Somewhere in the depths of the house something fell; a silver knife on a marble floor. The distant sound – for everything echoed in this house, as though it was a cathedral – struck a resonance of fear in her and she pushed the letters back into the compartment, not caring whether she crumpled them, slamming the doors shut and fumbling with the key. She put it back in its box on the dressing table and slammed the lid shut with shaking hands.

Her whole body was trembling uncontrollably.

She stood there, in the silence. There was no one there.

She took a few steps back, and sat down on one of the silk-covered chairs. She looked around the room; at the sheen of the hangings, the tall windows, the toilet service. Beside Harriet's bed, the small pile of books and the miniature of Mr Chichester.

I am justified, she thought. Why should a woman such as Harriet Chichester live unpunished when my child was left to die, crying for her mother and the father she would never see?

She sat there for a few minutes, speaking harsh words to herself, and cradling her now-imaginary daughter in her arms. Then she went to her room, got out the writing implements left her by her master, and, after straightening the pots containing the sand and the ink, began to write.

Alban approached the church of St James's Piccadilly from York Street. The church was illuminated for evening service, and he paused in the winter darkness to appreciate its effect, and to quieten his breathing, which had quickened at the thought of seeing Mary. To him the interior of the church did seem blessed; within the space contained by the huge windows, glazed with chequers of uneven glass, all was warmth and light, while everything outside languished in darkness. If it was an illusion of sanctity, he thought, it was a fine one.

He was late and, thinking only of Mary, he had not prepared himself for the eyes of the congregation: Piccadilly's finest in their silks and satins, looking askance at the stranger dressed in a black coat, his black hair unpowdered, his eyes searching. It reminded him of Jesse's words as he had left the house: 'They count the money in your purse before they even let you in there.' Despite entering amidst a great crash of organ music he still attracted glances and nudges as he nodded to the church warden, then the cross, and stood at the back of the church.

The great brass candle branches had been lit. He did not pause to count, but it seemed as though the white walls of the church and its gilded details glinted in the light of hundreds of candles.

His eyes scudded over the congregation: tall wigs, natural powdered curls, feathers, hats and hoods. When he finally found Mary, it gave him a tremor of shock, for she was sitting exactly where she had sat all those years ago, her back to him, looking ahead. Renard must have bought a pew here, long ago, he thought. Part of him had assumed that she would not be here, that this trip was just a sop to throw to Jesse. He allowed his eyes to rest on her in her widow's garb. A few powdered curls were visible at the edge of her cap, and his eyes lingered on her white neck.

So much has changed, he thought, though I try to set time under crystal. When she knew me first I was a much younger man. Do I differ, other than my back is stiffer, and my right elbow has begun to pain me, so that sometimes I have to put the hammer down? He thought that perhaps, day by day, he had changed by slight degrees, and the Alban Steele that stood here now was an entirely different man from the one that had stood here eleven years before.

He wondered how she had changed, and doubt crept into his mind.

It was Jesse who had sent him here. Jesse, carving a piece of wood, looking up at him this afternoon and saying: 'She came for you.'

'What do you mean?' he said.

'The day after you met her at church. She was out with her brother on an errand for her father, and she came near the house. I was on the step seeing someone out. Eli was running along the street; he nearly got in front of a carriage and I caught him. Little imp, he was, always laughing.'

'So you met her in the street,' said Alban, sardonically.

'She came for you,' said Jesse. 'Whether she knew it or not. I found a way to make it clear that you had gone.'

'Why did you not tell me?' said Alban.

'There was nothing to be done. You were already in the coach, going back to Chester. She was married within the week and the boy sent away. I did not speak of it before because I thought you would reproach yourself, and I only tell you now because I think it might make you do something.'

Standing in the church where he had first met Eli and Mary, he remembered the child's face so clearly, his blue eyes, the smile that lit up his face, and the weight of him as he threw him in the air. Then, the smile that Mary had given him.

'Who is she?' he had whispered to Jesse, after he had led the child back to the family pew and handed him to his mother. 'Mary Just,' said Jesse. 'Mallory's sister.' That little girl, he had thought – when he had visited as a fourteen-year-old apprentice, a child himself – I remember her, the girl with the mischievous eyes.

Of course it had only taken a moment for him to piece it all together; he had just heard her banns read, and for the last time of asking.

Weeks afterwards when he was back in Chester, he woke one morning and thought: I glimpsed the divine in that church. All those years I sought it, then I had it for one moment. But then he woke properly, and splashed cold water on his face, and was himself again. He reasserted it as he walked to work that day: I do not believe in serendipity. And I do not believe in God.

Mary kept her head bowed until the service came to a close. People were winding their way out, the babble of several hundred voices rising in the great white space of the church, when she felt Avery's hand on her arm. She turned, and saw Alban standing there, watching her as he had on the day of the funeral. The sight of him filled her with hope and a deep sense of relief. As she walked towards him, each step slow and measured so that she might look at him the longer, a hesitant smile filtered its way across his face.

He bowed and said her name, and took the hand she presented to him.

'I am glad to see you,' she said. 'It is a lucky chance. I normally worship at St George's, but friends allowed us a place in their pew this evening. I come here sometimes for my brother.'

She glanced over her shoulder, as though she might see

Eli there, running towards them. But there was no one there but the stragglers in the congregation, and Avery, who was speaking with two of the other worshippers. When she turned back she saw that her sadness was reflected in his eyes.

'Being here reminds me of him and my parents. It is the only place. My father's house was let long ago.'

'I am sorry,' he said.

Mary smiled. 'No,' she said. 'You have no need to be sorry. I remember the kindness you showed him.' She took a breath, wondering how she could lengthen the precious conversation. 'How do you find London?'

'Constantly changing, yet unchanging,' he said. 'It seems a hard place to me sometimes. A man here may wear a true-seeming face before a false heart, and not be discovered. But then I am an outsider. Perhaps I do not understand what it takes to succeed here.' He was looking around, as though agitated. When he spoke again, there was a note of decision in his voice.

'I came to tell you,' he said, and he swallowed. 'My accounts are all in order. I have some resources. I am not a rich man, but I have enough to be comfortable.'

She could not decipher his meaning; he had spoken too quickly, and she panicked a little. 'I am glad for you,' she said, taking refuge in politeness.

'Forgive me, I am not making myself clear,' he said urgently. 'I have come to ask you if you will consider becoming my wife. As I said, my accounts are all in order, and I can present them to Dr Taylor at his convenience.'

Mary searched for, but could not find, emotion in his

eyes. But of course, she thought; he speaks of money, why would he not? I was a fool to have imagined more. It felt to her as though the colour had drained out of the surroundings. She had placed meaning on such inconsequential events, so many years ago. All at once she felt ridiculous, and wronged, and angry. The memory of Mr Exham speaking to Benjamin on the stairs was still sharp.

'Despite all the rumours, Mr Steele,' she said, 'I am not a good investment. I thank you for your kind offer. I will pretend you never made it.' As she turned away, she felt as though every piece of warmth had fled to the core of her body, leaving her weak.

'Wait,' he said.

She stood still, her back to him.

'I did not think of the money,' he said in low voice. She felt, rather than heard, him take a step towards her. 'I ask you to consider my offer,' he said. 'It is honestly made.'

She waited for a moment, but no more words came from him. She felt no flicker of temper; only the leadenness of disappointment in her stomach.

'Do not make me repeat myself,' she said, but she did not move. There was something she had to ask. She didn't know whether it was because she had to guard the pillaged treasure of the past, or let it be finally trampled and laid waste.

'Did you think of me much these past years?' she said.

She saw Avery watching them, silently, from across the aisle.

'Why would I?' he said. 'You were married, and far from me.'

There was nothing she could say in response; she only looked at him, as though for the last time.

'I promise always to be honest with you,' he said.

Mary turned, curtseyed without meeting his eyes, then left the church. It was only out in the darkness of Jermyn Street that Avery finally caught up with her.

CHAPTER TWENTY-ONE

2nd June, 1792

I was looking over the ledgers tonight, when my wife interrupted me with her meaningless chatter. When she remarked that Benjamin seemed to be a good boy, but a little timid, I detected her cunning at work. I told her that she was not to criticize him, and that he meant more to me than she knew, and at this she protested.

It is my habit to keep things close to me and not to share them with Mary, but I could not help but tell her that there had been someone before her, far better than she. Yet when I spoke it did not quite come out so; there was a bitterness to my words. I am vexed that I did not keep myself more in check, but when a man has been wounded so many times, it is natural that a little venom should now and then escape. I must follow Dr Taylor's example, be patient, and pray, for I know God is just.

*

Alban lay back on the mattress, the footsteps of his nieces and nephews pounding backwards and forwards on the floorboards. He was exhausted, but the sound of their running feet comforted him. He remembered what it was like to be a child, to run thoughtlessly, when every day was like a new lifetime.

Jesse came down the stairs, yawning. 'Don't get up,' he said. 'What time did you work until?'

Alban shrugged.

'Listen to them. Doesn't it make you glad not to be a father?' said Jesse.

Alban said nothing. He did think that perhaps it was for the best that he would never be a father now; he did not want to watch his children become mired in the cares of the world. But he wished Jesse and Agnes would stop trying to prise acceptance out of him. He could seek it in his own way, though he did not wish to rebuff their kindness.

As he lay there he could not chase away his memory of eleven years before. We were not alone, he thought, for one moment long ago. I know we found each other. A brief illumination, as when a cloud moves away from the sun, before another passes over it.

He said to himself now that Mary had punished him for telling the truth. Her vanity had been unable to bear it. He had not had time to explain that there would have been no point in thinking of her, or torturing himself with a useless jealousy. Until that day on Bond Street he had believed himself dead to her, and it would have been as pointless as banging his head against a wall to have dwelt on the hope that had flared so briefly into life and then been snuffed out.

What he had not told her was that in those moments after their eyes had met, so many years ago, he had committed her name to memory, holding the swaying Eli in his arms, the child all warmth and life and glowing blue eyes. Mary Just. He had pictured the letters of it in the way he remembered decorative motifs, borders, edgings, designs, so that it could be assigned to his visual memory. He was a man who saved scraps of beauty, who buried precious things in his mind, hoarding them to be used later in the process of creation. So he had said her name, then buried it. He had not dwelt on her in the intervening years. Occasionally, in the long evenings when he drew, he would fall into a reverie, and return to London, and Mary, in his imagination. One evening he had designed a dinner service; drawn it completely to his own taste. He could see it on his own table, and the life he could have lived. She was there, in that life, even if she was only represented in the cypher he had drawn of their initials. Her name had always been there. If she could not see the sanctity of it, that was her fault.

When he had come home from church and told them what had happened, Agnes had left the room, her hand clamped across her mouth, and tears in her eyes.

'She is emotional, it's the breeding,' said Jesse. 'She wishes you to stay, as we all do. She had some vision of you with a wife and a houseful of children.'

'I will stay until you no longer need me,' said Alban.

'It is a cursed house, that Renard place,' said Jesse. His expression was grim and hard. 'And she is part of the curse.'

'Why would you say that?' said Alban. The cruelty in Jesse's tone chilled him; he was glad Agnes had left the room. 'Say you do not mean it, or we will have words.'

Jesse sighed. 'Forgive me. If I speak harshly, it is out of loyalty to you. That woman has grieved you, and I am sorry for my part in it. I wish I could make her suffer as you do now.'

'Do not say that,' said Alban. 'I do not wish her ill. She has done nothing wrong. And my injury is slight; I will forget it in a week. I was wrong to make a hasty proposal based on one look eleven years ago.'

When Mary entered the shop it was past ten in the morning. It did not seem as dark as usual, for Grisa had taken down some of the black velvet which had draped it in mourning, and the winter light reflected off the glass in the counter and presses. He held a salver up, turning it in his hands, inspecting the ornate chasing. It flashed in the light as he flipped it: white, grey, white, grey. Mary longed to rest her hands on its smooth coldness. Beside it, on the counter, a set of six salts had been placed, part unwrapped. A piece of sacking was still draped over one of them. With her right forefinger Mary unhooked it and let it fall silently on the counter.

'It is beautiful work,' she said. Grisa looked at her, taking his eyeglass out.

'Of course,' he said. 'Nothing but the best for the firm of Pierre Renard's, though we strike your mark on it now.'

'Who made it?' said Mary.

'Jesse Chamac's workshop,' said Grisa, and Mary felt

a sick stab of distress in her stomach. 'The new man, Alban, does fine work. I have asked him to send more pictures too, for he designs, and they have just the right look: clean, not like that ornate heavy stuff. Hullo there!' He waved his hand, and Mary looked back to see the watchman at the window, raising his hand in greeting. She nodded, and smiled, and he walked on. 'He keeps looking in,' said Grisa, raising an eyebrow. 'I feel looked-after.'

Mary touched one of the salts, its cold surface hard and unyielding. It was edged with beading.

'When were these made?' she said.

'They have just been delivered,' said Grisa.

Mary ran her fingers over the beading. The pieces of silver had been made by a confident hand. They had the charisma of things thought about, more than pleasing, as though the craftsmen had set his finger on the balance of nature. Alban may have made this, she thought: he may have turned it in his hands. She imagined him at work at his bench. It seemed the most natural thing in the world for him to be a silversmith, as though those hands – large, rough hands with long fingers, she remembered – had been made to shape metal. Despite the keenness of her disappointment in church, she had found that she could not shake off her good opinion of him. Now, when she thought of him she felt sad; a sadness that lay lightly over everything like a layer of dust.

'I'll have the boy polish them,' said Grisa, narrowing his eyes at her putting her hands all over the salts. 'Let's hope the customer pays this time.'

'What of that?' she said, pointing at a large monteith, plain but immense, on the floor beside Grisa's feet.

'It is to be melted down and refashioned,' said Grisa.

Mary nodded. Pierre had loved the melting down of old pieces to make new; it had reminded him of his own desire for constant reinvention. She remembered him with an old salver to be scrapped, bending it with his bare hands just for the sport of it, stamping on it, laughing. If she was truthful, she had despised him for his ready destruction of something that had been made with such care. Yet she had laughed when he urged her to. How she despised her pliability now.

There were no customers about, so Mary wrapped a cloak around her and, not heeding Grisa's silent disapproval, went out on to the street. She stood for a moment looking up and down, when she saw Mr Digby advancing towards her. The early morning light made his red hair appear even brighter, and his blue eyes fixed on her with a mournful expression.

'Good morning,' he said. 'It looks as though 'twill be a fine day.'

'Let us hope so,' she said. 'Forgive me, but sir, I have meant to thank you for some time. You helped me one day, when they were taking the table on to Bond Street from Dr Taylor's house. And then I saw you at my husband's funeral. Are you watching over me, Mr Digby?'

She smiled, and he smiled in return, though he seemed unaccustomed to it, wearing the expression with some awkwardness.

'I am meant to watch,' he said. 'It is what I am for. If I

have the reward of your good opinion, then there is no need for thanks.'

Mary opened her mouth to express acquiescence, but something told her that Digby did not wish for any more polite exchanges. He seemed comfortable in the silence between them, making no move to go. His hands clasped behind his back, he looked up at the sky as though pleased to feel the sun on his face.

'When I see the street all quiet in the morning light,' he said, 'it looks new to me. I could imagine myself a boy again, as I was when I first saw it. There is an art to looking so, do you not think?'

'It is art,' said Mary. 'It is money, too. This street keeps alive always. I used to think it the scenery where my life is lived, but now I think that Bond Street has its own life, which will continue when we are gone. But forgive me, you must think me a madwoman, venturing out without a hat on my head, talking away.'

'It is a pleasure to hear you speak,' he said.

'But such dark thoughts,' she said, 'I should keep to myself.'

'You do not seem, to me, to be a lady capable of dark thoughts,' he said.

'I am capable of it,' she said. 'I am frightened what I am capable of.'

'Yet if you will excuse me,' he said, 'I can't believe a bad thing would cross your mind, when I see you like this, with the light on your face.'

'There was a time when that was true,' she said. 'When I was young, and all my family was around me. As I remember it, I was surrounded by love, even amidst all the cares of life.'

'And what surrounds you now?' Digby said. He looked absorbed; his words were not formulated with intent, but spoken naturally.

She turned and looked at him. 'Nothing,' she said.

He knew that it would take some time for Mallory to come to the door, but he could not leave it. She struck him as the type of woman who did not like unexpected callers, especially if they were repeat offenders. Sure enough when she opened the door she stood motionless for a moment, looking at him with suspicion.

'How can I help you, Mr Digby?' she said.

'May I come in, Mrs Dunning?' he said.

She opened the door wider. 'Paying calls in the day now as well as the night, are you?' she said. 'We have none of the apple tart left, I'm afraid. It is buttered cabbage or nothing.'

The hallway smelt musty and closed-up to Digby. Mallory showed him into the parlour, and in the daylight it looked even more threadbare than he remembered it. She waved him into a seat, and when a child came hurtling through the door she pushed her, rather less than gently, back in the direction of the hall and kitchen where, he presumed, there would be someone else to look after her.

'I wanted to tell you myself,' he said, 'that a couple of us went to your shop and it was exactly as you say, nothing to worry about at all. There was a similar coffee pot, but it had been there some time, and the maid was mistaken.'

'I know you've been there, I get my report as I said,' she replied. 'But it's good of you to come and tell me that. It makes me sick to think that someone would slander me in that way, when they know it would mean the noose for such a crime.' She moved as though she might stand up, and see him out.

'And there was one more thing,' he said. 'The night Pierre Renard died, did you speak to him?'

She had backbone, he had to give her that; she sat completely still. There were no hysterics or fainting away, only her dark eyes, fixed on his face. 'Now who would have told you that?' she said.

'I've heard it from the lips of more than one person,' Digby lied. 'The thing is, Mrs Dunning, I don't feel like speaking with anyone about it. And I won't, if you tell me what you had to say to him.'

'Is there some other payment that you want?' she said. He saw the suspicion in her eyes. 'We may as well skip to that, if there is. I know what people think of me,' she said. 'Living alone as I do, with just the children.'

'I have just seen your sister, Mrs Renard,' he said. 'I would never think of either of you with anything less than respect.'

'My sister lives in a different world to me, as well you know. Well, I do not have the kind of life that she has, but she has paid dearly for it. What I am trying to say is, I don't like men coming here and demanding things of me.' Her voice was louder, resonating with firmness, almost aggression.

'Now, now,' said Digby. 'I know what you're driving at

and I'm not demanding anything. I just want to know what you had to say to him. I'm sure a charming creature such as yourself wouldn't have been involved in anything untoward. Though I am doubly sure there are men who would do anything for you, if you asked them. Men like Jesse Chamac, for example.'

Just beyond the window a disagreement had erupted and a man was shouting, but Mallory neither looked out nor flinched. She sat as though listening for her children, a distant background noise of small voices. Eventually, satisfied, she leaned forwards towards Digby.

'I can fight my own battles,' she said, in an undertone. 'If you must know, I did speak to Renard that evening. I went to ask him to give my son an apprenticeship. You see how I live, and I was just about done with having nothing from him but insults. It was understood by my parents that through marriage, Renard would be a help to us all; that my eldest boy, at least, could count on an apprenticeship from him. My parents may be in heaven now but I meant that man to honour the promise he made them. I went to call at Bond Street, but I met him before I got to his house, at the corner of Old Bond Street and Piccadilly. He had been drinking, and was in a hurry to get somewhere. But I wouldn't let him move on until I had an answer from him. It was my right.' Her eyes were bright with anger.

'What did he say to you?' said Digby.

Mallory gave a sharp exhalation; the anger seemed to move through her posture, her breath. 'That we were not his family,' she said. 'That he had suffered us long enough. That his home would not be a sanctuary for . . .' She took a breath. 'Idiot children.' It was then that her hard expression crumbled, and she put her hands to her face. After a minute's curiosity Digby realized that she was not weeping, but simply hiding herself for a moment so that she could regain her composure.

'He was referring to my brother, Eli,' she said, folding her hands in her lap again. 'He was infirm, and Pierre had him sent away. What kind of man, I ask you, having done that, would say such a thing? Only a wretch, who has no knowledge of what love is. Renard could speak of kinship and affection but it was an aping of something he had learned; the sound of it, and nothing more. He took Mary from us, and drained the life from her as surely as if he had opened her veins. And yet he lived, and laughed, as though the harm he did to others was a tonic to him. That night, I gave him the reply I had always longed to give: I said that my only prayer was that Mary would forgive us for chaining her to him. That I would curse him every day of his life.'

'How did he take that?' said Digby.

'I am sure it angered him. But he laughed, for he knew how to wound me, and like a malicious child he could not help but press on the point. He said that Eli should have been drowned at birth; that he would have done it, had he been there. That he would have,' she paused, 'managed things properly.'

She looked up at Digby, and the anger pouring from her eyes made him sit back a little. 'I struck him,' she said. 'He lit such a fury in me. I could not help it; I did not think; I was half-blind with anger. I only struck out. But I did not

SOPHIA TOBIN

harm him, I swear it. He cursed me, and raised his hand to me, but he did not hit me. He only set off wherever he was going, and at quite a pace. I'm glad I struck him, I tell you that. But I was not responsible for his death.'

Another small girl appeared in the doorway, her face framed by tangled pale curls, and Digby smiled at her wordless solemnity. 'Go back to the kitchen,' said Mallory. 'I'll be there directly.' She rose, and closed the door.

'Thank you for speaking freely,' said Digby. 'I keep my word, I will not speak to anyone of what you said.'

'I thank you for it,' said Mallory, her face turned to the door. 'I do not wish to hear that man's name again, not if I live until I'm a hundred.'

'I'll wish you a good day, Mrs Dunning,' said Digby.

As he turned out of Castle Street and set off for home, Digby no longer noticed the bright morning. He was deeply troubled. Maynard was bound to come after him soon, sniffing for more information, and he was damned if he knew what he was going to say. He had hoped for some titbits to feed the man, something to keep him satisfied. But he did not wish to drag Mallory and Mary into it all. He knew how precious the memory of love was; and if one of them had killed for it, his instinct was to protect them.

After the door had closed behind Digby, Mallory stood for a moment, leaning against the door in the suffocating darkness of the hallway. She did not know if she could move; if, suddenly, her legs might give way. I must keep on breathing, she thought, and tried to fix herself on the rhythm of it: in, out, in, out. If I keep on breathing, if I wait

252

through the moments, things will become calm again. I can carry on with my life.

'Mama?'

She moved her head slowly, glanced over her shoulder at her daughter, at the child's eyes – her own – and her tangled curls.

'Get your sister to brush your hair,' she said, her voice catching on the first word. The girl looked at her with her mother's sagacity, knowing that something was wrong.

It was not the first time Mallory had been spurred on by her children. She believed that she owed them nothing, not even if she thought about it with a quiet mind; but they were the reason she opened her eyes, some days. She pitched herself forwards. 'Come on,' she said, her fingers grazing the child's hair. Reassured, the little girl followed her, down the hall and into the noisy kitchen.

'Lis, brush your sister's hair,' said Mallory, and then she pushed through the smell of vegetables, the noise of her children's voices, walking through the darkness until she was out in the open air, if you could call the small courtyard that. She looked up, at the fragment of blue sky that was visible, the clouds moving quickly, twining and untwining themselves, until everything seemed to be moving too fast.

Then she knelt, and vomited.

CHAPTER TWENTY-TWO

1st September, 1792
I have, this day, written a codicil to my will, honouring the con-
nection I have with Sarah, through Benjamin. We must hold on
to the blessed connections we have in life, even if they are over in
the form we wished them to take.

Joanna had a half-day off. Always cherished, this week it was vital, for she felt the walls of the house closing in on her. She had written to the master, telling him what she knew of Harriet's love for Renard, and the letter lay folded in her locking box, haunting her.

It was her custom always to dream some tale of what she would do: she would walk further than before and see places she had not imagined. Maybe she would even reach green fields, where the air was not grey with smoke and people did not walk too close to you. They were always too close. Once she and Stephen had dreamed of opening a tavern far from London, and sometimes she thought if she walked far enough she would find the life she had been supposed to live, a cheerful tavern and him with their daughter, waiting for her.

As she checked her appearance in the fragment of looking glass from her locking box, she thought: it is gone. That elusive quality that made men look at you as you passed them in the street. There is not even the suggestion of it left; it stole away in the night.

Once outside, she followed her usual path, her feet carrying her by habit. She went to St James's Park, where the river was near freezing over. One or two people had lit fires on the banks, and she could smell chestnuts being roasted. She bought a handful, and ate them greedily, feeling the sweet, soft richness of each burst in her mouth. The young boy that had sold them to her watched her with impassive eyes. He is like me, she thought, always watching. 'If the Thames freezes solid,' she said to him, 'there will be a Frost Fair. They will roast an ox on the ice, just as they did in seventy-six.'

'I wasn't born then, missus,' he said.

'No,' she said. 'I don't suppose you were.'

She walked along beside the water, and watched a swan trapped by a thin tissue of encroaching ice. It swam forwards and nudged the edge with its body, as though it could swim a path through it. She stayed a moment to watch, and felt some of the tension in her muscles release.

In 1788 she had walked alone on the frozen Thames.

Stephen was dead, but she had conjured him so strongly in her mind it was as if he was beside her. For that afternoon she had taken his name, and she still had the ticket, set in one of the presses that sold souvenirs: printed for Mrs Joanna Best on the ice, 1788. She had walked past the crowds and games, not wanting the day to end, the snow making the city beautiful, and before her, a river of light. Joanna had been unafraid of the light then, or of whether men looked at her as she passed. It had felt as though she and the spectral Stephen could walk along the ice forever, her hand encompassed by his. She would find a place along the river where the ice was broken, and slip into its blue darkness, and there would be no more pain.

But she had stopped. Something had beckoned her back from death in the freezing river, some niggling invitation within her to live.

Now, she shook off all thoughts of the past and retraced her steps. When she reached home the other servants were about to eat their dinner, but Joanna felt no need for food. Light-headed, she was filled with a humming excitement: she didn't know if it was terror or delight, but it quenched everything else, leaving no room for thinking about normal concerns, and dissolving her customary hunger. The taste of the chestnuts was still in her mouth.

A small evening fire, thanks to Mr Chichester's orders, was built in the grate in her room. She took out the letter she had written to the master from her locking box, tore it, and surrendered the fragments to the flames, watching until they had burnt into ashes before she went back downstairs.

The light was nearly gone, and the staircase hall was still

and empty. In the cold air, and the half-light of sunset, Joanna felt the vibration of a kind of tension that was echoed in her own state. She suddenly felt very tired, the kind of deathly tiredness a street walker might feel at the end of a night that was dangerous to be surrendered to. She walked down the stairs. The space was hers alone: the black and white chequered tiles, the churchlike silence, the complex gilt ornament of the walls and ceiling which she did not understand. She wondered if it could be read, like some secret language.

She lay down on the floor. In the centre of the staircase hall, stretching out on the black and white tiled surface. The floor was cold and hard the length of her body, and her hair in its plain style pressed into the back of her head, barely cushioning her skull. She felt a lightening of her spirit; an unprecedented lack of fear. She didn't care if she was found. She stared up at the coffered dome of the ceiling, so far away in the failing light, decorated with squares of gilded plasterwork. The thought of Mr Chichester was her talisman: for wasn't she protected from on high by him, like one of the gods that flourished on the ceiling of the Salon? She had suffered much, and now she would be rewarded. Her uncertainty dissolved; she would survive, and her future would unfold in wonderful ways. Mr Chichester seemed like Jupiter himself: giver of favours and blessings, and she was bathed in his golden light.

She felt she could have lain there forever, until the dome crumbled and the house was open to the sky, and vines twined their way around the lyre-shaped ironwork on the balustrade, green around black, twines around twines.

Green luscious fronds grew up before her eyes, until she could not be sure if she was dreaming or awake.

Then she heard voices coming from the depths of the house. She sat up, got to her feet, and brushed her skirt off. With irritation she realized she had been listening, with heightened senses, all the time.

Digby was rather enjoying his evening in a new tavern; its liveliness was easing his disquiet. The Running Footman was so full that he was forced to stand. When he was also asked to pay for his drink he felt aggrieved, but decided that nothing would put him off his intended purpose. The place was full of servants, all bright-eyed and vigorous, laughing and gossiping as though they'd never done a day's work in their lives. Well, thought Digby, they are London servants. Everyone knew that London servants were sly and lazy and wanted to do less work for more money. And who could blame them. Still, their careless attitude to work and loyalty would be certain to help him.

Digby didn't care when people stared at him. He'd had little sleep, and Watkin had told him he looked hollow-eyed. His cough didn't seem so bad even though he had spent too long in the cold today, walking around the streets as though they offered the solution to his conundrum. The warmth of the tavern was welcome and long overdue.

He looked around hopefully, watchfully, standing tall, his hat off. He'd put the word out. He guessed it wouldn't take long. He saw people glance in his direction, some-times still talking, sometimes just looking. After a few minutes a man approached him. He was a tall young man with broad shoulders, a wide face and a too-wide smile. Digby instantly mistrusted him.

'I hear you've been asking questions about Pierre Renard,' the man said.

Digby smiled and signalled to the landlord for another drink.

CHAPTER TWENTY-THREE

5th September, 1792

Old man Maynard came to the shop today. He is all bustle and bluster. At the mention of the snuffbox, I put my hand in the air, to stop him from speaking, and turned my face away. It gave me great pleasure to tell him that, as his son has reneged on the terms of our other agreement, I am raising the percentage of interest to be charged. I thought he might be tipped into apoplexy, so purple he turned. It is a shame. For a long time, I hoped to cultivate him; a man does not do well to have too many enemies. But it soon became clear to me that he would never accept me, no matter my amiability or success in business. The man is old-fashioned; he cares only for the blood, and not for anyone who has risen, for he could never have done it himself. Anyhow, I told him of the new terms, gave him my word as a gentleman, and he said: 'You, sir, are not a gentleman. You are as far from a gentleman as can be.' There will be a day in the future when he will never dare to utter that. I can see it and feel it: one day, men will bow to me as their superior. I will have an estate in the country, as Thomas Havering has. And I will be the father of many children. My line will flourish.

As he regarded a pair of weighty silver bread baskets, it was with some surprise that Alban realized the smile that was flickering shyly across Grisa's face was meant for him. He was unprepared for it; lost in his own thoughts, it seemed remarkable that Renard's cynical manager was pleased to see him. Alban noticed that Grisa was less flamboyant than before; his French accent was even moderated a little, as though without Renard's influence the man was gradually becoming Anglicized. Alban handed over two design sheets with commissions drawn on them.

'More excellent work,' said Grisa. 'The mistress was most pleased with the last set of salts.'

Was she now, thought Alban. 'As long as the customer was satisfied,' he said. He had liked the designs, though it seemed strange to him that in the midst of lowness and lack of interest he could produce his best work, elegant wares with fine classical details, not overladen, but a perfect balance.

'It feels as though things are going to the devil, some days,' said Grisa, in a confiding tone. 'I was checking the inventory and a pair of candlesticks is gone – gone!' He gestured dramatically in the air. 'They were old-fashioned things, the old French style, with shells and flowers, but heavy enough – they could have been melted down and made a dozen à la mode pieces, but can I find them?

With the grief of monsieur's death, I cannot even think when I last saw them.'

'Perhaps they will turn up,' said Alban.

He looked around the Renard showroom. The shop still had an air of elegance, though he thought the stock was a little more thinly displayed, and the frisson of hard efficiency which he assumed had been Renard's had been eroded since his death. The place smelt of beeswax, and there was a faintly sulphurous odour emanating from the back room. 'Are you boiling silver back there?' said Alban.

Grisa nodded, and gave a little groan. 'It was black,' he said. 'And I hardly trust the boy to do it well. My nerves. What with the news from France, I wonder why I carry on. What is it all for? There will be revolution here soon enough, and I'm sure the ruffians will find a way to steal our plate and jewels first.' He shook his head, his eyes widening as they focused on something beyond the window.

Alban looked over his shoulder to see that a carriage had drawn up outside the shop. It was a fine equipage, painted a glossy brown, with a cypher on it in gold. As a man climbed down and approached the door Alban tried as best he could to be unobtrusive, stepping back against the wall. The door opened abruptly, the bell juddering as it was slammed shut.

The young man that entered was clearly a valued customer, though he was dressed in a greatcoat splashed with mud, and to Alban he looked little more than a child dressed in a man's clothes. He had a relaxed demeanour, and as he entered the shop he looked around, his eyes shining, keen and sharp, as though he wished to create the impression of taking everything in. Grisa bowed so low Alban wondered whether his nose might touch his knee.

'Mr Cheechester,' he said, the French accent returning with a vengeance.

The young man smiled as though accepting his customary admiration. 'Good day,' he said. He leaned on the glazed counter, his eyes running over the jewels and trinkets there. It took him only a minute. 'I would like that,' he said, his finger resting above a necklace. 'Will you wrap it? Add it to my bill.'

'Of course, sir,' said Grisa, opening the counter with a flourish. 'This is a new piece; would you care for a fitted box to be made?'

'No, no,' said Chichester. 'It is merely a trifle. Wrap it in whatever you have, but do it neatly.' Grisa scurried into the back room and returned in a moment with a piece of waxed paper. He laid the necklace down and began to wrap it gently.

'These are very fine,' said Mr Chichester, casually picking up one of the bread baskets that Alban had just delivered from the counter and feeling its weight. 'Something like this would suit me very well. I have been thinking of a large commission for some time. Silver for the dining table.'

Alban saw disquiet cross Grisa's face; he swallowed and stammered a little. 'That has just been delivered for another gentleman,' he said. 'But the man that made it is here. May I present Mr Steele?'

'Good day to you,' said Chichester. He looked surprised to see another person there, though Alban warranted he must have noticed him before. As he looked at Alban a smile flitted over his frosty countenance. 'The style of these seems perfect to me,' he said. 'Would you trouble yourself to call upon me in a day or so?'

'Of course,' said Grisa, before Alban could answer. 'We would be delighted.'

'Splendid,' said Chichester, pocketing the wrapped necklace. 'I am just returned to London from the country. I would be most pleased to see you on Tuesday, Mr Steele. This gentleman will direct you.' With a flourish, he left the shop, his greatcoat swirling around him in such a flurry that Alban wondered whether it might get shut in the door. Grisa closed the door carefully behind him and watched him leap up into his carriage.

'Why did you say that?' said Alban, as Grisa hung his head exaggeratedly. 'I am an outworker, that is all.' His impulse was to shout at the man, for he had no patience these last few days, but he kept his tone controlled, bearing his cousins' livelihood in mind.

'You do not say *non* to a man such as him,' said Grisa, in a wheedling tone. 'Besides, he liked you, I could see it at once, and that is worth more in our trade than anything else. I managed it well enough in the past but since Mr Renard left us I have suffered a ... *crise*. I expected madam to marry another silversmith quick enough, as any practical woman would, but she has not. There is too much work for me, and neither I nor,' he lowered his voice, 'that young fool monsieur left everything to has any real eye for design. I can recognize it though, Mr Steele, and you have it. I would ask for your assistance; it has been in my mind these past few days. The trustees will listen to me. You, and your cousin, will benefit from it.'

'I must think on it,' said Alban. He wasn't entirely sure what Grisa was driving at; he only wanted to be out of the place. 'In the meantime, I wish you good day.' He left before Grisa could babble further, ignoring whatever the man was saying as he went out.

Grisa's letter reached Foster Lane before Alban did. Alban wondered who Grisa had sent; some sprightly boy called up from the street and given a shining coin. It was lying on the table when he reached home; he broke the seal and frowned at the contents.

'What is it?' said Jesse, who was resting by the fire.

'It's that manager of Renard's,' said Alban. 'He wishes me to assist him with the business until some other partner can be found. He promises us handsome compensation for it.' He showed the letter to Jesse.

'Holy Jesus,' said Jesse, reading the amount. 'I knew he liked you. A strange one, that Grisa. I've often wondered what lies beneath all of his posturing.'

'He says he can authorize it with Taylor, though I think he should not be making offers without his knowledge. I do not wish to be dragged into whatever knot these people are tying themselves into,' said Alban. They had heard gossip at the Assay Office: all was not well in the Renard establishment.

'The widow?' said Jesse, seemingly unwilling to speak Mary's name. Alban shook his head impatiently, as though she meant nothing.

'Then you should do it,' said Jesse, sounding tired. 'If not for yourself, then us. When you leave us it will give us something to live on.'

He didn't mean it, Alban persuaded himself, but the words stuck in him: another small dagger. He would be glad to be away from it all, one day soon.

It was an excitable Grisa who arranged the meeting with Taylor. The doctor had taken to calling every day, he said. So it was that Alban found himself, looking at the shelves of stock in the Renard shop without enthusiasm, waiting for Taylor to call upon them. He was a patient man; but being at the beck and call of Dr Taylor disturbed him. Many things disturbed him about the situation.

'Is your mistress here?' he asked. He found it hard to concentrate with the knowledge that Mary was upstairs. It meant that every sound, every movement from above increased the tension in him.

'*Non*,' said Grisa. 'Miss Avery has taken her out.'

The shop door opened, and Taylor came in, removing his hat as he did so. He was short of breath. He made a study of avoiding Alban's direct gaze for a moment as Grisa babbled introductions, before bowing slightly. 'Have you worked silver all your life, Mr Steele?' he said, as he did so.

'Near enough,' said Alban, taken aback by the question. Grisa looked between the two of them, his face full of anxious confusion.

'Well,' said the doctor, as though ruminating on something. 'Well.'

'Dr Taylor, with respect,' said Grisa. 'We need Mr Steele here. He is a fine silversmith and a busy man.'

'I am not questioning his ability as a silversmith – believe me, Mr Steele, I am not – but this is a question of extreme delicacy and this decision has been rushed upon me. The other trustees are all agreeable to the idea, but I am closer to it than they. I feel a great sense of responsibility; which is why I pause. Do not be offended by it, I beg you.'

'I am not offended,' said Alban. 'But do you need me, or no?'

'If Mr Grisa says so,' said Taylor. 'There must be someone here to help. And with the boy, Benjamin – he has been turned over to Mrs Renard for now. I had hoped to find someone – to resolve the situation.'

'I am sure you will not need me for long,' said Alban. 'You may ask at Goldsmiths' Hall for my character. Has anyone come forwards to suggest a partnership?'

'Not at all,' said Taylor. 'Some damned fool has been putting word around that the place is cursed. Superstition: in this day and age. When people are rioting on the streets and the Tree of Liberty is erected on the green at Stockwell, you would think they have more real fears to think on.'

'Surely it is then that they turn to the imaginary ones,' said Alban.

'You may be right,' said Taylor. 'I am glad for your help, Mr Steele.' He still looked troubled, and cast a dark look at Grisa as he turned away. 'God save the King.' He cast the words behind him as he yanked open the door.

'God save the King,' said Alban.

CHAPTER TWENTY-FOUR

7th September, 1792

I received a note from Mrs Chichester today. She has decided that she wishes for the designs to be changed once again. It did me good to receive her note, and to think of her pretty face. It is strange how, to think of such an agreeable thing seems like a change of season to me. I have always felt things deeply, and this small degree of warmth did well for me. I was in good temper with Dr Taylor this evening; he came and we spoke of the newspapers, and amused each other with our jokes. I am glad of his company, for I already feel the chill of autumn in the air, and when I think of the long evenings that are to come, I would not wish always to be either out of doors, or alone with my wife.

Joanna lay fully dressed on her bed. They had sent one of the maids to hammer on the door, but Joanna only stared at the ceiling, and did not make a sound.

Mr Chichester had returned.

A gift from him lay on the bed next to her: a garnet neck-lace wrapped in waxen paper. The stones did not sparkle, but they had a vividness she liked: the viscous red of the good wine she had drunk on that evening in his library. Her hand found the necklace without her turning, and she picked it up and suspended it from her hand, moving it this way and that. What did such a gift mean? She allowed herself to think that desolate word, that word she had rejected for so long. Perhaps.

She was glad she had not sent the letter to him. Her writ-ing of it now seemed distant, like a dream, though it still troubled her. There was something terrible about a betrayal written down. Spoken, it was insubstantial, the words break-ing and dissolving in the air like bubbles. She had decided that she would speak to him about Harriet's infidelity.

She tried hard to picture him, but when she thought of his face it always disassembled, only leaving an impres-sion: of warmth beneath a crust of coldness, a warmth that she was determined to draw out.

She waited for the maid to go back downstairs before she got up and unlocked the door.

In the kitchen, Mrs Holland was eating a crust of bread spread thick with golden butter. A smear of it glistened on her upper lip. 'Where have you been?' she said. 'Madam was asking for you. I've sent Jane up with a tray, but she'll be whining all day about it.'

'I'll go up to her in a moment,' said Joanna. As she spoke Jane descended, her jerking steps sending the breakfast things clattering on the tray.

'She's calling for you,' she said, sullen. 'She said you were supposed to sleep in her room last night.'

'It was not practicable,' said Joanna. 'Not that I have to justify myself to you: no, nor anyone else, either.'

She turned and walked away. She could almost hear the glance that passed between Mrs Holland and the maid.

As she crossed the staircase hall the door of the library opened and Mr Chichester came out. 'Well met, Miss Dunning,' he said. She smiled, hoping that the heat she felt in her face wasn't conveying itself as a blush. She curtseyed.

'Will you come in here for a moment?' he said. Joanna saw the glances of Will and Oliver. As the library door closed behind her she longed to take her handkerchief and stuff it in the keyhole to prevent their spying eyes. Instead, she moved down to one end of the room, and vowed to keep her voice as low and soft as she could. Her movement seemed to intrigue Chichester and he followed her, smiling.'How was your time away, sir?' she said.

'Interesting,' he said. 'I paid a brief visit to my father and family. Do not tell Mrs Chichester, if you please; she will only complain. How have things been here?'

He watched her with a steady, frank gaze. It was so open, so concentrated, that she felt the seduction of it. It was a strange thing that had not happened in years; even her body reacted.

'They have been fairly quiet, sir,' she said. 'I am sure you had much more amusement and stimulation on your travels.'

'I doubt that,' he said. 'My parents are so shaken about

the events in France. All around it seems the old world is dissolving. Why, my father's steward has a daughter who is as fine a miss as you could ever wish for. She speaks French and plays the spinet better than my wife does. Should you wish to go up in the world, Joanna? To transcend where God or whoever has placed you?'

He said it archly, evidently enjoying the words. She could hardly breathe, under his gaze. She would have to take a next step, but she had no idea what it should be. She could not trust herself to weigh and balance the words quick enough; she was afraid.

'I know my place, sir,' she said. 'I have never questioned it.'

It was the best kind of lie: so essential that she said it with absolute conviction, a conviction that almost made it true.

'Well,' he said, nodding and smiling, holding her gaze. She was warm in a way that she could not remember feeling for years. In that moment she did not even think of betraying Harriet. She only wanted to stay beneath his gaze. To be seen.

'I saw my wife just now,' he said.

'You did?' she said, the words breaking from her before she had a moment to stop them.

'For a moment only,' he said. 'She looks well. You have done a marvellous job of patching her up. I have to go now. But I wish to speak to you later, perhaps this evening? You may slip out to me when I come in; I will light my own way.'

'Sir,' she said, curtseying, thinking how fine he looked as he opened the door and strode across the staircase hall.

Her happiness made Joanna merciful that day. She lived within a kind of dream world, smiling sweetly at every reprimand, and carrying out every want of Harriet's without even internal criticism.

She was still laced in, but her arms were bare, when she heard the master enter the house that night. When she checked her reflection in the fragment of looking glass the garnet necklace was vivid as blood against her white skin. She had brushed out her dark hair carefully by the light of the extra candles he had allowed her. The effect was pleasing; in the soft light, she could almost imagine that she was young again.

Without stopping to pull a wrap around her shoulders, she walked barefoot down the back stairs, carrying one of the new candles in a silver chamberstick she had taken from Harriet's dressing table. The stone stairs were cold under her feet and she trembled against her will, feeling the rush of cold from the winter night, a door opened somewhere in the house. She came out on the landing just as he approached his room, one hand brushing against the wall as he walked, a little unsteady. He was alone, as he had promised. But as she came out of the shadows he flinched, as though some reverie had been interrupted.

'Joanna,' he said.

'Sir,' she said.

'It is a cold night,' he said. 'You must be freezing.'

Her heart beat so hard she could hear it in her ears. She knew she must take this moment, while she had the courage. It did not feel right, as she thought it would; but she had only this moment, and as she had always chosen to live, she knew she must take it. She walked towards him, and put her hand on his face.

He started back. 'What are you doing?' he said.

'It is your right, sir,' she said, and drew his face towards her.

The next thing she knew she was stumbling away, her left cheek hot with pain. She fell into the banister, banging her back. The chamberstick fell to the floor, metal on stone, a dull ding. The light went out. Only after a moment or two did she realize he had slapped her, hard and quickly, with a flick of the wrist. A practised hand, she thought. She looked at him, unaware that her mask had fallen away, that pain shone in her eyes.

He was holding his candle up, between them. 'Forgive me,' he said. His voice was higher than usual, with an unpleasant note of justification. 'But you are presumptuous, Joanna.'

She snatched up the silver chamberstick, and before she could turn away he had picked up the candle stump from the floor and relit it. Her hand shaking, she allowed him to put it back into the silver nozzle. 'We will not speak of this again,' he said. But she had already turned away and was hurrying towards the door to the back stairs. Below her she saw a faint glow of light. Oliver was still up, and her mind registered that he must have seen her. Humiliation tightened her throat.

'Miss Dunning,' his sing-song voice rang out. 'Oh, Miss Dunning.' It was a whisper, but it carried through the great space, resonances overlapping each other as he padded up the stairs towards her. She heard the bang of the master's door behind her as Oliver reached her, blocking her way to the back stairs.

'They took you on because you are plain. It was your main advantage over all the others; never mind your French or your proficiency.' His voice changed slightly, its tone and phrasing a bass, but near-perfect imitation of Harriet's mother. 'Worry not, my dear, you will not suffer by comparison: the one I have chosen will make Chichester love you a hundredfold more.' He brought the candelabrum closer. 'You must learn your place, Miss Dunning.'

She pushed him hard, and he staggered back. She didn't stay to see him right himself; she hoped that his livery would catch on fire and burn him into ashes. She ran as fast as she could back to her room, sheltering the candle flame with her hand.

Ten minutes later she went down to the basement and woke the housekeeper. 'You must let me out,' she said. 'Doctor for the mistress.' Mrs Holland opened her mouth to say she would send one of the boys, but thought better of it. There was something steely in Joanna's glance tonight. She looked pale, her hair drawn back tightly against her face, wrapped in her cloak.

'Is she properly sick?' she said. 'Is it the babe?' Joanna shook her head. 'It's more a fancy than anything. I'll be no time. No need to bother anyone; it would make things worse.'

She ran out on to Hays Mews, hitting the coldness of the

night. The moon was bright and nearly full. The sight of a twine of straw on the cobbled street reminded her of Stephen. She bent double and sobbed, taking gasps of cold air, so cold it hurt her lungs. One stableman looked over his door, and decided to ignore her. One troubled woman wouldn't disturb the horses.

The familiar surroundings revolted her. Behind her the house towered, like a mountain, its dark mass like the shadow of death on her back. She began to run, clutching her cloak to her in the cold.

She thought of the river. It was too warm to be frozen. If she went to it, if she set her foot upon it, would Stephen be waiting? Knowing her luck, if she tried to drown herself she would be dragged out by some well-meaning member of the Humane Society and revived to continue in misery. She gave a little choke of a laugh at the thought. Tears filled her eyes, tears long unshed, and as they trickled on to her face, more came, tears upon tears, blurring her vision. But she kept running. She didn't care if she fell.

She ran into the man at full speed. It was like hitting a brick wall; if she shocked him he did not show it. He did not move an inch, and wiry arms closed around her, like a cage. She fought. But she knew as she lashed out she could not fight his superior strength. So she stopped almost as soon as she had begun, hopeless, thinking, her mind whirring and ticking.

The man, and the arms, stayed still. She let him take her weight, suddenly limp and exhausted. 'Easy there,' said the man's voice. 'Easy.' She thought of a groom calming a horse, and supposed he was one.

Joanna summoned the courage and looked up in the moonlight. She saw a familiar face. 'I know you,' she said.

The man smiled. 'Indeed you do, miss,' he said. 'I'm one of the night-watchmen.'

'What are you doing, hanging around here?' she said, her voice sharp.

He laughed. 'Watching,' he said. 'There's a murderer still walks these streets, you know. I let Watkin, my partner, do a turn of the square alone. He doesn't like it, but I like to keep an eye on this house special these days, make sure you're all safe. I was just walking back to join him when you came barrelling along there.'

His arms were still around her, the warmth becoming familiar. 'You can let go of me,' she said.

'Seems to me you don't want to be let go of,' he said. 'Not really.'

She didn't argue. It was so long since she had felt the closeness and the physical touch of another human being, she had forgotten what it was like. Relief surged through her. She would not have chosen this companion, but the warmth was already seeping into her blood. Although her tears had stopped, she could have wept again, but with something like happiness. Her mouth contorted into a bud as she tried to stop the sobs.

'Hush now,' the man said, as you would to a child, not taking his arms away in case she ran. 'Hush.' And he leaned forwards, and brushed her face with his own, as if to soak up the tears on her face.

'Digby!' The shout came from the square, and came again, getting nearer.

'My partner,' said Digby.

'Digby – have you got a wench in some alleyway?' The voice was nearly upon them. Finally, the man let her go.

'I'll be out here tomorrow, at nine, miss, if you want some comfort,' he said. Joanna said nothing. She stumbled over her own feet as she backed away. She shook her head. 'And the next night,' he said. Then he turned and shouted. 'Here! I thought I saw something, I'll be out directly.'

'I bet you did, you old bastard,' came the reply. 'Hurry on, will you?'

'I'll see you, miss,' he said.

'How dare you take such liberties,' said Joanna, but her voice sounded uncertain.

Digby shrugged. 'I reckon you'll come again, though,' he said. He turned away and began to walk quickly, without looking back. At the end of the mews before he moved out of sight she saw him bent double, coughing, a melancholy silhouette in the winter night.

CHAPTER TWENTY-FIVE

10th September, 1792

I came home from visiting a customer to find Grisa all aflutter, waving his handkerchief in the air like a gentle lady having a fainting fit, yet I was less amused when I saw that half the presses were unlocked, and he said a group of young gentlemen had come in, and asked to see this and that, and that Benjamin had been no use in assisting him. They told Grisa that they knew I lent money, and with what security, and how much was on the premises, and all in all he got them out. Nothing seems to have been taken – for I have a quick eye for the displays – but I suspect young Maynard is behind it, or some other scoundrel I have lent to.

At a quarter to eleven on a Monday morning Mary stood at the window and watched Alban Steele approach her home. He walked slowly, looking about him. The sight of him both galvanized and infuriated her. She turned sharply away.

'I would like to go from here,' she said to her cousin. 'I swear it, Avery, if my aunt would take us I would leave London with you this very night.'

Avery took Mary's place at the window. 'Why is he coming?' she said. 'It surely does not serve him in any way.'

Mary glanced at her cousin, and could not discern whether there was knowledge in her eyes. She had not confided the story of Alban's proposal to her, but she had the sense that Avery knew many things without being told.

'I do not know,' she said. 'There are so many cracks appearing in the firm; perhaps they wish to pin us all together again with some new fixture.'

Taylor had told Mary the news; Grisa had sought Alban's help and he had given it. A room had been put at his disposal for the days when he could not return to the City. It was business, she thought, all business: I must say that word to myself, until it becomes true.

Over the last few weeks she had learned to stare hard at Benjamin whenever she saw him: to meet his gaze without a flicker of weakness. But the effort of it exhausted her, as did Grisa's questions. He had been speaking to a man in a tavern who had insisted that Pierre was murdered for financial gain, and probably by one of his intimates. She had to tell Grisa again and again: Benjamin was here the night Pierre died; he could hardly have slipped out to Berkeley Square and slit his throat. And Pierre had trained her in self-doubt all those years, so now, although she had said it many times, she began to question her own judgement.

'It is best that you do not associate yourself with Mr Steele,' Taylor had said. 'For his assistance in the interim, we are of course in his debt. But he is merely a working silversmith; he is not the kind of man Pierre was, and he is not your social equal.'

She knew the doctor was discomfited by Grisa's determination to bring Alban on board. The shop manager had spoken to the other trustees, and they too had put pressure on Taylor. She had not spoken of Alban's proposal; she knew Taylor would disapprove, would begin piling objection upon objection until there was an insuperable barrier to him even entering the building. For now, it would remain her secret. The doctor's concern was touching, and his protectiveness was due to kindness, but it had begun to grate.

She left her parlour door open, so Alban's voice drifted up to her as Grisa answered the door. She heard its low, soft tone, and felt as though the sound was dredging her heart. Their last encounter at St James's might have tarnished her memory of him. But when his name was spoken her heart jumped at it, just as it had jumped when she had seen him on Bond Street a few days after her husband's death.

She left Avery sewing, and went to the top of the stairs to look down at Grisa and Alban, exchanging civilities in the doorway. At the sound of her footsteps they looked up at her, and Alban bowed. His expression was solemn, but she could see no disquiet in his eyes, no disturbance. He looked tired, she thought, and he had not shaved; his greatcoat was unbuttoned and it lay in haphazard folds.

'Mr Steele,' she said.

'Mrs Renard,' he said.

In the light from the shop window she noticed the colour of his eyes, and saw every contour of his face more clearly. When she heard Benjamin's heavy step, she turned away and went back to her parlour, a tight knot of tension in her stomach.

Half an hour later Avery had gone to the kitchen to speak to Ellen, when Alban tapped on the parlour door. He stood, hesitant, on the threshold. Though his reticence was a sign of respect, she saw that his expression had hardened since they had last spoken.

'Forgive me for interrupting you,' he said.

'You are not interrupting me,' she said. 'Please do come and sit down.'

He shook his head. 'I only need a moment of your time,' he said. The formality of his tone was so pronounced that she wondered whether Benjamin had already poisoned his mind against her. If he had, it was quick work.

'I have not come here to harass you,' he said. 'From your face I saw that perhaps my presence here is disagreeable to you.'

'Not at all,' she said, wondering how she could have been so misinterpreted.

'I came to say,' he said, 'if you do not wish me to be here, I will go. Please understand, what passed between us is over, and I wish to forget it. I was encouraged to speak and it was a lapse in my judgement. I misremembered the past and ... well, it is over now. I offer you my respect, and fellowship.'

'I do not wish for you to go,' she said, and meant it. But the emotion she sought to put into her words seemed not to register with him. She continued, falteringly. 'We are indebted to you for coming here, when others turn away from us. I am grateful to you, believe that.'

His expression did not show any satisfaction at her words. He took his leave and went down the stairs, rather more quickly than he had come up them.

Her vanity whispered to her: perhaps her refusal had wounded him. She admitted the thought only for a moment. Kept to her parlour, restricted in every way, she knew her mind had a way of converting the trivial to the significant. It was safer to believe he did not see her as someone worthy of love, but as an adjunct to his business that he wished to be on pleasant terms with. When people looked at her they did not see her, but her late husband's silver and gold plate. For all her memories, she knew she should remember that this man had spoken of money first. He had, at least, the honesty to do that. It had been a matter of chance that her memories of him had become intertwined with those of her brother.

Many times that day she heard him speaking with Benjamin: at least, she heard the apprentice's toneless voice answering him. As she struggled to discern the words, it reminded her of the night that Pierre had come to speak to her father in the days before their wedding. She wondered if the events of her life would always depend upon listening for the voices of men in another room. She unpicked a piece of sewing, and began it again, thinking with exasperation and frustration that if power was a habit, she had not established it, and she had no clue how to do it now.

She did not doubt that Alban would be able to gain and hold Benjamin's respect in a way she had not. She wondered if they would become friends, and her heart ached at the thought. She had cause to believe that Benjamin went, at night, with the other apprentices to Covent Garden, to see the girls that walked there, dressed in vivid colours with counterfeit jewels pinned on them and their hair feathered and piled high. For a few coins such a woman would take them to a tavern room; Mallory had told her of it, unflinching as always. She wondered if Alban would go with Benjamin one night to find such a woman, and the thought wounded her. It was part of her education, she supposed; she must learn to deaden herself to such wounds. Dressed in her mourning black, she knew she could not compete with such women in their reds and purples, and she told herself she did not want to.

Alban took himself out for an hour or so. He and Grisa had spent most of the afternoon hunting for a pendant that had gone missing. A woman had come asking for it, saying Mr Renard had promised it would be ready for her. It was nowhere to be found, and Grisa wondered how they would tell her, for she had watched them with her steady, mournful eyes as they had gone here and there, checking this place and that.

A drink was welcome. Alban only knew one person in the Red Lion, and it was Digby, hunched over his pint pot with a meditative expression on his face. The man's look when he saw Alban was not promising. 'It's you, then,' he said.

'Mr Digby,' said Alban. He felt worn with the effort of making polite conversation with Mary, Avery and Grisa at dinner, and wondered if he could manage another.

'How's Bond Street, then?'

'Quiet now. Has it always been your patch? My cousin tells me you were once a silversmith.' He tried to be easy and conversational, tried to forget the image of Mary stamping up the stairs after dinner, cloaked in her hideous mourning dress; the repetitive mutterings of Benjamin when Mary's name was mentioned.

'I'm no use to you,' said Digby. 'I'll make that clear to save you the trouble of speaking to me.'

'You mistake me,' said Alban. 'I meant only to be civil.'

'You've entered the Renard establishment,' said Digby. 'I know these things, you see. I keep my eye on things. How is she? The silversmith's wife?'

'She is well enough, I believe,' said Alban.

'So. You are tired of your cousin's house and all his brats crawling about you?'

'Not at all,' said Alban. 'I've lived alone for many years, and children bring life to a house. Now I'm in the quiet I think I'll miss them. I will go back there as much as business allows.'

'Playing your own game, are you, eh?' said Digby. 'Fancy yourself as the next husband of Mrs Renard? Where were you on the night of Mr Renard's death, by the way?'

'I take offence at that,' said Alban, feeling his heart jump with anger. 'And I was on the coach from Chester, if you must know. There are several hundred witnesses in the Charing Cross area.'

'Ach, don't get wild,' said Digby. 'I'm only playing with you.' He knocked back his drink, and called for another one. The landlord pointed at the board meaningfully, but brought him one anyway.

Alban stayed where he was, allowing his annoyance to die down. There was something interesting about Digby's face, unremarkable but with an air of delicacy that drew the eye. 'Do you not have children?' he said, hoping that interest would unlock some of the man's goodwill. But Digby only fixed him with a stare, and Alban noticed his blue eyes, piercing and vivid, the whites reddened. 'No,' he said.

'I'm sorry,' said Alban, remembering why he usually kept his mouth shut and why he disliked the prying words of others.

'Don't be sorry,' said Digby. 'I'd have sooner cut my children's throats than let them live the life I've had. Are you going to bother me with your company for long? I am expecting someone.'

Alban left him alone, and went up to pay the landlord. 'For his too,' he said.

'And welcome,' said the landlord. 'He owes more on tick than all my fine gentlemen put together.'

CHAPTER TWENTY-SIX

11th September, 1792
I visited the Chichesters today, on the excuse of delivering more
patterns, and was ushered into Mrs Chichester's chamber. When
I handed the papers to her, I touched her hand. An incidental
touch, but I still feel it, for it woke my heart in my breast. Not all
things result from reason.

Joanna had not slept. In the fragment of looking glass her
eyes were puffy, with purplish hollows beneath them. She
had tried to dress neatly, as usual, but there was something
dishevelled about her appearance that she could not tame,
and no matter how hard she tried she could not create the
impression of neatness and harmony.

The day after her encounter with Mr Chichester, she had
gone to Pierre Renard's shop, and it had been revealed to

her that the pendant was lost, and with it, the large lock of Stephen's hair. That night she had been unable to rest, had alternately argued with people not there, and wept, before finally falling into a fitful doze just before dawn. On waking her arm was curled against her chest. She was holding her child to her; there was a metallic taste in her mouth, and she knew within moments that unconsciousness had not brought her peace.

'Are you quite well?' said Harriet, as Joanna put one of the toilet service boxes down haphazardly and it collided with another. Joanna turned towards her mistress, and it occurred to her that she had not really looked Harriet in the eye, or observed her properly, for a long time. What she saw surprised her. Harriet's golden curls were pushed back from her forehead, and her skin, though fine, had lost its pinkish tinge of health. She looked rather fragile, and there was a certain nerve-ridden rawness about her gaze that made her look older.

Joanna shook her head. 'There is something I must tell you, madam,' she said. Harriet gestured to a chair.

Joanna sat down. She normally held herself straight, but some instinct made her curl forwards, examining her hands as she rubbed them together. 'You may hear of this soon enough from Mr Chichester,' she said. 'Though he may not couch it as directly as I do now, but only tell you that I have secrets, and that I am not a virtuous woman.' She continued without pausing, still staring at her hands, knowing that if she did not stop she could keep enough momentum to get her story out. 'Years ago, I fell in love. The man I loved is now dead – my husband.' She added the lie to protect her pride a little; she needed to paint a little respectability over it all. 'He died before I had our daughter. Our baby. I had to give the baby up.'

She did not cry. It astonished her. She had got the words out. When she looked up at Harriet, her mistress's eyes glistened with sorrow. But more than that; at the back of Harriet's gaze there was a spark of something, of joy at a secret shared.

'That is my secret. You must not send me away,' said Joanna. She heard a fervour in her own voice that startled her. 'Please,' she said, and then the tears came, falling fast, her breaths ragged as she sought to stifle her sobs.

'Why should I?' said Harriet, after a brief silence. She reached out and touched Joanna's hand. 'Do not cry; I do not judge you.'

But Joanna did not feel safe; she felt she was digging away the ground from under her feet, but she had to keep digging, as far as she dared. 'The master thinks I am a disreputable woman,' she said. 'He will tell you to send me away.'

'Why?' said Harriet. The question had more weight to it than it should have done, and terror rose in Joanna. She opened her mouth to answer it, when she did not know what answer would come. But, with the quickest of movements, Harriet put her finger out and touched Joanna's lips. 'Do not tell me,' she said. Her voice was soft. 'We can be disgraced together,' she said. 'You know, don't you, about my child? The father?'

Joanna looked; the tears were still falling, and she did not know what to say, but she nodded.

Harriet gave a small, sad smile. 'The silversmith loved

me,' she said. 'You are safe. We will weep over our children together.' And she sat back in her chair, her hands placed absentmindedly over her stomach.

Joanna was exhausted, but her head was clear, when she went to meet Dr Taylor in the staircase hall. It was mid-afternoon but the light was already beginning to fade, and a bored-looking Oliver was taking the doctor's cloak as Joanna descended the stairs. She prepared herself to be agreeable, but when the doctor turned to her she saw that he was unwilling to speak. He was still the same solid, for-ward-leaning figure all in black, his shoulders rounded. But he looked desperately tired and preoccupied. She knew of his popularity, and wondered at it; was he up every night, delivering gentle and noble infants, with the face of an undertaker? He apparently had so much work, he had been obliged to give some of his cases to a Mr Cracknell. But then, Harriet had told her that Taylor was the coroner too, which gave him much other work. It must be hard, she thought, moving so swiftly between the cradle and the graveside.

'Dr Taylor,' she said, with a curtsey.

He nodded and walked past her. He smelt of sweat and his clothes were emanating a damp stale odour, as though he had been out in the rain too long.

They found Harriet sitting as Joanna had left her: neat and obedient, though a little fidgety.

'Mr Chichester sent a message to me,' said Taylor. 'He said that you told him you were feeling unwell.'

Harriet's smile faded. Her voice faltered when she

replied. 'I simply said I thought I could feel something,' she said.

Taylor sat down on the chair Joanna had put beside the bed. His bag landed heavily on the floor next to him.

'Now, Mrs Chichester,' he said, rubbing his temples. 'What is it you felt? You may tell me. Speak with openness, for the sake of your child.' He put a particular emphasis on the word child. For some reason Joanna found it distasteful; she shivered, and felt her skin prickle, with the sense of trouble to come. Then there were his eyes: his gaze as before was detached, but with trouble at the back of it, as though there was some irritation that needed to be plucked out.

Harriet looked subdued. 'I care very much for the child,' she said. 'My feelings are worry for the child; distress when it moves so, as though it is disturbed.'

Taylor nodded. 'I should examine you,' he said. He turned to Joanna. 'If you could leave us.'

Surprisingly, Harriet said nothing, only sat mute as Joanna left the room to stand on the landing. She closed the door behind her, and stood a yard or so away from it, in case Harriet should call for her. Jane appeared, carrying a tray with two glasses of ratafia. The glasses rattled against each other with each step she took and as she stopped near her, Joanna reached forwards and separated them.

'Mrs Holland said the doctor might want some, and the mistress too,' Jane said.

I bet she knocked back a measure herself, thought Joanna. 'Give it to me,' she said. 'You can't go in there now. I'll take it myself.'

'I don't mind waiting,' said Jane.

Joanna heard Harriet calling her name.

'Here, get the door for me!' she snapped, seizing the tray and backing into the room as Jane released the door.

'All is well,' said Harriet brightly, but she sounded shaken. The doctor was standing near the window.

Joanna offered the doctor a drink. He took it and downed it in one gulp, turning away from her as he did so. Joanna put the other down carefully on the small table next to Harriet, then stood near to her, trying to look as inconspicuous as possible.

'Now then, Mrs Chichester,' said Dr Taylor, putting back his glass with a heavy clunk and sitting down. 'Nothing seems to be amiss. What is it that has really been disturbing you?'

'I am terrified,' said Harriet. 'About the birth.' The sadness in her voice unsettled Joanna. Harriet played with her dress fretfully, her little hands plucking at it. For all her artifice of the past, Joanna thought this must be the true Harriet, if there was such a thing. She felt sorry for her. Harriet knew the risks of her state. She had told Joanna she felt the chasm of death yawning in front of her. Joanna had almost laughed at the time, but mainly because she knew death, and it was not a chasm, but something unheralded and quick, almost ordinary: a change of light in a room, which you noticed from the corner of your eye.

It is hard for her to explain, thought Joanna. One is dull, when one is with child; she remembered that. Her mind had been like a familiar landscape with a low-hanging mist over it. She had searched for comfort and meaning, but everything had been strange, every step taken carefully with her hands out in front of her.

Harriet tried again. 'There are such twitchings, such flutterings inside me,' she said. 'It is like being possessed by a spirit, sometimes.'

'An unfortunate phrase to use,' said Taylor. 'Ladies do sometimes feel a little delicate; there is a certain sympathy between the womb and the emotions, so some disturbance is quite necessary, and normal. But you must work hard to overcome these strange impressions, especially if they are disagreeable.'

One kind word, thought Joanna. That is all she needs. But even as she thought it she saw Taylor take a breath, as though it took strength to summon his patience. She thought of the crowds on Piccadilly waiting to leave the metropolis from the White Bear. The doctor's patience is departing now.

'If you persist in indulging yourself, giving in to dark fancies,' said the doctor, 'you may harm the baby. You may leave some impression, all because of your weakness of will.'

'The feeling of strangeness is natural, surely,' said Joanna.

The doctor ignored her. 'It is your duty to rejoice in your state, and to embrace it,' he said. He seemed bowed down by his thoughts, his head too heavy for his neck. He stared at the floor. 'It is your duty as a mother,' he said.

Harriet's face bore an expression of exaggerated sadness, her lower lip trembling as though she might burst into a fit of weeping. Yet when Taylor raised his eyes to her face, he looked at her with clear contempt. The intensity of his expression scared Joanna. 'Doctor?' she said.

He looked at her as though he did not know how he had found his way to this room.

'I thought you were to be my doctor,' said Harriet. 'But I see you are in league with my husband. He wishes to keep me a prisoner.'

'Your husband is a gentleman,' said Taylor, 'and would you call this a prison?'

Joanna stepped forwards, placing a hand lightly but warningly on Harriet's arm. 'The mistress does not know what she says,' she said. 'She is exhausted. Surely you understand, sir, what a drain it has been for her. She is barely out of childhood herself, and this is her firstborn. She has tender regard for the baby and she weeps at the thought of him coming to any harm.'

She said 'him', clearly and purposefully. Her eyes said: she is a carrying an heir, and you are responsible for her. She was satisfied to see the doctor compose himself.

'I am sure all will be well,' he said. There was still no gentleness in his tone. He bowed. 'I wish you good day, Mrs Chichester. I will go and speak to your husband before I leave.'

As the door closed behind him, Harriet rose and put up her hand, to stop Joanna from speaking. After a minute or so, she went to the door and opened it as quietly as possible, and slipped out, closing it behind her.

Joanna waited in an agony of indecision. It was clear to her that Harriet did not wish her to follow, yet as the minutes ticked by she grew more and more afraid. She listened intently for any sounds of an outcry. When the door opened again it made her jump, and she stepped forwards eagerly.

It was Harriet. She looked, if anything, more delicate than before. She sat down. Her expression was set, her lips in a thin line.

'I listened at the door,' she said.

'But Will and Oliver . . .' said Joanna.

Harriet raised her eyebrows, an expression of grim amusement on her face. 'They could hardly stop me: I am their mistress,' she said. The amusement faded. 'Hackney,' she said. 'They mentioned Hackney. They think I am mad – or pretend to at least. They will wait and see; and if I do not improve,' her voice trembled, 'they will pile me into a private carriage and send me off to that village as if I never existed. That doctor . . .' She looked up at Joanna. 'I believe he hates me more than my husband does.'

Digby had watched long, and little had happened. He was cold, and tired of standing still in the grey light of the afternoon. He was about to turn away and head home when he saw Dr Taylor come out of the front door of the Chichester house. Digby observed him closely, seeing in Taylor's bowed head and sombre expression a person who was in their own world. But Taylor did something that no one else had done that day. He looked up and noticed Digby.

Digby turned his head away, looking in the opposite direction. But Taylor did not leave it; he crossed the road. As Digby looked back he raised his eyebrows in surprise and respect as with incongruous nimbleness Taylor leapt over a small pile of horse dung.

'Mr Digby,' said Taylor, as he reached the railings Digby

was leaning on. He was slightly breathless, and his cheeks were pink, whether from cold or exertion it was impossible to tell.

Digby looked at him, but did not take off his hat. 'Dr Taylor, sir,' he said, and ducked his head so briefly that Taylor blinked, clearly wondering whether he had seen it or not.

'I meant to say to you,' said Taylor. 'That is, I have meant to say for some time. On the night my good friend, Mr Renard, died, I was harsh to you, I believe. That is, I said some harsh words, and it has played on my conscience.'

Digby gazed at Taylor. He said nothing.

'I have had some sorrows of late,' said Taylor. 'I have been forced to reconsider my position, in many things. But that is by the by. I have come to beg your pardon, Mr Digby. As a Christian, and a man, will you forgive me?'

'It hardly matters, sir,' said Digby, his eyes now fixed over Taylor's shoulder on the front of the Chichester house. 'But if you wish me to say it, then I do.'

'Thank you,' said Taylor, before he turned and hurried away.

Joanna had thought she could slip away, but Harriet extracted a promise from her that she would stay near her during the evening gathering. After dinner Joanna accompanied her to the Salon. The chandelier was lit, and Joanna stood staring at it for some time, unable to take her eyes from the glittering cascade of glass. Harriet moved forwards, looking around the room. 'It is vast,' she said, her small voice drifting back to Joanna.

Joanna went to her. 'You are mistress here,' she said. 'It is tea and bread and butter, that is all.'

'Yes,' said Harriet. 'I must be brave, I suppose.'

As Nicholas Chichester walked in, he was pulling his long frock coat down, his hands running over the buttons. The light danced over the spangles and coloured silks of his waistcoat. Harriet trembled into life and smiled at him, her suffering giving her looks a piquancy that suited them. Joanna fixed her gaze on the middle distance as the master bowed and kissed his wife's hand. She knew he would not wish to be reminded of her existence.

'The room looks most wonderful, sir,' said Harriet. Her tone was pleasant and unforced, and Joanna imagined the surprise he must have felt.

'It was my aunt's favourite room,' she heard him say. 'I'm glad you like it.'

Then the first guests were announced, and Joanna felt herself begin to breathe again. She could not bear the thought of them together in that room, the master's eyes ribboning this way and that to avoid looking at her. Harriet, wrapped up in her own agony, would surely not notice, but the footmen would.

As more guests arrived Joanna moved back against the wall. She realized now that it suited her; that she would never have wanted to be in Harriet's position, holding her hand out to every person, a faint, anaemic little smile flitting across her white face. The crowds grew. People came dressed in their finery, smelling of the enormous dinners they had just consumed: onions and sauces and meats and wine; men belching surreptitiously before picking up slabs of bread and butter. Draped in white with a pale turquoise sash, Harriet moved like a ghost through the throng.

Time passed quickly enough. As the voices rose, the babble filling the room with echoing noise, Joanna slipped out on to the landing. The master walked past her. She felt the air move as he passed, felt revulsion rise in her at the clipped sound of his shoes on the floor. 'Mr Chichester,' she said, in a low voice.

He stopped, turned, and gave her an icy glance. Then he began to descend the stairs without a word.

The footman by the door glanced at her. He was a new boy; she was glad he was not Will or Oliver. 'Ungracious bastard, isn't he?' he said in an undertone, and she was able to breathe again. He took her little sigh as an assent, giving her a glance as he stood, stock-still. 'And we all know where he's off to, don't we?' he said.

'What are you talking about?' she said.

'I was in the Running Footman the other night. Heard them talking about him. Off to the molly house, he is. Unnatural. Doesn't care for his wife, longs only for young boys, very young boys, so I've heard. Someone'll give him the ending he deserves one of these days.'

With his index finger, he drew a line across his throat.

Joanna leaned against the wall. He glanced at her again. 'Didn't mean to offend you,' he said. 'I forget what I say sometimes, get carried away. Sorry, miss. You won't say anything, will you?'

Joanna shook her head.

CHAPTER TWENTY-SEVEN

12th September, 1792

Such a day this has been. A day to make me fall on my knees and thank God.

I went to Berkeley Square this morning. The Chichesters received me in the breakfast room. There was something amiss between them, I could see that at once. She insisted that I make some small alteration to the design of the dressing set and bring it to her that afternoon. As I left she slipped me a note.

These many changes mean I see you many times, *it said;* I will be alone this afternoon.

'Now that the French King is dead,' said Grisa, polishing a set of salts with small, ineffective, fretful movements, 'all people can talk of is bloodshed and the war with France. no one cares for beauty in such days. Before long, this business will be gone.' He clicked his fingers and sniffed.

One of the shop windows had been smashed a few nights before, startling them all as they sat at dinner. Though it was now fixed, out of the house's inhabitants it had seemed to destabilize Grisa the most; he veered between ecstatic cheerfulness and deep melancholy.

'You are not a companion for a winter's day,' said Alban. The window had discomforted him too; he had gone out into the evening, but the culprit was long gone. 'You are right, trade is quiet, but I am sure things will pick up.'

He was not so sure. He had not designed a piece of silver in weeks; he had only managed some small repairs in the quiet of the workshop, glad that Benjamin had been given leave to visit his parents. A letter from Dr Taylor had smoothed things out; he was to stay there for several weeks, and luxuriate in his family's company, for he was one day to own a silversmith's business in London, and was clearly enjoying some local fame.

'You do the apprentice's job better than him,' said Grisa, watching as Alban carefully rearranged a tray of mourning rings, seals and necklaces. Then, the shop manager gave a small, stifled sob, and cast his polishing rag down.

Alban sighed. Grisa's theatricality was no fun without Mary to share in his ridiculousness; over the past few weeks they had slowly become allies in the ill-assorted household.

'This is a cursed house,' said Grisa eventually, obviously annoyed that Alban was ignoring him.

The word needled Alban; he remembered Jesse saying it.

'Then why do you stay here?' he said. 'Out of loyalty to Mr Renard?'

'I know why *you* stay here,' said Grisa, sniffing.

'I have been inside long enough,' said Alban, with an air of finality, as he pushed the tray of jewellery back on to its shelf. 'And you have been melancholy long enough. I will get you some of those lozenges you have been asking for.'

Grisa wiped his eyes with the back of his hand, and began polishing again. 'You are a good friend, Mr Steele,' he said, with the weakest of smiles.

It was to be a trial of his new commercial approach, Alban thought, as he walked along Bond Street. It was not far to his intended stop. Mr Jones the apothecary had a shop a few yards down from Renard's on Bond Street. The shop floor was a fine room: plenty of dark wood, mirrors and gold writing advertising the potions anzd pills Jones sold, for he specialized in treatments for fashionable ailments.

Jones was a man who seemed to speak in swirls, and it was unclear whether he had been given this manner by nature or designed it himself. Alban thought he could have listened to his voice, rising and falling like the tides, for hours, for it had a strange musicality, and was often comic.

'Ah, Mr Steele, Mr Steele,' said Jones. 'How can I help you? Do you have the headache? Nausea? You can tell me, Mr Steele, if you supped too long with Bacchus last night.'

Alban laughed. 'I've come to get some of your best lozenges for Mr Grisa,' he said. 'He believes himself to be consumptive half the time; and an advert in *The Times* has convinced him that he will be well if he has your special lozenges.'

'Him, consumptive?' said Jones, losing a little of his delicate accent. 'The man grew up in Southwark. He has the constitution of a mule. But who am I to argue with my customers?' He handed the small packet over with a smile.

'By the by,' Alban said. He felt uncomfortable, but he hazarded that Pierre Renard would never have faltered at introducing business at any moment. 'Mr Holt mentioned that he was at dinner with you, and that you have a fine pair of candlesticks from our firm. Do they give satisfaction?'

The colour drained from Jones's face. 'What of it?' he said. His voice was faint. In the corner of the shop, a lady exclaimed over a pot of vegetable cream for the complexion.

'I wondered only if you cared for any more table wares to match?' said Alban, worried by the expression of annoyance on the apothecary's face.

'Not at present,' said Jones. He raised his voice. 'In fact, I regret buying them. It is unlikely I will venture to your shop again.'

'Are they faulty?' said Alban.

'No, not exactly – but they are old-fashioned, heavy French things. I believe I was talked into it by Mr Renard. God rest his soul. He was a friend of mine – and persuasive.'

'Perhaps we could exchange them?' said Alban, but this evidently dissatisfied Jones. He shook his head and took a step away, smoothing down his hair nervously.

'If you will excuse me, Mr Steele, I have customers to deal with. I wish you a pleasant day.'

'May I pay you for—'

'Just take them,' said Jones, adding, in a biting undertone, 'Do not come and see me about this again, and do not – I repeat, do not – mention this to anyone.'

'May we join you, Mr Steele?' said Mary that evening.

'If you don't mind watching me polish the stock,' he said. 'Mr Grisa began it today, but now he is laid up in bed.'

The shop was open late, the windows lit by candles, and as Mary walked past him, Alban caught the sweet scent of her.

Mallory crept down after her, a glass of red wine in her hand, looking rather merrier than usual. Her children's voices drifted down from upstairs, for they were being expertly cared for by Avery, who tirelessly involved them in conversation and games. Mary and Mallory moved around the shop, looking at pieces together and remarking on them. Mallory draped a chain of graduated amethysts around Mary's neck; the colour suited her pale skin, and as she turned in the candlelight, her eyes seemed bright in a way Alban had not seen before, so that for a moment he ceased to look at the silver, and put it down on the counter.

'Why do you powder your hair?' he said. 'It is such a colour.'

'Would you have me appear like a revolutionary?' she said, smiling. 'There are so many hidden things, so many signs. My husband taught me to look out for them, and now I am terrified of many transgressions. I hardly know how to keep up with them. You know how Dr Taylor thinks everyone a radical. If I left my hair as nature intended he would say God save the King every other sentence.'

'He already does,' he said, and she laughed.

Recently, their words and looks had begun to fit into each other, a puzzle that was gradually being constructed between them.

'You should not be afraid now,' he said to her, and saw Mallory tip another mouthful of red wine back.

There was a knock at the shop door. 'I'll go,' said Mallory, and she went to the door with a heavy step.

The door opened, banging the bell against the frame, and Dr Taylor peered in. 'Mrs Renard, Mrs Dunning, Mr Steele,' he said, removing his hat and bowing. 'I saw you at the window, Mrs Renard.' There was a tone of gentle disapproval in his voice. 'I know Mr Renard always said that you were dazzled by some of the jewels in this shop.'

'We have been surrounded by metal and stones our whole lives,' said Mallory. 'They hardly dazzle us, sir.'

'I did not mean to offend you, Mrs Dunning,' said Taylor. 'Though I see, as usual, you are quick to jump to it.'

'I will ask for tea,' said Mary, not daring to catch Alban's eye, for she knew he found Taylor and Mallory's irritation with each other amusing.

'There is no need,' said Taylor. 'I simply called to say that I have heard word from Thomas Havering, and I have given him leave to call on you, next week.'

Silence fell over the room.

Mallory spoke first. 'Well,' she said, 'it is a sensible thing, indeed, for him to visit.'

'You always hated him,' said Mary to Mallory, undoing the amethyst necklace, and crumpling it into her hands.

'Do you know him well?' said Taylor. He was leaning on his gold-topped cane, his eyes fixed on the floor.

'A little,' said Mary. 'My father did work for him. I used to hide behind his legs when Mr Havering came to call.'

She wished to add that Pierre had modelled himself on goldsmiths like Havering: bluff, thriving men, who knew how to woo and flatter, but never did anything unless it was to their advantage. She recalled Havering's square figure, his clothes enriched with gold lace, thick fingers adorned with an indecent number of rings as though he was a walking advertisement for his trade, and a nose that seemed wrinkled with permanent discontent.

As a child of nine, she had attended the burial of the goldsmith's first wife, Anne, at a country graveyard in St Pancras. She remembered chiefly the rain falling all around, and Havering expressing the worry that he might have caught a cold. Mary glanced at her sister, but Mallory was finding it hard to look at her, as was Taylor. Only Alban's eyes were fixed on her face.

'He has spoken warmly of you,' said Taylor. His voice was trembling slightly. 'Forgive me; this is an indelicate conversation, but an advantageous marriage, that would take you far away from these dangerous streets . . .' He let his voice trail off.

'Dr Taylor may have a point,' said Mallory. 'I am afraid for you, after everything that has happened.'

Alban put the ledger down hard on the counter, making everyone jump. 'Your book, Mrs Renard,' he said.

'What is this?' said Taylor.

'I have volunteered to keep the accounts,' said Mary.

'There is no need for you to involve yourself in the workings of the business,' he said.

'But I wish to be involved,' said Mary. 'My mother was a burnisher, you know. The women in my family were not always so helpless.'

'She writes a fine hand,' said Alban.

'I say again,' said Taylor, with a pained expression. 'There is no need. You must excuse me; Mrs Taylor has held the dinner long enough. Mrs Renard, do think on what I have said.'

He bowed, and went out on to the street, walking slowly, his eyes fixed on the ground as though he was deep in thought. Mallory brushed her skirts down. 'Avery must be rescued from the children,' she said. 'I have stayed too late. Mary, will you go up and bid them come down to me, if you please?'

Mary went, biting her lip, her face pale. Mallory put her empty glass down on the counter. She put her hands on her hips, as though she was gathering strength for something.

'Mr Steele,' she said, 'you must learn to hide your face, for in your expression I see everything, you know.'

Alban continued to polish the silver. 'I do not know,' he said.

She shook her head. 'You think me harsh,' she said, her voice slurring slightly, but only slightly, under his minute observation of her words. 'But it did grieve me to see all the life drain out of your face, and hers, when Havering was mentioned. I do not agree with Dr Taylor on much, but it will be best if Mary leaves here.'

'You have often said you wish to protect her,' he said.

'And so I do,' she said.

'Perhaps this is not the best way. She is stronger than you think,' he said.

Mallory stared at him. She leaned so close that he could see the pores in her fine skin.

'You were not there,' she said, 'on the day our brother was taken. I held the door shut when they carried him to the carriage. I stopped her from following him. The cry that came from her lips was unearthly. It froze my blood. I knew then she is not as I am. Not rooted in this world, but in some other.'

Her eyes dropped to the counter, as she heard her children's feet on the stairs. 'Proceed, if you must, Mr Steele,' she said quietly. 'But if you break her, I will break you.'

CHAPTER TWENTY-EIGHT

13th September, 1792

I return again to the blessings of yesterday, which have hardly left my mind for a moment except in the execution of business.

When the footman showed me to her boudoir there was nothing in his expression. After all, I have been sent up there many times by Mr Chichester. When I entered the room I hardly knew what awaited me. Only that, after the door had closed behind me, she went to it, and locked it, then turned to me, those beautiful eyes alight. Her expression lit such a fire in me that I hardly knew what I did. Only now can I savour it: the feeling of her lips beneath mine, the trembling of her body. I took her.

I had my satisfaction, as, may I hazard, did she: she did tremble so violently around and beneath me that it inflames me even to think of it. She cried out my name, so that I was obliged to put my hand over her mouth. Never had my wife cried out for me as she did; never for a moment looked at me in that way, as though I was a vision of heaven before her eyes. 'I am dying,' she said to me, and I held her to me, feeling her heart beat quick and fast, her body run through with pleasure.

'Come in with me,' Joanna said that night.

They managed it quietly enough, though Digby sensed her tension with every step on the stair. She had bribed Mrs Holland to let her borrow the key to the back door, but it was important that no other servant should see them. 'Never again,' she said, smiling, as she locked her bedroom door then, as an extra measure, dragged her locking box in front of it, and he reached out to pull her to him. He had given her a gift: a small folding knife with a mother-of-pearl handle, 'So you can defend yourself, when you come out to me at night,' he said.

She smiled. 'With a blade this short? I should have been better off with a dessert knife.'

'You are too practical,' he said, sounding hurt. 'I thought its prettiness would appeal to you.'

'And so it does,' she said, kissing it, and placing it on the locking box carefully, as though it was the most precious of love tokens.

It was the first time Digby had lain with her, and it had its own kind of unreality, like the dreams she had spoken of to him, so that afterwards he wondered if he really was there, in that garret room, with the moon shining in on them and all of London sleeping below.

'Shall we go to the theatre?' he said, his fingertips tapping up and down her spine slowly to the tune of a ballad singer he had heard in the street. 'I will buy you a seat in the first gallery.'

She took up his fantasy without hesitation. 'And shall we send our man ahead to save the seats?' she said.

'We shall,' he said, shifting, and kissing the top of her head.

She had told him things: of the things she saw and imagined, which seemed real to her. Nothing had been denied between them. He did not shrink from the slack, pale skin on her stomach, stretched long ago by pregnancy then let loose, so it lay as thin as tissue, with its small wrinkles and lines. He dipped his face to kiss it. She had thought men were incapable of such tenderness.

'I had a child once,' she said. 'A daughter. She is dead.'

'What of the father?' he said.

'He is dead too. I had only one thing of his, and it is gone. A lock of his hair, in a pendant. I gave it to Mr Renard to make, and now it is lost.'

Digby hid his face in her shoulder. He kissed her once, twice, three times, his mouth finding her neck. She held him, and after innumerable minutes, she heard his breathing deepen into sleep.

Her eyes moved across the room, taking in every detail, as she savoured the quiet moments, and the sound of his breathing. Her gaze halted on his clothes, hastily thrown to the floor. On the glint of gold, at the edge of his pocket.

She carefully moved out of his embrace, inching her way, stopping each time he stirred and letting him settle. She got out of bed, slowing every movement so as not to wake him. She took two steps across the floor, and crouched down beside the pile of clothes. What she had caught sight of was a gold link; part of a chain. She pulled it, felt the weight of something, then a watch emerged. The most beautiful watch she had ever seen.

The look on Joanna's face had unsettled Digby. He had woken suddenly, in the dense darkness of her room, and when he turned he saw that she was awake, but staring at the ceiling. She had submitted to his kiss, then had seen him out of the house quietly, with only the faintest of smiles. As he walked away, he knew he should be happy, but the tenderness they had shared had been diluted by the odd, sad look on her face, and the tentative way in which she had said goodnight.

He kept awake until morning, walking circuit after circuit of the square, and having received Watkin's pledge that he would be covered for the next night, went home. He slept a while, and woke, and coughed a good deal. It was a pattern he repeated over the day, until he checked his watch and knew he should take his place in the Red Lion, for he liked to be early for all appointments.

As Maynard entered the Red Lion, Digby could see he wasn't even making the effort to look cordial.

'So?' he said, taking his gloves off.

Digby gestured to the stool opposite him. He had chosen it on purpose, as he had liked its effect last time: a small, three-legged stool, shorter than the bench he sat upon, so Maynard's grand, elegant bulk sank until his eyes were lower than Digby's. He smiled at the displeasure filtering through Maynard's eyes; at the sense of him calculating whether he could rise again and cast the stool off for something more appropriate to his dignity.

'Don't mind if I do, sir,' said Digby, raising his drink high and then knocking back the dregs.

Maynard sighed and signalled to the landlord. 'I'm surprised you're not out on the watch,' he said. 'It's a bit late for you, isn't it?'

'Night off,' said Digby. 'It does happen sometimes. If one has important business.' As the landlord collected his tankard to refill it, he rubbed his hands together under the table, watching as Maynard wiped away a small tear of brown mucus trickling from his nostril. He almost asked for a pinch of snuff himself, then decided against it. He was glad he'd bribed Watkin and Brown to cover for him. He had no stomach for going out there tonight.

'You said you wanted me to keep an eye on things,' he said, glancing about him. When he looked back, Maynard seemed nonplussed. 'You know,' said Digby. 'This and that.'

'You'd better mean Renard,' said Maynard. His nose was twitching. Digby knew the man wanted to take his snuffbox out and take a good pinch of it, another, then another.

'Yes,' he said, and sat back as the landlord banged down his pint of porter. He noticed Mr Maynard had got a glass of red wine.

'I was thinking about him,' he said. 'That night I found him, the way he was lying. Clear to me someone came up from behind, surprised him. So what was he doing there, bang slap in the middle of Berkeley Square, middle of the night, putting himself at risk of footpads?'

'You are covering old ground, Digby,' said Maynard. He turned the glass by its stem, staring into the wine.

'We'll never know why he was there, that's what I think,' said Digby. 'But that doesn't mean we won't ever know why someone killed him. He was damn near one of the houses, too. One particular house: opposite it.'

He paused, and saw with satisfaction that Maynard was watching him. He knew the occupants of the houses: the Earl of Orford; two or three unoccupied; Lady Mary Clare; James Stewart; Lord Ducie; the list went on and on. Sitting before his meagre fire the day before, Digby had ruminated over the Chichesters and their connection with Renard. Once or twice he had seen Mrs Chichester at the first-floor window of their house. Not that a real lady would have allowed herself to be seen at the window so. He had only noticed her as one more thing to hate: a young woman with golden hair and empty features like those of a doll; her head an empty shell of porcelain, nodding on its slim neck.

'I went to the Running Footman the other night,' he said. 'Made enquiries.'

Maynard looked nonplussed, and Digby wondered whether his ignorance was real. Had the gentleman ever threaded his way through the press of servants, incognito, hearing their voices raised in description of their masters, their laughter, the room warmed by their breaths and bodies? One of the footmen hadn't wanted to stop talking.

'He had customers there, sir, on that side of the square. The Chichester family. Maybe he'd called on them, that night.'

There had been a scene in that house, the footman had said, his slippery face full of laughter. The maid he was tupping had seen the letter on the bed as Mrs Chichester was being calmed by her lady's maid after a crying fit. She was a smart girl, he said. She read enough to know the letter was telling of Mr Renard's death. 'There was more than one letter from that direction, when he lived,' he said, leering. 'Let's just say he called often on the master ... and, mainly, the mistress. But then, who can blame her?'

Digby held back from saying it. He took a sip of his drink, not caring for the silence and Maynard's blank expression. 'I've heard of the boy,' said Maynard, frowning. 'But not as anyone of influence.'

Digby weighed up how much he could say, and felt the unfamiliar taint of panic infect his judgement. Will the footman was hardly a reliable source. Apparently only three months ago he claimed to have bedded the chandler's wife and earned himself a sound beating that had temporarily blemished his good looks. The boy took great pleasure in hinting, in sliding his tongue around and making the ordinary seem suggestive. *He called mainly on the mistress.* To hint that Renard may have warmed the bed of Mrs Chichester would be like saying that the Virgin Mary had screwed a pimp in a back alley off Piccadilly.

'There was one other thing,' Digby said.

'Out with it then,' said Maynard, who seemed to be growing tenser by the moment.

Digby leaned forwards, projecting a whisper into Maynard's face. 'They happened to mention to me. Mr Chichester. His taste for entertainment – that is, he looks in the direction of young boys. I've seen him struggle with one myself of a night, though I could hardly swear to it that was what he was after. But he has a bad reputation amongst the servants, and he's so high and mighty, more than one of them would like to see him brought low. I wondered, sir. Mr Renard was killed right near Mr Chichester's house. It would have been mighty easy to mistake them in the night.'

Maynard stared at the table, with the expression of someone in the process of losing his self-control. 'I thought you had something of substance for me, Digby,' he said. 'I asked you to look into Renard's affairs. But you bring me servants' tittle-tattle about people who are so far above you, you should not even speak their names. Do not repeat that foul assertion, to anyone. Do you understand me?'

'I thought you wanted the truth, sir,' said Digby.

Maynard brought his fist down on to the table with a bang. The suddenness and force of it shocked Digby. He said nothing, only looked at Maynard's face, unsure of what to do or say, and fearful of the cold anger in his eyes.

'Go to the devil,' Maynard said. 'This is claptrap. There is something you're not telling me. I see it, behind your eyes. And I will find it out.'

CHAPTER TWENTY-NINE

14th September, 1792

One woman is surely not enough for a man. I mean that not in reference to my appetites, but in the simple matter of practicality. For when a woman is lacking in one element, or more, it is natural to tire of her, and to seek comfort elsewhere.

I am a reflective man. Others think me driven by money and business, and I understand that it may seem that way to them. But I also have a relationship with my maker. In the eyes of the world, what I did yesterday was a sin. Yet I know, and I think the knowledge God-given, that it was not. I know, with the certainty that God will be merciful to me, that I have planted a seed in the lady. It is God's will, perhaps, that my son will be born to her.

The man that arrived on Bond Street with his coach and four was dressed finely, but had never learned how to marry colours together. He wouldn't listen to his valet; he had his own regime, as he called it, his own scheme. Besides, he said, with evident pride, he had been used to working in one colour only, and that was silver.

Thomas Havering had once been a silversmith on Bond Street, and his reputation still stalked the street like a wraith, sometimes taking monstrous shapes. The money he had accumulated through his business and two judicious marriages had bought him a country seat near Uxbridge. Once a fixture in the clubs, societies and civic life of his London parish, he now breathed clean air and had a staff of fifteen. London might pulse only distantly on the horizon, but he monitored its heartbeat. He had learned of Pierre's death from the newspapers, and also because of a letter from Taylor, an old friend, notifying him that a debt Renard had owed him would shortly be settled by the dead man's administrators. Havering liked dabbling on Bond Street, as a grandparent dandles a small child on its knee: the distance between him and it provided a channel for agreeable feelings to flow in.

It was from pride that Mary dressed well on the morning of Havering's visit. She wore her best black gown and a thick black ribbon around her neck. She felt as though she was building her defences, adding rouge to her pale cheeks. When she had finished she looked feverish and unlike herself, but felt as though she had put in place another layer of protection between her and the world. When she came down the stairs and into the shop Alban and Grisa ceased speaking, and, in concert, looked her up and down.

'It is quiet,' she said. 'Is there no one about today?'

'It is early, madame,' said Grisa.

Alban said nothing. He leaned on the counter, and only took his eyes from her after a long moment, turning his whole body towards the shop manager. 'What were we saying?' he said to Grisa.

'The York designs,' said Grisa. 'I will get them from the workshop.'

As he bustled off Alban looked back at Mary; there was no warmth in his expression.

'Why are you looking at me so?' she said. 'Is there something amiss?'

He moved a piece of paper on the counter. 'No,' he said. 'Grisa tells me Thomas Havering is coming today. And I see you have prepared for him.'

Mary stared at him. The coldness of his voice shocked her. 'What do you mean by saying this to me?' she said. Her throat felt tight and constricted.

He gave a little shake of his head; she took a step forwards. 'We are friends, are we not?' she said firmly.

'I had thought so,' he said, but when he raised his eyes to her face they were blank and unfamiliar, as though every defence in his armoury had fallen into place. 'That day in church, you spoke to me as though I was motivated by money. You mistook me, and judged me, and I let it pass. And now this – for him. I will say only that we cannot go back in time, Mrs Renard. For a moment, I thought we could.'

Mary heard Grisa returning. As he came through the door she pushed past him, and ran upstairs. She went to her chamber, and when Avery came in, exclaiming that

Mary had got ready without her, she had already rubbed the rouge away.

When Thomas Havering approached the shop on Bond Street, it was with an exaggeratedly indulgent expression that could be seen from the upstairs window. He was projecting the expression as though he was on stage. His coachman struggled wildly with four nervy, ill-matched chestnuts.

'I bet he bought them cheap,' muttered Mallory under her breath. She and Avery stood, either side of the sash window, trying to keep out of sight.

'Good God, what a vehicle,' said Avery. 'He's driven the family manor into town.'

'Hush,' said Mary, as she heard the front door open. 'Oh no, you can hear him a mile away. He makes Grisa sound like a whispering maiden, and you know how his voice carries.' She felt faintly nauseous, and was still angry at Alban. Ponderous footsteps were heard ascending the stairs, and Mary and Mallory rose as the door opened. Avery sat in the corner, leafing through a book, playing the invisible companion.

'Ah, Mrs Renard. My condolences.' Havering made a low bow, raising himself with a slight wince. As he turned he looked fully at Mallory, and his eyes flickered.

So you do remember, thought Mary: Mallory as a child, pelting you with stones within the City walls because she'd taken against you. What a hiding our father gave her for that. You said she had eyes so hard they could chisel the heart out of a man.

Havering seated himself on a chair with his back half-turned to Mallory. 'I have been staying with my friend, the Reverend Mr Pincher, on Dover Street,' he said. 'Perhaps you know of him?'

'We are not closely connected,' said Mary.

Havering gave a little nod, and a grunt. 'I was most concerned to hear of your situation, my dear Mrs Renard,' he said. 'I remember you as a child. You have grown into a beauty, indeed.'

Mary felt unable to flatter him. Seeing the older man had brought back her image of the younger one. He had the same bulbous nose and protruding lower lip; the only change was that his features had grown coarser over the years. He had once spent much on his attire, and obviously still did, though the colours clashed terrifyingly. But age and success had taken away the need for beauty; and he bore himself as though his every feature was a thing to be proud of, from his reddened, vein-crazed face and large stomach to the small belch he now gave. He carried himself with a sense of pride and honour, and Mary wondered how well Pierre had known him, and whether he had studied him.

'And how is your family, sir?' she said, struggling to steer the conversation away from her situation.

'Alas, my poor Jane, I lost some months ago,' he said. 'I, myself, have designed a very handsome memorial for her in our parish church; it is a new church, and she is the first to go into the vault.'

'How agreeable for her,' said Mallory.

Havering licked his lips, and bit the bottom one, turning it an alarming purple colour. He ignored Mallory. 'If I could ever be a friend to you, my dear,' he said. 'I have a country estate, you know. Far from the reaches of the London smoke. The fresh air would do wonders for your beautiful complexion.'

'You are most kind to mention it,' said Mary. 'But I am well enough here.'

'Are you really?' he said. His face pantomimed astonishment. He looked around the room, as though he was making an inventory of its contents. 'Restricted to these small rooms, above a shop? Not mistress of your own house? Of course, you know I am owed no small amount. I will not call it in, yet, of course. I do not need it. But for you to be here, my dear, must be an almost intolerable burden. The business is for the men to deal with, and you must sit here, alone, isolated from society, it seems, with the rumours growing more poisonous as every day passes. Your window, I heard, was smashed. Your lodgers have deserted you.' He paused, and licked his lips again.

'Shall I call for tea?' said Mallory. Havering acknowledged her words with a startled and anticipatory look, but Mary shook her head.

'I am well aware of the state of Mr Renard's will,' said Havering, twirling his cane. 'And it only reinforced my impression that one should never trust a Frenchman.'

'You trusted him enough to do business with him,' said Mary. As Mallory tried to rise she reached out and held her arm.

'That was business,' said Havering. 'I have come here, and on seeing you, I resolve not to speak of business, but of something else. I am a wealthy man. There was a time,

Mrs Renard, when I thought of you as a bride for me, though your father thought you too young.'

Mary glanced at Mallory and saw that her sister was staring at the floor.

'The years have passed. They have been kind to me, and God has given me many blessings. They have not been so kind to you, but you are still the delicate creature I remember. I would dearly wish to watch you flourish. My house is near Uxbridge; it has a most comely view of my lands.'

'You have yet mentioned the house,' said Mary, standing. She felt her natural stubbornness spring to life: she had thought it long lost. Remembered her mother raising her hand to her as a child. 'Please excuse me, sir,' she said.

Mallory rose too, and smiled at Havering. 'My sister is unwell,' she said, in that resonant voice of hers, as if her words were meant to carry down the stairs and into the shop. 'She needs rest, as I'm sure you understand. We thank you for your visit.'

She half-dragged Mary into an unwilling curtsey.

Havering stared at them. 'Consider what I have said. I hear they never found the desperate person who killed Mr Renard. It would do you good, Mrs Renard, to be gone from here. I should hate to think of any harm befalling you.'

'She will think on it, sir,' said Mallory. 'We thank you for your visit.'

After he had gone, Mallory went to the window and watched him emerge on to Bond Street.

'You didn't even serve him tea,' said Avery, smiling as she turned another page of her book.

Mallory snorted. 'He is rich,' she said. 'And I am

persuaded of two things: that he would not be cruel to you, and that he would die fairly soon, if his complexion is anything to go by.'

'You wish me to be chained up again?' said Mary. 'After everything that has happened?'

'I wish to protect you. That wretched Benjamin is returning tomorrow. Every time I see him he becomes more vicious-looking – I can hardly sleep at the thought of him being under this roof with you. And better chained to Havering than to poverty,' said Mallory.

Avery sighed. 'Fie, Mall,' she said. 'You have answers for everything; and all of them so disagreeable.'

'Pierre wanted to be like that man,' said Mary.

'Yes, but Havering is nothing like him,' said Mallory. 'He is an indulgent old man. Look at him: his stomach precedes him.'

Mary joined her sister at the window, standing back in case he should turn and look up at them, taken by a fancy that he was being watched. Havering was traversing Bond Street, his carriage having taken a turn around the block. He was walking quickly, swinging his silver-knopped stick with some force. A young boy passing by must have made a comment, for he swung at him, and got a hit.

'Time was he was so powerful those crowds would have parted for him like the Red Sea,' said Mallory. 'Even now, he can still protect you.'

'I thought you wished me to become strong,' said Mary.

'So I do,' said Mallory. 'But a husband such as him would help you in that; and besides, there is the money.'

*

Mary did not go to dinner that evening. She lay on her bed, trying to imagine what life as Mrs Havering would be like, far from the city, and with such a husband as the old silversmith. She wondered whether Mallory was right. In this house she would never be free of Pierre; with every breath she breathed in the scent of him, she slept under the linen he had chosen, and told the hour of the day by his lantern clock. His death still haunted her; it would only take a moment's reverie before she saw him watching her dully as the tide of crimson spread around him. When the window had been broken in the shop she had not shown her fear, but inside she thought, just for a moment: he has come for me.

When she went down to lock the doors, Alban was still on the shop floor, putting away a display of seals.

'Mr Steele,' she said. He bowed, but would not look at her, only assisted her with the locking, and lifted the bar over the house door. When he had done it, he stood with his hands on the bar.

'I must beg your pardon,' he said quietly. 'I did not wish to wound you earlier. I was presumptuous. The subject of your marriage is none of my business.'

Mary clutched the keys tightly, and held her candlestick up so that the light would be clear between them. 'I should have told you, earlier,' she said. 'I have tried to go back in time myself, and if I could have done it by wishing, I would. But you are quite right, Mr Steele. It is impossible.'

CHAPTER THIRTY

20th September, 1792

My wife is unwell again. Her sister, that has all the strength, is tending to her. A hard one, that. I do not have the patience with invalids, and I never thought I would be married to one. Except for the toothache, I have been well recently, God be praised. The time alone suits me. I think of Harriet. Her very name carries her sweetness; I have only to say it and I am filled with agreeable feelings.

Joanna walked swiftly down the mews road, the knife hidden beneath the folds of her cloak. When she heard Digby's brief whistle her heart beat harder, but her pace did not slow, and her expression did not change. She stopped a foot or so in front of him.

She had thought of the watch many times since she had

crept back to bed, leaving it in his pocket. She had even begun to think that the object was his security; that it represented a chance for them to escape. Until today, when on an errand she had passed the Renard shop, and remembered where she had seen the watch before.

He was leaning against the wall. 'Are you not letting me in tonight?' he said. She could tell from the expression on his face that he had not sensed that anything was wrong. What fools we are, she thought: thinking that we fit together so perfectly, that we know each thought in the other's head, when we are just groping in the darkness.

'No,' she said. Then, her hand tight on the knife: 'Your watch, Edward.'

She saw the glint of his eyes as they narrowed in the darkness. Every instinct warned her of danger; so when he took a step towards her she was quicker than him, and Digby found a knife against his throat, not the small knife he had given her, but a dessert knife, with its sharpened blade, held by his lover's clenched fist.

'Jo,' he said.

'Did you kill him, or filch it from him? You would swing for it either way,' she said.

'I didn't kill him,' he said. 'Jo, Jo, put the knife down. Do you think I would hurt you?'

Grief welled up in her, as suddenly as fear had. 'No,' she said, but still she did not move.

'Will you put it down?' he said. 'And let me speak.' His voice was hushed, hoarse.

'I am not a fool,' she said. She heard a rushing sound in her ears, felt as though a thousand impulses were running through her. She did not know what was right, or who to trust; she could not even trust herself.

Digby gazed at her, his shoulders hunched. There was such a pitiful turn to his mouth that Joanna felt a sharp, keen sorrow. After a moment or two, it overtook the anger, and she let the knife fall a little way, an inch or two clear of his throat.

'I take it you know who it belonged to?' he said. She nodded. 'Well,' he said, as though to himself. 'That is no surprise. He was always flashing his tatler, so I gather, just like he flashed everything else. The silver, the clothes, the wife. Things are just as I told you. I found him, and he was already cold. I took the watch. There: that is all.'

In the darkness Joanna leaned closer, as though by seeing his eyes she would know the truth. But she could see nothing unusual in his face; he seemed to wear the same expression that he always wore when he looked at her. His apparent serenity chilled her more than any expression of anger would have done.

'What will you do?' he said. 'Will you betray me?'

'To whom?' she said, shivering. 'And for whose sake – Renard's? No, I will tell no one. You may take my word.'

Digby sighed. 'Will you come here?' He held his arms out to her hesitantly.

She shook her head. 'No,' she said. 'You must go now.'

'I will see you again?' he said.

'I cannot say. But you can rely on my word. Go now.'

He took a few steps away, backwards, looking at her. She saw his hand touch his pocket, and she realized, dully, that he was touching the watch. Then he turned his back to her and hurried away.

She was still holding the knife, tightly. She hid it in the folds of her sleeve. I could have killed someone tonight, she thought, and without a qualm. The thought distressed her, as though every firm boundary in her life was dissolving.

Alban said nothing as Grisa lurched through the door. It had been a long day, full of difficult customers. It was nearly ten o'clock; Alban had been about to close the shop, blowing out the many candles in the window display. He was holding a candlestick in his hands, about to lock it away in one of the glazed presses, when the door opened.

'At last,' he said, and he couldn't keep the irritation out of his voice.

'Are you my keeper, Mr Steele?' said Grisa. His breath smelt strongly of drink and as he walked to the counter his route veered wildly. 'Here, I will help you shut up.'

'There's no need,' said Alban. 'You will damage the goods in that state. Benjamin will help me.'

'Well, as you wish,' said Grisa, leaning back against the wall and half-sliding down it. 'I will do my part, Mr Steele, there is no need to give me such black looks. I will go through the ledgers tonight.'

'Mrs Renard has the books,' said Alban.

There was a dull thud as Benjamin's fist connected with the counter. 'You shouldn't have let her near the accounts,' he said. 'She'll curse the business, just like she's cursed everything else here. Nothing is safe once she touches it.

Mr Renard would tell you himself, if he could still speak. He is trying to tell us; his bench has a bloodstain on it – a new one. Have you not seen it?'

'Hold your tongue,' said Alban. He had wondered at the dark patch on the wood, and assumed some acid had been spilled. Benjamin's explanation maddened him. 'Mrs Renard is mistress of this establishment and I will not hear you speak of her in that way. I've had enough of this shop, and enough of your sour mutterings since you came back, to last me a lifetime.'

'You're an apprentice here, boy,' said Grisa. 'I or Mr Steele could beat you halfway round this house and not think anything of it, so do what he says.'

'I have a right to speak,' said Benjamin, a look of satisfaction on his face. 'This will all be mine one day and there's nothing you can do about it. And I tell you that woman is a witch. She went out the night Mr Renard died. She locked me in, and then I heard her at the door.'

Alban felt a prickle down the back of his neck, as though a cold rush of air had moved through the room. 'You are lying,' he said, thankful that his voice sounded steady. 'You have seen too many plays; I swear you are paid too much, and work too little, to have room for these fantasies in your tiny head.'

'It is not a lie!' Benjamin cried. 'I'll tell you, and I'll tell others, that she killed Mr Renard. They should bring back the old law and burn her for it, just as she should, under good old English law. Tom Doley told me a woman burnt for killing her husband, not so many years ago. They call it petty treason.'

Alban's temper snapped. Without thinking of the consequences, he put down the piece of silver he was holding and drove Benjamin up against the wall. The boy struggled, but Alban could see the fear in his eyes and after a moment he stopped, as though surrendering.

'I'll break your neck if you say another word against her, here or anywhere else,' Alban said.

'Will you?' said Benjamin, his voice thin and reedy with fear. 'I see you've thrown your lot in with the devil, Mr Steele.'

Alban felt Grisa's hands on his shoulders, pulling him back. He released the boy and Benjamin darted into the back room, slamming the door behind him.

'Let go of me,' said Alban. Grisa released him and stepped back. 'If you wish to be of use,' said Alban, 'you can help me put the stock away.'

After everything was done, Alban went to his room without another word to anyone. He sat with his head in his hands. He tried to calm himself, but Benjamin's words kept returning to him. There was a knot in the pit of his stomach, a sickening unease settling itself deep in him. He could not distance himself from it. Saying the words to himself, again and again, did not calm him: whispering them, trying to unpick them. But they never lost the terror they roused in him: Mary, my love, what have you done?

CHAPTER THIRTY-ONE

29th September, 1792

I have kept away from my wife. It was due to her poor attention, leaving the windows open at all times of the day and night, that made me so unwell last year. I am usually strong enough to over-come anything; but my wife tended to me inexpertly. Yet though I am frightened at the idea of my own sickness, the thought of her illness somehow cheers me, and raises a fierce sort of hope in my heart. If she were gone – the thought is seductive, though it should not be admitted to my mind.

A busy day. My patrons are returning to the city, and I feel the life-blood quickening in my veins. My wife, in trying to converse with me, gabbled on about the artistry of silver. I told her that the silversmith is part engineer, part banker. I said it to mock her, for I am strong and sure in my taste and judge-ment, and these are things that I know, from my experience of her, that she cannot understand. Besides, if she had any sense of taste, she would have responded to my gentle shaping of her in the first days of our marriage. I used to think it a pity I could not cast and chase her as I would a piece of silver; she will never be my masterpiece. I thought it possible, once, but that was long ago.

'The apothecary cannot come near this shop,' said Mary. 'It is almost amusing to see; he nearly crossed the road just now to avoid the front window.'

Alban said nothing. They had closed the shop early, and he was buttoning up his greatcoat. Mary watched him pensively; she was alone, Avery having gone to stay with Mallory.

'Where are you going, if you please?' she said. She tried to soften her voice, so he would not be offended, but still he looked it: wary, and tired.

'To visit my cousin and his family,' he said. She noticed that he could hardly bear to look at her.

'May I come with you?' she said, surprising herself with the question. It was almost a comfort to see his astonishment; to see that he recognized what a risk she was taking. 'The evenings are long and dark,' she said. 'And I do not want to be on my own. no one will see me with the hood of my cloak over my head.' And half of Bond Street already thinks me out of my wits, she added to herself.

'It's a long way,' said Alban. His face was still stern, and set. 'I am going by foot, and it would tire you.'

'It will not tire me,' she said. 'Unless you think it is not respectable?'

'I do not care for that,' he said, and sighed. 'You may come if you wish.'

They walked side by side in the fading light. The sky, partly obscured by clouds, was graduating from blue to that dark sapphire that showed that night was breathing over it. She sensed Alban was uncomfortable, staring straight ahead, saying nothing, and keeping a good foot between them, as though he did not dare to get too close. I am dangerous, she thought, and instead of giving her a thrill it saddened her, and she wondered if she should have stayed in the parlour, watching the fire.

At Alban's cousin's house on Foster Lane, the room fell silent when she entered it. But Alban stood, and looked around at his family, and in a moment Agnes came forwards, and held Mary tight. Mary stayed on the outside of their circle, partaking of their food and thanking them, but saying little, only smiling at the jokes that were made, and occasionally finding Alban's eyes upon her in the firelight, as they had fallen upon her so many times in the last few weeks on Bond Street. His look seemed to be a kind of declaration. At only one moment did he appear displeased: when Jesse, after several pints of beer, offered to show Mary the workshop, and she refused, gently but immediately.

When they left she declined Alban's offer of a chair or a carriage, and they walked home in silence. It was a long way. As they neared Piccadilly she slipped her hand around his arm, and he made no acknowledgement of it, only continued to walk. It had been an easy movement to make, and yet she sensed the power of it, and it made her feel drunk with excitement. It took all her effort to continue without saying anything, to leave the moment as it was.

'I am making you a cup of silver,' he said. It was abrupt, no tenderness in the tone, said in a rush. 'It is but half-finished. You were promised one, once. Benjamin said it. He knows too much, that boy.'

They continued to walk. Mary tried to think how Benjamin knew, imagining Pierre making a joke of it. Then the thought was overtaken with curiosity.

'Why make one?' she said. 'What does it mean?' She ventured it, after several minutes, as one turns over a card in a game played for high stakes.

'I wish you to have something you were promised,' he said. He stopped and turned to her, then shook his head with exasperation. 'It means what you wish it to mean. I am not a man to make speeches, or to speak verse to you. If you want that you should send to Thomas Havering and his like.' He turned back, and they walked on.

His words had stung her. She felt maddened by them. Why must she always occupy some limbo, some space where she had to interpret everything? She had already learned that a whole lifetime of interpretations may be wrong.

'Do you think me the kind of woman that wants verses?' she said. 'What Havering said was far from poetic. At least he spoke clearly to me.'

They moved through a group of people, hearing laughter in the darkness, and Mary kept her head down, leaning on him for guidance. When they were once again alone, she removed her hand.

He took it, and put it back where it had been.

'It seems I am constantly pursuing your good opinion,' she said.

'And yet,' he said, 'you did not care to come into the workshop.'

'In the cellar,' she said.

'Yes. What was it? Has Mr Renard trained you too well? Did you not wish to look at the dirt and the dust of the trade that keeps you? Has he made the knowledge of hard work sour to you?'

She stopped, pulling him to a halt. She looked at the ground, breathing steadily, and when she began to speak her words were clear and unhurried.

'When I was newly married, I told my husband that when I was a child I was frightened of the dark. That, in truth, I was still a little frightened of it. I was still a bride, and told him in a moment of confidence.'

She held his gaze. He stayed looking at her. She did not know if it cost him anything; she hoped that it did.

'Not long after, my brother was taken away for the second time. I still had some spirit then, and I confronted my husband, imagining my words might have some weight with him. He locked me in the cellar for the night. I thought I would die of the fear. I only dared to challenge him once more after that; and that was when I knew Eli was dying. Though much good that did, for Eli or me. But that is why I did not go down into your workshop. You know nothing of the life I have lived.'

'I am sorry,' he said. Her hand was locked on his arm, hard, rooted.

'I never did teach my husband,' she said, 'and I see

I have not taught you, that I am not a piece of silver. I cannot go through fire and emerge unscathed. I have been hardened by these things. I am not here to be worked, to be shaped.'

'I do not wish to shape you,' he said.

'Well, I must take your word for that,' she said. 'And to do so will be a sore test of my experience. What is there to gain? Not money. And I am no longer an ornament.'

'There,' he said, 'we must differ.'

She let go of his arm and turned her back to him, looking out into the darkness.

'I am not him,' he said, and his voice was soft. She turned back, and looked at him.

'What do you ask for?' she said.

'Only your presence,' he said. 'Your ... friendship.' It was an inadequate word.

'You are a mystery,' she said.

'We are all mysteries to each other,' he said.

'My husband was a stranger to me when I married him,' she said. 'And he was a stranger when he died. When I first saw you, I felt I knew you, completely. Yet I do not. And I have dealt too long with shadows.'

'I don't understand,' he said. Above them, the buildings of Bond Street stood, and they seemed to Mary as impenetrable as the world she was trying to occupy. 'I have always only spoken the truth to you.'

'Yes,' she said. 'But there is too much silence in between. I must know if what lies between us is real. You pretend to be a saint, but you are not a saint. Why did you come to Bond Street, after all that passed between us?'

'I cannot tell you why I came here,' said Alban. 'I barely know it myself.'

His face was half-hidden in the gloom. He looked as though he was far away. She wondered if he stood again in church, a younger man, with a small boy running towards him, his eyes alight with joy. It seemed to her then that there was no grand plan, only a succession of such moments. She took a step towards him, trying to see his eyes, to know just for a moment what he was thinking. She told herself this would be the last risk she would take.

He kissed her.

At the touch of his lips, the warmth of his body against hers, the coldness that had wrapped her heart for so long shifted slightly.

'I am not who you think I am,' she said, drawing away. 'There are things you do not know.'

He said nothing, only drew her to him again, and in the kiss she sensed a promise.

Neither of them saw the figure in the shadows turn away, and begin to walk in the direction of Berkeley Square, his hand tight around the hilt of a knife.

CHAPTER THIRTY-TWO

May, 1793

11th October, 1792

I have not written for some time. My head is so full of thoughts,
yet I can only live in them; to write them down would be to
deliver them of their power. I cannot make them real on the paper.
I think of Harriet every day and every night. I do not have suf-
ficient energy for my business; I do not care for my coffee house
or the fellowship of Taylor. Unable to see Harriet, I send her
notes. It is most disagreeable to have to find a different boy or
porter every day to take them to her.

Digby had been waiting some time in Ma Blacklock's when
Maynard found him. Several times the waiting girl had
passed him, glancing disapprovingly at him as he toyed
with his first drink. When Maynard arrived, her face was
transformed by a bright smile. Maynard spoke briefly to

her, then approached the table, his eyes trained on Digby's face.

'I've ordered some coffee,' he said. 'What are you drinking?'

'Small beer,' said Digby.

'Well?' said Maynard, flicking out the back of his coat as he sat down. 'You sent for me.' He raised a sardonic eyebrow. 'Most refreshing, to have a note from you. You write a fair hand.'

'There was a time when I couldn't move for seeing you,' said Digby. 'These last few days, you are a hard man to get hold of.'

Maynard gave him a warning glance as the waiting girl returned and laid her tray down on the table.

'What is it?' he said, once she had gone.

'I've been thinking,' said Digby. He saw Maynard's expression falter, and knew that he had been tempted to make some smart remark, but that he'd thought better of it. Instead, Maynard looked at his coffee.

'I was dwelling on the fact,' said Digby, 'that it never made much sense to me, sir, how you were so interested in Mr Renard's death. You came out with so many high ideals, about justice, about protecting Mrs Renard.'

'Does it surprise you?' said Maynard, with a frown. 'That a man of the world should also care about others?'

Digby fought back a laugh, but he could not help a smirk moving across his face. 'Now, sir,' he said. 'You truly sound like the silversmith himself. I would almost mistake you for one of his intimate circle. Yet in these last weeks, for some reason, you have drawn back from the mystery. After all your shouting and cursing at me, you have not sought me out again. Even though there are many unwholesome rumours circulating about the Renard house, and it cannot have escaped your attention that Mrs Renard's window was broken. Where is your concern now, sir?'

Maynard said nothing, though Digby could see he was searching for, and would probably find, a fluent response soon enough.

'As I say,' Digby continued, 'it got me thinking. Thought I'd keep an eye on things. You know how good I am at watching. Particularly around your house. How is young Mr Maynard, sir? Did he enjoy his trip to Europe? Just got back, so I hear.'

Maynard said nothing, but he had raised his eyes so quickly to Digby's that the watchman knew he was on to something. Still, as he looked at the other man's face, he could see vigilance, but no fear.

'Be good for Mrs Maynard, won't it?' said Digby. 'Seeing her boy again. He's been a bit of trouble to you though, hasn't he? Likes maidservants, according to tavern talk. Likes gambling. Too soft for violence – probably. But you sent him away, didn't you? When was it? The day after Renard's murder became known?'

Maynard looked back into the depths of his coffee cup as though reflecting on Digby's words. Then he sat back a little, and shrugged. 'You are right that I feared for him,' he said. 'Not that it matters now. He kept the wrong company. He never fought himself, but he was around those that did. He borrowed money from Renard, and bet away a snuffbox that had some sentimental value to me. When this murder happened, I would have left it, but it was driving my wife to distraction. She had to know. He is our only son, and the knowledge that he might have been involved was making her ill; every day she spoke of it. That is why I asked you to look into it.' He glanced up. 'I thought I would shake the tree, and if anything fell out . . .' He let his sentence peter out.

'What if I had found something out?' said Digby.

'I would have paid you off. Don't tell me you can't be bought. And, if not . . . as I said to you before, I am not womanish, like Taylor. I would have found a solution, shall we leave it at that? Everyone knows you are crooked, Digby. You are hardly some guardian of the law. Besides, I knew you had nothing that could harm me, the last time I saw you. I apologize for my – shall we say, intensity? I had to get your attention, to see if there was anything there. And when I did, there wasn't any real fear in your eyes. Real fear is the fear we have for ourselves.'

Digby watched the surface of his own drink: a small black mote floating in it, the surface trembling with every vibration of the floorboards. He felt tired. 'You're right,' he said.

'I know that,' said Maynard. 'If there was anything to be known you would have found it out and I'd have seen it in a moment.' He leaned close again, his hands resting on the table, his voice a whisper. 'There is nothing that can tie my son to Renard's death, I am confident of it; and you're right, with the rumours, and the broken windows, there may be something else going on, but he has been far away from here until this week. I, for one, do not care to concern myself with Renard any more.'

'So much for your high ideals,' said Digby, taking a gulp of his beer.

'A bit much coming from you,' said Maynard. He gave a throaty laugh. 'no one cares. Londoners are so heartless, aren't they? Here a death, there a death, and they just keep moving forwards, with not even a glance behind. You're looking mighty thoughtful though. Indulge me. Who do you think murdered Renard, after all your scraping about?'

Digby thought of Mary. He had wanted to protect her and, in a way, he still did. She had awoken something in him: a certain sensitivity, and the knowledge that his life might be put to use protecting, as well as hating. When he thought of her, and Mallory, a kind of tenderness rose in him. But when he had seen her in Alban Steele's arms, he had let go of that obligation. He felt no bitterness towards her, but he owed her no loyalty either.

'I've no proof,' he said. 'But I think it was the silversmith's wife and her sister, sir. They had a little brother. Renard was cruel to him, and he died. All in all, I think they found a way to have their revenge.'

He looked at Maynard's face. The man was frowning, and he gave a little shake of his head. Then he put his finger to his lips. Digby nodded.

'I'll leave you to your beer,' Maynard said. 'I suppose we'll have to let the dead rest.'

It was only after he had gone that Digby looked up to see the coin he'd left, as bright as if he'd polished it, glinting silver in the dim light.

CHAPTER THIRTY-THREE

12th October, 1792

I fancy Taylor has a liking for icy women. His wife barely speaks without something saucy coming out of her mouth. I could not live with such a woman, her tongue always sharpened. He had a glass too much of Hermitage tonight and was expounding on Mary's delicacy, and I had to tell him the truth. That her father was a mere box-maker in the City; that his worth, and hers, rested solely in the contents of his strong-box. It is the truth. When I first met him I was keen for the association, for I knew he had amassed enough to set me up as I wished, that he was sell-ing his daughters so high because of that boy of his.

I told him all of this, but he would not see it; he only laughed his booming, stupid laugh, and shook his head, as though I was in jest, and Mary is all he believes her to be. He angered me, and I put my fist down on the table, hard enough to knock over my glass. I did not know how to make him see the depths of my despair, so I said it: there are days when I wish her dead. He fell silent, and I could only rouse him again by pouring him another glass of wine.

Alban set out his wares on a small mahogany table that had been specially covered with a white cloth for the purpose. He did it slowly, and with great care. Mr Chichester moved around him, pacing up and down in front of the windows, and giving him a history of the Berkeley Square town house with an air of generous condescension. Since their first meeting in the Renard shop several months before, Chichester had postponed the appointment for ordering plate several times, so that Alban had wondered whether he would ever come here at all. Now, Alban felt he could have done well without it; he was in a dark humour, and having to flatter this boy, barely out of his teens, felt like a bad day's work. As Alban had bowed to him he had noticed the contrast between the white of Chichester's cravat and the grimy yellowish shade of his neck. He knew he was unusually fastidious, that most of the men walking around London probably looked as Chichester did if he cared to observe them, but it still jarred. He never envied privilege, but thought it had its obligations, and neatness was one of them.

Outside, Mattie was waiting for him, his fists ready lest anyone make an attempt on the silver. He had walked there with Alban, revelling in his new role as guard, so much so that Alban found it hard not to laugh. If he was going to have to pay house calls there was no one he would rather have with him, for if anything was certain it was that Mallory's son would be more than capable of beating the hell out of anyone who tried to steal something. He couldn't blame the boy for not wanting to enter the house, and had not encouraged it, for Mallory hadn't raised her son for servitude, and he thought it would take a good deal of time before Mattie cared to ingratiate himself with those above him.

'Most excellent,' said Chichester as Alban put the last piece of silver, a tureen, out on the table. He said it in a way that was hail-fellow-well-met, yet Alban heard the false note in his voice, as though he hadn't quite the confidence, or conviction, to believe his compliment. He smiled, but stayed silent, as Chichester shifted on his feet, bending down to observe the pieces closely, his hands clasped tightly behind his back as though it might harm him to touch something.

'My wife always dealt with the silversmith before,' he said. 'Came to a bad end, I believe, the Frenchman?' He looked at Alban questioningly, and seemed unnerved by the steady gaze that was returned to him. 'He did, sir,' said Alban, and was glad when no further questions followed.

'This is exquisite,' Chichester said, picking up a finely chased creamer, 'though a little feminine for my taste. It is something my wife would have liked at one time.' He straightened up and smiled conspiratorially. 'I am master in my own house at last,' he said. Alban found it hard to return the smile. There was something desperately unappealing about this boy-man in his gilded interior, moving affectedly like an automaton in a music box, dancing to somebody else's tune.

He smiled as best he could, and cleared his throat. 'What kind of thing are you thinking of, sir?' he said. 'I'm sure the firm would be able to supply your wants.'

Chichester smiled with unaffected pleasure. 'My goal is to assemble a family silver collection to be passed on through the generations,' he said. 'We have my father's plate at the estate, of course, but I wish to branch out; to acquire things that reflect my taste for exquisite craftsmanship. Mr Renard always spoke to me of fashions, he hardly listened at all; everything he brought me was the same. I would take pleasure in knowing that my taste, my education, my discrimination will be passed down to my children and my children's children.' His voice was most warm when he spoke of his education and taste, rather than his children.

'But I am a collector, you see,' said Chichester. He seemed determined to cordially prove his credentials. 'There is not much here – most of my collection is held in my family home. I have some prints and fragments of sculpture I salvaged during my time in Italy – but ...' His expression darkened. 'I cannot show you them now. My wife is in the library. Another day, I will show you.'

'I would like to see them very much,' said Alban. 'Such things are always of use to men such as me. We are plunderers, you see, snatching up fragments of beautiful things so that we might use them again.'

'Yes, yes,' said Chichester, his face turning pinkish with pleasure. 'I am most glad we have met. In the future I will deal with the commissioning of plate myself.' He gave an unaffected laugh. 'I think, to start, a pair of bread baskets, Mr Steele. With guilloche handles, as on this sugar basket you have here, and the sides similar. Make them refined, but strong. And with my arms engraved in the centre on the bottom. Every time anyone takes a roll I want them to see it.' He smiled at Alban. 'Send through a sketch for my approval – you understand the idea I have?'

Alban tapped his own forehead. 'It is all in here, Mr Chichester,' he said.

'That is all for now, I think,' said Chichester. 'I have a fancy for some epergnes and sauce boats, but they can wait till next time.' His abruptness and sense of mastery was already returning. Alban sensed the awkwardness in him, as though he was not sure how to balance the conversation. 'I have business to attend to. But I am glad to have met you again.'

'And I you, sir,' said Alban, beginning to wrap up the items he had brought only marginally quicker than he had unwrapped them.

'I will send for you again soon,' said Chichester. 'There is much I would like to order in the future.' Alban inclined his head, and watched as the man rushed from the room, still flushed and leaving the door open.

One of the footmen put his head through the door. 'Hurry up,' he said.

Alban slowed his movements purposely, neatly wrapping up and tucking in every piece, with a considered precision. What a strange house this is, he thought, looking at the footman swaggering around the room as though he owned it, even reaching out to flick one of the pieces of silver. Alban caught his wrist before he did it. 'Don't,' he said. 'Or I will have a quarrel with you.'

Harriet tilted her head. 'Do I hear someone in the hall?' she said. 'It may be Mama. Go and check. If you please.' She added those three words to the end of almost every request these days; it was a habit, used to pacify her husband, and now everyone else, too.

'It will only be the silversmith,' said Joanna, then realized with a jolt what she had said. But Harriet seemed not to have noticed. Joanna put her sewing down and rose. Before she crossed the room, she tucked Harriet's blanket in. Since the day of Harriet's forgiveness of her, Joanna had grown fonder of the girl, the strengthening mutual sympathy of the trapped. She kept asking for her mother, even though there had been no word that the lady would visit.

'It is Mr Chichester,' Joanna said, as the door opened, and she sank into a curtsey, lowering her face so she would not have to look him in the eyes.

The young man passed her, and sat down next to his wife.

'How are you, my dear?' he said, his voice soft.

'Very well,' said Harriet, smiling slightly.

'I have been seeing the silversmith, and ordering plate,' he said. And he began to describe pieces. He talked for a long time, his tone smooth and confident as he described each detail of what he had in mind.

At each stage, he asked Harriet her opinion, and she would incline her head and say, soft-voiced: 'That will meet my approval.'

It was so different from all those months before, when the toilet service had been ordered, that Joanna, invisible, standing against the wall like a piece of furniture, felt a chill. We are all in your power now, she thought, looking at Mr Chichester's animated face as he spoke.

As the door closed behind him, Harriet turned to her. 'Where do they find all the silversmiths?' she said, her voice pure and clear, almost musical. 'When Pierre went, were they lining up, ready to replace him? And yet he cannot be replaced. I believe he loved me more than any person ever has.'

CHAPTER THIRTY-FOUR

16th October, 1792
I sent a box of sweetmeats from Gunter's to my dearest girl. I,
always so careful, would bankrupt myself for her sake. She sends
me the most affecting letters. I write back, of course; I give her
what she wishes for. And the truth is that my own feelings are
not far behind. I imagine so many things. Just yesterday I was
able to see her; she slipped away and we met at a secluded spot in
the park. Her coachman is loyal and sees nothing. We drank
sweet milk wrung from the udder. God, the taste of her mouth.
Had she allowed me I would have taken her again right there, and
sent everything else in my life to hell for her sake.

A coroner's meeting had been called, and the poor suicide
had been carried to the tavern in St James's from the
house that had once been his home in a backstreet near

Piccadilly. His mother had held on so tightly to him that the tears her fingernails had made showed clearly on his frayed coat. Brass and Jennings, the watchmen from St James's parish who had carried him here, stood nearby under Digby's watchful, interested eye. Digby had no business being here other than his ghoulish interest, but no one questioned his presence. With a glance at each other Brass and Jennings agreed that it was best to leave such an odd 'un alone.

Digby watched Taylor look at the body and sigh heavily. He seemed a different man today from the one that had presided over the coroner's meeting for Pierre Renard so many months ago. For that man, his duty as coroner had been borne as a conspicuous honour to him. He had held himself upright, as an observer of human life and death, a preserver of law and justice. But looking at the wracked face of the suicide, he looked like someone on the same level as the dead, not a representative of a higher justice. It was as though his own vitality was being eroded, one death at a time.

'Exham the engraver. He drank laudanum,' said the constable. 'That's what his mother told me. I couldn't bring her here. She's still wailing in her parlour.' He produced a bottle, the label's contents long faded. 'This was it. The manservant's come to testify.' He nodded towards an eager-eyed man, waiting obediently in the corner.

'How interesting,' said one of the younger men, stepping forwards and looking over the body with a kind of cool interest. 'He was an engraver, you say? Was he an associate of Renard's, Dr Taylor?'

'I believe Mr Renard had some small dealings with him,' said Taylor.

'How strange,' said the man, with a snigger. 'It seems that the silverworkers of London have much to fear in this parish.'

'He was in debt, I understand,' said Taylor. The young man shrugged.

Digby saw Taylor's distressed expression, and almost felt compassion for him; almost, but not quite. He was in agreement with Taylor. There was something chilling about the young pup, something unfeeling in his detachment. Were we all like that once, he thought? In our youth, so unaware of suffering, so arrogant of its effects, that we were impervious to it? When I, I who have seen so much, do not care, it is because I am hardened to it, because I have steeled myself. Not this young man. Suffering has never touched him, and he believes it never will, because he is righteous. An involuntary shudder ran through him. Righteous; my God. To think yourself righteous is the worst crime of all.

Taylor passed a hand over his brow. 'I am satisfied there is no link between the two. To me, the verdict is clear. Poor wretch. May his soul rest in peace.'

'You have many cares at the moment, sir,' said the young man, in an easy tone. 'I hear there is much talk of Mrs Renard, that she is increasingly delicate.'

'The lady is well enough,' said Taylor. Digby guessed the doctor was trying to keep a light tone, but the words came out wrong, all sour and over-sharp, like a scold.

The young man raised his eyebrows and moved off

without another word, or a bow. Digby saw Taylor take a step towards the boy's retreating back. Was he feeling a tremor of panic, wondered Digby? Taylor seemed lost in this strange, post-Pierre world. The word was he was no longer welcomed by some of his cronies on Bond Street; was the world's respect melting away?

Digby was startled out of his musings by Maynard, who had just entered, and patted him heartily on the shoulder as he passed. This rather bothered Digby, and not just because of his dealings with Maynard; he considered himself invisible, moving in and out of people's lives like a ghost. Having given him startling proof of his visibility, Maynard saluted the company.

'Can we get on, gentlemen?' he said, his voice booming out above the general conversation. 'I have pressing business elsewhere.' There was a general rumble of discontent, but the irritation entered Taylor's blood; Digby saw it flicker across his face.

The coroner's meeting progressed quickly, with everyone agreeing on the verdict of suicide. Brass and Jennings covered the body. It would be cold enough in the night not to give the undertaker too much trouble.

'A word with you, Mr Maynard,' said Taylor, as people began to disperse.

Maynard's lip gave that sardonic little twist that was familiar to Digby. The watchman moved further back into the shadows, in case he was noticed. He leaned against the wall, but it was too cold, and he soon stood up again. Maynard gave a slight bow and came over to the corner where Taylor stood.

'I know you to be an honourable man, Maynard,' Taylor said, and Digby saw surprise permeate Maynard's disinterested expression. 'I was most displeased to hear, therefore, that you have been speaking of Mrs Renard about the town.'

Maynard's eyebrows remained up. 'Am I to know why you level such a charge at me?' he said, in his most imperious tone.

'Come now, man,' Taylor said. 'I heard directly from a member of your club that you had been speaking of Mr Renard, and slandering him.'

'Oh, Mr Renard,' said Maynard, sounding bored, though Digby guessed he was far from it. 'He is dead. What can it possibly matter? And if the slander, as you put it, is not fiction, but fact, then I have the perfect right to say what I wish.'

'Damn you!' cried Taylor. The shout broke from him with such suddenness that Digby jumped, as though a gun had been fired. Maynard leaned on his cane and looked at the floor. 'Come about, now, Taylor,' he murmured.

Taylor leaned in so close that Digby had to strain his sharp ears to hear him: he took the risk of leaning forwards out of the shadows. 'I am telling you, Maynard, to act with some honour,' he said. 'Have some respect for the dead, and those left behind. Mrs Renard has enough to contend with without your malicious tongue.'

Maynard's icy stare never wavered. 'It's chivalrous of you, Taylor, but Mrs Renard has nothing to fear from me,' he said. 'I have never slandered her in any way. If I spoke against anyone it is Renard, who ...' he leaned close

'. . . was as damnable a rogue as I ever knew, friend of yours or not.' He seemed angry now. 'And shall I tell you what the talk is of now, Taylor? Word is you are sick with love for Mrs Renard, and that *your* behaviour to *her* has been far from honourable. And a gentleman said to me last night that on visiting the shop, he could already see the effects of it.'

'What do you mean?' said Dr Taylor.

'Good God, man,' said Maynard, in a low voice. 'What a fool you are. She is with child. Look to yourself and your own reputation before bothering to defend that of a dead man. I wish you good day, sir.' He went out, his cane tip ringing on the tavern's stone floor.

Dr Taylor had frozen, his lips parted, as though he might cry out.

There was something compelling about it: the stricken doctor standing still and alone, staring into space. In the man's expression, Digby thought he saw the movement of God. He wondered at the doctor's surprise, for in his daily wanderings, Digby had noticed the bloom on Mrs Renard's face; he knew there was love, and where love was, children would follow. He wanted to stay longer, perhaps offer a word or two of comfort to the doctor, for the enmity he had felt for Taylor had faded. But he had to go; his hand, as always, closed around the precious watch within his pocket. The way he moved his fingers over it was a kind of routine now, a comforting thing done by rote rather than choice. He took one long, last look at Taylor, then moved towards the door, keeping near the wall and walking carefully so as not to make any noise.

Time was ticking on; and he had his own appointment to keep.

Joanna slipped out of the house. As she walked away from it she had the delicious feeling that she was dissolving into the darkness of the night, her new hat warming her head. The night had once made her shiver with fear, but now she welcomed it. It was her camouflage, the enabler of her freedom, and that freedom gave her courage. If there were robbers and villains about, she thought, she would be one too. She knew how to defend herself.

She didn't come out every night. Sometimes she stayed with Harriet, sitting guard over her, keeping her calm and entertained. But as the girl's belly grew larger so she grew more lethargic, and tonight her eyelids had been drooping by eight. Joanna made her way out of the house quietly, passing the butler as he snored loudly near the silver store, past Mrs Holland who had recently been trying to ingratiate herself. Her plot to topple Joanna lay in ruins. Joanna knew Holland had gone to Mr Chichester to report her for slipping out at night. But he had said nothing, and done nothing, and now Mrs Holland worshipped Joanna as a higher power, even as the household hierarchy began to falter and crumble, its master and mistress barely worthy of the names, such ineffective keepers of their servants as they were.

As Joanna neared the end of the mews she heard Digby's low whistle. He was there, at the corner, and when he saw her, a sad smile spread across his face. 'No Watkin tonight?' she said.

'Poetry,' said Digby, with exaggerated pronunciation. 'I hoped you'd come.'

'Only for a moment,' she said. 'I can't walk the circuit with you. I don't care to take the risk of being seen tonight.'

'Your face is half-covered,' he said. 'Who would know?' He pulled her to him. In the shadows, she could not see his face clearly until he was near her. She pushed him away and shook her head.

'I could come into the house,' he said, a spark in his eyes.

'And make me lose my place?' she said. 'I am not in the mood to gamble. It was made clear enough to me when I came here: no followers allowed. I am in trouble enough as it is.' She tried not to say it: I cannot let you close to me again. They had not spoken about the watch, but sometimes, in the middle of the night, she thought of it, and the fear was enough to keep her awake until dawn crept over the London sky.

'You are a temptation to a man, Jo,' he said. 'Stay with me a while. Take pity on me. I've been to see a poor suicide looked over by the coroners.'

'How dreadful,' she said.

'It doesn't normally bother me,' he said. 'But he was an engraver and knew Renard. And as I walked here, I thought of Renard, and wondered if he who killed him is still out there, waiting in the shadows in the square.'

She said nothing, but let one hand rest on the back of his neck. Moving close, he hooked his chin over her shoulder, and huddled into her.

'The warmth of you does me good,' he said. 'We understand each other, Jo, do we not?'

'Yes. But why, I do not know,' she said. The heat of his body had a soporific effect. She had spent so long wound tight that to be lulled by his embrace was a luxury. She pulled herself away unwillingly.

'We understand each other because you have a heart as black as my own,' he said, with a smile, a genuine smile that filled his eyes.

'No,' she said. 'Stop teasing me.'

He leaned back against the wall, and sighed. 'Why do we not have the liberty to do as we wish?' he said. 'And these wretches, within their high walls, with their fires and their food and their jewels. I hate them.'

'All that envy,' she said, stroking his hair. She understood it; but it made her feel cold inside to see the look on his face.

'You understand me,' he said. 'I know you do.'

'I thought I hated them once,' she said. 'But now, I cannot explain it.'

'How is your mistress?' he said.

'Fractious. The master barely speaks to her.'

'If he bought her and she does not give him kindness . . . her father recognized a plum when he saw him.'

'No,' said Joanna, quickening in defence of Harriet. 'The money came from her family. Chichester's a good name, an old name, and madam's father wanted to marry his new money with old blood. It is all hers really, though she is owned by him now. He is a cold man.'

He leaned his forehead against hers, then looked up at the walls surrounding them. 'I've done her an injustice then,' he said. 'They all seem the same to me. They built this place in my grandfather's time. He told me they made the bricks here, made them in their kilns with the London clay. How the fine ladies and gentlemen in the streets nearby complained. They said the smoke ruined their fine drapes and furnishings.' He kissed her again. 'I wish I'd been the brickmaker,' he said, and in the darkness she saw the glint of his teeth as he smiled.

CHAPTER THIRTY-FIVE

17th October, 1792

A quarrel with one of Harriet's footmen, a low-born scoundrel. The man said I have second-hand airs. That I spend so long with 'my lady this and my lady that' each day that I act like one. I damned him to hell and back. He is lucky I was not carrying a sword.

It shook me, and later I said more than I should have done. I told Taylor of my love for Harriet, thinking I could trust him. Surely any reasonable man would see her worth, and the comparative poverty of my wife's character. Yet the look he gave me was terrible, as though he had been blinded by the knowledge, as though he saw nothing for a good few minutes. For a moment I thought he might weep. Is he, like Mary, about to succumb to acting as though he is on stage at Drury Lane? I clapped him on the back and tried to ease him with some lighter words. I am lucky that I did not tell him more.

Mary. The very name is hateful to me. How can I explain what it is to live, year after year, with a person who is a sore irritation. The very sound of her footstep on the stair sends a shadow over my evening.

'So,' said Grisa, as Mary and Alban entered the shop. 'It is done.' His expression was one of relief, tinged with sadness.

'It is. And Miss Avery has left us to return to her family. Where's Benjamin?' said Alban.

'I did as I told you I would. He has been sent to collect the hallmarked wares from Goldsmiths' Hall; I did not wish him to see you return.'

'We must keep things quiet for a while longer,' said Mary.

'Go upstairs, my dear, and rest,' said Alban. 'I will come and see you in a few moments.' He turned to Grisa, but his expression showed that he was listening to his wife's footsteps with solicitude.

'She is delicate,' said Grisa.

'So would you be, if you had lived her life,' said Alban. 'Grief etches its way through us, leaving its mark like salt on silver.' The emotion of the morning had loosened his instinct for concealment; he had been opened up by it. 'How has trade been?' he said, trying to inject briskness into his voice.

'Quiet,' said Grisa. 'Until Mr Maynard called in.'

In her chamber, Mary undid her hair and sat on the bed. That morning, Avery had helped her dress, both she and

Mary laughing and crying as they fumbled over their clothes and hair. It was not long past seven on the clock when they went down to the hackney carriage where Mallory waited, walking as quietly as they could down the stairs of the silent house, Ellen letting them out while Benjamin still slept.

The weather was dry, but the sky was covered with clouds. White light poured in through the carriage windows as it rattled through the London streets towards the City and the places she had known as a child.

'I am glad you are going to be married at St Vedast's,' said Mallory, as the carriage tumbled along. 'The goldsmiths' church. Our father would have been proud.' She had made an uneasy peace with the situation; Mary had insisted that Alban and her sister shake hands, and now she watched a faint smile dawn on Mallory's face as the carriage turned into Foster Lane.

Their father had worked the metal all his life, and his father before him. With his death that legacy had been lost. Yet, here they were, the carriage bringing them back to the heart of the City, steps from Goldsmiths' Hall, where the metal that had kept them their whole lives was assayed and hallmarked.

It was just before eight o'clock. The time was the only thing in common with Mary's first marriage, and she panicked for a moment, hoping that it would not lay some kind of curse on this ceremony, before reminding herself to stay calm. The special licence had been secured in the utmost secrecy.

Jesse Chamac stood in the doorway of the church,

waiting for her as Avery and Mallory helped her out of the carriage. He looked frail, and as she got down she noticed how green his eyes were: a hard tourmaline brightness that unnerved her for a moment.

'How does he?' she said. Though she could see, ahead of her, the figure of Alban waiting for her at the altar, she could not help herself. Jesse smiled. 'He is nervous, and can barely believe it is true,' he said. Then he offered her his arm, looking this way and that down the street, as though someone might come to interrupt them. 'Come now,' he said.

Mary sought to savour every moment, but she shook with nerves, and knew that she would not hold the memory in her mind. As the service began she wanted to slow it somehow, for the very words seemed too quick and disjointed.

Behind them, the church door opened, and a cold gust laid the candle flames flat and blue for a moment, almost snuffing them out. Mary turned, and at that first moment her eyes fell on the doorway, she saw them: her parents, a small figure linking them. It was only their silhouettes, but it was unmistakable, the light of the church door behind them: her mother, her father, and Eli. But when she blinked, it was only an acquaintance of Jesse's and his wife, trying to slip into the church, embarrassed by the stir their entrance had caused. When Mary glanced at Mallory's face, it was as though her sister had seen nothing at all: she stared ahead, at the gold words of the commandments inscribed on the black board behind the altar.

'I thought,' she said, and felt Alban's hand tighten on

hers. As the priest continued, she wondered what he had made of it; and she wanted to halt things, to explain to Alban what this blessing meant. But Alban was so rooted in the world, so calm, that he would never have thought such a thing, she knew.

He did not pause as he leaned over the register, and signed his name: his hand small, neat, precise and graceful; Mary's curving, elaborate, as though she sought to inject all her lost potential for artistry into this one moment.

As they left the church to return to Bond Street, she remembered the first night they had lain together, and how she had woken to feel the warmth of his hand on her back, him reaching out to her even as they slept. Their bond, forged in heat, had finally been blessed.

She was brushing her hair when her husband came into their chamber. She was smiling to herself, remembering Avery's joy as she had kissed them on the church steps.

'Avery says she is going back to her brother's shop to find herself a husband,' she said. 'That she hopes she may find one as fine as you.'

Alban laughed. She loved the sound; it seemed to make everything in the world right, and she wondered if marriage would change things between them. They had lain together many times since that first night, a handful of days from their first kiss. On that first night they had undressed frantically, as though knowing if either paused they would draw back, forever, from what they had started. In their urgency, if they had heeded anything it was the need for silence; the only sound their breathing, the creak of the bed beneath them. In a matter of weeks she said to him that she thought she was with child, delight and fear flaring in her eyes at the idea of it.

One evening, held close by him, she had told him of her hatred for Pierre. Told him in a hushed voice, as though their lovemaking would be dissolved by her words, daring him to leave her. 'I should have been stronger with Pierre; I should have seen, should have known who he was. He took everything I loved from me, and did I turn on him? No, I let him take my soul instead. I ask you: what would you do to the person that did that?'

He had said nothing, holding her, shushing her. But she had seen the fear twist in his eyes, fighting with the love that she knew he felt for her. They both knew the answer: I would want to kill them.

But on this day, she would admit to only joy.

She smiled brightly at him. 'Do you have any family you wish to inform, or wish me to meet?'

He shook his head. 'My parents are both dead,' he said. 'You have met Jesse and Agnes; I have some other cousins you may meet but they are rooted in Chester, so a journey will be necessary.'

She watched him. 'Were you ever married before?' she said. 'Forgive me if the question seems indelicate. You do not offer information about yourself, and there are some things that I need to know.'

'I should have been more forthcoming, perhaps,' he said. 'But it does not come easily to me. I have nothing I do not wish you to know, and nothing to tell.' He took her gently by the shoulders. In the light he saw the many colours in her eyes, colours that all seemed to mingle to make that piercing stare. 'There are no other wives, no other children,' he said. 'No ghosts.'

'All the ghosts are here, then,' she said, and flushed, for she could see from the look in his eyes that she had wounded him. Just as quickly the hurt melted away, and he smiled at her; no, she thought, you are not Pierre.

'We will be gone from here soon,' he said. 'And you are showing. You will be a subject of gossip, Mrs Steele.'

She smiled, plaiting her hair slowly. 'I thought,' she said, 'that it might not be true. I was growing thinner by the day, before.' She stroked her stomach.

'Well, I will see you eat well,' said Alban. 'And I have strict orders from Avery. If I do not make you grow until you are large and hearty, she will return, and make you eat every hour that you are in her company.'

'I saw Eli,' she said. She hardly knew what impulse prompted her to say it.

'What?' he said.

'In the church. I glanced behind, and he was there, with my parents. They wanted me to know that they bless us.'

'My love,' he said, and she could see the disquiet in his eyes. 'You must rest. Get into bed, or you will be cold.' He came forwards and pulled up the covers. Before he covered her over he allowed his hand to rest on her stomach. He could not help it; he had to bless his unborn child with tenderness every time he came near her.

As she lay down, his fingers traced a pattern that she had sewed into her nightgown: a delicate web of red thread on the cream. 'It has its own kind of beauty,' he said.

'Like the small things we work into silver. It shows me you and I are matched, Mary.' He looked at her. 'I will protect you. I will do whatever I have to do, to protect you.'

Mary slid down under the covers and let him tuck her in. He kissed her lips gently. 'You must rest,' he said, standing up, and stretching, as though he was preparing for work.

'Are you leaving me?' she asked.

'There is work to be done, and we must keep things as normal as possible,' he said. 'Grisa tells me a man called Mr Maynard called. He says that he has only just recalled that he left a snuffbox here, some months ago. Grisa has not seen it, and I must search the place top and bottom, for he is most insistent. Will you give me the keys to the chests?' He held his hand out.

She hesitated. Apart from the two occasions with Benjamin and Mallory, she had not surrendered the keys to anyone since Pierre's death. She had begun to think of them as her own. They lay beside the bed, and she looked at them for a long moment. Then she saw the impatience in his eyes, and she remembered how shyly they had spoken their vows to each other, as though they were strangers.

'We will be happy, won't we?' she said.

'Yes, of course. Mary?'

'Yes, my dear?'

'Give me the keys.'

CHAPTER THIRTY-SIX

1st November, 1792

I happened to walk by Berkeley Square today. I saw Chichester pass, carried in a sedan. He looked thin, as weak as water. He seems to fade day by day. My apprentice, malnourished as he is, could beat him in the ring. And his wife is such a woman: my dearest girl.

At our meeting in the park I happened to mention to her of a legal separation I had heard of. I must have been mad to say it, but when her skin is beneath my fingertips, the thoughts flow from my lips. She is so beautiful, dressed in the most delicate silks and satins, her white neck warmed by sable. It is like that day I first entered a jeweller's shop: her eyes are the sapphires, her skin the silver. I am racked by the need to have her, not just to possess her bodily, but to make the jewel entirely my own, and keep it in a case of my own devising.

Of course it is madness to talk of a separation; it would never be possible and it is fantastical to think of it. But God has given me the vision of what could be: the boy will die, and if my wife is not there . . . God knows I have wished her gone long enough. Yes, I will write it: I see a day when Harriet could be my wife. To write it brings tears to my eyes, tears of gladness and longing. They blur my sight and fall on to this page.

The next day dawned bright. When Mary came out of the shop on to Bond Street, she felt that the world had been transformed, and all her fears from the night before, dissolved. It was as though her senses had been sharpened, and she saw everything anew. Her sight was clearer, and she noticed details everywhere. A weed in the guttering, a crack in a brick, the specks of dirt in a pail of milk as it was carried past her, the milkmaid mewing her wares.

It was like that first morning after she had taken Alban into her bed. The sense of life had surged in her. Strange as it was, she felt sure it was not mainly from the physical act. She had felt connected to the world again. She was free to feel sympathy for others again, and free to see beauty where it lay.

She smiled to think that her husband had learned about women the way he had learned to draw designs and work silver: carefully, slowly, persistently. This morning, he had left her silver wedding cup on the table, so that she found it when she came in to breakfast. Its surfaces pure and sheer, he had rubbed every fingerprint away. It shone, drawing light into itself, and casting light out. It seemed to say to her: have patience, and you will have everything.

'You and I are so different,' he had said to her, when she had run to him and kissed him for it. And she didn't know if she saw pleasure or misgiving in his eyes.

'Madam?'

The woman's voice made her turn in the street, and her gaze met with a pair of blue eyes. The lady that had spoken to her had one hand placed on the wall of the shop, as though it was taking her weight. She was dressed finely, her hat trimmed with feathers that bobbed and spun in the breeze. She wore gloves, and was well wrapped against the cold, but Mary could see she was heavily pregnant. She recognized her from somewhere, and as she moved towards her she mentally began flicking through the lists of names she had consulted in the ledger, hoping that an identity would emerge. There was such a stricken look on the woman's face that Mary's first instinct was to offer her comfort.

'Are you well?' said Mary. 'Can I help you?'

The woman shook her head, and looked at the ground. When she spoke, her voice was soft, without any harshness. 'I may be in error,' she said, and again turned her eyes to Mary's face, as though searching for something there. 'Yet I had to come here, and speak to you. I hope you will understand.'

'Please, do speak,' said Mary.

'Oh,' said the woman. 'This is much harder than I thought. I have imagined this moment many times, yet now, all of the things I have to say to you have dissolved, like smoke.' She gave a small, girlish laugh, but Mary noticed that her eyes remained steady. 'I suppose there is only one important thing I must say,' said the lady. She took a deep breath, then drew herself up, as though bracing herself. 'I loved your husband once,' she said.

Mary said nothing. Her first thought was: Alban. But before she could formulate any question, the woman had pitched herself forwards, and began to walk down the street, quickly. She did not look back, and moved surprisingly fast. Mary watched her bobbing head until it disappeared from view.

She didn't know how long she stood there. A customer went into the shop, glancing at her strangely as he passed. She turned a little, and saw Alban and Grisa dancing in attendance through the glass. Her husband smiled as he spoke to the customer, but his eyes were sad.

Then the bell went again, the customer passed by, and Alban was beside her.

'What's the matter?' he said. 'Grisa noticed your dress fluttering in the wind. And here you are, stock-still as though in a trance. Don't the neighbours think you strange enough?'

He meant it as a joke, she knew. But she turned away from him, unable to look at him. 'What is it?' he said. She shook her head, silently, and pushed past him to go into the shop and up the stairs. As she did it, she could tell he was maddened by her silence, and it grieved her, yet she could not speak.

Two hours had passed and Alban came to their chamber door, knocking and knocking until she opened it.

'What is it?' he said.

'I have a headache,' she said. 'Go back to your bench.'

He was dressed in his work clothes: the pale brown shirt and breeches, the leather apron still tied around his waist. His hands were stained grey with toil. 'Did you not even wash before you came up here?' she said. Her voice sounded disdainful, even to herself.

'Not until you tell me what happened,' he said.

'What's wrong with your hand?' she said. His right thumbnail was black; she caught sight of it as his hands twitched slightly in the anxiety of the moment. 'I mis-struck,' he said. 'Are you going to tell me?'

She stared at his hand, reached out to touch it. He put his hands on her waist, and pulled her to him. 'Tell me,' he said. His left hand brushed her face, then slid down gently to the back of her neck, and rested there. Mary found she couldn't look up at him.

'A woman on the street,' she said. 'Came up to me and said, "I loved your husband once".'

Alban let her go. 'I see,' he said. 'Did you recognize her?'

'Yes, but I don't know who she was. For a moment, I thought she meant you. And the sadness came upon me – and I thought – what hope is there? After everything that has happened? How can we be free of it all?'

He shook his head. 'We can be free if you will only let him go. You think I am like him, don't you? Do you know me?'

She sagged forwards at the disbelief on his face. She clung to him, and kissed him, until he answered her kisses with his own, turning the key in the lock. Afterwards she was too sensitive to be touched, and twisted on the bed, not knowing how to be soothed. 'I am sorry,' she said. 'Forgive me.'

'Will you never have faith in me?' he said, and his voice was sad.

'I will,' she said. 'I do.'

'No,' he said. 'You don't.'

A door slammed in the depths of the house and Joanna woke suddenly.

As she rubbed her eyes the details of her dream stayed vivid in her mind. She'd come across the master with one of the boys he had picked off the street. She had been walking along, her heart full of cheer having just left Digby; she had seen someone struggling with a young boy, had paused, her hand clenched around a knife, yet not wanting to use it. And out of the darkness, her master's face, then a cry of fear.

Unnerved, Joanna got up and left her room, locking the door behind her. She went down through the back stairs.

Harriet's room was empty. A window had been left open, the air blowing through. Joanna hurried to it and shut it, with a crash. I put too much force into things, she thought, I must still myself, I cannot be angry with the world forever.

Down in the hall no one had seen Harriet. Alarm began to unfurl itself in Joanna's chest. She spoke sharply to the footmen, and they looked at each other. She had an image in her mind of Harriet, hopeless dramatic Harriet, doing some injury to herself. She picked up her skirts and ran up the stairs.

As she did, the front door opened and Harriet walked in. She looked well. Joanna wondered how she had even managed to dress herself properly; to bind her hat to her head. Joanna ran to her, fussed over her, and called for them to mix the mistress a hot sillabub. Then she folded Harriet's hand over her arm and led her upstairs.

'I am well,' said Harriet, settling down on a chair. 'Dearest Joanna, you must not worry.'

'Where did you go?' said Joanna, fussing around her.

'I went to see Mr Renard's shop,' said Harriet. 'I never went there, while he lived. He always came here. One only had to write a note, and he would come running.'

'You should not have gone out,' said Joanna. 'You should not distress yourself.'

'I am not distressed,' said Harriet. 'I wished to go to his shop.' Her voice was soft. 'I owed him that.'

'Now, now,' said Joanna. 'You have no obligation to him.'

'He deserved an honest answer,' said Harriet. 'I should not have left him to wait outside for me on a cold November night, at the mercy of whoever should pass. I knew my answer before that night. I could have written to him, made him understand without bringing him to stand outside this house. You see, Joanna, he thought he could persuade me, still. The day before that terrible night, he had sent me money. I still have it. It is in my secretaire. Proof of his circumstances, he said. Insurance, security, I did not know what he meant.'

'A man such as him should not have been discussing money with you,' said Joanna.

Harriet looked away in irritation. 'He was not thinking rightly. He said he was wildly in love with me. I thought it was a game. I had not been flattered so. But then, he tried to speak to me, in such serious terms. I laughed it off.'

'Serious terms?' said Joanna.

Harriet looked up. Even now there was something of the coquette about her gaze. 'He told me I could separate from my husband.'

Joanna tried to swallow back her amazement. She fixed her gaze on Harriet. No, she thought, no. Pierre Renard was not that kind of man.

'He even spoke of us marrying,' said Harriet. 'And when I laughed, he told me not to, for it killed him.'

'And what of his wife?' said Joanna.

'I do not know,' she said. 'He promised me all would be well, that he would "deal properly with the situation". He said I should wait and see, and that he would prove it to me. That he would do everything to make me contented, if only I would promise to be his.'

'What did you say?' said Joanna.

'What could I say? I was all astonishment. I told him to come back that evening, that I would get some message to him. But I knew, already. I could not look him in the eyes and say it. He gave me full proof of his affection.' Her eyes flickered. 'But I, the silversmith's wife?' She paused, as though she expected Joanna to say something. 'The shame would have killed my father. To leave this, for a trades-man? I may as well have been the grocer's wife or the chandler's wife.'

Joanna said nothing. It was amazing, she thought, that

the Harriet who wept over the stirrings of her baby would give this same cool, pragmatic stare. She wondered whether the emotion there was all play-acting, if it rippled any further than the surface of those blue eyes. And she felt dread twist its way around her heart.

'That night,' said Harriet, 'I knew he would be there. He had begged me to reconsider, to let him know my thoughts and feelings on the matter. I should have sent out to him, some message. It was a cold night. But my husband had someone in the house. I was jealous and afraid. And I knew Pierre would return. Though,' she paused, 'he too had frightened me, a little. Shown me his temper. He said he would chalk,' she paused again, 'a word, on our door. When I think of it now, I cannot bear it. I was so distraught, I told it all to my coachman. Such a loyal servant. Poor Pierre.'

She hid her face with her hands. Automatically, Joanna reached out to her, and gently touched her arm. But you were there, she thought. You told me you went out, fearlessly, into the night; you told me you stood on the step. Terrified, she did not speak. When Harriet lowered her hands her eyes were dry.

'I went to see Mrs Renard today,' she said. 'I wanted to tell her not to mourn, for she meant nothing to him. But when I got there, I did not know what to say. He hated her, you see, and how could that be a comfort?'

'How was she?' said Joanna.

'She is striking enough, I suppose,' said Harriet. 'But not pretty like me.'

Joanna could say nothing.

'She looked happy,' said Harriet. 'So there was no reason to tell her. She is happy.'

Joanna shook her head, and felt Harriet's hand rest on hers, then tighten. I will say nothing, she thought: it is not my place, I am a good servant. And when she raised her eyes to Harriet's, Harriet smiled.

'We all receive what we deserve in the end,' said Harriet. 'Do you not think so?'

But Joanna could not speak, recognizing for the first time a nature as twisted as her own.

CHAPTER THIRTY-SEVEN

17th November, 1792

Taylor came this evening, and without invitation. He was not his usual cheerful self, and though I called for wine, and was all fit to welcome him – despite the fact that I had not invited him – he did not respond to my jollity. I noticed that he kept looking about, in a distracted way, and before long he asked where Mary was. I said that she was above, for she had a headache, and this seemed to disturb him even more, so that for a moment I thought he might ask to see her.

I admit this did vex me, and so I made a few barbed comments, and I was a little forced in my humour. I made a jape about her sickliness, which he reprimanded me on; and later when I joked about a gentlemen I had read of in the newspaper who had left a large fortune, and said that it was strange that rich husbands did not live long, he interjected forcefully. He brought up some

*strange thing of the past – a person who was an apprentice of
mine, who had a weak character – and accused me of hounding
him. He told me he had often excused me of things in the past,
and let my words go when he should have spoken up. I have seen
that look on your face before, Pierre, he said – you know I love
you as I would a brother or a son, but I do not like what I see in
your eyes. I am pleased to say that I did not respond with wrath;
I was silent, and cold, and eventually he begged my pardon, as
I knew he would, and left.*

Mary knew that, some day soon, she would have to learn
to be harder. For now, every time Alban was absent from
her, she felt it keenly, as though death was close. The sound
of Pierre's step in the hall, the suggestion of his voice, even
when she couldn't hear the words, had made her heart
quicken with dread. Alban's step ended her suffering, for
she knew that he lived.

She knew that what Mallory termed her 'nervous com-
plaint' would taint everything if she let it. She had to learn
to leave joy alone, to enjoy it, not always to look forward to
loss. Summer was coming, and she hoped that the length-
ening days would reawaken her hope, and quicken the
calm Mary who she was sure had once existed. She tried,
but it was the kind of work that could not be achieved by
effort alone, and she felt as though the sun was always
behind her, on her back, and her shadow always cast ahead.

This evening, she was playing cards alone, a solitary
game her father had taught her as a child. The cards felt
greasy under her fingertips. Pierre had been used to playing with them. She did not dare to look out of her own

pool of light. She would not whisper it, even to herself: he is here. But she felt sure he was: in the darkness in the hall, the unexpected flaring of the fire, and the ticking of the clock. She longed to know that Alban was safe, but she did not dare move herself to go to the workshop, where he was carrying out repairs with Benjamin.

A knock on the door made her jump, but when it opened Ellen was there, looking bored. 'Please, Mrs Renard,' she said. 'Dr Taylor is here.'

He was standing directly behind Ellen, a dim figure. As Mary rose she knocked the table, and some of the cards fell on to the floor. She thought that surely he must see it: the dreadful symmetry of this night, and the night he had come to tell her Pierre was dead. But his face was blank.

He had come on other evenings, she supposed, though not usually this late, and usually with Amelia.

'Good evening, Dr Taylor,' she said. 'I was not expecting you. Is Mrs Taylor well?'

'Perfectly, thank you, madam,' said Taylor, bowing to her. She caught the scent of spirits as she came closer.

'It is late,' she said. 'Mr Steele is still in the workshop, if you wish to speak to him about the business. Mr Grisa is out. Shall I ask for tea?'

'No,' said Taylor. 'Thank you. It is you I wish to speak to.' His temper seemed to be fluctuating with every moment: he moved his head, as though he longed to shake something off. 'I meant to call earlier,' he said, 'but I have been unwell these last few days. Mr Cracknell took my visits on for me.'

'I am sorry to hear that,' she said, seeking some sign of

his normal gentleness. There was none. He sat half-turned away from her, and the firelight shadowed his face. There was a certain harshness to his expression, and the change from his usually kind demeanour troubled her.

He continued without encouragement. 'You know I have always tried to be a good friend to you,' he said. 'And it is as such a friend I speak now. I hope I have done my duty to you, and to Pierre's memory. You, and this business, were his most precious possessions. It is my duty to protect you, and it, and that is why I speak.'

'Well, then,' she said. 'Speak.'

Taylor kept his eyes down. 'I have been looking at the books,' he said. 'There has been a falling-off in trade, a marked falling-off. Not just due to the season,' he added, more loudly. 'Mr Steele was most kind to help us, but it is time to find someone more fitting.'

'More fitting?' said Mary, struggling to keep her temper. 'He is the finest craftsman I have ever seen.'

'I am sure, I am sure,' said Taylor. He rocked a little, and would not look at her. 'But he is a working silversmith, not a retailing goldsmith. This business is a going concern. I'm sure his skills are manifold, but he is no salesman, and though Mr Grisa is half-entranced with him, better management is needed.' He nodded, seeming more comfortable.

'He may not be a salesman,' she said. 'But he knows what beauty is, and how to create it. If he does not court people as Pierre did, maybe he is better for it. If I have any say in the matter, I do not accept your recommendation.'

Taylor looked at her face sorrowfully. 'My dear Mrs

Renard,' he said. 'I have failed you. I had come here hoping that what I had heard is not true, but now I see what has happened here. This man has enchanted you in some way.' He leaned forwards, and touched her hand. She snatched it away. 'I do not blame you,' he said. 'Let me say it, I do not blame you. After losing such a husband as Pierre, such a man.'

'What have your spies been telling you?' she said. 'Is Mr Digby one of your men? Is that why he haunts this stretch of Bond Street as if his soul was tethered here? What are you paying him?'

'Mr Digby?' said Taylor. 'What do you mean?'

She shook her head. 'I do not care, anyway. I will tell you the truth: I am not afraid of it. I am married to Mr Steele. I am expecting his child. And you are mistaken, quite mistaken, in what you said about Pierre. My husband is a better man than Pierre Renard ever was.'

Taylor stared at her as though she was raving. But she had heard his sharp intake of breath, and saw his fists clench. 'God,' he said, under his breath.

'I am not ashamed,' she said, her voice wavering, though she could hardly hear it. 'If we have married too quickly in the eyes of the world, still I know my heart is pure, and I know his is too.'

'You don't know what you are saying,' he said. 'I fear for you, Mrs Renard. I fear for you.'

'There is no need,' she said. She did not search for anger; it rose quick in her. 'I will not be controlled. You sought to find another Pierre, but I would not wish for him again. I hated him.'

'Stop it,' he said. 'You don't know what you saying. My dear Mary.'

'I am not your dear Mary!' she cried. 'I am not a child. It has been long since I have been grateful for your protection. For God's sake go now, before I say anything else.'

The ugliness of Taylor's former expression had crumbled away, like plaster chiselled from a flint wall. He was all raw anguish now, painful to look upon. He stood up, and held his hands out to her, as one would to a difficult child. As she turned away, the door opened.

'Mary?' It was Alban, holding a rag to his hands. 'What is it, dear?' he said. 'I heard you shouting.' He looked at Taylor. 'So you've heard. Come to speak of your disapproval, have you? Come to say you wish to exert your powers?'

'You will have to go,' said Taylor.

'Well, I knew that,' said Alban. 'Why not call in daylight hours instead of sneaking around in the dark? What business did you come here with this evening? Or did you come merely to trouble my wife?' He stood in front of the door. His eyes were dark with anger, unreadable in intent. His customary calmness threw his anger into strong relief.

Taylor sensed his menace and rose quickly. 'Let me go home. It was a mistake to come here,' he said.

'I'll show you out myself,' said Alban.

Mary heard the bang of the front door, and her husband calling to Benjamin to tidy the benches.

'High emotion,' he said, when he came back into the room. 'Was that his sole reason for coming here? Our marriage? What other business did he have?'

Mary was tidying the cards up, heaping them together in a haphazard way. 'Nothing,' she said.

'When will you learn to be honest with me?' he said.

'Very well, then, if you will know. He came to say that the business was not working as it should. That a different approach was needed.'

Alban nodded. 'I see,' he said.

'He said that you do not woo the customers in the way Pierre did.'

She looked at him. His face was delineated by shadow. He had not shaved for days, and his hair was roughly pushed back from his face.

She tried to be gentle. 'It is new for you, to run a shop on Bond Street. There are many clients. You must learn to read them all, and flatter them all. I know that this is not, perhaps, the way you imagined it.'

'It is not.' He was still holding the rag in his hands, as though he didn't know what to do with it. 'I didn't come to London for this,' he said. 'I came to be myself. To be a silversmith. To do my work. That, at least, is real and true.'

'Your work is beautiful,' she said, shying at the inadequacy of the word. 'no one can dispute its quality or its mastery. But the shop makes certain demands. Clients may not want something new and beautiful; they want what Lady So-and-so has.'

He threw the rag down. 'I should not have taken this on,' he said.

'Oh, come now,' she said. 'It does not matter. We will go.'

'It was never what I wanted,' he said. 'It came with

you. That's why I did it. All these years I have been too cautious. I wanted you and rushed into this place of misery. And now I am here, after all your angry words about him, you seek to make me into the model of your dead husband.'

She thought her heart might stop. She sat down quickly, hearing him go out into the London night. Her first instinct was to follow him, but she knew it would be pointless. She slammed the parlour door. She couldn't bear for Benjamin to come in, and triumph over her.

Alban turned right, and kept walking. He didn't know where he was walking to, only that he had to be gone from Bond Street. His first thought was Jesse; but that was too far, and he had no idea what he would say once he got there. He didn't want to speak, or explain anything. He was tired, there was the pain in his elbow, and now he was walking away from his wife.

All those years of calm, he thought, and now this. It is like being thrown into a wild sea, with only the stars to guide you, and the stars were often hidden by clouds.

What kind of man does it make me, he thought. That within a few months I have disappointed my wife, failed in her eyes and in the eyes of the world. I am nothing when compared to him, he thought. She might cling to me, but even now she watches, wondering why I am not like him. Even when Pierre's woman had come to lay her tears at Mary's feet, she had doubted him, and not Pierre, not that wretch who he had loathed at first glance, whose every word, whose every breath, seemed to fill the air with the aroma of his bloated ambition like stale tobacco.

He reached Piccadilly, and stopped. He looked left and right. Carriages and people everywhere, things brewing. Up and down these streets people were drinking themselves into unconsciousness, wagering livelihoods on the turn of a card, losing their virtues in golden palaces and dirty hovels. That old wretch Digby was right, perhaps; he said that London would chew me up and spit me out. I should have turned right round and got back on the mail coach again. I'll see my grave sooner than I will the long grass dancing in a field, under the full moon.

'Care for some company, sir?'

Of course, it had taken only a moment for her to find him. Girls like her could sniff out a conquest; or did they hit everyone? She was ageless, in the way some of these whores were; young, yet old enough to have seen too much.

'For one of your kind looks I'll give you a good price,' she said.

She took him to an alleyway nearby. She could tell he needed the shadows, the seclusion.

Her hands upon him were practised and skilful. Their dexterity surprised him, and his hand went to his pocket. The best whores in the world, he remembered a man saying. Who was that man? Was it Digby again? Was he the repository of truth and wisdom?

Alban took her wrists. His feeling surged in him, but it was mainly aggression, only edged by lust. He felt like he wanted to punch through a wall. Yet he was at a distance from his desire. He felt like he was fighting his way through a thicket. Something stood between him and the fulfilment of the desire.

The girl's face was passive before him: not comprehending, her eyes as glassy as moonstones.

'No,' he said. Then, 'I'm sorry.' He saw something cross her face, the beginning of a snarl. 'Keep the money,' he said.

She lapsed against the wall as he turned and walked away from her. He had to go back to Mary. His anger had melted away, found its home in the darkness of the London night. It belonged to someone else now.

CHAPTER THIRTY-EIGHT

24th November, 1792

I counted out the pills and doubled the amount Jones told me when I asked him how many for her headache, and how many more for a long sleep. He did not question me further, such is our sympathy. I have separated the dose in a piece of waxed paper, and put it in Maynard's snuffbox, and stowed it away with this book, beyond the prying eyes of everyone.

I have sent a pair of silver candlesticks for my friend the apothecary. They please me: chased with laurels, the signifiers of victory. He will not recognize my little joke. There are ways out of all things.

I would not have myself so callous towards Mary. I will not let our last parting be unkind. I would not like that as a memory. I feel a kind of tenderness for her, for she is sickly, and I see the trouble in her soul. A rest from the world is what she needs.

*

Joanna woke in the dim room, and sensed Digby's body beside her even before she turned. When he slept so soundly, she would wonder at him. Observe his face in repose, a face that, relaxed, looked so unlike him. Her eyes ran over the shadows of his ribs, his tough limbs. His body was so hard, so wiry, it was though there was no flesh on him.

Tonight, he did not look serene. The furrows remained in his brow, and sometimes his lips moved, as though he was recounting his troubles to the silence. He looked as though he was worrying rather than resting.

We found each other, she thought, without sentiment: trouble found trouble. Last week their lovemaking had been like drinking laudanum, lulling her into peace, into darkness. Afterwards, she had slept so deeply, in such a blackness that it seemed she was falling through the night sky, with no stars and no moon. When she woke she didn't know where she was. Then she saw him, watching her, not with a smile, simply watching. He had spread her dark hair out on the pillow with his hands, as though it was a halo. 'You talk when you fall asleep,' he said. 'I could ask you anything, and you would answer it truthfully.'

'My hair,' she said crossly, and sat up, patting it down.

He had gone without another word, not even kissing her, only placing a touch on her shoulder.

She wondered why she still invited him in, when she did not love him, or feel a fraction of what she had felt for Stephen. She was petrified at the idea of being discovered, and even more petrified by the thought that he would be taken up one day and hung for the watch. But still, he lit a spark in her, and when he held her, his arms hard around her, she felt enclosed and safe.

The hammering on her door shocked them both. She had turned the key in it, and put her locking box against it. Digby rose swiftly, alarm in his eyes. Wordlessly, he slipped under the bed. Joanna wrapped herself in a gown and opened the door. It was Mrs Holland, carrying two candles, two fat plaits of grey hair framing her face. 'You'd better come quickly,' she said. 'Missus has her pains.'

'Is it time?' said Joanna, dazed. She knew it was an inexact thing, but she was sure Dr Taylor had said it would be some time before the baby came. 'I'll be down directly,' she said, taking one of the candles. 'Let me dress.'

After Mrs Holland's footsteps had died away Digby slid out from under the bed. He watched her pin back her hair and slip on a gown in one clean, athletic movement. 'I never noticed how graceful you are,' he said.

'You can make your own way out?' she said.

He looked pained. 'The place will be in uproar,' he said.

'Well, wait here, then,' she said. She left the room quickly.

As he heard her footsteps retreating, Digby took Renard's watch from his coat, and checked the time.

Harriet's screams could be heard halfway across the house. Unlike that day months before when she had heard of Renard's death, there was no artifice to them; they were screams of agony and terror. At the sound, Joanna broke into a run. Mrs Holland was standing just outside the

389

chamber door. When she saw Joanna she shook her head. 'I cannot go in there,' she said. 'I remember my sister.'

Joanna nodded curtly. 'Has the doctor been sent for?' she said. Mrs Holland nodded. 'And the master?' said Joanna.

'Hadn't gone to bed yet,' said Mrs Holland, a look of distaste on her face. 'He's in the library, playing with his prints. He just asked for more wine.'

'Joanna?' Harriet's voice floated out, a thin thread. Joanna went straight in and across the room, lit with many candles in large silver candelabra. Harriet's face was red, but her expression had a vulnerability to it, the fragility of a reed pulled tight. The shadows beneath her eyes made them seem larger, and they glowed a kind of celestial blue. Joanna thought, unaccountably, that they were the blue of a distant heaven, the blue of an ever-opening sky. She felt afraid for her mistress. 'I can see silver all around,' said Harriet, smiling mistily. It seemed she could not focus. Joanna fumbled for one of the silver vinaigrettes on the dressing table, and held it to Harriet's nose. The girl jerked back into consciousness.

'Is there water?' called Joanna, gripping Harriet's hand as she grimaced, her body arcing in pain.

Mrs Holland was a dim shape in the doorway. 'It is coming,' she said. 'And linen.'

'The doctor is coming,' said Joanna, close to Harriet's ear.

'And what of Pierre?' said Harriet, in a whisper. 'What of him? Is he coming, Joanna? Is he coming for me?'

'Hush!' Joanna looked behind her. Mrs Holland stood, impassive. Joanna could not tell whether she had heard or not. She leaned even closer to Harriet, feeling the warmth of her own breath reflected back at her as she whispered in her ear. 'You do not know what you are saying,' she said. 'Do not speak of him – your life depends on it, do not speak.'

Harriet took a breath, and screamed. Joanna felt the bones of her hand compress and shift under Harriet's grip, and pushed back the pain. She felt the urge to pray, a long-forgotten defence against the agony of the moment, but all she could remember were the words that had been read at Stephen's brief burial service. Still, they were something, and she whispered them under her breath so Harriet did not hear them. 'Man that is born of woman hath but a short time to live, and is full of misery. He cometh up, and is cut down, like a flower; he fleeth as it were a shadow, and never continueth in one stay.' She thought of Digby, alone in her room, or creeping down through the passages of the house, and of his arms around her.

When Taylor arrived, his expressionless face comforted Joanna. She already felt exhausted with empathy. Harriet's pain seemed to be infusing her own mind, as Stephen's had during his last illness. She wondered where her defences had gone. Had Digby's wordless touch, his hard arms around her, dissolved them so effectively? She slumped back in a chair as Taylor commenced his examination, seemingly impervious to Harriet's howls. She had taken to calling for her mother.

'The baby is almost here,' Taylor said to Joanna. 'Are all the necessary arrangements in place? Is the nursery prepared?'

Joanna shook her head. 'Mr Chichester has engaged his own wet nurse, but she has not arrived in London yet. She is in Kent.'

Taylor tut-tutted under his breath as he searched through his bag.

The boy was born just after half past midnight. There was a long minute before he let out his first scream. There was a shock of recognition in Joanna's heart; still holding Harriet's hand, she rose to her feet.

Harriet lay uncovered, every ivory-pale limb trembling, smeared with blood. Joanna turned to her, trying to find her gaze and make her focus. 'A healthy boy, madam,' she said, loudly, and was rewarded with a blink. Harriet's eyes, she realized, were not looking into nothing, but were following the child, as Taylor washed and dried him with practised roughness.

After he was swaddled, Joanna held out her arms to him. He lay like a blessing, heavy and warm, in her arms. The weight and warmth of him, the motion of him, his quivering life, drew something long-dormant from her. 'He has brown hair, like the master, and eyes as blue as your own,' she said to her mistress, unable to disguise the emotion in her voice. She wept.

Harriet said nothing. Joanna arranged the crook of Harriet's arm against the pillow, and put the child there. Harriet looked at him, a long look as though she sought to memorize his face. 'She needs rest,' Taylor said to Joanna, dipping his hands in the bloody water, then drying them. 'The child is small, though he screams healthily enough. I will tell Mr Chichester that the priest should be sent for as a precaution.'

'It hardly seems necessary,' said Joanna, gazing at the baby's face. He seemed the embodiment of life. The words of death had dried up on her lips.

'Of course it is necessary,' said Taylor. 'We must be sure that the germ of sin that is already in him does not send him plummeting to hell if he dies.' He left the room without a backward glance. When Joanna went to search for him a few minutes later, she found him in the staircase hall, the heels of his hands against his eyes, as though he was weeping. She moved back before he saw her, and left him alone.

CHAPTER THIRTY-NINE

August, 1793

Joanna had thought she would have been sorry to leave this house, for it was where her life had begun again, but as she moved around its rooms she felt nothing at all. They would be back, she supposed. The only thing she could think of missing was the quality of the light in the staircase hall; and light was everywhere, after all. It had never taken much for her to pack up and move on, and now she had more to move: two new gowns, several books, and a white paste brooch that glittered in candlelight, a gift from her grateful mistress.

On her way to see Harriet, Joanna slipped into the Grand Salon. It was sheeted up, muffled in white like a landscape under snow. But it wasn't cold. In the slowly simmering heat of the August afternoon, the room smelt shut-up already. It had languished since winter. She went to the window and looked out over Berkeley Square. In the two months since baby Charles had been born, the square had set its growth forwards: the plane trees were larger now, though still saplings, and was that sprinkling of colour she could see a patch of flowers? What had once seemed dark and corrupt now seemed benign to her. But she also knew she would not miss it, for she travelled with her heart, and with the child that had such a place there. Here, he had been born, and she felt as if she had been born again in her own way, her dead feelings unhusked, her heart made new.

Though Charles stared through Harriet's blue eyes, he resembled neither Renard nor Chichester. 'We must wait,' said Harriet, one day, without being questioned, 'for him to grow.' Joanna said nothing more, and over time, silence lay on silence, and dulled her misgivings. Harriet played with the child and dandled him on her knee, but she kept a distance from him that surprised Joanna, who loved him with an intensity that consumed all her energy.

Harriet was writing in her boudoir. 'I must write to Mama before we leave,' she said. She sat straight, upright. The expressions that crossed her face were light, and subtle, but Joanna knew that you could never mistake this Harriet for the empty-headed bride who had come to this house. Joanna had not seen her shed a tear since Charles had been born.

'My husband wished me to write to the silversmith, and make enquiries about our new service,' she said. 'I have written it; will you kindly instruct one of the footmen to take it there?' There was not so much as a flicker of her eyelids; she spoke as though there would be no connection in her mind with Renard. You have shed his ghost, thought Joanna, and it occurred to her that Harriet had done what she never could.

'I will take it myself, madam, if you allow,' said Joanna. 'I wish to take a walk before we leave. Say goodbye to the London streets.'

'Very well,' said Harriet. 'Goodness. How truly sentimental you are. I would never have thought it of you.' She handed the letter to Joanna.

As Joanna put on her cloak, she thought of Digby. She had not seen him since the night of Charles's birth, though she had gone to look for him. She thought he must have been in the shadows, watching her. She did not call to him. She had too much pride to do that. She felt, with a touch of shame, that she could let him go easily. His sins were not her own. She had not loved him. And now there was Charles, who absorbed all her love and attention.

The pendant had come back to her too. A small packet, delivered by a boy who shrugged when she asked who had paid him. It had been the night after Charles's birth and, like the baby, it had seemed to be a gift from the angels. She wore the pendant against her heart; Harriet approved of this, smiling tartly, and saying she was a woman of sensibility.

Joanna had faith again. She knew that Stephen was still working for her. He was with God, but he was still working for her in the world: Stephen and their daughter, little Lottie. Tonight, she thought, I will light the candles and think of you, every time a flame flares into life.

CHAPTER FORTY

The sun had risen. Orange strips of light fell diagonally across the grey rippled stone of the courtyard where Digby lived. Glowing golden light chased the darkness out of his room. He had lain awake all night, sleep banished by the prospect of deliverance. He had decided on his course of action, and even though he could not sleep, as the hours passed he became more and more accustomed to the idea. The knowledge made the decision for him; he felt peaceful, having abdicated responsibility. The peace made him almost ready to believe in a higher power; he had been on the brink of it for so long. He supposed Mary Steele was to be thanked for that.

He got up, as quietly as possible. He dressed carefully. He had extracted his best clothes from the chest before going to bed. He donned his best linen shirt, and his collarless black coat. These were the clothes he had sworn he would leave this dwelling in; these were the clothes he would wear when he escaped, and it wouldn't be in his coffin.

He transferred the precious watch into his pocket. Only then did he set out for Berkeley Square. He walked quicker than usual; it took him less time than he had expected. He waited by the fence to the gardens.

He was disappointed in himself, for he had thought of this moment for a long time, and he had expected to enjoy it. Yet his hands were shaking, and when he observed closely he saw that the pounding of his heart trembled his shirt. He felt safe in the spot he had chosen and didn't want to leave it.

When he saw Joanna turn from Hay's Mews he felt even more shaken. She did not see him, walking briskly, her dark head up, on some mission. He felt a pang of longing for her. His memory of her had not had the power she had in the flesh. How straight she walked, he thought, how fine she looked; what a woman she was. 'I wish I could take you with me,' he said, in a whisper. He thought of running after her, calling her name. The thought of her turning, and looking at him with that smile she had, made his mouth water as though in anticipation of a feast. It would be so easy. But he had come so far, and if he spoke to her she could bring him down, or even worse, learn to look at him with contempt, one day.

He mounted the steps of the fine town house, then reached out, and banged the knocker. He tried to imprint its appearance in his mind, to remember this moment always: the brass studs in the door, the lion's head gazing at him with its unseeing eyes.

The door opened and the butler's face showed his disapproval; Digby saw the hesitation, and knew the man thought he might just slam the door in his face. He produced the coins, and put them in his hand. With a nod, the man opened the door further and leaned in to hear what he had to say.

'Mrs Chichester will want to see me,' he said. 'Tell her it concerns Mr Pierre Renard.' This was the exact moment to call: after breakfast, before visiting. He knew their routine of old.

He could hardly believe it, though, when the man waved him through into the hall. As he followed him, he looked up, and saw the light streaming in. It was as he had imagined it, but he was taller now, not a cowed child. He walked slowly towards a pair of double doors, which opened to show a small, plump woman: Mrs Chichester. The butler closed the door. It was the library, he thought, and looked around, trying to take every detail in.

'What is it you have to say?' she said, after the door had closed. He looked at her interestedly. She was more matronly now, more substantial; she had lost the slenderness she had as a bride, when he used to see her staring from her window. She had the layered toughness of a woman with experience. Digby wondered, just for a moment, if he had waited too long.

Digby took a deep breath, then removed the watch from his pocket and held it up so it swung like a pendulum. He watched her follow it with her eyes, see the slices of coloured stone, the finely chased gold case. Saw horror dawn on her face. She tried to get to the bell, but he was too quick for her. 'Whoa there, madam,' he said. He had her wrists. He had the sensation that if he just squeezed, he could break her; that one hand could easily encircle her neck. It was tempting in the way he had always found it tempting when a stagecoach came towards him at full pelt: a kind of curiosity about what would happen if he threw himself beneath the horses' hooves.

'Release me,' she said. But the note of command in her voice was mixed with fear.

'Only if you promise you'll be good,' he said. 'No screaming, no shouting. It will serve you as well as me. For we both know the young lad isn't your husband's child, don't we? If I were to say all that I knew, all hell would break loose.'

He observed with satisfaction that her eyes had widened. It had crossed his mind that she might call his bluff. From the far reaches of the house, he heard a baby cry. She nodded, and he released her.

'What do you want?' she said.

'First, I want you to get me a drink,' he said. He slipped the watch back into his pocket. He sat down in the nearest chair and looked around him, at the marble fireplace, the great pier glass, and beyond, the gardens. It was a view he had never seen before. He heard a clink, the sound of a silver wine label tinging against glass, and the sound of her pouring a drink. She was more sensible than he thought. A woman like her must have the hang of deception.

She offered him the glass. 'I thank you,' he said, and drank it back. It tasted as good as he thought it would: as sweet and cleansing as liquid fire.

'You killed him,' Harriet said. He looked up at her, in her fine white gown, her hands resting by her side. She looked calm. Quite the lady, he thought.

'Not me,' he said, putting the glass down a little heavily. Now he was here, he didn't feel the urge to smash it in the fireplace. 'He was cold when I found him.'

She sat down opposite him, her eyes never leaving his face.

'He didn't just have the watch,' he said, 'he had a letter for you, madam, that's how I know what I know.'

'What did it say?' she said.

Poor lamb, he thought. Nothing. It said nothing. Your maid said it all, as she slept.

He shrugged. 'Enough,' he said.

'May I see it?' she said.

'As if I'd bring it here,' he said. 'My security. You know it exists, and that's enough. When you've settled with me, I'll burn it, and you and your little baby boy can rest easy in your beds.'

'I'll settle with you,' she said, with a swiftness that impressed him. 'Name the price, and I will send you the money by way of one of my servants, tomorrow evening. My maid, Joanna.'

He nodded. He knew the wait would be agony. 'Eight o'clock tomorrow, by the corner of Hill Street. Don't send some gabbling maid. Send a man. He needn't know what he carries. Make sure it's not that Will. Talks a lot, he does.'

He was watching her close enough to see that something crumbled in her: her sense of secrets kept, scattered to the air like dust. We all have to learn, he thought. This is the gift I give you: knowledge.

CHAPTER FORTY-ONE

It was a simple bloodstone box: a dark, dead green, spotted through with red. Its beauty lay in its simplicity, for the lid was carved into a shell shape, and the whole held in a delicate cage of gold, small flowers chased into it.

'Forget-me-nots,' said Mary. She took Alban's glass from his hand, and looked over the gold work, smiling.

'My father made this box,' she said. 'It is a type I recognize.'

'Well, Mr Maynard will be pleased,' said Alban. 'It answers the description of his box. There were pills in it. I found it with a box of documents, which I will go through when I have leisure. But I have other things to think about.'

He looked towards the letter that lay on the workbench, a pale rectangle on the dark blemished wood. He had heard the distant jangle of the bell, and a low female voice. Grisa had brought it in, handing it to him with a sympathetic smile. Alban had read it once, briefly, his eyes flickering over the spiky characters in black ink before he cast it down.

'What is that, my love?' said Mary. He couldn't bear the look of dread on her face. 'You look so fatigued,' she said. He couldn't help but smile at her, so tiny in stature and so rounded. She came over to where he stood with laboured steps, and picked up the letter.

'The Chichesters want their silver,' said Alban. 'It will be ready soon, but it seems that it is not soon enough for them.' It was a reproach, he knew. Jesse and a couple of other outworkers were completing the service; it wanted only to be marked at the Hall. Alban had wanted to leave the business with the books clear, with everything paid for. But it was impossible. And he sensed that the Chichesters, the very customers he had courted, would take a long time to pay their bill, and much money had been laid out for their commission. He and Mary would be gone soon, though no date had been settled on, and he didn't want to leave things in a tangle. It was his pride. He wanted a neat ending.

'If it is nearly ready there is no need to worry, surely?' said Mary.

He held out his arms, embraced her, and held her tightly. 'My dear,' he said, and she moved her head to settle it against his shoulder, the small adjustment of love. 'I am not a businessman, it seems,' he said. 'Will all turn out well?'

She moved away from him and looked up at him. 'Of course,' she said. 'We must believe that, if we believe nothing else.'

She padded away, and he heard her ascending the stairs slowly.

Grisa returned, carrying the design for a wine cooler. 'May we discuss the changes?' he said. His accent was all but gone now. 'I wish to make use of you while you are here.'

'I wish we had been gone long since,' said Alban. 'While I must, I suppose, be grateful to Taylor for allowing us to stay here until now. I would we were far from here. When does Benjamin return?'

'Not for a month or so,' said Grisa. 'And do not feel grateful to Taylor. There is no one who wants to take this place on. Not as it stands.'

Alban conversed with him for a while, making changes to the design that had been suggested by the patron. When Grisa left him alone he thought of Mary, her hands supporting her back as she stretched, her hair loose down her back. I would do it all again, he thought.

He busied himself with tidying through papers that he and Mary had left untended. Mallory's son Mattie was only just beginning an apprenticeship with Jesse, to whom he had been bound. Alban had been happy for him, but the boy's enthusiasm was a source of vague unease, for he knew one day it would go. 'Perhaps not,' said Mary, when he told her that. 'Perhaps he will not be as hard on himself as you are.' And she had smiled, and sipped her wine from her wedding cup.

Alban went to a chest of papers to look for another old design spoken of by Grisa's client. As it was so often, he spoke in his mind to an imaginary Pierre. You were a sharp businessman, he thought, yet you left such disorder. The outside appearance had been clean and smooth, but underneath there was darkness and chaos. The accounts had been neat enough, but there had been a whole chest of other things. And then there was the dark wood box that Alban had found, taking up a floorboard to remove the corpse of a mouse. When he opened the chest he saw it where he had left it. He had tossed it there having glimpsed the interior; some papers, with Maynard's snuffbox on top. Now, he burrowed his hands into it. Alban did not like irregularities. He decided he would know everything of Renard.

He did not think much as he went through the papers, tasting the dust. They seemed meaningless: receipts for confectionary and perfumes. He swallowed hard, wondering if Renard had bought them for Mary. He hardly felt them in his hands, he was so preoccupied with his own misery and sense of failure. His wife told him he should cast it off, as if it was an outmoded coat, but she did not realize that it was as inescapable to him as the sky. It had come again, and he could only hope one day it would dissolve. As he delved through the scraps of paper his hand hit something firm.

It was a small book, covered with ruddy calfskin, smooth and cool in his hand from its resting place. He opened it, and read the words written on the first page. There was an immediate familiarity to the hand and the tone; and Alban faltered for a moment, astonishment releasing the tension in him. Then he took a breath, and rocked back on to his heels as he read.

This book has been ordered special for me from Mr Laveen. The best marbled paper, the finest calfskin, although we had a dispute about the quality of the gilding; but it is well enough. One day, all of the things in my house will be as beautiful as this book.

I wish to keep a record of my thoughts; not just for myself (for there are few persons I can confide in), but because the generations that follow me will wish to know of Pierre Renard. Founder of a dynasty of silversmiths. Gentleman. This is not mere intention, but resolution; I have my eyes set high. This precious record will serve as a reminder of the rough road I have travelled, when I one day come to write of my life. For now, I will keep it tucked away: as safe as silver.

CHAPTER FORTY-TWO

Mary was aware of nothing but the pain. The agony filled her head, pushing out all reasonable thoughts. I will die, she thought: and she opened her mouth to tell Mallory, but could not speak.

Before her, Eli walked. He was not in the aisle of St James's Church, but on Foster Lane, running his hand along the stones of the houses, laughing, zig-zagging here and there. She waited for him to turn and smile at her, feeling the tears on her face, knowing that once she took his hand there would be no way back.

She wanted to say: bring Alban. Let me kiss him. Let me say goodbye. But she could not speak.

Mallory's face swam before her, and she saw softness there. I know the pain, she wanted to tell her, I understand it now. She was proud with herself, for she was not making a sound.

She had never thought a child would be born alive here, in Bond Street, in this wretched house full of shadows. She should have made Alban take her to Chester. She was sure there, the air would be clearer, there would be no corruption waiting to claim her or her baby, and the dark shadow of Pierre would not stand in the corner, waiting to take her happiness. She heard footsteps, and gasped for air as Mallory left the room.

'Get Taylor,' said Mallory to Alban. She shoved him in the shoulder. 'Whatever is wrong between you and him, he is the best man for this business, and he will help her. For the sake of your wife and child!'

He went out into the night without a word. It was against every instinct to go to the house, with its black door and polished step. But he went, knowing that Mallory always spoke the truth. He went, and he hammered on the door, then when no one came, called up, the desperate cry ripping its way out of his throat.

Amelia Taylor came to the door when she heard Alban's voice, its notes piercing in the night, half-hysterical. Her hair was loose about her shoulders, and she carried a candle. 'He is not here,' she said. 'Is it her time? God bless her. Go to Cracknell.'

Mr Cracknell nodded at Mallory as he passed her in the corridor. Mallory nodded back. 'He attended my first child,' she said to Alban. 'In the days when I had better standing than I do now, and when he was learning his trade.' She did not want to go into the next room, and neither did she want Alban to go. There was too much blood.

After a few minutes Cracknell came out, his hands only half-washed. Mallory passed him, and went back into the room. Alban listened for his wife's voice, but could hear nothing.

'I can save her, or the child,' said Cracknell. 'She's not a brood mare like her sister. If you want a son, Steele, this might be your only chance.'

'Save her,' Alban said. He saw a frown cross Cracknell's face. He leaned forwards, his eyes prising a glance from the doctor. 'Her.' He gave the word full weight, as he would put the weight into a hammer strike. Cracknell nodded.

Alban went to Mary, and laid a kiss on her forehead, though she did not see him, her expression confused. Then he went to the parlour and sat alone. Ellen had left the house, finding a place with some respectable tradesman. But Grisa came in, in his nightgown and his ridiculous red nightcap, and poured Alban a glass of wine, which Alban pushed away. Had he thought it would do any good, he would have prayed.

The clock ticked. He heard running feet. It was Mallory. 'She lives,' she said. Her eyes were red. 'And so does your son, but he is weak, Alban, he is weak.'

Alban ran past her. He wrung Cracknell's hand. Mary lay, prone and pale. Alban put his face into his wife's hair, and stared at her until her eyes focused on him. She smiled. There was a slight mewling sound. Alban raised his eyes and looked at his son, lying beside Mary. 'Mrs

Dunning has gone to fetch the priest,' said Cracknell. Alban shook his head. He didn't have the strength to resist.

He lay next to Mary until the priest came. 'What will you call him?' the man said. Mary smiled at Alban.

'Edmund,' he said.

'Your father's name?' asked Cracknell, who had agreed to stand godparent. 'No,' said Alban. 'He was the man who first taught me to work silver.'

Light was only barely touching the sky when Dr Taylor came to the Steele house on Bond Street, and knocked until he was admitted by Grisa. 'The sky is the colour of mud,' he said. 'No stars, no moon. I could barely find my way. My wife told me. I waited, until I could wait no longer.'

Alban came down the stairs, protecting his flickering candle with one hand, dressed as though for a day's work. 'I will speak to you in the shop,' he said, and nodded at Grisa to go.

Taylor went into the shop. Around him, the silver that had not been locked in the safe glowed dully, in dim coldness. He looked around as though he felt enclosed by the shelves, by the counter that he had seen his friend Pierre lean on so many times. When he stopped looking around he stared at Alban. Alban pulled out a chair for him from behind the counter, but Taylor shook his head.

'Does she live?' he said eventually. His voice sounded hoarse. His neckcloth was undone, and he had come out without his coat. Alban saw the glint of spittle on his lips.

'Yes,' said Alban. 'She lives, and so does our son, at

present. Mrs Dunning is with them. They are both very weak.'

'I am glad she lives,' said Taylor. 'Even though I have not played my part in it, now. I failed her tonight. Had I known, I would have come – you must know that.'

'Would you like to see our son?' said Alban; it cost him everything to say it. Taylor shook his head, and moved as if to withdraw. 'Stay a moment,' said Alban. 'There are things we have to say to each other.'

'No,' said Taylor. 'I do not wish to discuss your marriage. It is beneath her – it pains me to say it – but it is so. But it is done, before God, and I cannot undo it.'

'Surely you wish her to be happy?' said Alban.

Taylor looked at him with amazement. 'Of course I do,' he said. 'But I do not believe that marriage to you will bring her that. Forgive me – my words sound harsh as I say them. But Pierre was a person who could not be replaced.'

'Tell me of him,' said Alban. 'And then I will tell you what I have to say to you; and it does not concern my marriage, or your poor opinion of me.'

He gestured towards the chair, and at last Taylor sat down, heavily, bowed forwards.

'He was an exceptional man,' said Taylor. 'It is true, there was a sharpness to him, and he made enemies – not least because of his handsome face. But there was a true sympathy between him and me. To me, he confided his hopes – of a family, of building this business. And he told me of his past, though he was ashamed of it. He was a true friend to me, almost a son. We all have our fears, our hopes. We all have sadnesses to bear, and he knew of mine. And Mary,' his face lit up, 'she is of true delicacy, of sensitivity, of depth. She has a beautiful soul.'

'On that,' said Alban, 'we can agree.'

As he looked at the doctor's face, Alban felt sorry for him. He looked like an old man, his eyes with heavy bags, his face riven with lines of worry. Alban held out Pierre's book. Taylor looked at it. 'What is it?' he said.

Alban continued to hold it out until Taylor took it. He opened it, found the first page and began to read, squinting as Alban held the candle near his face. Alban saw the truth begin to dawn on Taylor's face. But when he looked up, there was only resignation there. 'Did he write everything?' he said. Alban nodded.

'What do you know?' said Taylor. He kept his eyes fixed on the book, even as he closed it.

'I know that Pierre was obsessed with Harriet Chichester,' said Alban. 'I know that he never loved Mary. That he intended to be rid of her. And I know he told you that. I also know, though not from this book, that you hold Mary dear to you, almost like a daughter.'

Taylor looked up at him.

'That is all I know,' said Alban.

'I thought he was drunk when he spoke of wanting Mary's death,' said Taylor. 'But he kept returning to it. I did not believe it at first. My friend. He was not a bad man, Mr Steele. He had his head turned. That was all. Only wait, I thought, and it will pass. But on the night he died, he told me he had spoken to the apothecary, that he was willing to put the plan into action.' He stopped. There were tears in his eyes. 'My immortal soul,' he said. 'I have prayed, but there is no relief. I see what you think, and you are right.'

He was trembling, and he put his head in his hands.

'What am I right about?' said Alban. 'I must hear it from your lips.' He held the candle steady, watched the doctor wipe his tears away with his large hands.

'Do you seek to torture me?' said the doctor.

'You know me so little,' said Alban. 'You may find comfort in facing the truth.'

Dr Taylor nodded.

'I killed him,' he said. 'I did it quickly. One fast slice, across the throat. He never saw me. He never knew it was me.' He met Alban's gaze. 'It is the only thing I am thankful for.'

He closed his eyes, and the tears fell again. Alban leaned forwards, and put his hand on Taylor's arm. The only noise was the doctor's ragged in-and-out breaths.

'Will you tell them?' he said. 'I deserve nothing less, I suppose. I did it for the love of him, too, you know. He was a good man, but he angered too quickly. A resentment, once rooted, was impossible to dig up. He always wanted to be known as a gentleman. I always saw him as someone good; good, as Mary was good. I couldn't let him hurt her. I couldn't let him hurt himself.'

'You saved what I love most,' said Alban. 'Why would I wish to tell anyone?'

'And Mary?'

'She has borne a sense of guilt for it all these past months. She was so convinced of her own wrongdoing that I had even begun to believe her. I will say enough to relieve her mind, but no more. I keep nothing from her, but this. This is not my secret.' He let the book rest in Taylor's hand.

Taylor went out into the dawn. He walked home, and went to bed. He was woken early, with the news that Digby, the watchman, had absconded. When he returned from investigating this, he slept most of the day, even as the sun gained heat outside the shutters. Amelia tiptoed around the house, brought him supper, and told him to sleep the night.

When he returned a day later, he found the Renard house shut up, the silver secure in the plate room, and the occupants of it all gone.

EPILOGUE

August, 1799

The stones of the cottage seemed to hold the summer's heat within them. The sun was just setting; soon it would be completely dark, but for the stars and moon.

In the six years since they had left London, Mary had hardly ever thought of the city. It troubled her a little that the place she had grown up in had such a small hold on her heart; that the threads were so easily broken. Mallory always tutted when she said that, and told her she had always been too sentimental. The place was nothing, she said, it was just another stage set.

Of Mallory's children only Mattie had stayed in London, learning his trade as a silversmith in the workshop on Foster Lane with Jesse. It was Mattie who had written to his aunt Mary in his careful hand, telling her that Dr Taylor had died, his body found floating in the Thames near Chelsea, a year to the day after the Steeles had left London. Some said he must have lost his footing, but others spoke of how his nature had darkened, and thought he had sought the bottom of the Thames. He had taken to spending his days in the church, was the rumour, and whatever he had found there, it was not enough to save him in the end.

Mallory had just now returned from London. She had gone to see Mattie, tend to her investments, and to visit Francis Dunning's sister, who had returned to the city and seemed as devoted as ever to the little boy in her care. Her master had died, and the mistress had promised her a handsome pension one day. 'I think,' Mallory had said, carefully, 'she is happy.'

When Mary walked through the house in the evenings, she felt no fear of the shadows. Her grief for Eli was always there, but when she thought of him, as she often did, she could see his face clearly; he no longer turned his back to her. More often than not, he was smiling.

Mary went into the small building next to the cottage, where her husband was working. He made small table wares, did repairs for goldsmiths in nearby Chester, and, occasionally, his own work. He struck his initials on it, and sent his pieces to be assayed at Chester. He did not care, he said, if others overstruck his mark.

'How will anyone ever know your work, if you hide away here?' she would chide him.

'I like the mystery,' he would say, smiling that same quiet smile that he had always had, half-sadness, half-delight, which had stayed with her throughout the years of her first marriage.

He made parcels of designs: carefully drawn, persistently worked on, packaged up and sent off. The best things, he did not share; he locked them away.

He was drawing tonight, and when she put her hand on his back, he turned and smiled. He drew her to him and put his head against her heart, and she thought, how will they know this? Posterity should remember you, but how will they know you, even when they hold a piece of your silver in their hands?

'Alban Steele,' she said. 'Do you know nothing of time?'

He laughed, and kissed her. 'I forget it,' he said. 'I'll be in directly.'

'I'll check on Edmund,' she said.

She found their son at his casement window. She normally closed the shutters and tucked him in long before this time. He was kneeling there and looking out. When he saw his mother he looked guilty. 'The light woke me, Mama,' he said. She went to him and put her arms around him. She inhaled the smell of his hair and skin: that familiar, mineral-like smell, of newness.

'It is bright,' she said. The moon seemed closer tonight.

'What is it?' asked Edmund, his face turned up to her, all young babyish curves; it pained her to think how like an angel he looked, with that light on his face.

'It is the full moon,' she said, and stroked his hair. 'It is the full moon, Edmund.' She wanted to say: people walk abroad by the light of it. They fall in love, they steal, they kill by the light of it. Stay in the house, my boy: never venture out under such a moon. She didn't say it, of course. She had begun to realize that her success as a mother would depend on learning to stay silent about so much.

She kissed her son, and tucked him in, telling him that the full moon would watch over him while he slept. He seemed pleased by this, and closed his eyes. He fell asleep almost immediately. When she went to close the shutters she stared up at the moon as though for the first time. She saw its shadows and its mysteries. She was surprised by it, surprised anew. Because it didn't look like silver. It didn't look like silver at all.

ACKNOWLEDGEMENTS

I am indebted to my agent, Jane Finigan, and the staff at Lutyens & Rubinstein, for championing this book from its earliest stages. I am also immensely grateful to my editor, Clare Hey, and to all at Simon & Schuster for their hard work and enthusiasm.

The Lucy Cavendish College Fiction Competition was an invaluable source of encouragement and I am grateful to everyone who is involved in the competition. I am also indebted to the Trustees of the London Library who granted me Carlyle membership of the Library, allowing me to complete the research for this book.

My colleagues at the Goldsmiths' Company have provided much encouragement and I am grateful to all of them.

A big thank you to all of the friends who have cheered

me on, especially Sian Robinson, Ruth Seward and Samantha Woodward. I am grateful to Luke Schrager for reading the manuscript and discussing eighteenth-century detail with me. All errors are my own.

Finally, huge thanks to my family: my parents; my sister Lisa and her sons Samuel and Harrison; my sister Angela and her family; and above all my husband, without whose love and practical assistance not a page would have been written.

Author's note
The wording of the advertisement for the Foundling Hospital which upsets Joanna is adapted from an original that appeared in *The Times*, on Monday, 9th May, 1791.

An exclusive extract from

THE WIDOW'S CONFESSION

*The new novel from Sophia Tobin,
coming January 2015*

PROLOGUE

Delphine's letter, April, 1852

I still remember the first girl we found on the sand. I think of her name, and she is there. Her features have the softness of youth, only marred by the frown that remains on her brow, even in death. She is lying on her back, a bright shape on dark sand, and the folds of her white gown have been made translucent by the sea. That sea is coming to claim her, each wave easing forwards, then retreating, each retreat a little less than its previous progress. The deepening of the water around her is almost imperceptible; gently, it floats a few of her golden curls.

I sometimes wonder whether my mind is playing tricks

on me with this vividness. Perhaps, in reality, when we found her the hungry tide had already retreated from her, and the morning sun had begun to dry the sand. I suspect it is so.

I could not paint her, if you asked me to. Even though I see her face so clearly, I could not describe a single line of it with charcoal or watercolour. The memory of her is stored in some other place; at the thought of her there is a jolt of emotion, and she is there, before my eyes, in her totality. I cannot observe the memory of her. I can only feel it.

Having thought myself detached and clear-sighted, my reaction to her and to the other dead girls surprised me. I thought that I had hardened myself and put my emotions away; folded neatly, like the ball gowns of my youth, with dried lavender pressed in paper between them. Yet that summer, with its sea mists and storms, unlocked something in me. A thing I had not killed; just denied.

I write to you now as Delphine Beck, and I write only because you have asked me to. Hitherto, if we are truthful, we have been little more than strangers. To write to you seems dangerously intimate somehow. The paper is passive; it accepts my words as you may not. But I believe you when you tell me that you have to know everything. If we are to begin our lives together, all concealment must be put aside, and sunlight let into a room which has been dark and cold for so long.

My love, I promised you my confession.

Here it is.

*

CHAPTER ONE

Edmund Steele went to Broadstairs to escape a love affair. It was the first dishonourable act of his life towards a woman. As the train crawled its way through a country-side deep in the lushness of late spring, he pictured the shape of Mrs Craven's white neck when her face was turned away from him; he remembered the sheen of the reddish-brown gown she had worn at their last meeting. And, knowing that she had expected him to propose to her, he also remembered the painful sense of shame, and was burned by the thought as though he had held his hand too close to a candle flame. I made her no promises, he thought, as the train neared the coast, and he watched the stuttering shadow of its outline on the ground as it moved on: I made her no promises. But he felt no better.

At Margate Sands, Edmund hired a man with a cart to

take him to Broadstairs, the horse sweating in the sun, and switching its tail. They travelled through deep narrow lanes of the countryside. When they emerged from the green darkness of the last hedgerowed lane, onto the coast road near Kingsgate Bay, Edmund put his head back. He felt the sunlight, warm and harsh, slick across his city-worn face. 'Will you pull up?' he said. 'I'll pay you extra for the lost time.'

The man found a place to stop near the edge of the cliff. There was a sharpness to the air, bitterly cold, but welcome to Edmund. He hoped the clean air would reach the depths of his lungs. He had wanted to see the sea, the distant breakers, the vast sky and the curve of the tan-coloured sands beneath the bone grey, crumbling cliffs.

'Is it far to Holy Trinity?' he said.

'Less than half a mile. Past the North Foreland light-house over yonder, then we're on the road to Stone, and near enough to the town. Come for a holiday, sir?'

'I think so,' said Edmund.

The church of Holy Trinity and its parsonage were mere steps away from the town, at a point where the road narrowed to a single carriage width. Edmund said he would take his own trunk to the house, and sent the carrier off, but the driveway was long and the exertion tired him swiftly and without warning. He was breathing heavily as he knocked on the door of the parsonage.

When the door opened he blinked at the darkness, his gaze suddenly clouded by the contrast with the sunlight as he peered at the young man who was saying his name. He guessed from the clerical collar it was Theo Hallam.

He saw immediately that his face had once been marked by illness, and exposed to the scourges of the most brutal heat. Now only the signs were left behind – fading freckles on a face pocked with scars. Yet, it was still a handsome face in its way, its disfigurements giving its underlying beauty a certain power.

Hallam hung back, in the shadows of the hallway. 'Do come out of the sun, Mr Steele,' he said. 'It is merciless today. The sea breeze takes the edge off the heat, which means you do not feel it as it beats down on you, but it will punish you if you stay out in it.'

Edmund wondered whether he really did look so bad that he needed to be sheltered from the sun like some delicate maiden, and it pinched his pride. The penalties of easy London living, he thought; too much claret, too much meat. 'You must be Mr Hallam,' he said. 'I admit I did not expect you to be answering your own door.'

Theo Hallam laughed. It suited him. 'I should be working on a sermon. But my housekeeper Martha is fretting over our supper in the kitchen, and as she is sadly over-stretched at the moment, it would have been unfair to expect her to look out for you as well.'

'Well, I am pleased to meet you,' said Edmund, holding out his hand.

Theo shook his hand briskly. 'And I you. But do come out of the heat, Mr Steele, I beg of you.'

The coolness of the tiled hallway was a relief to Edmund, as was the tea Theo ordered from Martha, who looked with frank curiosity at Edmund as she unloaded the tray. They took tea in the immaculate drawing room, which was uncluttered but tastefully decorated with paintings and ceramics. Its austere beauty surprised Edmund, for he knew the clergyman lived alone, and he did not link such clean serenity with the habits of a bachelor.

'I must thank you for allowing a perfect stranger a room for the season,' Edmund said, trying to take in the details of the room without his eyes lingering too much.

'A friend of Mr Venning is a friend of mine,' said Theo. 'He has known my family since I was a boy, and went to Oriel College, as I did. And I admit, that what he told me of your work piqued my interest – I understand you have medical connections, and that you are interested in the study of the mind.'

'I fear Charles has overrated me,' said Edmund, with an uneasy laugh. 'It is true that I count many medical men as my friends, but I do not practise myself. I am comfortable enough – I worked in a city counting house in my youth, and invested in railways at the right time – so I have the leisure to study what interests me. I have been concerned in one or two cases.'

'And the mind is your area of interest?' said Theo.

Edmund swallowed. 'Yes – that is, it was. I think it is a subject which is in its infancy.'

A warmth had crept over Theo's previously neutral expression. 'You speak of healing the mind, and I the soul. Perhaps we may discuss the way in which these areas overlap.' There was a faint glow in the young man's blue eyes; an enthusiasm which Edmund moved quickly to quash.

'If you would be so kind, I am glad to take a rest from it. Do not mention my interest to any of the sea-bathers, I beg you. I wish to be nothing but a tourist here.' He thought of his study at home, with the labelled drawers and cabinets of papers, the neatly written indices. 'I am of robust health, but my friends tell me that I have over-exerted myself recently. I do not feel it myself – I am quite merry – but I trust their opinions. Mr Venning has instructed me to rest. I am sure you can imagine his firmness on the matter.'

Theo nodded, without any offence. 'Very well. You are here before most of the incomers – forgive me, the tourists, I should say. "Incomers" sounds so bare and unwelcoming. Well, you are among the first, so you will be settled in before the rest arrive. My aunt, Mrs Quillian, will be here in a few days or so. She comes every season to the town, and always stays at the Albion. She does not care to dwell with her poor parson nephew; she prefers to be surrounded by people.' He smiled.

'I thought this was a quiet place,' said Edmund, feeling slightly alarmed.

Theo laughed. 'It is not always so. And any increase in numbers is doubly noticeable to its inhabitants. Many of the local people claim to prefer the rough seas and empty streets of January, but we would be ruined without our guests. We are to have gaslight soon, you know, so the modern age has reached us. You may read of the London arrivals in the newspaper – we have the occasional Duke and Marquis, and Mr Dickens, of course.' He offered Edmund a slice of bread and butter. Edmund took it. The butter was spread thinly, as though it had been spread on, then scraped off, then scraped again.

'Empty streets are unknown to me,' said Edmund, biting

into the bread and discovering it was stale. 'Perhaps I should have come in January – I would have liked to see that.' He chewed, slowly. 'Mr Venning says clean air and pleasant company will restore me to my normal ways.'

'Have you been truly unwell?' said Theo. The beauty of the question was all in the way he said it: without the sharpness of gossiping curiosity, but with enough steadiness to assure Edmund he had an interested listener.

Edmund took a gulp of tea to wash down the bread, then put his teacup down, gently, on the small table beside him. 'Well asked,' he said. 'Charles sent me here with good reason. I can see you will be drawing my confessions from me like poison from a wound.'

'Any gifts I have are given me by the Lord, Mr Steele. I will not press you – I do not seek to force confidences – but I am here if there is some burden you wish to discuss. And if we only talk of trivial things, that is welcome too.'

'Do you find it lonely, living in such a small town, without many diversions?' said Edmund. He caught the slight flinch Theo gave, an almost imperceptible movement.

'I would never say that,' said Theo. He folded his hands in his lap, and sat, straight-backed, without leaning in his chair. 'I am where I have been called to be, to serve God's purpose. I am following my faith. But your company is welcome.'

It was only later that Edmund thought he had not answered the question.

It had been many years since Edmund had attended Evening Prayer on a weekday, but when his host asked him to, he agreed in a moment. The church of Holy Trinity stood a few steps from the parsonage; built as a chapel-of-ease to the Parish of St Peter-in-Thanet, it had been dedicated only twenty years, Theo informed him. It was a flint construction, black and glittering in the summer light, but within, it changed character from brooding to serene. The interior was a large open space, with white walls. The only division was an elaborately carved rood screen. The sweet, stale scent of incense hung in the air.

Edmund took his place quietly in the front pew Theo had pointed out, fearing that, fatigued as he was, he might doze off in the warmth of the summer evening. He could not help but think that he would normally have been in his club at this time, but reminded himself of his resolve to be open to new impressions and new places. London had been his whole life since his teens, which was a good while ago, for he was in his late fifties now. With the exception of his intermittent visits to his parents in Cheshire, which had ceased on their deaths, he had known few other places. It was true he had travelled abroad, but those experiences were like mere framed prints on the wall: distant, separate, as though they had happened to other people. Nothing had touched or changed him. Now, suddenly aware of his advancing years, he felt a little ashamed of it.

He rubbed his eyes. Despite his distance from London, there was much to think of, not least the pressing matter of Mrs Craven and her happiness. He had written a thousand letters to her in his mind, but the outcome was never definite. To ask her for her hand in marriage, or not? Just as he decided on one course, he would think, *and yet . . .*

He heard the church door open and close behind him. Theo looked up from his prayer book. Edmund glanced over his shoulder. A lady had entered the church, and was standing a few steps from the door, in the centre, looking over the church and the few worshippers, her gaze sweeping them without any embarrassment. Slim and tall, she was dressed entirely in black. A widow. Edmund thought her striking, but did not want to stare. He turned back to see that Theo had paused in the deep hush. He gazed long at her, before he returned his eyes to the page and continued reading, his voice moving fluidly over the elements of the service.

The last Amen woke Edmund from his reverie, and he heard the cries of seagulls seeping through the stone walls of the church. When he glanced back, the widow had gone.

Prayers, supper and bed; these would be the things, Edmund thought, which would soothe his troubled mind. He retired as ten chimed on the grandfather clock at the turn of the stairs, and inspected his room by the light of a candle. It was pristine. There was a neat four-poster bed, with heavy hangings drawn back for him; a wardrobe; a washstand with clean towels, soap, a basin and a ewer filled with cold water. A table had been set out in the bay window with writing equipment, and beside his bed was a chair where, neatly placed, there was a box of matches and another two candles. There was no dust, no cobwebs; knowing that Martha was Theo's only servant made Edmund wonder. Already, Theo had struck him as the kind of man who was concerned with details, and he thought he saw the priest's own taste in the careful preparation of the writing desk, and provision of candles. For a moment he wondered if his host had even made the bed with his own hands. He pulled back the top cover and saw that four blankets had been layered on the bed, but then he had been warned about the fierce sea breezes.

His host's room was situated at the other end of the hall. Edmund heard his feet travelling the length of the corridor, the boards squeaking with every light step.

He settled down at the writing desk, where everything had been prepared for him, and dipped the pen.

My dear Venning,

I have arrived, and find the young man very much as you told me he would be: warm and hospitable. But there are depths to him, Charles, as you said. This evening we passed his study door, and I glimpsed within a portrait of Saint Sebastian. It was a mournful sight, that saintly face full of suffering, his sides pierced with many arrows. Mr Hallam closed the door as soon as he saw my eyes upon it. It is clear that he has not taken a role in the church for the sake of a profession, or convenience, but I will not complain of his intensity. His fireside is warm, his port and brandy good, and, for now, he is short on lectures for a clergyman. I see nothing to trouble me yet.

Did you really only send me here to 'recover my spirits' as you so charmingly put it? I blame myself, for confiding in you that, as a bachelor, long past fifty, I look dully at my life and am weighed down by the burden of my accumulated wisdom. Are you giving me a rest cure, as you claimed, or another diversion?

I doubt I will receive a full explanation by return. I will breathe in the sea air, and smile benignly, and pray that I get through this 'holiday' of mine alive.

Your good friend, Edmund Steele

Edmund left the letter open so that the black ink, glossy in the candlelight, would sink into the paper. Then he got up and walked around the room, not worrying too much about the creaking boards, for his host was way down the corridor. In London he would have been drinking and playing cards, laughing at foolish jokes and talking nonsense. He had shied away from mentioning Mrs Craven in the letter, though Charles Venning and his wife had encouraged the match. He thought of his father, as he often did these last months, and wondered if he had disappointed Alban Steele by not being as pure in intention as him. It was in his recent studies that he had sought to close this gap, and to add some seriousness to a life that had been full of trivialities. He had also wished to examine the darkness which had haunted his father, the shadow which, despite Alban's happiness, had yet come over him sometimes.

'Too late, too late,' he said, under his breath. Amusement and diversion, these were the things that made his life bearable. If his father, a silversmith and an artist in his way, had bequeathed him something, it was exactness; a precision which had served him well in the building and keeping of his fortune, and was at odds with his otherwise relaxed nature.

Fretfully, he went over to the window and lifted the drape. Dense, blue-black darkness greeted him. It was perfect night in this seaside town, deeper and darker than any city night. He could not hear a sound, not even the cry of a gull. He wondered if it was the trees, waving in the growing breeze, that swathed the parsonage in such complete darkness, but after a minute or two he saw there was a gap in them, a line of sight intermittently blocked by their movement.

He saw a light.

He tilted his head, and took a step to the right. Across the narrow road at the end of the driveway, someone was standing on the step of one of the cottages. He narrowed his eyes at the pale column and made out the figure of a woman, holding a candle, shielded from the sea breeze by a glass shade. He caught the glint of it. He raised his hand, but the pale shape showed no sign that she was aware of his presence. She stayed still, seeming to stare straight ahead. He had no idea what she was looking at; the building he was in was surely cloaked in leaves, a mass of darkness to her eyes.

He waved a little more, until he felt foolish and dropped the drape. He took a turn around the room and closed his letter. Then he could not help himself. He went to the window and looked out again. But the figure was gone. There was no light behind the shutters of the cottage, no sign that there was anyone within.

He undressed and got into bed. The balminess of the day had quite gone. The bed was cool and he was aware that his heart was beating hard, and that he wanted to know who had been watching the parsonage from a cottage step. It is a quaint little place, Venning had told him, but do not listen to the local people: they can talk only of wrecks, and they try to scare the ladies by speaking of sea-monsters and ghosts.

Ghosts, thought Edmund. Foolish, so foolish. He closed his eyes, and thought of his childhood, imagining that he was in his parents' cottage again, his mother stirring a pot on the range. He thought of the London streets, the chaos and energy, the messenger boy running to him, bringing news of the money he had made through no labour of his own. He heard the chink of Mrs Craven's wine glass as she set it down on the silver salver bought by her first husband. And at last, as he fell asleep, he saw the pale shape of a woman on a step, and the dark and glittering sea.

If you enjoyed the extract from *The Widow's Confession*, read on for more information …

Broadstairs, Kent, 1851. Once a sleepy fishing village, now a select sea-bathing resort, this is a place where people come to take the air, and where they come to hide …

Delphine and her cousin Julia have come to the seaside with a secret, one they have been running from for years. The clean air and quiet outlook of Broadstairs appeal to them and they think this is a place they can hide from the darkness for just a little longer. Even so, they find themselves increasingly involved in the intrigues and relationships of other visitors to the town.

But this is a place with its own secrets, and a dark past. And when the body of a young girl is found washed up on the beach, a mysterious message scrawled on the sand beside her, the past returns to haunt Broadstairs and its inhabitants. As the incomers are drawn into the mystery and each others' lives, they realise they cannot escape what happened here years before …

A compelling story of secrets, lies and lost innocence …

Publishing 15 January 2015

HB ISBN: 978-1-47112-812-7
eBook ISBN: 978-1-47112-815-8